George MacDonald (10 December 1824 – 18 September 1905) was a Scottish author, poet and Christian minister. He was a pioneering figure in the field of fantasy literature and the mentor of fellow writer Lewis Carroll. In addition to his fairy tales, MacDonald wrote several works on Christian apologetics. His writings have been cited as a major literary influence by many notable authors including W. H. Auden, J. M. Barrie, Lord Dunsany, Hope Mirrlees, Robert E. Howard, L. Frank Baum, T.H. White, Lloyd Alexander, C. S. Lewis, J. R. R. Tolkien, Walter de la Mare, E. Nesbit, Peter S. Beagle, Neil Gaiman and Madeleine L'Engle. C. S. Lewis wrote that he regarded MacDonald as his "master": "Picking up a copy of Phantastes one day at a train-station bookstall, I began to read. A few hours later", said Lewis, "I knew that I had crossed a great frontier." G. K. Chesterton cited The Princess and the Goblin as a book that had "made a difference to my whole existence". (Source: Wikipedia)

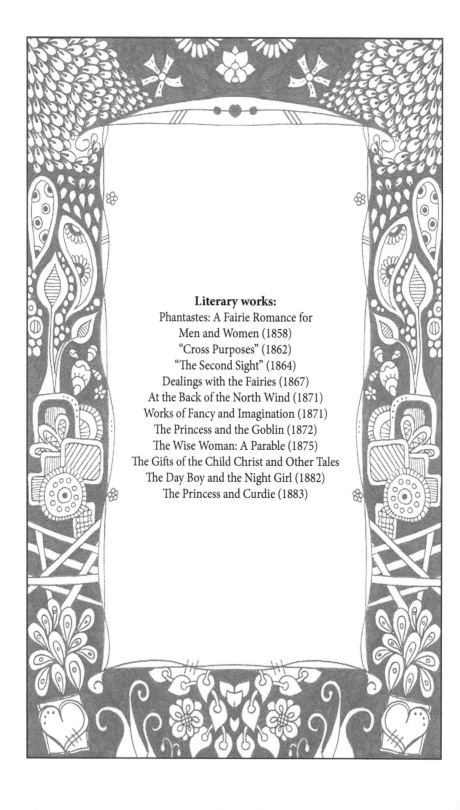

Literary works:
Phantastes: A Fairie Romance for
Men and Women (1858)
"Cross Purposes" (1862)
"The Second Sight" (1864)
Dealings with the Fairies (1867)
At the Back of the North Wind (1871)
Works of Fancy and Imagination (1871)
The Princess and the Goblin (1872)
The Wise Woman: A Parable (1875)
The Gifts of the Child Christ and Other Tales
The Day Boy and the Night Girl (1882)
The Princess and Curdie (1883)

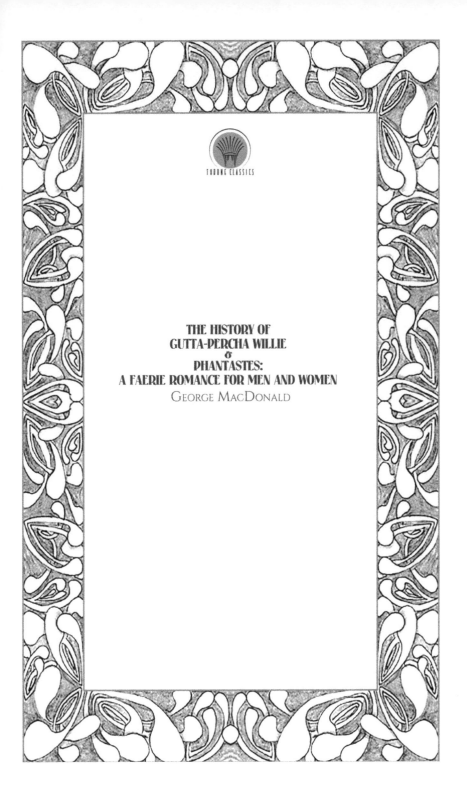

THE HISTORY OF
GUTTA-PERCHA WILLIE
&
PHANTASTES:
A FAERIE ROMANCE FOR MEN AND WOMEN
George MacDonald

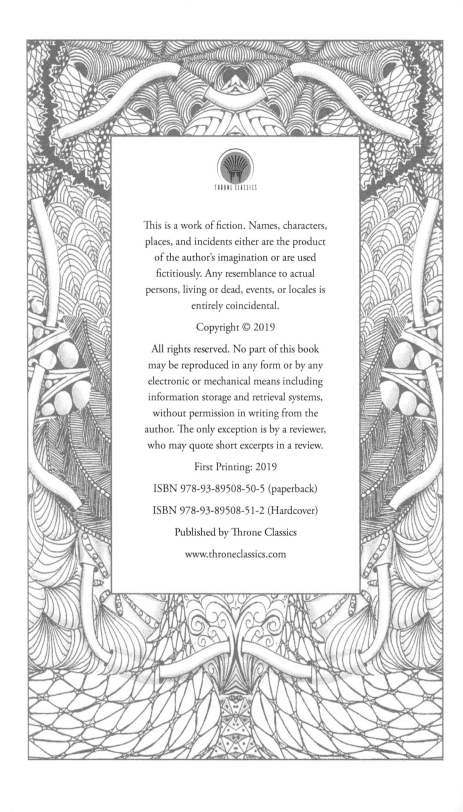

Copyright © 2019

First Printing: 2019

ISBN 978-93-89508-50-5 (paperback)

ISBN 978-93-89508-51-2 (Hardcover)

Published by Throne Classics

www.throneclassics.com

Contents

THE HISTORY OF
GUTTA-PERCHA WILLIE
&
PHANTASTES:
A FAERIE ROMANCE FOR MEN AND WOMEN

THE HISTORY OF GUTTA-PERCHA WILLIE

CHAPTER I. WHO HE WAS AND WHERE HE WAS.

When he had been at school for about three weeks, the boys called him Six-fingered Jack; but his real name was Willie, for his father and mother gave it him—not William, but Willie, after a brother of his father, who died young, and had always been called Willie. His name in full was Willie Macmichael. It was generally pronounced Macmickle, which was, by a learned anthropologist, for certain reasons about to appear in this history, supposed to have been the original form of the name, dignified in the course of time into Macmichael. It was his own father, however, who gave him the name of Gutta-Percha Willie, the reason of which will also show itself by and by.

Mr Macmichael was a country doctor, living in a small village in a thinly-peopled country; the first result of which was that he had very hard work, for he had often to ride many miles to see a patient, and that not unfrequently in the middle of the night; and the second that, for this hard work, he had very little pay, for a thinly-peopled country is generally a poor country, and those who live in it are poor also, and cannot spend much even upon their health. But the doctor not only preferred a country life, although he would have been glad to have richer patients, and within less distances of each other, but he would say to any one who expressed surprise that, with his reputation, he should remain where he was—"What's to become of my little flock if I go away, for there are very few doctors of my experience who would feel inclined to come and undertake my work. I know every man, woman, and child in the whole country-side, and that makes all the difference." You see, therefore, that he was a good kind-hearted man, and loved his work, for the sake of those whom he helped by it, better than the money he received for it.

Their home was necessarily a very humble one—a neat little cottage in the village of Priory Leas—almost the one pretty spot thereabout. It lay in a valley in the midst of hills, which did not look high, because they rose with a gentle slope, and had no bold elevations or grand-shaped peaks. But they rose to a good height notwithstanding, and the weather on the top of them in the wintertime was often bitter and fierce—bitter with keen frost, and fierce with as wild winds as ever blew. Of both frost and wind the village at their feet had its share too, but of course they were not so bad down below, for the hills were a shelter from the wind, and it is always colder the farther you go up and away from the heart of this warm ball of rock and earth upon which we live. When Willie's father was riding across the great moorland of those desolate hills, and the people in the village would be saying to each other how bitterly cold it was, he would be thinking how snug and warm it was down there, and how nice it would be to turn a certain corner on the road back, and slip at once out of the freezing wind that had it all its own way up among the withered gorse and heather of the wide expanse where he pursued his dreary journey.

For his part, Willie cared very little what the weather was, but took it as it came. In the hot summer, he would lie in the long grass and get cool; in the cold winter, he would scamper about and get warm. When his hands were as cold as icicles, his cheeks would be red as apples. When his mother took his hands in hers, and chafed them, full of pity for their suffering, as she thought it, Willie first knew that they were cold by the sweet warmth of the kind hands that chafed them: he had not thought of it before. Climbing amongst the ruins of the Priory, or playing with Farmer Thomson's boys and girls about the ricks in his yard, in the thin clear saffron twilight which came so early after noon, when, to some people, every breath seemed full of needle-points, so sharp was the cold, he was as comfortable and happy as if he had been a creature of the winter only, and found himself quite at home in it.

For there were ruins, and pretty large ruins too, which they called the Priory. It was not often that monks chose such a poor country to settle in, but I suppose they had their reasons. And I dare say they were not monks at all, but begging friars, who founded it when they wanted to reprove the luxury and greed of the monks; and perhaps by the time they had grown as bad themselves, the place was nearly finished, and they could not well move it. They had, however, as I have indicated, chosen the one pretty spot, around which, for a short distance on every side, the land was tolerably good, and grew excellent oats if poor wheat, while the gardens were equal to apples and a few pears, besides abundance of gooseberries, currants, and strawberries.

The ruins of the Priory lay behind Mr Macmichael's cottage—indeed, in the very garden—of which, along with the house, he had purchased the fen—that is, the place was his own, so long as he paid a small sum—not more than fifteen shillings a year, I think—to his superior. How long it was since the Priory had come to be looked upon as the mere encumbrance of a cottage garden, nobody thereabouts knew; and although by this time I presume archaeologists have ferreted out everything concerning it, nobody except its owner had then taken the trouble to make the least inquiry into its history. To Willie it was just the Priory, as naturally in his father's garden as if every garden had similar ruins to adorn or encumber it, according as the owner might choose to regard its presence.

The ruins were of considerable extent, with remains of Gothic arches, and carvings about the doors—all open to the sky except a few places on the ground-level which were vaulted. These being still perfectly solid, were used by the family as outhouses to store wood and peats, to keep the garden tools in, and for such like purposes. In summer, golden flowers grew on the broken walls; in winter, grey frosts edged them against the sky.

I fancy the whole garden was but the space once occupied by the huge building, for its surface was the most irregular I ever saw in a garden. It was up and down, up and down, in whatever direction you went, mounded with heaps of ruins, over which the mould had gathered. For many years bushes and flowers had grown upon them, and you might dig a good way without coming to the stones, though come to them you must at last. The walks wound about between the heaps, and through the thick walls of the ruin, overgrown with lichens and mosses, now and then passing through an arched door or window of the ancient building. It was a generous garden in old-fashioned flowers and vegetables. There were a few apple and pear trees also on a wall that faced the south, which were regarded by Willie with mingled respect and desire, for he was not allowed to touch them, while of the gooseberries he was allowed to eat as many as he pleased when they were ripe, and of the currants too, after his mother had had as many as she wanted for preserves.

Some spots were much too shady to allow either fruit or flowers to grow in them, so high and close were the walls. But I need not say more about the garden now, for I shall have occasion to refer to it again and again, and I must not tell all I know at once, else how should I make a story of it?

CHAPTER II. WILLIE'S EDUCATION.

Willie was a good deal more than nine years of age before he could read a single word. It was not that he was stupid, as we shall soon see, but that he had not learned the good of reading, and therefore had not begun to wish to read; and his father had unusual ideas about how he ought to be educated. He said he would no more think of making Willie learn to read before he wished to be taught than he would make him eat if he wasn't hungry. The gift of reading, he said, was too good a thing to give him before he wished to have it, or knew the value of it. "Would you give him a watch," he would say, "before he cares to know whether the sun rises in the east or the west, or at what hour dinner will be ready?"

Now I am not very sure how this would work with some boys and girls. I am afraid they might never learn to read until they had boys and girls of their own whom they wanted to be better off than, because of their ignorance, they had been themselves. But it worked well in Willie's case, who was neither lazy nor idle. And it must not be supposed that he was left without any education at all. For one thing, his father and mother used to talk very freely before him—much more so than most parents do in the presence of their children; and nothing serves better for teaching than the conversation of good and thoughtful people. While they talked, Willie would sit listening intently, trying to understand what he heard; and although it not unfrequently took very strange shapes in his little mind, because at times he understood neither the words nor the things the words represented, yet there was much that he did understand and make a good use of. For instance, he soon came to know that his father and mother had very little money to spare, and that his father had to work hard to get what money they had. He learned also that everything that came into the house, or was done for them, cost money; therefore, for one thing, he must not ill-use his clothes. He learned, too, that there was a great deal of suffering in the world, and that his father's business was to try to make it less, and help people who were ill to grow well again, and be able to do their work; and this made him see what a useful man his father was, and wish to be also of some good in the world. Then he looked about him and saw that there were a great many ways of getting money, that is, a great many things for doing which people would give money; and he saw that some of those ways were better than others, and he thought his father's way the very best of all. I give these as specimens of the lessons he learned by listening to his father and mother as they talked together. But he had another teacher.

Down the street of the village, which was very straggling, with nearly as many little gardens as houses in it, there was a house occupied by several poor people, in one end of which, consisting just of a room and a closet, an old woman lived who got her money by spinning flax into yarn for making linen. She was a kind-hearted old creature—widow, without any relation near to help her or look after her. She had had one child, who died before he was as old as Willie. That was forty years before, but she had never forgotten her little Willie, for that was his name too, and she fancied our Willie was like him. Nothing, therefore, pleased her better than to get him into her little room, and talk to him. She would take a little bit of sugar-candy or liquorice out of her cupboard for him, and tell him some strange old fairy tale or legend, while she sat spinning, until at last she had made him so fond of her that he would often go and stay for hours with her. Nor did it make much difference when his mother begged Mrs Wilson to give him something sweet only now and then, for she was afraid of his going to see the old woman merely for what she gave him, which would have been greedy. But the fact was, he liked her stories better than her sugar-candy and liquorice; while above all things he delighted in watching the wonderful wheel go round and round so fast that he could not find out whether her foot was making it spin, or it was making her foot dance up and down in that curious way. After she had explained it to him as well as she could, and he thought he understood it, it seemed to him only the more wonderful and mysterious; and ever as it went whirring round, it sung a song of its own, which was also the song of the story, whatever it was, that the old woman was telling him, as he sat listening in her high soft chair, covered with long-faded chintz, and cushioned like a nest. For Mrs Wilson had had a better house to live in once, and this chair, as well as the chest of drawers of dark mahogany, with brass handles, that stood opposite the window, was part of the furniture she saved when she had to sell the rest; and well it was, she used to say, for her old rheumatic bones that she had saved the chair at least. In that chair, then, the little boy would sit coiled up as nearly into a ball as might be, like a young bird or a rabbit in its nest, staring at the wheel, and listening with two ears and one heart to its song and the old woman's tale both at once.

One sultry summer afternoon, his mother not being very well and having gone to lie down, his father being out, as he so often was, upon Scramble the old horse, and Tibby, their only servant, being busy with the ironing, Willie ran off to Widow Wilson's, and was soon curled up in the chair, like a little Hindoo idol that had grown weary of sitting upright, and had tumbled itself into a corner.

Now, before he came, the old woman had been thinking about him, and wishing very much that he would come; turning over also in her mind, as she spun, all her stock of stories, in the hope of finding in some nook or other one she had not yet told him; for although he had not yet begun to grow tired even of those he knew best, it was a special treat to have a new one; for by this time Mrs Wilson's store was all but exhausted, and a new one turned up very rarely. This time, however, she was successful, and did call to mind one that she had not thought of before. It had not only grown very dusty, but was full of little holes, which she at once set about darning up with the needle and thread of her imagination, so that, by the time Willie arrived, she had a treat, as she thought, quite ready for him.

I am not going to tell you the story, which was about a poor boy who received from a fairy to whom he had shown some kindness the gift of a marvelous wand, in the shape of a common blackthorn walking-stick, which nobody could suspect of possessing such wonderful virtue. By means of it, he was able to do anything he wished, without the least trouble; and so, upon a trial of skill, appointed by a certain king, in order to find out which of the craftsmen of his realm was fittest to aid him in ruling it, he found it easy to surpass every one of them, each in his own trade. He produced a richer damask than any of the silk-weavers; a finer linen than any of the linen-weavers; a more complicated as well as ornate cabinet, with more drawers and quaint hiding-places, than any of the cabinet-makers; a sword-blade more cunningly damasked, and a hilt more gorgeously jewelled, than any of the sword-makers; a ring set with stones more precious, more brilliant in colour, and more beautifully combined, than any of the jewellers: in short, as I say, without knowing a single device of one of the arts in question, he surpassed every one of the competitors in his own craft, won the favour of the king and the office he wished to confer, and, if I remember rightly, gained at length the king's daughter to boot.

For a long time Willie had not uttered a single exclamation, and when the old woman looked up, fancying he must be asleep, she saw, to her disappointment, a cloud upon his face—amounting to a frown.

"What's the matter with you, Willie, my chick?" she asked. "Have you got a headache?"

"No, thank you, Mrs Wilson," answered Willie; "but I don't like that story at all."

"I'm sorry for that. I thought I should be sure to please you this time; it is one I never told you before, for I had quite forgotten it myself till this very afternoon. Why don't you like it?"

"Because he was a cheat. He couldn't do the things; it was only the fairy's wand that did them."

"But he was such a good lad, and had been so kind to the fairy."

"That makes no difference. He wasn't good. And the fairy wasn't good either, or she wouldn't have set him to do such wicked things."

"They weren't wicked things. They were all first-rate—everything that he made—better than any one else could make them."

"But he didn't make them. There wasn't one of those poor fellows he cheated that wasn't a better man than he. The worst of them could do something with his own hands, and I don't believe he could do anything, for if he had ever tried he would have hated to be such a sneak. He cheated the king, too, and the princess, and everybody. Oh! shouldn't I like to have been there, and to have beaten him wand and all! For somebody might have been able to make the things better still, if he had only known how."

Mrs Wilson was disappointed—perhaps a little ashamed that she had not thought of this before; anyhow she grew cross; and because she was cross, she grew unfair, and said to Willie—

"You think a great deal of yourself, Master Willie! Pray what could those idle little hands of yours do, if you were to try?"

"I don't know, for I haven't tried," answered Willie.

"It's a pity you shouldn't," she rejoined, "if you think they would turn out so very clever."

She didn't mean anything but crossness when she said this—for which probably a severe rheumatic twinge which just then passed through her shoulder was also partly to blame. But Willie took her up quite seriously, and asked in a tone that showed he wanted it accounted for—

"Why haven't I ever done anything, Mrs Wilson?"

"You ought to know that best yourself," she answered, still cross. "I suppose because you don't like work. Your good father and mother work very hard, I'm sure. It's a shame of you to be so idle."

This was rather hard on a boy of seven, for Willie was no more then. It made him look very grave indeed, if not unhappy, for a little while, as he sat turning over the thing in his mind.

"Is it wrong to play about, Mrs Wilson?" he asked, after a pause of considerable duration.

"No, indeed, my dear," she answered; for during the pause she had begun to be sorry for having spoken so roughly to her little darling.

"Does everybody work?"

"Everybody that's worth anything, and is old enough," she added.

"Does God work?" he asked, after another pause, in a low voice.

"No, child. What should He work for?"

"If everybody works that is good and old enough, then I think God must work," answered Willie. "But I will ask my papa. Am I old enough?"

"Well, you're not old enough to do much, but you might do something."

"What could I do? Could I spin, Mrs Wilson?"

"No, child; that's not an easy thing to do; but you could knit."

"Could I? What good would it do?"

"Why, you could knit your mother a pair of stockings."

"Could I though? Will you teach me, Mrs Wilson?"

Mrs Wilson very readily promised, foreseeing that so she might have a good deal more of the little man's company, if indeed he was in earnest; for she was very lonely, and was never so happy as when he was with her. She said she would get him some knitting-needles—wires she called them—that very evening; she had some wool, and if he came to-morrow, she would soon see whether he was old enough and clever enough to learn to knit. She advised him, however, to say nothing about it to his mother till she had made up her mind whether or not he could learn; for if he could, then he might surprise her by taking her something of his own knitting—at least a pair of muffetees to keep her wrists warm in the winter. Willie went home solemn with his secret.

The next day he began to learn, and although his fingers annoyed him a good deal at first by refusing to do exactly as he wanted them, they soon became more obedient; and before the new year arrived, he had actually knitted a pair of warm white lamb's-wool stockings for his mother. I am bound to confess that when first they were finished they were a good deal soiled by having been on the way so long, and perhaps partly by the little hands not always being so clean as they might have been when he turned from play to work; but Mrs Wilson washed them herself, and they looked, if not as white as snow, at least as white as the whitest lamb you ever saw. I will not attempt to describe the delight of his mother, the triumph of Willie, or the gratification of his father, who saw in this good promise of his boy's capacity; for all that I have written hitherto is only introductory to my story, and I long to begin and tell it you in a regular straightforward fashion.

Before I begin, however, I must not forget to tell you that Willie did ask his father the question with Mrs Wilson's answer to which he had not been satisfied—I mean the question whether God worked; and his father's answer, after he had sat pondering for a while in his chair, was something to this effect:—

"Yes, Willie; it seems to me that God works more than anybody—for He works all night and all day, and, if I remember rightly, Jesus tells us somewhere that He works all Sunday too. If He were to stop working, everything would stop being. The sun would stop shining, and the moon and the stars; the corn would stop growing; there would be no more apples or gooseberries; your eyes would stop seeing; your ears would stop hearing; your fingers couldn't move an inch; and, worst of all, your little heart would stop loving."

"No, papa," cried Willie; "I shouldn't stop loving, I'm sure."

"Indeed you would, Willie."

"Not you and mamma."

"Yes; you wouldn't love us any more than if you were dead asleep without dreaming."

"That would be dreadful."

"Yes it would. So you see how good God is to us—to go on working, that we may be able to love each other."

"Then if God works like that all day long, it must be a fine thing to work," said Willie.

"You are right. It is a fine thing to work—the finest thing in the world, if it comes of love, as God's work does."

This conversation made Willie quite determined to learn to knit; for if God worked, he would work too. And although the work he undertook was a very small work, it was like all God's great works, for every loop he made had a little love looped up in it, like an invisible, softest, downiest lining to the stockings. And after those, he went on knitting a pair for his father; and indeed, although he learned to work with a needle as well, and to darn the stockings he had made, and even tried his hand at the spinning—of which, however, he could not make much for a long time—he had not left off knitting when we come to begin the story in the next chapter.

CHAPTER III. HE IS TURNED INTO SOMETHING HE NEVER WAS BEFORE.

Hitherto I have been mixing up summer and winter and everything all together, but now I am going to try to keep everything in its own place.

Willie was now nine years old. His mother had been poorly for some time—confined to her room, as she not unfrequently was in the long cold winters. It was winter now; and one morning, when all the air was dark with falling snow, he was standing by the parlour window, looking out on it, and wondering whether the angels made it up in the sky; for he thought it might be their sawdust, which, when they had too much, they shook down to get melted and put out of the way; when Tibby came into the room very softly, and looking, he thought, very strange.

"Willie, your mamma wants you," she said; and Willie hastened upstairs to his mother's room. Dark as was the air outside, he was surprised to find how dark the room was. And what surprised him more was a curious noise which he heard the moment he entered it, like the noise of a hedgehog, or some other little creature of the fields or woods. But he crept gently up to his mother's bed, saying—

"Are you better this morning, mamma?"

And she answered in a feeble sweet voice—

"Yes, Willie, very much better. And, Willie, God has sent you a little sister."

"O-o-o-oh!" cried Willie. "A little sister! Did He make her Himself?"

"Yes; He made her Himself; and sent her to you last night."

"How busy He must have been lately!" said Willie. "Where is she? I should like to see her. Is she my very own sister?"

"Yes, your very own sister, Willie—to love and take care of always."

"Where is she?"

"Go and ask nurse to let you see her."

Then Willie saw that there was a strange woman in the room, with something lying on her lap. He went up to her, and she folded back the corner of a blanket, and revealed a face no bigger than that of the big doll at the clergyman's house, but alive, quite alive—such a pretty little face! He stood staring at it for a while.

"May I kiss her, nurse?"

"Yes—gently—quite gently."

He kissed her, half afraid, he did not know of what. Her cheek was softer and smoother than anything he had ever touched before. He sped back to his mother, too full of delight to speak. But she was not yet well enough to talk to him, and his father coming in, led him down-stairs again, where he began once more to watch the snow, wondering now if it had anything to do with baby's arrival.

In the afternoon, it was found that the lock of his mother's room not only would not catch easily, but made a noise that disturbed her. So his father got a screwdriver and removed it, making as little noise as he could. Next he contrived a way, with a piece of string, for keeping the door shut, and as that would not hold it close enough, hung a shawl over it to keep the draught out—all which proceeding Willie watched. As soon as he had finished, and the nurse had closed the door behind them, Mr Macmichael set out to take the lock to the smithy, and allowed Willie to go with him. By the time they reached it, the snow was an inch deep on their shoulders, on Willie's cap, and on his father's hat. How red the glow of the smith's fire looked! It was a great black cavern with a red heart to it in the midst of whiteness.

The smith was a great powerful man, with bare arms, and blackened face. When they entered, he and two other men were making the axle of a wheel. They had a great lump of red-hot iron on the anvil, and were knocking a big hole through it—not boring it, but knocking it through with a big punch. One of the men, with a pair of tongs-like pincers, held the punch steady in the hole, while the other two struck the head of it with alternate blows of mighty hammers called sledges, each of which it took the strength of two brawny arms to heave high above the head with a great round swing over the shoulder, that it might come down with right good force, and drive the punch through the glowing iron, which was, I should judge, four inches thick. All this Willie thought he could understand, for he knew that fire made the hardest metal soft; but what he couldn't at all understand was this: every now and then they stopped heaving their mighty sledges, the third man took the punch out of the hole, and the smith himself, whose name was Willet (and will it he did with a vengeance, when he had anything on the anvil before him), caught up his tongs in his hand, then picked up a little bit of black coal with the tongs, and dropped it into the hole where the punch had been, where it took fire immediately and blazed up. Then in went the punch again, and again the huge hammering commenced, with such bangs and blows, that the smith was wise to have no floor to his smithy, for they would surely have knocked a hole in that, though they were not able to knock the anvil down halfway into the earth, as the giant smith in the story did.

While this was going on, Mr Macmichael, perceiving that the operation ought not to be interrupted any more than a surgical one, stood quite still waiting, and Willie stood also—absorbed in staring, and gradually creeping nearer and nearer to the anvil, for there were no sparks flying about to make it dangerous to the eyes, as there would have been if they had been striking the iron itself instead of the punch.

As soon as the punch was driven through, and the smith had dropped his sledge-hammer, and begun to wipe his forehead, Willie spoke.

"Mr Willet," he said, for he knew every man of any standing in the village by name and profession, "why did you put bits of coal into the hole you were making? I should have thought it would be in the way rather than help you."

"So it would, my little man," answered Willet, with no grim though grimy smile, "if it didn't take fire and keep getting out of the way all the time it kept up the heat. You see we depend on the heat for getting through, and it's much less trouble to drop a bit of coal or two into the hole, than to take up the big axle and lay it in the fire again, not to mention the time and the quantity of coal it would take to heat it up afresh."

"But such little bits of coal couldn't do much?" said Willie.

"They could do enough, and all that's less after that is saving," said the smith, who was one of those men who can not only do a thing right but give a reason for it. "You see I was able to put the little bits just in the right place."

"I see! I see!" cried Willie. "I understand! But, papa, do you think Mr Willet is the proper person to ask to set your lock right?"

"I haven't a doubt of it," said Mr Macmichael, taking it out of his greatcoat pocket, and unfolding the piece of paper in which he had wrapped it. "Why do you make a question of it?"

"Because look what great big huge things he does! How could those tremendous hammers set such a little thing as that right? They would knock it all to pieces. Don't you think you had better take it to the watchmaker?"

"If I did, Willie, do you know what you would say the moment you saw him at work?"

"No, papa. What should I say?"

"You would say, 'Don't you think, papa, you had better take it back to the smith?"

"But why should I say that?"

"Because, when you saw his tools beside this lock, you would think the tools so small and the lock so huge, that nothing could be done between them. Yet I daresay the watchmaker could set the lock all right if he chose to try. Don't you think so, Mr Willet?"

"Not a doubt of it," answered the smith.

"Had we better go to him then?"

"Well," answered the smith, smiling, "I think perhaps he would ask you why you hadn't come to me. No doubt he could do it, but I've got better tools for the purpose. Let me look at the lock. I'm sure I shall be able to set it right."

"Not with that great big hammer, then," said Willie.

"No; I have smaller hammers than that. When do you want it, sir?"

"Could you manage to do it at once, and let me take it home, for there's a little baby there, just arrived?"

"You don't mean it!" said the smith, looking surprised. "I wish you joy, sir."

"And this is the lock of the room she's in," continued the doctor.

"And you're afraid of her getting out and flying off again!" said the smith. "I will do it at once. There isn't much wrong with it, I daresay. I hope Mrs Macmichael is doing well, sir."

He took the lock, drew several screws from it, and then forced it open.

"It's nothing but the spring gone," he said, as he took out something and threw it away.

Then he took out several more pieces, and cleaned them all. Then he searched in a box till he found another spring, which he put in instead of the broken one, after snipping off a little bit with a pair of pincers. Then he put all the pieces in, put on the cover of it, gave something a few taps with a tiny hammer, replaced the screws, and said—

"Shall I come and put it on for you, sir?"

"No, no; I am up to that much," said Mr Macmichael. "I can easily manage that. Come, Willie. I'm much obliged to you for doing it at once. Good-night."

Then out they went into the snowstorm again, Willie holding fast by his father's hand.

"This is good," said his father. "Your mother will have a better day all to-morrow, and perhaps a longer sleep to-night for it. You see how easy it is

27

to be both useful and kind sometimes. The smith did more for your mother in those few minutes than ten doctors could have done. Think of his great black fingers making a little more sleep and rest and warmth for her—and all in those few minutes!"

"Suppose he couldn't have done it," said Willie. "Do you think the watchmaker could?"

"That I can't tell, but I don't think it likely. We should most probably have had to get a new one."

"Suppose you couldn't get a new one?"

"Then we should have had to set our wits to work, and contrive some other way of fastening the door, so that mamma shouldn't take cold by its being open, nor yet be disturbed by the noise of it."

"It would be so nice to be able to do everything!" said Willie.

"So it would; but nobody can; and it's just as well, for then we should not need so much help from each other, and would be too independent."

"Then shouldn't a body try to do as many things as he can?"

"Yes, for there's no fear of ever being able to do without other people, and you would be so often able to help them. Both the smith and the watch maker could mend a lock, but neither of them could do without the other for all that."

When Willie went to bed, he lay awake a long time, thinking how, if the lock could not have been mended, and there had been no other to be had, he could have contrived to keep the door shut properly. In the morning, however, he told his father that he had not thought of any way that would do, for though he could contrive to shut and open the door well enough, he could not think how a person outside might be able to do it; and he thought the best way, if such a difficulty should occur, would be to take the lock off his door, and put it on mamma's till a better one could be got. Of this suggestion his father, much to Willie's satisfaction, entirely approved.

CHAPTER IV. HE SERVES AN APPRENTICESHIP.

Willie's mother grew better, and Willie's sister grew bigger; and the strange nurse went away, and Willie and his mother and Tibby, with a little occasional assistance from the doctor, managed the baby amongst them. Considering that she had been yet only a short time at school, she behaved wonderfully well. She never cried except she was in some trouble, and even then you could seldom have seen a tear on her face. She did all that was required of her, grew longer and broader and heavier, and was very fond of a lighted candle. The only fault she had was that she wouldn't give Willie quite so many smiles as he wanted. As to the view she took of affairs, she seemed for a long time to be on the whole very well satisfied with life and its gifts. But when at last its troubles began to overtake her, she did not approve of them at all. The first thing she objected to was being weaned, which she evidently considered a very cruel and unnecessary experience. But her father said it must be, and her mother, believing him to know best, carried out his decree. Little Agnes endured it tolerably well in the daytime, but in the night protested lustily—was indeed so outrageously indignant, that one evening the following conversation took place at the tea-table, where Willie sat and heard it.

"Really, my dear," said Mrs Macmichael, "I cannot have your rest disturbed in this way another night. You must go to Willie's room, and let me manage the little squalling thing myself."

"Why shouldn't I take my share of the trouble?" objected her husband.

"Because you may be called up any moment, and have no more sleep till next night; and it is not fair that what sleep your work does let you have should be so unnecessarily broken. It's not as if I couldn't manage without you."

"But Willie's bed is not big enough for both of us," he objected.

"Then Willie can come and sleep with me."

"But Willie wants his sleep as much as I do mine."

"There's no fear of him: he would sleep though all the babies in Priory Leas were crying in the room."

"Would I really?" thought Willie, feeling rather ashamed of himself.

"But who will get up and warm the milk-and-water for you?" pursued his father.

"Oh! I can manage that quite well."

"Couldn't I do that, mamma?" said Willie, very humbly, for he thought of what his mother had said about his sleeping powers.

"No, my pet," she answered; and he said no more.

"It seems to me," said his father, "a very clumsy necessity. I have been thinking over it. To keep a fire in all night only to warm such a tiny drop of water as she wants, I must say, seems like using a steam-engine to sweep up the crumbs. If you would just get a stone bottle, fill it with boiling water, wrap a piece of flannel about it, and lay it anywhere in the bed, it would be quite hot enough even in the morning to make the milk as warm as she ought to have it."

"If you will go to Willie's room, and let Willie come and sleep with me, I will try it," she said.

Mr Macmichael consented; and straightway Willie was filled with silent delight at the thought of sleeping with his mother and the baby. Nor because of that only; for he resolved within himself that he would try to get a share in the business of the night: why should his mother have too little sleep rather than himself? They might at least divide the too little between them! So he went to bed early, full of the thought of waking up as soon as Agnes should begin to cry, and finding out what he could do. Already he had begun to be useful in the daytime, and had twice put her to sleep when both his mother and Tibby had failed. And although he quite understood that in all probability he would not have succeeded if they hadn't tried first, yet it had been some relief to them, and they had confessed it.

But when he woke, there lay his mother and his sister both sound asleep; the sun was shining through the blind; he heard Tibby about the house; and, in short, it was time to get up.

At breakfast, his father said to him—

"Well, Willie, how did Agnes behave herself last night?"

"So well!" answered Willie; "she never cried once."

"O Willie!" said his mother, laughing, "she screamed for a whole hour, and was so hungry after it that she emptied her bottle without stopping once. You were sound asleep all the time, and never stirred."

Willie was so much ashamed of himself, although he wasn't in the least to blame, that he could hardly keep from crying. He did not say another word, except when he was spoken to, all through breakfast, and his father and mother were puzzled to think what could be the matter with him: He went about the greater part of the morning moodily thinking; then for advice betook himself to Mrs Wilson, who gave him her full attention, and suggested several things, none of which, however, seemed to him likely to succeed.

"If I could but go to bed after mamma was asleep," he said, "I could tie a string to my hair, and then slip a loop at the other end over mamma's wrist, so that when she sat up to attend to Agnes, she would pull my hair and wake me. Wouldn't she wonder what it was when she felt it pulling her?"

He had to go home without any help from Mrs Wilson. All the way he kept thinking with himself something after this fashion—

"Mamma won't wake me, and Agnes can't; and the worst of it is that everybody else will be just as fast asleep as I shall be. Let me see—who is there that's awake all night? There's the cat: I think she is, but then she wouldn't know when to wake me, and even if I could teach her to wake me the moment Agnes cried, I don't think she would be a nice one to do it; for if I didn't come awake with a pat of her velvety pin-cushions, she might turn out the points of the pins in them, and scratch me awake. There's the clock; it's always awake;

31

but it can't tell you the time till you go and ask it. I think it might be made to wind up a string that should pull me when the right time came; but I don't think I could teach it. And when it came to the pull, the pull might stop the clock, and what would papa say then? They tell me the owls are up all night, but they're no good, I'm certain. I don't see what I am to do. I wonder if God would wake me if I were to ask Him?"

I don't know whether Willie did or did not ask God to wake him. I did not inquire, for what goes on of that kind, it is better not to talk much about. What I do know is, that he fell asleep with his head and heart full of desire to wake and help his mother; and that, in the middle of the night, he did wake up suddenly, and there was little Agnes screaming with all her might. He sat up in bed instantly.

"What's the matter, Willie?" said his mother. "Lie down and go to sleep."

"Baby's crying," said Willie.

"Never you mind. I'll manage her."

"Do you know, mamma, I think I was waked up just in time to help you.

I'll take her from you, and perhaps she will take her drink from me."

"Nonsense, Willie. Lie down, my pet."

"But I've been thinking about it, mamma. Do you remember, yesterday, Agnes would not take her bottle from you, and screamed and screamed; but when Tibby took her, she gave in and drank it all? Perhaps she would do the same with me."

As he spoke he slipped out of bed, and held out his arms to take the baby. The light was already coming in, just a little, through the blind, for it was summer. He heard a cow lowing in the fields at the back of the house, and he wondered whether her baby had woke her. The next moment he had little Agnes in his arms, for his mother thought he might as well try, seeing he was awake.

"Do take care and don't let her fall, Willie."

"That I will, mamma. I've got her tight. Now give me the bottle, please."

"I haven't got it ready yet; for you woke the minute she began to cry."

So Willie walked about the room with Agnes till his mother had got her bottle filled with nice warm milk-and-water and just a little sugar. When she gave it to him, he sat down with the baby on his knees, and, to his great delight, and the satisfaction of his mother as well, she stopped crying, and began to drink the milk-and-water.

"Why, you're a born nurse, Willie!" said his mother. But the moment the baby heard her mother's voice, she forsook the bottle, and began to scream, wanting to go to her.

"O mamma! you mustn't speak, please; for of course she likes you better than the bottle; and when you speak that reminds her of you. It was just the same with Tibby yesterday. Or if you must speak, speak with some other sound, and not in your own soft, sweet way."

A few moments after, Willie was so startled by a gruff voice in the room that he nearly dropped the bottle; but it was only his mother following his directions. The plan was quite successful, for the baby had not a suspicion that the voice was her mother's, paid no heed to it, and attended only to her bottle.

Mr Macmichael, who had been in the country, was creeping up the stair to his room, fearful of disturbing his wife, when what should he hear but a man's voice as he supposed! and what should he think but that robbers had broken in! Of course he went to his wife's room first. There he heard the voice plainly enough through the door, but when he opened it he could see no one except Willie feeding the baby on an ottoman at the foot of the bed. When his wife had explained what and why it was, they both laughed heartily over Willie's suggestion for leaving the imagination of little Agnes in repose; and henceforth he was installed as night-nurse, so long as the process of weaning should last; and very proud of his promotion he was. He slept as sound as ever, for he had no anxiety about waking; his mother always woke him the instant Agnes began to cry.

"Willie!" she would say, "Willie! here's your baby wanting you."

And up Willie would start, sometimes before he was able to open his eyes, for little boys' eyelids are occasionally obstinate. And once he jumped out of bed crying, "Where is she, mamma? I've lost her!" for he had been dreaming about her.

You may be sure his mamma let him have a long sleep in the morning always, to make up for being disturbed in the night.

Agnes throve well, notwithstanding the weaning. She soon got reconciled to the bottle, and then Willie slept in peace.

CHAPTER V. HE GOES TO LEARN A TRADE.

Time passed, and Willie grew. Have my readers ever thought what is meant by growing? It is far from meaning only that you get bigger and stronger. It means that you become able both to understand and to wonder at more of the things about you. There are people who the more they understand, wonder the less; but such are not growing straight; they are growing crooked. There are two ways of growing. You may be growing up, or you may be growing down; and if you are doing both at once, then you are growing crooked. There are people who are growing up in understanding, but down in goodness. It is a beautiful fact, however, that you can't grow up in goodness and down in understanding; while the great probability is, that, if you are not growing better, you will by and by begin to grow stupid. Those who are growing the right way, the more they understand, the more they wonder; and the more they learn to do, the more they want to do. Willie was a boy of this kind. I don't care to write about boys and girls, or men and women, who are not growing the right way. They are not interesting enough to write about.

But he was not the only one to grow: Agnes grew as well; and the more Willie grew capable of helping her, the more he found Agnes required of him. It was a long time, however, before he knew how much he was obliged to Agnes for requiring so much of him.

She grew and grew until she was capable of a doll; when of course a doll was given her—not a new one just bought, but a most respectable old doll, a big one that had been her mother's when she was a little girl, and which she had been wise enough to put in her trunk before she left her mother's house to go home with Mr Macmichael. She made some new clothes for it now, and Tibby made a cloak and bonnet for her to wear when she went out of doors. But it struck Willie that her shoes, which were only of cloth, were very unfit for walking, and he thought that in a doctor's family it was something quite amazing that, while head and shoulders were properly looked after, the feet should remain utterly neglected. It was clear that must be his part in the affair; it could not be anybody else's, for in that case some one else would have attended to it. He must see about it.

I think I have said before that Willie knew almost everybody in the village, and I might have added that everybody without exception knew him. He was a favourite—first of all, because his father was much loved and trusted; next, because his mother spoke as kindly to her husband's poor patients as to the richer ones; and last, because he himself spoke to everybody with proper respect. Some of the people, however, he knew of course better than others. Of these Mrs Wilson we know was one. But I believe I also mentioned that in the house in which she lived there were other poor people. In the room opposite to hers, on the ground-floor, lived and worked a shoemaker—a man who had neither wife nor child, nor, so far as people knew, any near relative at all. He was far from being in good health, and although he worked from morning to night, had a constant pain in his back, which was rather crooked, having indeed a little hump on it. If his temper was not always of the best, I wonder what cleverest of watches or steam-engines would go as well as he did with such a twist in its back? To see him seated on his low stool—in which, by the way, as if it had not been low enough, he sat in a leather-covered hole, perhaps for the sake of the softness and spring of the leather—with his head and body bent forward over his lapstone or his last, and his right hand with the quick broad-headed hammer hammering up and down on a piece of sole-leather; or with both his hands now meeting as if for a little friendly chat about something small, and then suddenly starting asunder as if in astonished anger, with a portentous hiss, you might have taken him for an automaton moved by springs, and imitating human actions in a very wonderful manner—so regular and machine-like were his motions, and so little did he seem to think about what he was at. A little passing attention, a hint now and then from his head, was sufficient to keep his hands right, for they were so used to their work, and had been so well taught by his head, that they could pretty nearly have made a pair of shoes of themselves; so that the shoemaking trade is one that admits of a great deal of thought going on in the head that hangs over the work, like a sun over the earth ripening its harvest. Shoemakers have distinguished themselves both in poetry and in prose; and if Hector Macallaster had done so in neither, he could yet think, and that is what some people who write both poetry and prose cannot do. But it is of infinitely more importance to be able to think well than merely to write ever so well; and, besides, to think well is what everybody ought to be or to become able to do.

Hector had odd ways of looking at things, but I need not say more about that, for it will soon be plain enough. Ever since the illness from which he had risen with a weak spine, and ever-working brain, and a quiet heart, he had shown himself not merely a good sort of man, for such he had always been, but a religious man; not by saying much, for he was modest even to shyness with grown people, but by the solemnity of his look when a great word was spoken, by his unblamable behaviour, and by the readiness with which he would lend or give of his small earnings to his poor neighbours. The only thing of which anybody could complain was his temper; but it showed itself only occasionally, and almost everybody made excuse for it on the ground of his bodily ailments. He gave it no quarter himself, however. He said once to the clergyman, to whom he had been lamenting the trouble he had with it, and who had sought to comfort him by saying that it was caused by the weakness of his health—

"No, sir—excuse me; nobody knows how much I am indebted to my crooked back. If it weren't for that I might have a bad temper and never know it. But that drives it out of its hole, and when I see the ugly head of it I know it's there, and try once more to starve it to death. But oh dear! it's such a creature to burrow! When I think I've built it in all round, out comes its head again at a place where I never looked to see it, and it's all to do over again!"

You will understand by this already that the shoemaker thought after his own fashion, which is the way everybody who can think does think. What he thought about his trade and some other things we shall see by and by.

When Willie entered his room, he greeted him with a very friendly nod; for not only was he fond of children, but he had a special favour for Willie, chiefly because he considered himself greatly indebted to him for something he had said to Mrs Wilson, and which had given him a good deal to think about. For Mrs Wilson often had a chat with Hector, and then she would not unfrequently talk about Willie, of whose friendship she was proud. She had told him of the strange question he had put to her as to whether God worked, and the shoemaker, thinking over it, had come to the same conclusion as Willie's father, and it had been a great comfort and help to him.

"What can I do for you to-day, Willie?" he said; for in that part of the country they do not say Master and Miss. "You look," he added, "if you wanted something."

"I want you to teach me, please," answered Willie.

"To teach you what?" asked Hector.

"To make shoes, please," answered Willie.

"Ah! but do you think that would be prudent of me? Don't you see, if I were to teach you to make shoes, people would be coming to you to make their shoes for them, and what would become of me then?"

"But I only want to make shoes for Aggy's doll. She oughtn't to go without shoes in this weather, you know."

"Certainly not. Well, if you will bring me the doll I will take her measure and make her a pair."

"But I don't think papa could afford to pay for shoes for a doll as well as for all of us. You see, though it would be better, it's not necessary that a doll should have strong shoes. She has shoes good enough for indoors, and she needn't walk in the wet. Don't you think so yourself, Hector?"

"But," returned Hector, "I shall be happy to make Agnes a present of a pair of shoes for her doll. I shouldn't think of charging your papa for that. He is far too good a man to be made to pay for everything."

"But," objected Willie, "to let you make them for nothing would be as bad as to make papa pay for them when they are not necessary. Please, you must let me make them for Aggy. Besides, she's not old enough yet even to say thank you for them."

"Then she won't be old enough to say thank you to you either," said Hector, who, all this time, had been losing no moment from his work, but was stitching away, with a bore, and a twiddle, and a hiss, at the sole of a huge boot.

"Ah! but you see, she's my own—so it doesn't matter!"

If I were writing a big book, instead of a little one, I should be tempted to say not only that this set Hector a thinking, but what it made him think as well. Instead of replying, however, he laid down his boot, rose, and first taking from a shelf a whole skin of calf-leather, and next a low chair from a corner of the room, he set the latter near his own seat opposite the window.

"Sit down there, then, Willie," he said; adding, as he handed him the calf-skin, "There's your leather, and my tools are at your service. Make your shoes, and welcome. I shall be glad of your company."

Having thus spoken, he sat down again, caught up his boot hurriedly, and began stitching away as if for bare life.

Willie took the calf-skin on his lap, somewhat bewildered. If he had been asked to cut out a pair of seven-leagued boots for the ogre, there would have seemed to his eyes enough of leather for them in that one skin. But how ever was he to find two pieces small enough for doll's shoes in such an ocean of leather? He began to turn it round and round, looking at it all along the edge, while Hector was casting sidelong glances at him in the midst of his busyness, with a curiosity on his face which his desire to conceal it caused to look grim instead of amused.

Willie, although he had never yet considered how shoes are made, had seen at once that nothing could be done until he had got the command of a manageable bit of leather; he found too much only a shade better than too little; and he saw that it wouldn't be wise to cut a piece out anywhere, for that might spoil what would serve for a large pair of shoes or even boots. Therefore he kept turning the skin round until he came to a small projecting piece. This he contemplated for some time, trying to recall the size of Dolly's feet, and to make up his mind whether it would not be large enough for one or even for both shoes. A smile passed over Hector's face—a smile of satisfaction.

"That's it!" he said at last. "I think you'll do. That's the first thing—

39

to consider your stuff, and see how much you can make of it. Waste is a thing that no good shoemaker ever yet could endure. It's bad in itself, and so unworkmanlike! Yes, I think that corner will do. Shall I cut it off for you?"

"No, thank you—not yet, please. I think I must go and look at her feet, for I can't recollect quite how big they are. I'll just run home and look."

"Do you think you will be able to carry the exact size in your head, and bring it back with you?"

"Yes, I think I shall."

"I don't. I never could trust myself so far as that, nearly. You might be pretty nigh it one way and all wrong another, for you have to consider length and breadth and roundabout. I will tell you the best way for you to do. Set the doll standing on a bit of paper, and draw a pencil all round her foot with the point close to it on the paper. Both feet will be better, for it would be a mistake to suppose they must be of the same size. That will give you the size of the sole. Then take a strip of paper and see how long a piece it takes to go round the thickest part of the foot, and cut it off to that length. That will be sufficient measurement for a doll's shoe, for even if it should not fit exactly, she won't mind either being pinched a little or having to walk a little loose."

Willie got up at once to go and do as Hector had told him; but Hector was not willing to part with him so soon, for it was not often he had anybody to talk to while he went on with his work. Therefore he said—

"But don't you think, Willie, before you set about it, you had better see how I do? It would be a pity to spend your labour in finding out for yourself what shoemakers have known for hundreds of years, and which you could learn so easily by letting me show you."

"Thank you," said Willie, sitting down again.

"I should like that very much. I will sit and look at you. I know what you are doing. You are fastening on the sole of a boot."

"Yes. Do you see how it's done?"

"I'm not sure. I don't see yet quite. Of course I see you are sewing the one to the other. I've often wondered how you could manage with small shoes like mine to get in your hand to pull the needle through; but I see you don't use a needle, and I see that you are sewing it all on the outside of the boot, and don't put your hand inside at all. I can't get to understand it."

"You will in a minute. You see how, all round the edge of the upper, as we call it, I have sewn on a strong narrow strip, so that one edge of the strip sticks out all round, while the other is inside. To the edge that sticks out I sew on the sole, drawing my threads so tight that when I pare the edges off smooth, it will look like one piece, and puzzle anybody who did not know how it was done."

"I think I understand. But how do you get your thread so sharp and stiff as to go through the holes you make? I find it hard enough sometimes to get a thread through the eye of a needle; for though the thread is ever so much smaller than yours, I have to sharpen and sharpen it often before I can get it through. But yours, though it is so thick, keeps so sharp that it goes through the holes at once—two threads at once—one from each side!"

"Ah! but I don't sharpen my thread; I put a point upon it."

"Doesn't that mean the same thing?"

"Well, it may generally; but I don't mean the same thing by it. Look here."

"I see!" cried Willie; "there is a long bit of something else, not thread, upon it. What is it? It looks like a hair, only thicker, and it is so sharp at the point!"

"Can't you guess?"

"No; I can't."

"Then I will tell you. It is a bristle out of a hog's back. I don't know what a shoemaker would do without them. Look, here's a little bunch of them."

"That's a very clever use to put them to," said Willie.

"Do you go and pluck them out of the pigs?"

"No; we buy them at the shop. We want a good many, for they wear out. They get too soft, and though they don't break right off, they double up in places, so that they won't go through."

"How do you fasten them to the thread?"

"Look here," said Hector.

He took several strands of thread together, and drew them through and through a piece of cobbler's wax, then took a bristle and put it in at the end cunningly, in a way Willie couldn't quite follow; and then rolled and rolled threads and all over and over between his hand and his leather apron, till it seemed like a single dark-coloured cord.

"There, you see, is my needle and thread all in one."

"And what is the good of rubbing it so much with the cobbler's wax?"

"There are several good reasons for doing that. In the first place, it makes all the threads into one by sticking them together. Next it would be worn out before I had drawn it many times through but for the wax, which keeps the rubbing from wearing it. The wax also protects it afterwards, and keeps the wet from rotting it. The waxed thread fills the hole better too, and what is of as much consequence as anything, it sticks so that the last stitch doesn't slacken before the next comes, but holds so tight that, although the leather is very springy, it cannot make it slip. The two pieces are thus got so close together that they are like one piece, as you will see when I pare the joined edges."

I should tire my reader if I were to recount all the professional talk that followed; for although Willie found it most interesting, and began to feel as if he should soon be able to make a shoe himself, it is a very different thing merely to read about it—the man's voice not in your ears, and the work not going on before your eyes. But the shoemaker cared for other things besides shoemaking, and after a while he happened to make a remark which led to the following question from Willie:—

"Do you understand astronomy, Hector?"

"No. It's not my business, you see, Willie."

"But you've just been telling me so much about the moon, and the way she keeps turning her face always to us—in the politest manner, as you said!"

"I got it all out of Mr Dick's book. I don't understand it. I don't know why she does so. I know a few things that are not my business, just as you know a little about shoemaking, that not being your business; but I don't understand them for all that."

"Whose business is astronomy then?"

"Well," answered Hector, a little puzzled, "I don't see how it can well be anybody's business but God's, for I'm sure no one else can lay a hand to it."

"And what's your business, Hector?" asked Willie, in a half-absent mood.

Some readers may perhaps think this a stupid question, and perhaps so it was; but Willie was not therefore stupid. People sometimes appear stupid because they have more things to think about than they can well manage; while those who think only about one or two things may, on the contrary, appear clever when just those one or two things happen to be talked about.

"What is my business, Willie? Why, to keep people out of the dirt, of course."

"How?" asked Willie again.

"By making and mending their shoes. Mr Dick, now, when he goes out to look at the stars through his telescope, might get his death of cold if his shoemaker did not know his business. Of the general business, it's a part God keeps to Himself to see that the stars go all right, and that the sun rises and sets at the proper times. For the time's not the same any two mornings running, you see, and he might make a mistake if he wasn't looked after, and that would be serious. But I told you I don't understand about astronomy, because it's not my business. I'm set to keep folk's feet off the cold and wet earth, and stones and broken glass; for however much a man may be an astronomer and look up at the sky, he must touch the earth with some part of him, and generally does so with his feet."

"And God sets you to do it, Hector?"

"Yes. It's the way He looks after people's feet. He's got to look after everything, you know, or everything would go wrong. So He gives me the leather and the tools and the hands—and I must say the head, for it wants no little head to make a good shoe to measure—and it is as if He said to me—'There! you make shoes, while I keep the stars right.' Isn't it a fine thing to have a hand in the general business?"

And Hector looked up with shining eyes in the face of the little boy, while he pulled at his rosin-ends as if he would make the boot strong enough to keep out evil spirits.

"I think it's a fine thing to have to make nice new shoes," said Willie; "but I don't think I should like to mend them when they are soppy and muddy and out of shape."

"If you would take your share in the general business, you mustn't be particular. It won't do to be above your business, as they say: for my part, I would say below your business. There's those boots in the corner now. They belong to your papa. And they come next. Don't you think it's an honour to keep the feet of such a good man dry and warm as he goes about from morning to night comforting people? Don't you think it's an honour to mend boots for him, even if they should be dirty?"

"Oh, yes—for papa!" said Willie, as if his papa must be an exception to any rule.

"Well," resumed Hector, "look at these great lace-boots. I shall have to fill the soles of them full of hobnails presently. They belong to the best ploughman in the parish—John Turnbull. Don't you think it's an honour to mend boots for a man who makes the best bed for the corn to die in?"

"I thought it was to grow in," said Willie.

"All the same," returned Hector. "When it dies it grows—and not till then, as you will read in the New Testament. Isn't it an honour, I say, to mend boots for John Turnbull?"

"Oh, yes—for John Turnbull! I know John," said Willie, as if it made any difference to his merit whether Willie knew him or not!

"And there," Hector went on, "lies a pair of slippers that want patching. They belong to William Webster, the weaver, round the corner. They're very much down at heel too. But isn't it an honour to patch or set up slippers for a man who keeps his neighbours in fine linen all the days of their lives?"

"Yes, yes. I know William. It must be nice to do anything for William Webster."

"Suppose you didn't know him, would that make any difference?"

"No," said Willie, after thinking a little. "Other people would know him if I didn't."

"Yes, and if nobody knew him, God would know him; and anybody God has thought worth making, it's an honour to do anything for. Believe me, Willie, to have to keep people's feet dry and warm is a very important appointment."

"Your own shoes aren't very good, Hector," said Willie, who had been casting glances from time to time at his companion's feet, which were shod in a manner that, to say the least of it, would have prejudiced no one in favour of his handiwork. "Isn't it an honour to make shoes for yourself Hector?"

"There can't be much honour in doing anything for yourself," replied Hector, "so far as I can see. I confess my shoes are hardly decent, but then I can make myself a pair at any time; and indeed I've been thinking I would for the last three months, as soon as a slack time came; but I've been far too busy as yet, and, as I don't go out much till after it's dusk, nobody sees them."

"But if you should get your feet wet, and catch cold?"

"Ah! that might be the death of me!" said Hector. "I really must make myself a pair. Well now—let me see—as soon as I have mended those two pairs—I can do them all to-morrow—I will begin. And I'll tell you what," he added, after a thoughtful pause, "if you'll come to me the day after to-morrow, I will take that skin, and cut out a pair of shoes for myself, and you shall see how I do it, and everything about the making of them;—yes, you shall do some part of them yourself, and that shall be your first lesson in shoemaking."

"But Dolly's shoes!" suggested Willie.

"Dolly can wait a bit. She won't take her death of cold from wet feet. And let me tell you it is harder to make a small pair well than a large pair. You will do Dolly's ever so much better after you know how to make a pair for me."

CHAPTER VI. HOW WILLIE LEARNED TO READ BEFORE HE KNEW HIS LETTERS.

The next day his thoughts, having nothing particular to engage them, kept brooding over two things. These two things came together all at once, and a resolution was the consequence. I shall soon explain what I mean.

The one thing was, that Hector had shown considerable surprise when he found that Willie could not read. Now Willie was not in the least ashamed that he could not read: why should he be? It was nowhere written in the catechism he had learnt that it was his duty to be able to read; and if the catechism had merely forgotten to mention it, his father and mother would have told him. Neither was it a duty he ought to have known of himself—for then he would have known it. So why should he be ashamed?

People are often ashamed of what they need not be ashamed of. Again, they are often not at all ashamed of what they ought to be ashamed of, and will turn up their faces to the sun when they ought to hide them in the dust. If, for instance, Willie had ever put on a sulky face when his mother asked him to hold the baby for her, that would have been a thing for shame of which the skin of his face might well try to burn itself off; but not to be able to read before he had even been made to think about it, was not at all a thing to be ashamed of: it would have been more of a shame to be ashamed. Now that it had been put into his head, however, to think what a good thing reading was, all this would apply no longer. It was a very different thing now.

The other subject which occupied his thoughts was this:

Everybody was so kind to him—so ready to do things for him—and, what was of far more consequence, to teach him to do them himself; while he, so far as he could think, did nothing for anybody! That could not be right; it could not be—for it was not reasonable. Not to mention his father and mother, there was Mrs Wilson, who had taught him to knit, and even given him a few lessons in spinning, though that had not come to much; and here was Hector Macallaster going to teach him to make shoes; and not one thing that he could think of was he capable of doing in return! This must be looked into, for things could not be allowed to go on like that. All at once it struck him that Hector had said, with some regret in his voice, that though he had plenty of time to think, he had very little time to read; also that although he could see well enough by candlelight to work at his trade, he could not see well enough to read. What a fine thing it would be to learn to read to Hector! It would be such fun to surprise him too, by all at once reading him something!

The sun was not at his full height when Willie received this illumination. Before the sun went down he knew and could read at sight at least a dozen words.

For the moment he saw that he ought to learn to read, he ran to his mother, and asked her to teach him. She was delighted, for she had begun to be a little doubtful whether his father's plan of leaving him alone till he wanted to learn was the right one. But at that precise moment she was too busy with something that must be done for his father to lay it down and begin teaching him his letters. Willie was so eager to learn, however, that he could not rest without doing something towards it. He bethought himself a little—then ran and got Dr Watts's hymns for children. He knew "How doth the little busy bee" so well as to be able to repeat it without a mistake, for his mother had taught it him, and he had understood it. You see, he was not like a child of five, taught to repeat by rote lines which could give him no notions but mistaken ones. Besides, he had a good knowledge of words, and could use them well in talk, although he could not read; and it is a great thing if a child can talk well before he begins to learn to read.

He opened the little book at the Busy Bee, and knowing already enough to be able to divide the words the one from the other, he said to himself—

"The first word must be How. There it is, with a gap between it and the next word. I will look and see if I can find another How anywhere."

He looked a long time before he found one; for the capital H was in the way. Of course there were a good many how's, but not many with a big H, and he didn't know that the little h was just as good for the mere word. Then he looked for doth, and he found several doth's. Of the's he found as great a swarm as if they had been the bees themselves with which the little song was concerned. Busy was scarce; I am not sure whether he found it at all; but he looked at it until he was pretty sure he should know it again when he saw it. After he had gone over in this way every word of the first verse, he tried himself, by putting his finger at random here and there upon it, and seeing whether he could tell the word it happened to touch. Sometimes he could, and sometimes he couldn't. However, as I said, before the day was over, he knew at least a dozen words perfectly well at sight.

Nor let any one think this was other than a great step in the direction of reading. It would be easy for Willie afterwards to break up these words into letters.

It took him two days more—for during part of each he was learning to make shoes—to learn to know anywhere every word he had found in that hymn.

Next he took a hymn he had not learned, and applied to his mother when he came to a word he did not know, which was very often. As soon as she told him one, he hunted about until he found another and another specimen of the same, and so went on until he had fixed it quite in his mind.

At length he began to compare words that were like each other, and by discovering wherein they looked the same, and wherein they looked different, he learned something of the sound of the letters. For instance, in comparing the and these, although the one sound of the two letters, t and h, puzzled him, and likewise the silent e, he conjectured that the s must stand for the hissing sound; and when he looked at other words which had that sound, and perceived an s in every one of them, then he was sure of it. His mother had no idea how fast he was learning; and when about a fortnight after he had begun, she was able to take him in hand, she found, to her astonishment, that he could read a great many words, but that, when she wished him to spell one, he had not the least notion what she meant.

"Isn't that a b?" she said, wishing to help him to find out a certain word for himself.

"I don't know," answered Willie. "It's not the busy bee," he added, laughing;—"I should know him. It must be the lazy one, I suppose."

"Don't you know your letters?" asked his mother.

"No, mamma. Which are they? Are the rest yours and papa's?"

"Oh, you silly dear!" she said.

"Of course I am!" he returned;—"very silly! How could any of them be mine before I know the names of them! When I know them all, then they'll all be mine, I suppose—and everybody else's who knows them.—So that's Mr B—is it?"

"Yes. And that's C," said his mother.

"I'm glad to see you, Mr C," said Willie, merrily, nodding to the letter. "We shall know each other when we meet again.—I suppose this is D, mamma. How d'e do, Mr D? And what's this one with its mouth open, and half its tongue cut off?"

His mother told him it was E.

"Then this one, with no foot to stand on, is Fe, I suppose."

His mother laughed; but whoever gave it the name it has, would have done better to call it Fe, as Willie did. It would be much better also, in teaching children, at least, to call H, He, and W, We, and Y, Ye, and Z, Ze, as Willie called them. But it was easy enough for him to learn their names after he knew so much of what they could do.

What gave him a considerable advantage was, that he had begun with verse, and not dry syllables and stupid sentences. The music of the verse repaid him at once for the trouble of making it out—even before he got at the meaning, while the necessity of making each line go right, and the rhymes too, helped him occasionally to the pronunciation of a word.

The farther he got on, the faster he got on; and before six weeks were over, he could read anything he was able to understand pretty well at sight.

By this time, also, he understood all the particulars as to how a shoe is made, and had indeed done a few stitches himself, a good deal of hammering both of leather and of hob-nails, and a little patching, at which last the smallness of his hands was an advantage.

At length, one day, he said to the shoemaker—

"Shall I read a little poem to you, Hector?"

"You told me you couldn't read, Willie."

"I can now though."

"Do then," said Hector.

Looking for but a small result in such a short time, he was considerably astonished to find how well the boy could read; for he not merely gave the words correctly, but the sentences, which is far more difficult; that is, he read so that Hector could understand what the writer meant. It is a great thing to read well. Few can. Whoever reads aloud and does not read well, is a sort of deceiver; for he pretends to introduce one person to another, while he misrepresents him.

In after life, Willie continued to pay a good deal of attention not merely to reading for its own sake, but to reading for the sake of other people, that is, to reading aloud. As often as he came, in the course of his own reading, to any verse that he liked very much, he always read it aloud in order to teach himself how it ought to be read; doing his best—first, to make it sound true, that is, to read it according to the sense; next, to make it sound beautiful, that is, to read it according to the measure of the verse and the melody of the words.

He now read a great deal to Hector. There came to be a certain time every day at which Willie Macmichael was joyfully expected by the shoemaker—to read to him for an hour and a half—beyond which time his father did not wish the reading to extend.

CHAPTER VII. SOME THINGS THAT CAME OF WILLIE'S GOING TO SCHOOL.

When his father found that he had learned to read, then he judged it good for him to go to school. Willie was very much pleased. His mother said she would make him a bag to carry his books in; but Willie said there was no occasion to trouble herself; for, if she would give him the stuff, he would make it. So she got him a nice bit of green baize, and in the afternoon he made his bag—no gobble-stitch work, but good, honest back-stitching, except the string-case, which was only run, that it might draw easier and tighter. He passed the string through with a bodkin, fixed it in the middle, tied the two ends, and carried the bag to his mother, who pronounced it nearly as well made as if she had done it herself.

At school he found it more and more plain what a good thing it is that we haven't to find out every thing for ourselves from the beginning; that people gather into books what they and all who went before them have learned, so that we come into their property, as it were; and, after being taught of them, have only to begin our discoveries from where they leave off. In geography, for instance, what a number of voyages and journeys have had to be made, and books to record them written; then what a number of these books to be read, and the facts gathered out of them, before a single map could be drawn, not to say a geography book printed! Whereas now he could learn a multitude of things about the various countries, their peoples and animals and plants, their mountains and rivers and lakes and cities, without having set his foot beyond the parish in which he was born. And so with everything else after its kind. But it is more of what Willie learned to do than what he learned to know that I have to treat.

When he went to school, his father made him a present of a pocket-knife. He had had one before, but not a very good one; and this, having three blades, all very sharp, he found a wonderful treasure of recourse. His father also bought him a nice new slate.

Now there was another handy boy at school, a couple of years older than Willie, whose father was a carpenter. He had cut on the frame of his slate, not his initials only, but his whole name and address,—Alexander Spelman, Priory Leas. Willie thought how nice it would be with his new knife also to cut his name on his slate; only he would rather make some difference in the way of doing it. What if, instead of sinking the letters in the frame, he made them stand up from the frame by cutting it away to some depth all round them. There was not much originality in this, for it was only reversing what Spelman had done; but it was more difficult, and would, he thought, be prettier. Then what was he thus to carve? One would say, "Why, William Macmichael, of course, and, if he liked, Priory Leas" But Willie was a peculiar little fellow, and began to reason with himself whether he had any right to put his own name on the slate. "My father did not give me the slate," he said, "to be my very own. He gave me the knife like that, but not the slate. When I am grown up, it will belong to Agnes. What shall I put on it? What's mine's papa's, and what's papa's is his own," argued Willie.—"I know!" he said to himself at last.

The boys couldn't imagine what he meant to do when they saw him draw first a D and then an O on the frame. But when they saw a C and a T follow, they thought what a conceited little prig Willie was!

"Do you think you're a doctor because your father is, you little ape?" they said.

"No, no," answered Willie, laughing heartily, but thinking, as he went on with his work, that he might be one some day.

When the drawing of the letters was finished, there stood, all round the slate, "Doctor Macmichael's Willie, The Ruins, Priory Leas."

Then out came his knife. But it was a long job, for Willie was not one of those slovenly boys that scamp their work. Such boys are nothing but soft, pulpy creatures, who, when they grow to be men, will be too soft for any of the hard work of the world. They will be fit only for buffers, to keep the working men from breaking their heads against each other in their eagerness. But the carving was at length finished, and gave much satisfaction—first to

Willie himself, because it was finished; next, to Alexander Spelman, Priory Leas, because, being a generous-minded boy, he admired Willie's new and superior work; third, to Mr and Mrs Macmichael, because they saw in it, not the boy's faculty merely, but his love to his father as well; for the recognition of a right over us is one of the sweetest forms love can take. "I am yours" is the best and greatest thing one can say, if to the right person.

It led to a strong friendship between him and Spelman, and to his going often to the workshop of the elder Spelman, the carpenter.

He was a solemn, long-faced, and long-legged man, with reddish hair and pale complexion, who seldom or ever smiled, and at the bench always looked as if he were standing on a stool, he stooped so immoderately. A greater contrast than that between him and the shoemaker could hardly have been found, except in this, that the carpenter also looked sickly. He was in perfect health, however, only oppressed with the cares of his family, and the sickness of his wife, who was a constant invalid, with more children her husband thought than she could well manage, or he well provide for. But if he had thought less about it he would have got on better. He worked hard, but little fancied how many fewer strokes of his plane he made in an hour just because he was brooding over his difficulties, and imagining what would be the consequences if this or that misfortune were to befall him—of which he himself sought and secured the shadow beforehand, to darken and hinder the labour which might prevent its arrival. But he was a good man nevertheless, for his greatest bugbear was debt. If he could only pay off every penny he owed in the world, and if only his wife were so far better as to enjoy life a little, he would, he thought, be perfectly happy. His wife, however, was tolerably happy, notwithstanding her weak health, and certainly enjoyed life a good deal—far more at least than her husband was able to believe.

Mr Macmichael was very kind and attentive to Mrs Spelman; though, as the carpenter himself said, he hadn't seen the colour of his money for years. But the Doctor knew that Spelman was a hard-working man, and would rather have given him a little money than have pressed him for a penny. He told him one day, when he was lamenting that he couldn't pay him even yet, that he was only too glad to do anything in the least little bit like what the

Saviour did when he was in the world—"a carpenter like you, Spelman—think of that," added the Doctor.

So Spelman was as full of gratitude as he could hold. Except Hector Macallaster, the Doctor was almost his only creditor. Medicine and shoes were his chief trials: he kept on paying for the latter, but the debt for the former went on accumulating.

Hence it came that when Willie began to haunt his shop, though he had hardly a single smile to give the little fellow, he was more than pleased;—gave him odds and ends of wood; lent him whatever tools he wanted except the adze—that he would not let him touch; would drop him a hint now and then as to the use of them; would any moment stop his own work to attend to a difficulty the boy found himself in; and, in short, paid him far more attention than he would have thought required of him if Willie had been his apprentice.

From the moment he entered the workshop, Willie could hardly keep his hands off the tools. The very shape of them, as they lay on the bench or hung on the wall, seemed to say over and over, "Come, use me; come, use me." They looked waiting, and hungry for work. They wanted stuff to shape and fashion into things, and join into other things. They wanted to make bigger tools than themselves—for ploughing the earth, for carrying the harvest, or for some one or other of ten thousand services to be rendered in the house or in the fields. It was impossible for Willie to see the hollow lip of the gouge, the straight lip of the chisel, or the same lip fitted with another lip, and so made into the mouth of the plane, the worm-like auger, or the critical spokeshave, the hammer which will have it so, or the humble bradawl which is its pioneer—he could see none of them without longing to send his life into theirs, and set them doing in the world—for was not this what their dumb looks seemed ever to implore? At that time young Spelman was busy making a salt-box for his mother out of the sound bits of an old oak floor which his father had taken up because it was dry-rotted. It was hard wood to work, but Willie bore a hand in planing the pieces, and was initiated into the mysteries of dovetailing and gluing. Before the lid was put on by the hinges, he carved the initials of the carpenter and his wife in relief upon it, and many years after they used to show his work. But the first thing he set about making for himself was a water-wheel.

If he had been a seaside boy, his first job would have been a boat; if he had lived in a flat country, it would very likely have been a windmill; but the most noticeable thing in that neighbourhood was a mill for grinding corn driven by a water-wheel.

When Willie was a tiny boy, he had gone once with Farmer Thomson's man and a load of corn to see the mill; and the miller had taken him all over it. He saw the corn go in by the hopper into the trough which was the real hopper, for it kept constantly hopping to shake the corn down through a hole in the middle of the upper stone, which went round and round against the lower, so that between them they ground the corn to meal, which, in the story beneath, he saw pouring, a solid stream like an avalanche, from a wooden spout. But the best of it all was the wheel outside, and the busy rush of the water that made it go. So Willie would now make a water-wheel.

The carpenter having given him a short lecture on the different kinds of water-wheels, he decided on an undershot, and with Sandy's help proceeded to construct it—with its nave of mahogany, its spokes of birch, its floats of deal, and its axle of stout iron-wire, which, as the friction would not be great, was to run in gudgeon-blocks of some hard wood, well oiled. These blocks were fixed in a frame so devised that, with the help of a few stones to support it, the wheel might be set going in any small stream.

There were many tiny brooks running into the river, and they fixed upon one of them which issued from the rising ground at the back of the village: just where it began to run merrily down the hill, they constructed in its channel a stonebed for the water-wheel—not by any means for it to go to sleep in!

It went delightfully, and we shall hear more of it by and by. For the present, I have only to confess that, after a few days, Willie got tired of it—and small blame to him, for it was of no earthly use beyond amusement, and that which can only amuse can never amuse long. I think the reason children get tired of their toys so soon is just that it is against human nature to be really interested in what is of no use. If you say that a beautiful thing is always interesting, I answer, that a beautiful thing is of the highest use. Is not a diamond that flashes all its colours into the heart of a poet as useful as the diamond with which the glazier divides the sheets of glass into panes for our windows? Anyhow, the reason Willie got tired of his water-wheel was that it went round and round, and did nothing but go round. It drove no machinery, ground no grain of corn—"did nothing for _no_body," Willie said, seeking to be emphatic. So he carried it home, and put it away in a certain part of the ruins where he kept odds and ends of things that might some day come in useful.

Mr Macmichael was so devoted to his profession that he desired nothing better for Willie than that he too should be a medical man, and he was more than pleased to find how well Willie's hands were able to carry out his contrivances; for he judged it impossible for a country doctor to have too much mechanical faculty. The exercise of such a skill alone might secure the instant relief of a patient, and be the saving of him. But, more than this, he believed that nothing tended so much to develop common sense—the most precious of faculties—as the doing of things with the hands. Hence he not only encouraged Willie in everything he undertook, but, considering the five hours of school quite sufficient for study of that sort, requested the master not to give him any lessons to do at home. So Willie worked hard during school, and after it had plenty of time to spend in carpentering, so that he soon came to use all the common bench-tools with ease, and Spelman was proud of his apprentice, as he called him—so much so, that the burden of his debt grew much lighter upon his shoulders.

But Willie did not forget his older friend, Hector Macallaster. Every half-holiday he read to him for a couple of hours, chiefly, for some time, from Dick's Astronomy. Neither of them understood all he read, but both understood much, and Hector could explain some of the things that puzzled Willie. And when he found that everything went on in such order, above and below and all about him, he began to see that even a thing well done was worth a good deal more when done at the right moment or within the set time; and that the heavens themselves were like a great clock, ordering the time for everything.

Neither did he give up shoemaking, for he often did a little work for Hector, who had made him a leather apron, and cut him out bits of stout leather to protect his hands from the thread when he was sewing. For twelve months, however, his chief employment lay in the workshop of the carpenter.

CHAPTER VIII. WILLIE DIGS AND FINDS WHAT HE DID NOT EXPECT.

He had been reading to Hector Sir Walter Scott's "Antiquary," in which occurs the narration of a digging for treasure in ruins not unlike these, only grander. It was of little consequence to Willie that no treasure had been found there: the propriety of digging remained the same; for in a certain spot he had often fancied that a hollow sound, when he stamped hard, indicated an empty place underneath. I believe myself that it came from above, and not from beneath; for although a portion of the vaulted roof of the little chamber had been broken in, the greater part of it still remained, and might have caused a reverberation. The floor was heaped up with fallen stones and rubbish.

One Wednesday afternoon, instead of going to Hector, whom he had told not to expect him, he got a pickaxe and spade, and proceeded to dig in the trodden heap. At the first blow of the pickaxe he came upon large stones—the job of clearing out which was by no means an easy one—so far from it, indeed, that, after working for half an hour, and only getting out two large and half a dozen smaller ones, he resolved to ask Sandy Spelman to help him. So he left his pickaxe with one point fast between two stones, and ran to the shop. Sandy was at work, but his father was quite willing to let him go. Willie told them he was digging for a treasure, and they all laughed over it; but at the same time Willie thought with himself—"Who knows? People have found treasures buried in old places like that. The Antiquary did not—but he is only in a story, not in a high story" (for that was Willie's derivation of the word history). "The place sounds likely enough. Anyhow, where's the harm in trying?"

They were both so eager—for Sandy liked the idea of digging in the ruins much better than the work he was at—that they set off at full speed the moment they were out of the shop, and never slackened until they stood panting by the anchored pickaxe, upon which Spelman pounced, and being stronger than Willie, and more used to hard work, had soon dislodged both the stones which held it. They were so much larger, however, than any Willie had come upon before, that they had to roll them out of the little chamber, instead of lifting them; after which they got on better, and had soon piled a good heap against the wall outside. After they had had their tea, they set to work again, and worked till the twilight grew dark about them—by which time they had got the heap down to what seemed the original level of the floor. Still there were stones below, but what with fatigue and darkness, they were now compelled to stop, and Sandy went home, after promising to come as early as he could in the morning and call Willie, who was to leave the end of a string hanging out of the staircase window, whose other end should pass through the keyhole of his door and be tied to his wrist. He seemed to have hardly been in bed an hour, when he woke with his arm at full length, and the pulling going on as if it would pull him out of bed. He tugged again in reply, and jumped out.

It was a lovely summer morning—the sun a few yards up the sky; the grass glittering with dew; the birds singing as if they were singing their first and would sing their last; the whole air, even in his little room, filled with a cool odour as of blessed thoughts, and just warm enough to let him know that the noontide would be hot. And there was Sandy waiting in the street to help him dig for the treasure! In a few minutes he had opened the street door and admitted him. They went straight to the scene of their labour.

Having got out a few more stones, they began to fancy they heard a curious sound, which they agreed was more like that of running water than anything else they could think of. Now, except a well in the street, just before the cottage, there was no water they knew of much nearer than the river, and they wondered a good deal.

At length Sandy's pickaxe got hold of a stone which he could not move, do what he would. He tried another, and succeeded, but soon began to suspect that there was some masonry there. Contenting himself therefore with clearing out only the loose stones, he soon found plainly enough that he was working in a narrow space, around which was a circular wall of solid stone and lime. The sound of running water was now clear enough, and the earth in the hole was very damp. Sandy had now got down three or four feet below the level.

"It's an old well," he said. "There can be no doubt of it."

"Does it smell bad?" asked Willie, peeping down disappointed.

"Not a bit," answered Sandy.

"Then it's not stagnant," said Willie.

"You might have told that by your ears without troubling your nose," said Sandy. "Didn't you hear it running?"

"How can it be running when it's buried away down there?" said Willie.

"How can it make a noise if it isn't running?" retorted Sandy—to which question Willie attempted no reply.

It was now serious work to get the stones up, for Sandy's head only was above the level of the ground; it was all he could do to lift some of the larger ones out of the hole, and Willie saw that he must contrive to give him some help. He ran therefore to the house, and brought a rope which he had seen lying about. One end of it Sandy tied round whatever stone was too heavy for him, and Willie, laying hold of the other, lifted along with him. They got on faster now, and in a few minutes Sandy exclaimed—

"Here it is at last!"

"The treasure?" cried Willie. "Oh, jolly!"

Sandy burst out laughing, and shouted—

"The water!"

"Bother the water!" growled Willie. "But go on, Sandy; the iron chest may be at the bottom of the water, you know."

"All very well for you up there!" retorted Sandy. "But though I can get the stones out, I can't get the water out. And I've no notion of diving where there's pretty sure to be nothing to dive for. Besides, a body can't dive in a stone pipe like this. I should want weights to sink me, and I mightn't get them off in time. I want my breakfast dreadful, Willie."

So saying, he scrambled up the side of the well, and the last of him that appeared, his boots, namely, bore testimony enough to his having reached the water. Willie peered down into the well, and caught the dull glimmer of it through the stones; then, a good deal disappointed, followed Sandy as he strode away towards the house.

"You'll come and have your breakfast with me, Sandy, won't you?" he said from behind him.

"No, thank you," answered Sandy. "I don't like any porridge but my mother's."

And without looking behind him, he walked right through the cottage, and away home.

Before Willie had finished his porridge, he had got over his disappointment, and had even begun to see that he had never really expected to find a treasure. Only it would have been fun to hand it over to his father!

All through morning school, however, his thoughts would go back to the little vault, so cool and shadowy, sheltering its ancient well from the light that lorded it over all the country outside. No doubt the streams rejoiced in it, but even for them it would be too much before the evening came to cool and console them; while the slow wells in the marshy ground up on the mountains must feel faint in an hour of its burning eye. This well had always been, and always would be, cool and blessed and sweet, like—like a precious thing you can only think about. And wasn't it a nice thing to have a well of your own? Tibby needn't go any more to the village pump—which certainly was nearer, but stood in the street, not in their own ground. Of course, as yet, she could not draw a bucketful, for the water hardly came above the stones; but he would soon get out as many as would make it deep enough—only, if it was all Sandy could do to get out the big ones, and that with his help too, how was he to manage it alone? There was the rub!

I must go back a little to explain how he came to think of a plan.

After Hector and he had gone as far in Dr Dick's astronomy as they could understand, they found they were getting themselves into what seemed quite a jungle of planets, and suns, and comets, and constellations.

"It seems to me," said the shoemaker, "that to understand anything you must understand everything."

So they laid the book aside for the present; and Hector, searching about for another with which to fill up the remainder of the afternoon, came upon one in which the mechanical powers were treated after a simple fashion.

Of this book Willie had now read a good deal. I cannot say that he had yet come to understand the mechanical power so thoroughly as to see that the lever and the wheel-and-axle are the same in kind, or that the screw, the inclined plane, and the wedge are the same power in different shapes; but he did understand that while a single pulley gives you no advantage except by enabling you to apply your strength in the most effective manner, a second pulley takes half the weight off you. Hence, with the difficulty in which he now found himself, came at once the thought of a block with a pulley in it, which he had seen lying about in the carpenter's shop. He remembered also that there was a great iron staple or eye in the vault just over the well; and if he could only get hold of a second pulley, the thing was as good as done—the well as good as cleared out to whatever depth he could reach below the water.

As soon as school was over, he ran to Mr Spelman, and found to his delight that he could lend him not only that pulley but another as well. Each ran in a block which had an iron hook attached to it. With the aid of a ladder he put the hook of one of the blocks through the staple, and then fastened the end of his rope to the block. Next he got another bit of rope, and having pulled off his shoes and stockings, and got down into the well, tied it round the largest stone within reach, loosely enough to allow the hook of the second pulley to lay hold of it. Then, as a sailor would say, he rove the end of the long rope through this block, and getting up on the ladder again, rove it also through the first block which he had left hanging to the staple. All preparations thus completed, he stood by the well, and hauled away at the rope. It came slipping through the pulleys, and up rose the stone from the well as if by magic. As soon as it came clear of the edge, he drew it towards him, lowered it to the ground, took off its rope collar, and rolled it out of the doorway. Then he got into the well again, tied the collar about another stone, drew down the pulley, thrust its hook through the collar, got out of the well, and hauled up the second stone.

In this way he had soon got out so many that he was standing far above his ankles in the water, which was so cold that he was glad to get out to pull up every stone. By this time it was perfectly explained how the water made a noise, for he saw it escape by an opening in the side of the well.

He came at last to a huge stone, round which it was with difficulty he managed to fasten the rope. He had to pull away smaller stones from beneath it, and pass the rope through under it. Having lifted it a little way with the powerful help of his tackle, to try if all was right before he got out to haul in earnest, he saw that his knot was slipping, and lowered the stone again so as to set it on one end, leaning against the side of the well—when he discovered that his rope collar had got so frayed, that one of the strands was cut through; it would probably break and let the stone fall again into the well, when he would still more probably tumble after it. He was getting tired too, and it was growing very dusky in the ruins. He thought it better to postpone further proceedings, and getting out of the well, caught up his shoes and stockings, and went into the house.

CHAPTER IX. A MARVEL.

Early the next morning Mr Macmichael, as he was dressing, heard a laugh of strange delight in the garden, and, drawing up the blind, looked out. There, some distance off, stood Willie, the one moment staring motionless at something at his feet, the other dancing and skipping and singing, but still looking down at something at his feet. His father could not see what this something was, for Willie was on the other side of one of the mounds, and was turning away to finish his dressing, when from another direction a peculiar glitter caught his eye.

"What can this mean?" he said to himself. "Water in the garden! There's been no rain; and there's neither river nor reservoir to overflow! I can hardly believe my eyes!"

He hurried on the remainder of his clothes, and went out. But he had not gone many steps when what should he meet but a merry little brook coming cantering down between two of the mounds! It had already worn itself a channel in the path. He followed it up, wondering much, bewildered indeed; and had got to a little turfy hollow, down the middle of which it came bubbling and gabbling along, when Willie caught sight of him, and bounded to meet him with a radiant countenance and almost inarticulate cries of delight.

"Am I awake, Willie? or am I dreaming?" he asked.

"Wide awake, papa," answered Willie.

"Then what is the meaning of this? You seem to be in the secret: where does this water come from? I feel as if I were in a fairy tale."

"Isn't it lovely?" cried Willie. "I'll show you where it comes from. This way. You'll spoil your boots there. Look at the rhubarb-bed; it's turned into a swamp."

"The garden will be ruined," said his father.

"No, no, papa; we won't let it come to that. I've been watching it.

There's no soil carried away yet. Do come and see."

In mute astonishment, his father followed.

As I have already described it, the ground was very uneven, with many heights and hollows, whence it came that the water took an amazing number of twists and turns. Willie led his father as straight as he could, but I don't know how often they crossed the little brook before they came to where, from the old stone shaft, like the crater of a volcano, it rolled over the brim, an eruption of cool, clear, lucid water. Plenteous it rose and overflowed, like a dark yet clear molten gem, tumbling itself into the open world. How deliciously wet it looked in the shadow I——how it caught the sun the moment it left the chamber, grew merry, and trotted and trolled and cantered along!

"Is this your work, Willie?" asked his father, who did not know which of twenty questions to ask first.

"Mostly," said Willie.

"You little wizard! what have you been about? I can't understand it. We must make a drain for it at once."

"Bury a beauty like that in a drain!" cried Willie. "O papa!"

"Well, I don't know what else to do with it. How is it that it never found its way out before—somewhere or other?"

"I'll soon show you that," said Willie. "I'll soon send it about its business."

He had thought, when he first saw the issuing water, that the weight of the fallen stones and the hard covering of earth being removed, the spring had burst out with tenfold volume and vigour; but had satisfied himself by thinking about it, that the cause of the overflow must be the great stone he had set leaning against the side the last thing before dropping work the previous night: it must have blocked up the opening, and prevented the water from getting out as fast as before, that is, as fast as the spring rose. Therefore he now laid hold of the rope, which was still connected with the stone, and, not aware of how the water would help him by partly floating it, was astonished to find how easily he moved it. At once it swung away from the side into the middle of the well; the water ceased to run over the edge, with a loud gurgling began to sink, and sank down and down and down until the opening by which it escaped was visible.

"Ah! now, now I understand!" cried Mr Macmichael. "It's the old well of the Priory you've come upon, you little burrowing mole."

"Sandy helped me out with the stones. I thought there might be a treasure down there, and that set me digging. It was a funny treasure to find—wasn't it? No treasure could have been prettier though."

"If this be the Prior's Well, and all be true they said about it in old times," returned his father, "it may turn out a greater treasure than you even hoped for, Willie. Why, as I found some time ago in an old book about the monasteries of the country, people used to come from great distances to drink the water of the Prior's Well, believing it a cure for every disease under the sun. Run into the house and fetch me a jug."

"Yes, papa," said Willie, and bounded off.

There was no little brook careering through the garden now—only a few pools here and there—and its channel would soon be dry in the hot sun. But Willie thought how delightful it was to be able to have one there whenever he pleased. And it might be a much bigger brook too, for, instead of using the stone which could but partly block the water from the underground way, he would cut a piece of wood large enough to cover the opening, and rounded a little to fit the side of the well; then he would put the big stone just so far from the opening that the piece of wood could get through between it and the side of the well, and so be held tight. Then all the water would be forced to mount up, get out at the top, and run through the garden.

Meantime Mr Macmichael, having gone to see what course the water had taken, and how it had left the garden, found that, after a very circuitous route, it had run through the hedge into a surface drain in the field, and so down the hill towards the river.

When Willie brought him the jug, he filled it from the well, and carried the water into his surgery. There he put a little of it into several different glasses, and dropping something out of one bottle into one glass, and something out of another bottle into another glass, soon satisfied himself that it contained medicinal salts in considerable quantities. There could be no doubt that Willie had found the Prior's Well.

"It's a good thing," said his father at breakfast, "that you didn't flood the house, Willie! One turn more and the stream would have been in at the back-door."

"It wouldn't have done much harm," said Willie. "It would have run along the slabs in the passage and out again, for the front door is lower than the back. It would have been such fun!"

"You mischievous little thing!" said his mother, pretending to scold him,—"you don't think what trouble you would have given Tibby!"

"But wouldn't it have been fun? And wouldn't it have been lovely— running through the house all the hot summer day?"

"There may be a difference of opinion about that, Master Willie," said his mother. "You, for instance, might like to walk through water every time you went from the parlour to the kitchen, but I can't say I should."

Curious to know whether the village pump might not be supplied from his well, Mr Macmichael next analysed the water of that also, and satisfied himself that there was no connection between them. Within the next fortnight Willie discovered that as often as the stream ran through the garden, the little brook in which he had set his water-wheel going was nearly dry.

He had soon made a nice little channel for it, so that it should not get into any of the beds. He laid down turf along its banks in some parts, and sowed grass and daisy-seed in others; and when he found a pretty stone or shell, or bit of coloured glass or bright crockery or broken mirror, he would always throw it in, that the water might have the prettier path to run upon. Indeed, he emptied his store of marbles into it. He was not particularly fond of playing with marbles, but he had a great fancy for those of real white marble with lovely red streaks, and had collected some twenty or thirty of them. He kept them in the brook now, instead of in a calico bag.

The summer was a very hot and dry one. More than any of the rest of the gardens in the village, that of The Ruins suffered from such weather; for not only was there a deep gravel-bed under its mould, but a good part of its produce grew on the mounds, which were mostly heaps of stones, and neither gravel nor stones could retain much moisture. Willie watered it a good deal out of the Prior's Well; but it was hard work, and did not seem to be of much use.

One evening, when he had set the little brook free to run through the garden, and the sun was setting huge and red, with the promise of another glowing day to-morrow, and the air was stifling, and not a breath of wind stirring, so that the flowers hung their heads oppressed, and the leaves and little buttons of fruit on the trees looked ready to shrivel up and drop from the boughs, the thought came to him whether he could not turn the brook into a little Nile, causing it to overflow its banks and enrich the garden. He could not, of course, bring it about in the same way; for the Nile overflows from the quantities of rain up in the far-off mountains, making huge torrents rush into it faster than its channel, through a slow, level country, can carry the water away, so that there is nothing for it but overflow. If, however, he could not make more water run out of the well, he could make it more difficult for what did come from it to get away. First, he stopped up the outlet through the hedge with stones, and clay, and bits of board; then watched as it spread, until he saw where it would try to escape next, and did the same; and so on, taking care especially to keep it from the house. The mounds were a great assistance to him in hemming it in, but he had hard enough work of it notwithstanding; and soon perceived that at one spot it would get the better of him in a few minutes, and make straight for the back-door. He ran at once and opened the sluice in the well, and away the stream gurgled underground.

Before morning the water it left had all disappeared. It had soaked through the mounds, and into the gravel, but comforting the hot roots as it went, and feeding them with dissolved minerals. Doubtless, also, it lay all night in many a little hidden pool, which the heat of the next day's sun drew up, comforting again, through the roots in the earth, and through the leaves in the air, up into the sky. Willie could not help thinking that the garden looked refreshed; the green was brighter, he thought, and the flowers held up their heads a little better; the carrots looked more feathery, and the ferns more palmy; everything looked, he said, just as he felt after a good drink out of the Prior's Well. At all events, he resolved to do the same every night after sunset while the hot weather lasted—that was, if his father had no objection.

Mr Macmichael said he might try it, only he must mind and not go to bed and leave the water running, else they would have a cartload of mud in the house before morning.

So Willie strengthened and heightened his barriers, and having built a huge one at the last point where the water had tried to get away, as soon as the sun was down shut the sluice, and watched the water as it surged up in the throat of the well, and rushed out to be caught in the toils he had made for it. Before it could find a fresh place to get out at, the whole upper part of the garden was one network of lakes and islands.

Willie kept walking round and round it, as if it had been a wild beast trying to get out of its cage, and he had to watch and prevent it at every weak spot; or as if he were a magician, busily sustaining the charm by which he confined the gad-about creature. The moment he saw it beginning to get the better of him, he ran to the sluice and banished it to the regions below. Then he fetched an old newspaper, and sitting down on the borders of his lake, fashioned boat after boat out of the paper, and sent them sailing like merchant ships from isle to blooming isle.

Night after night he flooded the garden, and always before morning the water had sunk away through the gravel. Soon there was no longer any doubt that everything was mightily refreshed by it; the look of exhaustion and hopelessness was gone, and life was busy in flower and tree and plant. This year there was not a garden, even on the banks of the river, to compare with it; and when the autumn came, there was more fruit than Mr Macmichael remembered ever to have seen before.

CHAPTER X. A NEW ALARUM.

Willie was always thinking what uses he could put things to. Only he was never tempted to set a fine thing to do dirty work, as dull-hearted money-grubbers do—mill-owners, for instance, when they make the channel of a lovely mountain-stream serve for a drain to carry off the filth from their works. If Dante had known any such, I know where he would have put them, but I would rather not describe the place. I have told you what Willie made the prisoned stream do for the garden; I will now tell you what he made the running stream do for himself, and you shall judge whether or not that was fit work for him to require of it.

Ever since he had ceased being night-nurse to little Agnes, he had wished that he had some one to wake him every night, about the middle of it, that he might get up and look out of the window. For, after he had fed his baby-sister and given her back to his mother in a state of contentment, before getting into bed again he had always looked out of the window to see what the night was like—not that he was one bit anxious about the weather, except, indeed, he heard his papa getting up to go out, or knew that he had to go; for he could enjoy weather of any sort and all sorts, and never thought what the next day would be like—but just to see what Madame Night was thinking about—how she looked, and what she was doing. For he had soon found her such a changeful creature that, every time he looked at her, she looked at him with another face from that she had worn last time. Before he had made this acquaintance with the night, he would often, ere he fell asleep, lie wondering what he was going to dream about; for, with all his practical tendencies, Willie was very fond of dreaming; but after he had begun in this manner to make acquaintance with her, he would just as often fall asleep wondering what the day would be dreaming about—for, in his own fanciful way of thinking, he had settled that the look of the night was what the day was dreaming. Hence, when Agnes required his services no longer, he fell asleep the first night with the full intention of waking just as before, and getting up to have a peep into the day's dream, whatever it might be, that night, and every night thereafter.

But he was now back in his own room, and there was nothing to wake him, so he slept sound until the day had done dreaming, and the morning was wide awake.

Neither had he awoke any one night since, or seen what marvel there might be beyond his windowpanes.

Does any little boy or girl wonder what there can be going on when we are asleep? Sometimes the stars, sometimes the moon, sometimes the clouds, sometimes the wind, sometimes the snow, sometimes the frost, sometimes all of them together, are busy. Sometimes the owl and the moth and the beetle, and the bat and the cat and the rat, are all at work. Sometimes there are flowers in bloom that love the night better than the day, and are busy all through the darkness pouring out on the still air the scent they withheld during the sunlight. Sometimes the lightning and the thunder, sometimes the moon-rainbow, sometimes the aurora borealis, is busy. And the streams are running all night long, and seem to babble louder than in the day time, for the noises of the working world are still, so that we hear them better. Almost the only daylight thing awake, is the clock ticking with nobody to heed it, and that sounds to me very dismal. But it was the look of the night, the meaning on her face that Willie cared most about, and desired so much to see, that he was at times quite unhappy to think that he never could wake up, not although ever so many strange and lovely dreams might be passing before his window. He often dreamed that he had waked up, and was looking out on some gorgeous and lovely show, but in the morning he knew sorrowfully that he had only dreamed his own dream, not gazed into that of the sleeping day. Again and again he had worked his brains to weariness, trying and trying to invent some machine that should wake him. But although he was older and cleverer now, he fared no better than when he wanted to wake himself to help his mother with Agnes. He must have some motive power before he could do anything, and the clock was still the only power he could think of, and that he was afraid to meddle with, for its works were beyond him, and it was so essential to the well-being of the house that he would not venture putting it in jeopardy.

One day, however, when he was thinking nothing about it, all at once it struck him that he had another motive power at his command, and the thought had hardly entered his mind, before he saw also how it was possible to turn it to account. His motive power was the stream from the Prior's Well, and the means of using it for his purpose stood on a shelf in the ruins, in the shape of the toy water-wheel which he had laid aside as distressingly useless. He set about the thing at once.

First of all, he made a second bit of channel for the stream, like a little loop to the first, so that he could, when he pleased, turn a part of the water into it, and let it again join the principal channel a little lower down. This was, in fact, his mill-race. Just before it joined the older part again, right opposite his window, he made it run for a little way in a direct line towards the house, and in this part of the new channel he made preparations for his water-wheel. Into the channel he laid a piece of iron pipe, which had been lying about useless for years; and just where the water would issue in a concentrated rush from the lower end of it, he constructed a foundation for his wheel, similar to that Sandy and he had built for it before. The water, as it issued from the pipe, should strike straight upon its floats, and send it whirling round. It took him some time to build it, for he wanted this to be a good and permanent job. He had stones at command: he had a well, he said, that yielded both stones and water, which was more than everybody could say; and in order to make it a sound bit of work, he fetched a lump of quick-lime from the kiln, where they burned quantities of it to scatter over the clay-soil, and first wetting it with water till it fell into powder, and then mixing it with sand which he riddled from the gravel he dug from the garden, he made it into good strong mortar. When its bed was at length made for it, he took the wheel and put in a longer axis, to project on one side beyond the gudgeon-block, or hollow in which it turned; and upon this projecting piece he fixed a large reel. Then, having put the wheel in its place, he asked his father for sixpence, part of which he laid out on a large ball of pack-thread. The outside end of the ball he fastened to the reel, then threw the ball through the open window into his room, and there undid it from the inside end, laying the thread in coils on the floor. When it was time to go to bed, he ran out and turned the water first into the garden, and then into the new channel; when suddenly the wheel began to spin about, and wind the pack-thread on to the reel. He ran to his room, and undressed faster than he had ever done before, tied the other end of the thread around his wrist, and, although kept awake much longer than usual by his excitement, at length fell fast asleep, and dreamed that the thread had waked him, and drawn him to the window, where he saw the water-wheel flashing like a fire-wheel, and the water rushing away from under it in a green flame. When he did wake it was broad day; the coils of pack-thread were lying on the floor scarcely diminished; the brook was singing in the garden, and when he went to the window, he saw the wheel spinning merrily round. He dressed in haste, ran out, and found that the thread had got entangled amongst the bushes on its way to the wheel, and had stuck fast; whereupon the wheel had broken it to get loose, and had been spinning round and round all night for nothing, like the useless thing it was before.

That afternoon he set poles up for guides, along the top of which the thread might run, and so keep clear of the bushes. But he fared no better the next night, for he never waked until the morning, when he found that the wheel stood stock still, for the thread, having filled the reel, had slipped off, and so wound itself about the wheel that it was choked in its many windings. Indeed, the thread was in a wonderful tangle about the whole machine, and it took him a long time to unwind—turning the wheel backwards, so as not to break the thread.

In order to remove the cause of this fresh failure, he went to the turner, whose name was William Burt, and asked him to turn for him a large reel or spool, with deep ends, and small cylinder between. William told him he was very busy just then, but he would fix a suitable piece of wood for him on his old lathe, with which, as he knew him to be a handy boy, he might turn what he wanted for himself. This was his first attempt at the use of the turning-lathe; but he had often watched William at work, and was familiar with the way in which he held his tool. Hence the result was tolerably satisfactory. Long before he had reached the depth of which he wished to make the spool, he had learned to manage his chisel with some nicety. Burt finished it off for him with just a few touches; and, delighted with his acquisition of the rudiments of a new trade, he carried the spool home with him, to try once more the possibility of educating his water-wheel into a watchman.

That night the pull did indeed come, but, alas before he had even fallen asleep.

Something seemed to be always going wrong! He concluded already that it was a difficult thing to make a machine which should do just what the maker wished. The spool had gone flying round, and had swallowed up the thread incredibly fast. He made haste to get the end off his wrist, and saw it fly through the little hole in the window frame, and away after the rest of it, to be wound on the whirling spool.

Disappointing as this was, however, there was progress in it: he had got the thing to work, and all that remained was to regulate it. But this turned out the most difficult part of the affair by far. He saw at once that if he were only to make the thread longer, which was the first mode that suggested itself, he would increase the constant danger there was of its getting fouled, not to mention the awkwardness of using such a quantity of it. If the kitten were to get into the room, for instance, after he had laid it down, she would ruin his every hope for the time being; and in Willie's eyes sixpence was a huge sum to ask from his father. But if, on the contrary, he could find out any mode of making the machine wind more slowly, he might then be able to shorten instead of lengthening the string.

At length, after much pondering, he came to see that if, instead of the spool, he were to fix on the axis a small cogged wheel—that is, a wheel with teeth—and then make these cogs fit into the cogs of a much larger wheel, the small wheel, which would turn once with every turn of the water-wheel, must turn a great many times before it could turn the big wheel once. Then he must fix the spool on the axis of this great slow wheel, when, turning only as often as the wheel turned, the spool would wind the thread so much the more slowly.

I will not weary my reader with any further detail of Willie's efforts and failures. It is enough to say that he was at last so entirely successful in timing his machine, for the run of the water was always the same, that he could tell exactly how much thread it would wind in a given time. Having then measured off the thread with a mark of ink for the first hour, two for the second, and so on, he was able to set his alarum according to the time at which he wished to be woke by the pull at his wrist.

But if any one had happened to go into the garden after the household was asleep, and had come upon the toy water-wheel, working away in starlight or moonlight, how little, even if he had caught sight of the nearly invisible thread, and had discovered that the wheel was winding it up, would he have thought what the tiny machine was about! How little would he have thought that its business was with the infinite! that it was in connection with the window of an eternal world—namely, Willie's soul—from which at a given moment it would lift the curtains, namely, the eyelids, and let the night of the outer world in upon the thought and feeling of the boy! To use a likeness, the wheel was thus ever working to draw up the slide of a camera obscura, and let in whatever pictures might be abroad in the dreams of the day, that the watcher within might behold them.

Indeed, one night as he came home from visiting a patient, soon after Willie had at length taught his watchman his duty, Mr Macmichael did come upon the mill, and was just going to turn the water off at the well, which he thought Willie had forgotten to do, when he caught sight of the winding thread—for the moon was full, and the Doctor was sharp-sighted.

"What can this be now?" he said to himself. "Some new freak of Willie's, of course. Yes; the thread goes right up to his window! I dare say if I were to stop and watch I should see something happen in consequence. But I am too tired, and must go to bed."

Just as he thought thus with himself, the wheel stopped. The next moment the blind of Willie's window was drawn up, and there stood Willie, his face and his white gown glimmering in the moonlight. He caught sight of his father, and up went the sash.

"O papa!" he cried; "I didn't think it was you I was going to see!"

"Who was it then you thought to see?" asked his father.

"Oh, nobody!—only the night herself, and the moon perhaps."

"What new freak of yours is this, my boy?" said his father, smiling.

"Wait a minute, and I'll tell you all about it," answered Willie.

Out he came in his night-shirt, his bare feet dancing with pleasure at having his father for his midnight companion. On the grass, beside the ruins, in the moonlight, by the gurgling water, he told him all about it.

"Yes, my boy; you are right," said his father. "God never sleeps; and it would be a pity if we never saw Him at his night-work."

CHAPTER XI. SOME OF THE SIGHTS WILLIE SAW.

I fancy some of my readers would like to hear what were some of the scenes Willie saw on such occasions. The little mill went on night after night—almost everynight in the summer, and those nights in the winter when the frost wasn't so hard that it would have frozen up the machinery. But to attempt to describe the variety of the pictures Willie saw would be an endless labour.

Sometimes, when he looked out, it was a simple, quiet, thoughtful night that met his gaze, without any moon, but as full of stars as it could hold, all flashing and trembling through the dew that was slowly sinking down the air to settle upon the earth and its thousand living things below. On such a night Willie never went to bed again without wishing to be pure in heart, that he might one day see the God whose thought had taken the shape of such a lovely night. For although he could not have expressed himself thus at that time, he felt that it must be God's thinking that put it all there.

Other times, the stars would be half blotted out—all over the heavens—not with mist, but with the light of the moon. Oh, how lovely she was!—so calm! so all alone in the midst of the great blue ocean! the sun of the night! She seemed to hold up the tent of the heavens in a great silver knot. And, like the stars above, all the flowers below had lost their colour and looked pale and wan, sweet and sad. It was just like what the schoolmaster had been telling him about the Elysium of the Greek and Latin poets, to which they fancied the good people went when they died—not half so glad and bright and busy as the daylight world which they had left behind them, and to which they always wanted to go back that they might eat and drink and be merry again—but oh, so tender and lovely in its mournfulness!

Several times in winter, looking out, he saw a strange sight—the air so full of great snowflakes that he could not see the moon through them, although her light was visible all about them. They came floating slowly down through the dusky light, just as if they had been a precipitate from that solution of moonbeams. He could hardly persuade himself to go to bed, so fascinating was the sight; but the cold would drive him to his nest again.

Once the wheel-watchman pulled him up in the midst of a terrible thunder-storm—when the East and the West were answering each other with alternate flashes of forked lightning that seemed to split the black clouds with cracks of blinding blue, awful in their blasting silence—followed by great, billowy, shattering rolls of thunder, as loud as if the sky had been a huge kettledrum, on which the clubs of giant drummers were beating a terrible onset; while at sudden intervals, down came the big-dropped rain, pattering to the earth as if beaten out of the clouds by the blows of the thunder. But Willie was not frightened, though the lightning blinded and the thunder deafened him—not frightened any more than the tiniest flower in the garden below, which, if she could have thought about it, would have thought it all being done only that she might feel cooler and stronger, and be able to hold up her head better.

And once he saw a glorious dance of the aurora borealis—in all the colours of a faint rainbow. The frosty snow sparkled underneath, and the cold stars of winter sparkled above, and between the snow and the stars, shimmered and shifted, vanished and came again, a serried host of spears. Willie had been reading the "Paradise Lost," and the part which pleased him, boy-like, the most, was the wars of the angels in the sixth book. Hence it came that the aurora looked to him like the crowding of innumerable spears— in the hands of angels, themselves invisible—clashed together and shaken asunder, however, as in the convolutions of a mazy dance of victory, rather than brandished and hurtled as in the tumult of the battle.

Another vision that would greatly delight him was a far more common one: the moon wading through clouds blown slowly across the sky—especially if by an upper wind, unfelt below. Now she would be sinking helpless in a black faint—growing more and more dim, until at last she disappeared from the night—was blotted from the face of nature, leaving only a dim memorial light behind her; now her soul would come into her again, and she was there once more—doubtful indeed: but with a slow, solemn revival, her light would grow and grow, until the last fringe of the great cloud swung away from off her face, and she dawned out stately and glorious, to float for a space in queenly triumph across a lake of clearest blue. And Willie was philosopher enough to say to himself, that all this fainting and reviving, all this defeat and conquest, were but appearances; that the moon was her own bright self all the time, basking contented in the light of her sun, between whom and her the cloud could not creep, only between her and Willie.

But what delighted him most of all was to catch the moon dreaming. That was when the old moon, tumbled over on her back, would come floating up the east, like a little boat on the rising tide of the night, looking lost on the infinite sea! Dreaming she must be surely!—she looked nothing but dreaming; for she seemed to care about nothing—not even that she was old and worn, and withered and dying,—not even that, instead of sinking down in the west, into some deep bed of dim repose, she was drifting, haggard and battered, untidy and weak and sleepy, up and up into the dazzling halls of the sun. Did she know that his light would clothe her as with a garment, and hide her in the highest recesses of his light-filled ceiling? or was it only that she was dreaming, dreaming—sweet, cool, tender dreams of her own, and neither knew nor cared about anything around her? What a strange look all the night wore while the tired old moon was thus dreaming of the time when she would come again, back through the vanishing and the darkness—a single curved thread of a baby moon, to grow and grow to a great full-grown lady moon, able to cross with fearless gaze the gulf of the vaulted heavens—alone, with neither sleep nor dreams to protect her!

There were many other nights, far more commonplace, which yet Willie liked well to look out upon, but which could not keep him long from his bed. There was, for instance, the moonless and cloudy night, when, if he had been able to pierce the darkness to the core, he would have found nothing but blackness. It had a power of its own, but one cannot say it had much to look at. On such a night he would say to himself that the day was so sound asleep he was dreaming of nothing at all, and make haste to his nest. Then again there was the cold night of black frost, when there was cloud enough to hide the stars and the moon, and yet a little light came soaking through, enough to reveal how hopeless and dreary the earth was. For in such nights of cold, when there is no snow to cover them, the flowers that have crept into their roots to hide from the winter are not even able to dream of the spring;—they grow quite stupid and benumbed, and sleep outright like a polar bear or a dormouse. He never could look long at such a night.

Neither did he care to look long when a loud wind was out—except the moon was bright; for the most he could distinguish was the trees blowing against the sky, and they always seemed not to like it, and to want to stop. And if the big strong trees did not like it, how could the poor little delicate flowers, shivering and shaking and tossed to and fro? If he could have seen the wind itself, it would have been a different thing; but as it was, he could enjoy it more by lying in bed and listening to it. Then as he listened he could fancy himself floating out through miles and miles of night and wind, and moon-and-star-light, or moony snowflakes, or even thick darkness and rain; until, falling asleep in the middle of his fancy, it would thicken around him into a dream of delight.

Once there was to be an eclipse of the moon about two o'clock in the morning.

"It's a pity it's so late, or rather so early," said Mr Macmichael.

"You, Willie, won't be able to see it."

"Oh, yes, I shall, father," answered Willie.

"I can't let you sit up so late. I shall be in the middle of Sedgy Moor most likely when it begins—and who is to wake you? I won't have your mother disturbed, and Tibby's not much to depend upon. She's too hard-worked to wake when she likes, poor old thing."

"Oh, I can be woke without anybody to do it!" said Willie.

"You don't mean you can depend on your water-wheel to wake you at the right time, do you?"

"Yes, I do, father. If you will tell me exactly when the eclipse is going to begin, I will set my wakener so that it shall wake me a quarter-of-an-hour before, that I may be sure of seeing the very first of it."

81

"Well, it will be worth something to you, if it can do that!" said Mr Macmichael.

"It's been worth a great deal to me, already," said Willie. "It would have shown me an eclipse before now, only there hasn't been one since I set it going."

And wake him it did. While his father was riding across the moor, in the strange hush of the blotted moon, Willie was out in the garden beside his motionless wheel, watching the fell shadow of the earth passing over the blessed face of the moon, and leaving her pure and clear, and nothing the worse.

CHAPTER XII. A NEW SCHEME.

I have said that Willie's father and mother used to talk without restraint in his presence. They had no fear of Willie's committing an indiscretion by repeating what he heard. One day at dinner the following conversation took place between them.

"I've had a letter from my mother, John," said Mrs Macmichael to her husband. "It's wonderful how well she manages to write, when she sees so badly."

"She might see well enough—at least a great deal better—if she would submit to an operation, said the doctor.

"At her age, John!" returned his wife in an expostulatory tone. "Do you really think it worth while—for the few years that are left her?"

"Worth while to see well for a few years!" exclaimed the doctor.

"Indeed, I do."

"But there's another thing I want to talk to you about now," said Mrs Macmichael. "Since old Ann's death, six months ago, she says she has been miserable, and if she goes on like this, it will shorten the few days that are left her. Effie, the only endurable servant she has had since Ann, is going to leave at the end of her half-year, and she says the thought of another makes her wretched. She may be a little hard to please, but after being used to one for so many years, it is no wonder if she be particular. I don't know what is to be done."

"I don't know, either—except you make her a present of Tibby," said her husband.

"John!" exclaimed Mrs Macmichael; and "John" burst out laughing.

"You don't think they'd pull together?" he said.

"Two old people—each with her own ways, and without any memories in common to bind them together! I'm surprised at your dreaming of such a thing," exclaimed his wife.

"But I didn't even dream of it; I only said it," returned her husband.

"It's time you knew when I was joking, wifie."

"You joke so dreadfully like earnest!" she answered.

"If only we had one more room in the house!" said the doctor, thoughtfully.

"Ah!" returned his wife, eagerly, "that would be a blessing! And though Tibby would be a thorn in every inch of grandmamma's body, if they were alone together, I have no doubt they would get on very well with me between them."

"I don't doubt it," said her husband, still thoughtfully.

"Couldn't we manage it somehow, John?" said Mrs Macmichael, half timidly, after a pause of some duration.

"I can't say I see how—at this moment," answered the doctor, "much as I should like it. But there's time yet, and we'll think it over, and talk about it, and perhaps we may hit upon some plan or other. Most things may be done; and everything necessary can be done _some_how. So we won't bother our minds about it, but only our brains, and see what they can do for us."

With this he rose and went to his laboratory.

Willie rose also and went straight to his own room. Having looked all round it thoughtfully several times, he went out again on the landing, whence a ladder led up into a garret running the whole length of the roof of the cottage.

"My room would do for grannie," he said to himself; "and I could sleep up there. A shake-down in the corner would do well enough for me."

He climbed the ladder, pushed open the trap-door, crept half through, and surveyed the gloomy place.

"There's no window but a skylight!" he said; and his eyes smarted as if the tears were about to rush into them. "What shall I do? Wheelie will be useless!—Well, I can't help it; and if I can't help it, I can bear it. To have grannie comfortable will be better than to look out of the window ever so much."

He drew in his head, came down the ladder with a rush, and hurried off to school.

At supper he laid his scheme before his father and mother.

They looked very much pleased with their boy. But his father said at once—

"No, no, Willie. It won't do. I'm glad you've been the first to think of something—only, unfortunately, your plan won't work. You can't sleep there."

"I'll engage to sleep wherever there's room to lie down; and if there isn't I'll engage to sleep sitting or standing," said Willie, whose mother had often said she wished she could sleep like Willie. "And as I don't walk in my sleep," he added, "the trap-door needn't be shut."

"Mice, Willie!" said his mother, in a tone of much significance.

"The cat and I are good friends," returned Willie. "She'll be pleased enough to sleep with me."

"You don't hit the thing at all," said his father. "I wonder a practical man like you, Willie, doesn't see it at once. Even if I were at the expense of ceiling the whole roof with lath and plaster, we should find you, some morning in summer, baked black as a coal; or else, some morning in winter frozen so stiff that, when we tried to lift you, your arm snapped off like a dry twig of elder."

"Ho! ho! ho!" laughed Willie; "then there would be the more room for grannie."

His father laughed with him, but his mother looked a little shocked.

"No, Willie," said his father again; "you must make another attempt. You must say with Hamlet when he was puzzled for a plan—'About my

85

brains!' Perhaps they will suggest something wiser next time."

Willie lay so long awake that night, thinking, that Wheelie pulled him before he had had a wink of sleep. He got up, of course, and looked from the window.

The day was dreaming grandly. The sky was pretty clear in front, and full of sparkles of light, for the stars were kept in the background by the moon, which was down a little towards the west. She had sunk below the top of a huge towering cloud, the edges of whose jags and pinnacles she bordered with a line of silvery light. Now this cloud rose into the sky from just behind the ruins, and looking a good deal like upheaved towers and spires, made Willie think within himself what a grand place the priory must have been, when its roofs and turrets rose up into the sky.

"They say a lot of people lived in it then!" he thought with himself as he stood gazing at the cloud.

Suddenly he gave a great jump, and clapped his hands so loud that he woke his father.

"Is anything the matter, my boy?" he asked, opening Willie's door, and peeping in.

"No, papa, nothing," answered Willie. "Only something that came into my head with a great bounce!"

"Ah!—Where did it come from, Willie?"

"Out of that cloud there. Isn't it a grand one?"

"Grand enough certainly to put many thoughts into a body's head, Willie.

What did it put into yours?"

"Please, I would rather not tell just yet," answered Willie, "—if you don't mind, father."

"Not a bit, my boy. Tell me just when you please, or don't tell me at all.

I should like to hear it, but only at your pleasure, Willie."

"Thank you, father. I do want to tell you, you know, but not just yet."

"Very well, my boy. Now go to bed, and sleep may better the thought before the morning."

Willie soon fell asleep now, for he believed he had found what he wanted.

He was up earlier than usual the next morning, and out in the garden.

"Surely," he said to himself, "those ruins, which once held so many monks, might manage even yet to find room for me!"

He went wandering about amongst them, like an undecided young bird looking for the very best possible spot to build its nest in. The spot Willie sought was that which would require the least labour and least material to make it into a room.

Before he heard the voice of Tibby, calling him to come to his porridge, he had fixed upon one; and in the following chapter I will tell you what led him to choose it. All the time between morning and afternoon school, he spent in the same place; and when he came home in the evening, he was accompanied by Mr Spelman, who went with him straight to the ruins. There they were a good while together; and when Willie at length came in, his mother saw that his face was more than usually radiant, and was certain he had some new scheme or other in his head.

CHAPTER XIII. WILLIE'S NEST IN THE RUINS.

The spot he had fixed upon was in the part of the ruins next the cottage, not many yards from the back door of it. I have said there were still a few vaulted places on the ground-level used by the family. The vault over the wood-house was perfectly sound and weather-tight, and, therefore, as Willie and the carpenter agreed, quite safe to roost upon. In a corner outside, and now open to the elements, had once been a small winding stone stair, which led to the room above, on the few broken fragments of which, projecting from the two sides of the corner, it was just possible to climb, and so reach the top of the vault. Willie had often got up to look out through a small, flat-arched window into the garden of the manse. When Mr Shepherd, the clergyman, who often walked in his garden, caught sight of him, he always came nearer, and had a chat with him; for he did not mind such people as Willie looking into his garden, and seeing what he was about. Sometimes also little Mona, a girl of his own age, would be running about; and she also, if she caught sight of Willie, was sure to come hopping and skipping like a bird to have a talk with him, and beg him to take her up, which, he as often assured her, was all but impossible. To this place Mr Spelman and Willie climbed, and there held consultation whether and how it could be made habitable. The main difficulty was, how to cover it in; for although the walls were quite sound a long way up, it lay open to the sky. But about ten feet over their heads they saw the opposing holes in two of the walls where the joists formerly sustaining the floor of the chamber above had rested; and Mr Spelman thought that, without any very large outlay either of time or material, he could there lay a floor, as it were, and then turn it into a roof by covering it with cement, or pitch, or something of the sort, concerning which he would take counsel with his friend Mortimer, the mason.

"But," said Willie, "that would turn it into the bottom of a cistern; for the walls above would hold the rain in, and what would happen then? Either it must gather till it reached the top, or the weight of it would burst the walls, or perhaps break through my roof and drown me."

"It is easy to avoid that," said Mr Spelman. "We have only to lay on the cement a little thicker at one side, and slope the surface down to the other, where a hole through the wall, with a pipe in it, would let the water off."

"I know!" cried Willie. "That's what they called a gurgoyle!"

"I don't know anything about that," said the carpenter; "I know it will carry off the water."

"To be sure," said Willie. "It's capital."

"But," said Mr Spelman, "it's rather too serious a job this to set about before asking the doctor's leave. It will cost money."

"Much?" asked Willie, whose heart sank within him.

"Well, that depends on what you count much," answered Spelman. "All I can say is, it wouldn't be anything out of your father's pocket."

"I don't see how that can be," said Willie. "—Cost money, and yet be nothing out of my father's pocket! I've only got threepence ha'-penny."

"Your father and I will talk about it," said the carpenter mysteriously, and offered no further information.

"There seems to be always some way of doing a thing," thought Willie to himself.

He little knew by what a roundabout succession of cause and effect his father's kindness to Spelman was at this moment returning to him, one of the links of connection being this project of Willie's own.

The doctor being out at the time, the carpenter called again later in the evening; and they had a long talk together—to the following effect.

Spelman having set forth his scheme, and the doctor having listened in silence until he had finished—

"But," said Mr Macmichael, "that will cost a good deal, I fear, and I have no money to spare."

"Mr Macmichael," said Spelman solemnly, his long face looking as if some awful doom were about to issue from the middle of it, "you forget how much I am in your debt."

"No, I don't," returned the doctor. "But neither do I forget that it takes all your time and labour to provide for your family; and what will become of them if you set about this job, with no return in prospect but the satisfaction of clearing off of an old debt?"

"It is very good of you, sir, to think of that," said the carpenter; "but, begging your pardon, I've thought of it too. Many's the time you've come after what I'd ha' called work hours to see my wife—yes, in the middle of the night, more than once or twice; and why shouldn't I do the same? Look ye here, sir. If you're not in a main hurry, an' 'll give me time, I'll do the heavy work o' this job after six o'clock o' the summer nights, with Sandy to help me, and I'll charge you no more than a journeyman's wages by the hour. And what Willie and Sandy can do by themselves—he's a clever boy Sandy; but he's a genius Willie—what they can do by themselves, and that's not a little, is nothing to me. And if you'll have the goodness, when I give you the honest time, at fourpence ha'penny an hour, just to strike that much off my bill, I'll be more obliged to you than I am now. Only I fear I must make you pay for the material—not a farthing more than it costs me at the saw-mills, up at the Grange, for the carriage 'll come in with other lots I must have."

"It's a generous offer, Spelman," said the doctor, "and I accept it heartily, though you are turning the tables of obligation upon me. You'll have done far more for me than I ever did for you."

"I wish that were like to be true, sir, but it isn't. My wife's not a giantess yet, for all you've done for her."

Spelman set to work at once. New joists were inserted in the old walls, boarded over, and covered, after the advice of Mortimer, with some cunning mixture to keep out the water. Then a pipe was put through the wall to carry it off—which pipe, if it was not masked with an awful head, as the remains of more than one on the Priory showed it would have been in the days of the monks, yet did it work as faithfully without it.

When it came to the plastering of the walls, Mr Spelman, after giving them full directions, left the two boys to do that between them. Although there was no occasion to roughen these walls by clearing away the old mortar from between the stones, the weather having done that quite sufficiently, and all the preparation they wanted for the first thin coat was to be well washed down, it took them a good many days, working all their time, to lay on the orthodox three coats of plaster. Mr Spelman had wisely boarded the ceiling, so that they had not to plaster that.

Meantime he was preparing a door and window-frames in the shop. The room had probably been one of the prior's, for it was much too large and lofty for a mere cell, and had two windows. But these were fortunately small, not like the splendid ones in the chapel and refectory, else they would have been hard to fill with glass.

"I'm afraid you'll be starved with cold, Willie," said his father one day, after watching the boys at work for a few minutes. "There's no fireplace."

"Oh! that doesn't signify," answered Willie. "Look how thick the walls are! and I shall have plenty of blankets on my bed. Besides, we can easily put a little stove in, if it's wanted."

But when the windows were fitted and fixed, Mr Macmichael saw to his dismay that they were not made to open. They had not even a pane on hinges.

"This'll never do, Willie," he said. "This is far worse than no chimney."

Willie took his father by the coat, and led him to a corner, where a hole went right through the wall into another room—if that can be called a room which had neither floor nor ceiling.

"There, father!" he said; "I am going to fit a slide over this hole, and then I can let in just as much or as little air as I please."

"It would have been better to have one at least of the windows made to open. You will only get the air from the ruins that way, whereas you might have had all the scents of Mr Shepherd's wallflowers and roses."

"As soon as Mr Spelman has done with the job," said Willie, "I will make them both to come wide open on hinges; but I don't want to bother him about it, for he has been very kind, and I can do it quite well myself."

This satisfied his father.

At length the floor was boarded; a strong thick door was fitted tight; a winding stair of deal inserted where the stone one had been, and cased in with planks, well pitched on the outside; and now Willie's mother was busy making little muslin curtains for his windows, and a carpet for the middle of the room.

In the meantime, his father and mother had both written to his grandmother, telling her how Willie had been using his powers both of invention and of labour to make room for her, and urging her to come and live with them, for they were all anxious to have her to take care of. But, in fact, small persuasion was necessary, for the old lady was only too glad to accept the invitation; and before the warm weather of autumn was over, she was ready to go to them. By this time Willie's room was furnished. All the things from his former nest had been moved into it; the bed with the chintz curtains, covered with strange flowers and birds; the old bureau, with the many drawers inside the folding cover, in which he kept all his little treasures; the table at which he read books that were too big to hold, such as Raleigh's History of the World and Josephus; the old oblong mirror that hung on the wall, with an outspread gilt eagle at the top of it; the big old arm-chair that had belonged to his great-grandfather, who wrote his sermons in it—for all the things the boy had about him were old, and in all his after-life he never could bear new furniture. And now his grandmother's furniture began to appear; and a great cart-load of it from her best bedroom was speedily arranged in Willie's late quarters, and as soon as they were ready for her, Mrs Macmichael set out in a post-chaise to fetch her mother.

CHAPTER XIV. WILLIE'S GRANDMOTHER.

Willie was in a state of excitement until she arrived, looking for her as eagerly as if she had been a young princess. So few were the opportunities of travelling between Priory Leas and the town where his grandmother lived, that he had never seen her, and curiosity had its influence as well as affection. Great, therefore, was his delight when at last the chaise came round the corner of the street, and began to draw up in order to halt at their door. The first thing he caught sight of was a curious bonnet, like a black coal-scuttle upside down, inside which, when it turned its front towards him, he saw a close-fitting widow's cap, and inside that a kind old face, and if he could have looked still further, he would have seen a kind young soul inside the kind old face. She smiled sweetly when she saw him, but was too tired to take any further notice of him until she had had tea.

During that meal Willie devoted himself to a silent waiting upon her, watching and trying to anticipate her every want. When she had eaten a little bread and butter and an egg, and drunk two cups of tea, she lay back in her own easy chair, which had been placed for her by the side of the parlour fire, and fell fast asleep for ten minutes, breathing so gently that Willie got frightened, and thought she was dead. But all at once she opened her eyes wide, and made a sign to him to come to her.

"Sit down there," she said, pushing a little footstool towards him.

Willie obeyed, and sat looking up in her face.

"So," she said, "you're the little man that can do everything?"

"No, grannie," answered Willie, laughing. "I wish I could; but I am only learning to do a few things; and there's not one of them I can do right yet."

"Do you know what they call you?"

"The boys at school call me Six-fingered Jack," said Willie.

"There!" said his grandmother. "I told you so."

"I'm glad it's only a nickname, grannie; but if it weren't, it would soon be one, for I'm certain the finger that came after the little one would be so much in the way it would soon get cut off."

"Anyhow, supposing you only half as clever a fellow as you pass for, I want to try you. Have you any objection to service? I should like to hire you for my servant—my own special servant, you understand."

"All right, grannie; here I am!" cried Willie, jumping up. "What shall I do first?"

"Sit down again instantly, and wait till we've finished the bargain. I must first have you understand that though I don't want to be hard upon you, you must come when I call you, and do what I tell you."

"Of course, grannie. Only I can't when I'm at school, you know."

"I don't want to be told that. And I'm not going to be a tyrant. But I had no idea you were such a silly! For all your cleverness, you've positively never asked me what wages I would give you."

"Oh! I don't want any wages, grannie. I like to do things for people; and you're my very own grandmother, besides, you know."

"Well, I suppose I must settle your wages for you. I mean to pay you by the job. It's an odd arrangement for a servant, but it will suit me best. And as you don't ask any, I needn't pay you more than I like myself."

"Certainly not, grannie. I'm quite satisfied."

"Meantime, no engagement of a servant ought to be counted complete without earnest."

"I'm quite in earnest, grannie," said Willie, who did not know the meaning of the word as his new mistress used it. They all laughed.

"I don't see what's funny," said Willie, laughing too, however.

But when they explained to him what earnest meant, then he laughed with understanding, as well as with good will.

"So," his grandmother went on, "I will give you earnest, which, you know, binds you my servant. But for how long, Willie?"

"Till you're tired of me, grannie. Only, you know, I'm papa and mamma's servant first, and you may have to arrange with them sometimes; for what should I do if you were all to want me at once?"

"We'll easily manage that. I'll arrange with them, as you say. And now, here's your earnest."

As she spoke, she put into his hand what Willie took to be a shilling.

But when he glanced at it, he found himself mistaken.

"Thank you, grannie," he said, trying not to show himself a little disappointed, for he had had another scheme in his head some days, and the shilling would have been everything towards that.

"Do you know what grannie has given you, Willie?" said his mother.

"Yes, mother—such a pretty brass medal!"

"Show it me, dear. Why, Willie! it's no brass medal, child;—it's a sovereign!"

"No-o-o-o! Is it? O grannie!" he cried, and went dancing about the room, as if he would actually fly with delight.

Willie had never seen a sovereign, for that part of the country was then like Holland—you never saw gold money there. To get it for him, his grandmother had had to send to the bank in the county town.

After this she would often give him sixpence or a shilling, and sometimes even a half-crown when she asked him to do anything she thought a little harder than usual; so that Willie had now plenty of money with which to carry out his little plans. When remonstrated with by her daughter for giving him so much, his grandmother would say—

"Look how the boy spends it!—always doing something with it! He never wastes it on sweets—not he!—My Willie's above that!"

The old lady generally spoke of him as if she were the chief if not the sole proprietor of the boy.

"I'm sure I couldn't do better with it," she would add; "and that you'll see when he comes to be a man. He'll be the making of you all."

"But, mother, you can't afford it."

"How do you know that? I can afford it very well. I've no house-rent to pay; and I am certain it is the very best return I can make you for your kindness. What I do for Willie will prove to have been done for us all."

Certainly Willie's grandmother showed herself a very wise old lady. The wisest old ladies are always those with young souls looking out of their eyes. And few things pleased Willie more than waiting upon her. He had a passion for being useful, and as his grandmother needed his help more than any one else, her presence in the house was an endless source of pleasure to him.

But his father grew anxious. He did not like her giving Willie so much money—not that he minded Willie having or spending the money, for he believed that the spending would keep the having from hurting him; but he feared lest through her gifts the purity of the boy's love for his grandmother might be injured, and the service which at first had looked only to her as its end might degenerate into a mere serving of her for the sake of her shillings.

He had, therefore, a long talk with her about it. She was indignant at the notion of the least danger of spoiling Willie, but so anxious to prove there was none that she agreed to the test proposed by his father—which was, to drop all money transactions between them for a few months, giving Willie no reason for the change. Grannie, however, being in word and manner, if possible, still kinder to him than ever—and no wonder, seeing she could no more, for the present, let her love out at her pocket-hole—and Willie having, therefore, no anxiety lest he should have displeased her, he soon ceased to think even of the change; except, indeed, sometimes when he wanted a little money very much, and then he would say to himself that he was afraid poor grannie had been too liberal at first, and had spent all her money upon him; therefore he must try to be the more attentive to her now. So the result was satisfactory; and the more so that, for all her boasting, his grandmother had not been able to help trembling a little, half with annoyance, half with anxiety, as she let the first few of his services pass without the customary acknowledgment.

"There!" she said one day, at length, triumphantly, to Mr Macmichael; "what do you think of my Willie now? Three months over and gone, and where are your fears? I hope you will trust my judgment a little better after this."

"I'm very glad, anyhow, you put him to the trial," said his father. "It will do him good."

"He wants less of that than most people, Mr Macmichael—present company not excepted," said the old lady, rather nettled, but pretending to be more so than she really was.

CHAPTER XV. HYDRAULICS.

The first thing Willie did, after getting his room all to himself, was to put hinges on the windows and make them open, so satisfying his father as to the airiness of the room. Finding himself then, as it were, in a house of his own, he began to ask his friends in the village to come and see him in his new quarters. The first who did so was Mrs Wilson, and Mr Spelman followed. Hector Macallaster was unwell, and it was a month before he was able to go; but the first day he could he crawled up the hill to the Ruins, and then up the little winding stair to Willie's nest. The boy was delighted to see him, made him sit in his great arm-chair, and, as the poor man was very tired with the exertion, would have run to the house to get him something; but Hector begged for a little water, and declared he could take nothing else. Therefore Willie got a tumbler from his dressing-table, and went to the other side of the room. Hector, hearing a splashing and rushing, turned round to look, and saw him with one hand in a small wooden trough that ran along the wall, and with the other holding the tumbler in a stream of water that fell from the side of the trough into his bath. When the tumbler was full, he removed his hand from the trough, and the water ceased to overflow. He carried the tumbler to Hector, who drank, and said the water was delicious.

Hector could not imagine how the running water had got there, and Willie had to tell him what I am now going to tell my reader. His grandmother's sovereign and his own hydraulics had brought it there.

He had been thinking for some time what a pleasure it would be to have a stream running through his room, and how much labour it would save poor old Tibbie; for it was no light matter for her old limbs to carry all the water for his bath up that steep narrow winding stair to his room. He reasoned that as the well rose and overflowed when its outlet was stopped, it might rise yet farther if it were still confined; for its source was probably in the heart of one of the surrounding hills, and water when confined will always rise as high as its source. Therefore, after much meditation as to how it could be accomplished in the simplest and least expensive manner, he set about it as follows.

First of all he cleared away the floor about the well, and built up the circular wall of it a foot or two higher, with stones picked from those lying about, and with mortar which he made himself. By means of a spirit-level, he laid the top layer of stones quite horizontal; and he introduced into it several blocks of wood instead of stones.

Next he made a small wooden frame, which, by driving spikes between the stones, he fastened to the opening of the underground passage, so that a well-fitting piece of board could move up and down in it, by means of a projecting handle, and be a more manageable sluice than he had hitherto had.

Then he made a strong wooden lid to the mouth of the well, and screwed it down to the wooden blocks he had built in. Through a hole in it, just large enough, came the handle of the sluice.

Next, in the middle of the cover, he made a hole with a brace and centre-bit, and into it drove the end of a strong iron pipe, fitting tight, and long enough to reach almost to the top of the vault. As soon as this was fixed he shut down the sluice, and in a few seconds the water was falling in sheets upon him, and flooding the floor, dashed back from the vault, against which it rushed from the top of the pipe. This was enough for the present; he raised the sluice and let the water escape again below. It was plain, from the force with which the water struck the vault, that it would yet rise much higher.

He scrambled now on the top of the vault, and, examining the ruins, soon saw how a pipe brought up through the breach in the vault could be led to the hole in the wall of his room which he had shown his father as a ventilator. But he would not have a close pipe running through his room. There would be little good in that. He could have made a hole in it, with a stopper, to let the water out when he wanted to use it, but that would be awkward, while all the pleasure lay in seeing the water as it ran. Therefore he got Mr Spelman to find him a long small pine tree, which he first sawed in two, lengthways, and hollowed into two troughs; then, by laying the small end of one into the wide end of the other, he had a spout long enough to reach across the room, and go through the wall on both sides.

The chief difficulty was to pierce the other wall, for the mortar was very hard. The stones, however, just there were not very large, and, with Sandy's help, he managed it.

The large end of one trough was put through the ventilator-hole, and the small end of the other through the hole opposite; their second ends met in the middle, the one lying into the other, and were supported at the juncture by a prop.

They filled up the two openings round the ends with lime and small stones, making them as tidy as they could, and fitting small slides by which Willie could close up the passages for the water when he pleased. Nothing remained but to solder a lead pipe into the top of the iron one, guide this flexible tube across the ups and downs of the ruins, and lay the end of it into the trough.

At length Willie took his stand at the sluice, and told Sandy to scramble up to the end of the lead pipe, and shout when the water began to pour into the trough. His object was to find how far the sluice required to be shut down in order to send up just as much water as the pipe could deliver. More than that would cause a pressure which might strain, and perhaps burst, their apparatus.

He pushed the sluice down a little, and waited a moment.

"Is it coming yet, Sandy?" he cried.

"Not a drop," shouted Sandy.

Willie pushed it a little further, and then knew by the change in the gurgle below that the water was rising in the well; and it soon began to spout from the hole in the cover through which the sluice-handle came up.

"It's coming," cried Sandy, after a pause; "not much, though."

Down went the sluice a little further still.

"It's pouring," echoed the voice of Sandy amongst the ruins; "as much as ever the pipe can give. Its mouth is quite full."

Willie raised the sluice a little.

"How is it now?" he bawled.

"Less," cried Sandy.

So Willie pushed it back to where it had been last, and made a notch in the handle to know the right place again.

So the water from the Prior's Well went careering through Willie's bed-chamber, a story high. When he wanted to fill his bath, he had only to stop the run with his hand, and it poured over the sides into it; so that Tibbie was to be henceforth relieved of a great labour, while Willie's eyes were to be delighted with the vision, and his ears with the sounds of the water scampering through his room.

An hour or so after, as he was finishing off something about the mouth of the well, he heard his father calling him.

"Willie, Willie," he shouted, "is this any more of your kelpie work?"

"What is it, father?" cried Willie, as he came bounding to him.

He needed no reply when he saw a great pool of water about the back door, fed by a small stream from the direction of the woodhouse. Tibbie had come out, and was looking on in dismay.

"That's Willie again, sir," she was saying. "You never can tell where he'll be spouting that weary water at you."

The whole place'll be bog before long, and we'll be all turned into frogs, and have nothing to do but croak. That well 'll be the ruin of us all with cold and coughs."

"You'll be glad enough of it to-night, Tibbie," said Willie, laughing prophetically.

"A likely story!" she returned, quite cross. "It'll be into the house if you don't stop it."

"I'll soon do that," said Willie.

Neither he nor Sandy had thought what would become of the water after it had traversed the chamber. There it was pouring down from the end of the wooden spout, just clearing the tarred roof of the spiral stair, and plashing on the ground close to the foot of it; in their eagerness they had never thought of where it would run to next. And now Willie was puzzled. Nothing was easier than to stop it for the present, which of course he ran at once to do; but where was he to send it?

Thinking over it, however, he remembered that just on the other side of the wall was the stable where his father's horses lived, close to the parson's garden; and in the corner, at the foot of the wall, was a drain; so that all he had to do was to fit another spout to this, at right angles to it, and carry it over the wall.

"You needn't take any water up for me tonight, Tibby," he said, as he went in to supper, for he had already filled his bath.

"Nonsense, Willie," returned Tibbie, still out of temper because of the mess at the door. "Your papa says you must have your bath, and my poor old bones must ache for 't."

"The bath's filled already. If you put in one other pailful, it'll run over when I get into it."

"Now, don't you play tricks with me, Willie. I won't have any more of your joking," returned Tibbie.

Nettled at the way she took the information with which he had hoped to please her, he left her to carry up her pail of water; but it was the last, and she thanked him very kindly the next day.

The only remaining question was how to get rid of the bath-water. But he soon contrived a sink on the top step of the stair outside the door, which was a little higher than the wall of the stable-yard. From there a short pipe was sufficient to carry that water also over into the drain.

I may mention, that although a severe winter followed, the Prior's Well never froze; and that, as they were always either empty, or full of running water, the pipes never froze, and consequently never burst.

CHAPTER XVI. HECTOR HINTS AT A DISCOVERY.

The next day after Hector's visit, Willie went to see how he was, and found him better.

"I certainly am better," he said, "and what's more, I've got a strange feeling it was that drink of water you gave me yesterday that has done it. I'm coming up to have some more of it in the evening, if you'll give it me."

"As much of it as you can drink, Hector, anyhow," said Willie. "You won't drink my cow dry."

"I wonder if it could be the water," said Hector, musingly.

"My father says people used to think it cured them. That was some hundreds of years ago; but if it did so then, I don't see why it shouldn't now. My mother is certainly better, but whether that began since we found the well, I can't be very sure. For Tibbie—she is always drinking at it, she says it does her a world of good."

"I've read somewhere," said the shoemaker, "that wherever there's a hurt there's a help; and when I was a boy, and stung myself with a nettle, I never had far to look for a dock-stalk with its juice. Who knows but the Prior's Well may be the cure for me? It can't straighten my back, I know, but it may make me stronger for all that, and fitter for the general business."

"I will lay down a pipe for you, if you like, Hector, and then you can drink as much of the water as you please, without asking anybody," said Willie.

Hector laughed.

"It's not such a sure thing," he replied, "as to be worth that trouble; and besides, the walk does me good, and a drink once or twice a day is enough— that is, if your people won't think me a trouble, coming so often."

"There's no fear of that," said Willie; "it's our business, you know, to try to cure people. I'll tell you what—couldn't you bring up a bit of your work, and sit in my room sometimes? It's better air there than down here."

"You're very kind, indeed, Willie. We'll see. Meantime, I'll come up morning and evening, and have a drink of the water, as long at least as the warm weather lasts, and by that time I shall be pretty certain whether it is doing me good or not."

So Hector went on drinking the water and getting a little better.

Next, grannie took to it, and, either from imagination, or that it really did her good, declared it was renewing her youth. All the doctor said on the matter was, that the salts it contained could do no one any harm, and might do some people much good; that there was iron in it, which was strengthening, and certain ingredients besides, which might possibly prevent the iron from interfering with other functions of the system. He said he should not be at all surprised if, some day or other, it regained its old fame as a well of healing.

Mr Spelman, in consequence of a talk he had with Hector, having induced

his wife to try it, she also soon began to think it was doing her good.

Beyond these I have now mentioned, no one paid any attention to the

Prior's Well or its renascent reputation.

CHAPTER XVII. HOW WILLIE WENT ON.

As soon as Willie began a new study, he began trying to get at the sense of it. This caused his progress to be slow at first, and him to appear dull amongst those who merely learned by rote; but as he got a hold of the meaning of it all, his progress grew faster and faster, until at length in most studies he outstripped all the rest.

I need hardly repeat that the constant exercise of his mind through his fingers, in giving a second existence outside of him to what had its first existence inside him—that is, in his mind, made it far easier for him to understand the relations of things that go to make up a science. A boy who could put a box together must find Euclid easier—the Second Book particularly—than one who had no idea of the practical relations of the boundaries of spaces; one who could contrive a machine like his water-wheel, must be able to understand the interdependence of the parts of a sentence better than one equally gifted otherwise, but who did not know how one wheel could move another. Everything he did would help his arithmetic, and geography, and history; and these and those and all things besides, would help him to understand poetry.

In his Latin sentences he found the parts fit into each other like dove-tailing; finding the terms of equations, he said, was like inventing machines, and he soon grew clever at solving them. It was not from his manual abilities alone that his father had given him the name of Gutta-Percha Willie, but from the fact that his mind, once warmed to interest, could accommodate itself to the peculiarities of any science, just as the gutta-percha which is used for taking a mould fits itself to the outs and ins of any figure.

He still employed his water-wheel to pull him out of bed in the middle of the night. He had, of course, to make considerable alterations in, or rather additions to, its machinery, after changing his bed-room, for it had then to work in a direction at right angles to the former; but this he managed perfectly.

It is well for Willie's reputation with a certain, and that not a small class of readers, that there was something even they would call useful in several of his inventions and many of his efforts; in his hydraulics, for instance, by means of which he saved old Tibby's limbs; in his house-building, too, by means of which they were able to take in grannie; and, for a long time now, he had been doing every little repair wanted in the house. If a lock went wrong, he would have it off at once and taken to pieces. If less would not do, he carried it to the smithy, but very seldom troubled Mr Willett about it, for he had learned to do small jobs, and to heat and work and temper a piece of iron within his strength as well as any man. His mother did not much like this part of his general apprenticeship, for he would get his hands so black sometimes on a Saturday afternoon that he could not get them clean enough for church the next day; and sometimes he would come home with little holes burnt here and there in his clothes by the sparks from the red-hot iron when beaten on the anvil. Concerning this last evil, she spoke at length to Hector, who made him a leather apron, like Mr Willett's, which thereafter he always wore when he had a job to do in the smithy.

It is well, I say, that the utility of such of his doings as these will be admitted by all; for some other objects upon which he spent much labour would, by most people, be regarded as utterly useless. Few, for instance, would allow there was any value in a water-wheel which could grind no corn, and was of service only to wake him in the middle of the night—not for work, not for the learning of a single lesson, but only that he might stare out of the window for a while, and then get into bed again. For my part, nevertheless, I think it a most useful contrivance. For all lovely sights tend to keep the soul pure, to lift the heart up to God, and above, not merely what people call low cares, but what people would call reasonable cares, although our great Teacher teaches us that such cares are unjust towards our Father in Heaven. More than that, by helping to keep the mind calm and pure, they help to keep the imagination, which is the source of all invention, active, and the judgment, which weighs all its suggestions, just. Whatever is beautiful is of God, and it is only ignorance or a low condition of heart and soul that does not prize what is beautiful. If I had a choice between two mills, one that would set fine dinners on my table, and one that would show me lovely sights in earth and sky and sea, I know which I should count the more useful.

Perhaps there is not so much to be said for the next whim of Willie's; but a part at least of what I have just written will apply to it also.

What put it in his head I am not sure, but I think it was two things together—seeing a soaring lark radiant with the light of the unrisen sun, and finding in a corner of Spelman's shop a large gilt ball which had belonged to an old eight-day clock he had bought. The passage in which he set it up was so low that he had to remove the ornaments from the top of it, but this one was humbled that it might be exalted.

The very sight of it set Willie thinking what he could do with it; for he not only meditated how to do a thing, but sometimes what to make a thing do. Nor was it long ere he made up his mind, and set about a huge kite, more than six feet high—a great strong monster, with a tail of portentous length—to the top of the arch of which he attached the golden ball. Then he bought a quantity of string, and set his wheel to call him up an hour before sunrise.

One morning was too still, another too cloudy, and a third wet; but at last came one clear and cool, with a steady breeze which sent the leaves of the black poplars all one way. He dressed with speed, and, taking his kite and string, set out for a grass field belonging to Farmer Thomson, where he found most of the daisies still buttoned up in sleep, their red tips all together, as tight and close as the lips of a baby that won't take what is offered it—as if they never meant to have anything more to do with the sun, and would never again show him the little golden sun they had themselves inside of them. In a few minutes the kite had begun to soar, slowly and steadily, then faster and faster, until at length it was towering aloft, tugging and pulling at the string, which he could not let out fast enough. He kept looking up after it intently as it rose, when suddenly a new morning star burst out in golden glitter. It was the gilt ball; it saw the sun. The glory which, striking on the heart of the lark, was there transmuted into song, came back from the ball, after its kind, in glow and gleam. He danced with delight, and shouted and sang his welcome to the resurrection of the sun, as he watched his golden ball alone in the depth of the air.

He never thought of any one hearing him, nor was it likely that any one in the village would be up yet. He was therefore a good deal surprised when he heard the sweet voice of Mona Shepherd behind him; and turning, saw her running to him bare-headed, with her hair flying in the wind.

"Willie! Willie!" she was crying, half-breathless with haste and the buffeting of the breeze.

"Well, Mona, who would have thought of seeing you out so early?"

"Mayn't a girl get up early, as well as a boy? It's not like climbing walls and trees, you know, though I can't see the harm of that either."

"No more can I," said Willie, "if they're not too difficult, you know.

But what brought you out now? Do you want me?"

"Mayn't I stop with you? I saw you looking up, and I looked up too, and then I saw something flash; and I dressed as hard as I could, and ran out. Are you catching the lightning?"

"No," said Willie; "something better than the lightning—the sunlight."

"Is that all?" said Mona, disappointed.

"Why, Mona, isn't the sunlight a better thing than the lightning?" said philosophical Willie.

"Yes, I dare say; but you can have it any time."

"That only makes it the more valuable. But it's not quite true when you think of it. You can't have it now, except from my ball."

"Oh, yes, I can," cried Mona; "for there he comes himself."

And there, to be sure, was the first blinding arc of the sun rising over the eastern hill. Both of them forgot the kite, and turned to watch the great marvel of the heavens, throbbing and pulsing like a sea of flame. When they turned again to the kite they could see the golden ball no longer. Its work was over; it had told them the sun was coming, and now, when the sun was come, it was not wanted any more. Willie began to draw in his string and roll it up on its stick, slowly pulling down to the earth the soaring sun-scout he had sent aloft for the news. He had never flown anything like such a large kite before, and he found it difficult to reclaim.

"Will you take me out with you next time, Willie?" asked Mona, pleadingly. "I do so like to be out in the morning, when the wind is blowing, and the clouds are flying about. I wonder why everybody doesn't get up to see the sun rise. Don't you think it is well worth seeing?"

"That I do."

"Then you will let me come with you? I like it so much better when you are with me. Janet spoils it all."

Janet was her old nurse, who seemed to think the main part of her duty was to check Mona's enthusiasm.

"I will," said Willie, "if your papa has no objection."

Mona did not even remember her mamma. She had died when she was such a little thing.

"Come and ask him, then," said Mona.

So soon as he had secured Sun-scout, as he called his kite with the golden head, she took his hand to lead him to her father.

"He won't be up yet," said Willie.

"Oh, yes, long ago," cried Mona. "He's always up first in the house, and as soon as he's dressed he calls me. He'll be at breakfast by this time, and wondering what can have become of me."

So Willie went with her, and there was Mr Shepherd, as she had said, already seated at breakfast.

"What have you been about, Mona, my child?" he asked, as soon as he had shaken hands with Willie.

"We've been helping the sun to rise," said Mona, merrily.

"No, no," said Willie; "we've only been having a peep at him in bed,

109

before he got up."

"Oh, yes," chimed in Mona. "And he was so fast asleep!—and snoring," she added, with a comical expression and tone, as if it were a thing not to be mentioned save as a secret.

But Willie did not like the word, and her father was of the same mind.

"No, no," said Mr Shepherd; "that's not respectful, Mona. I don't like you to talk that way, even in fun, of the great light of the earth. There are more good reasons for objecting to it than you would quite understand yet. Willie would not talk like that, I am sure. Tell me what you have been about, my boy."

Willie explained the whole matter, and asked if he might call Mona the next time he went out with his kite in the morning.

Mr Shepherd consented at once; and Mona said he had only to call from his window into their garden, and she would be sure to hear him even if she was asleep.

The next thing Willie did was to construct a small windlass in the garden, with which to wind up or let out the string of the kite; and when the next fit morning arrived, Mona and he went out together. The wind blowing right through the garden, they did not go to the open field, but sent up the kite from the windlass, and Mona was able by means of the winch to let out the string, while Willie kept watching for the moment when the golden ball should catch the light. They did the same for several mornings after, and Willie managed, with the master's help, to calculate exactly the height to which the ball had flown when first it gained a peep of the sun in bed.

One windy evening they sent the kite up in the hope that it would fly till the morning; but the wind fell in the night, and when the sun came near there was no golden ball in the air to greet him. So, instead of rejoicing in its glitter far aloft, they had to set out, guided by the string, to find the fallen Lucifer. The kite was of small consequence, but the golden ball Willie could not replace. Alas! that very evening he had added a great length of string—so much, that when the wind ceased the kite could just reach the river, into which it fell; and when the searchers at length drew Sun-scout from the water they found his glory had departed; the golden ball had been beaten and ground upon the stones of the stream, and never more did they send him climbing up the heavens to welcome the lord of day.

Indeed, it was many years before Willie flew a kite again, for, after a certain conversation with his grandmother, he began to give a good deal more time to his lessons than hitherto; and while his recreations continued to be all of a practical sort, his reading was mostly such as prepared him for college.

CHAPTER XVIII. WILLIE'S TALK WITH HIS GRANDMOTHER.

One evening in winter, when he had been putting coals on his grannie's fire, she told him to take a chair beside her, as she wanted a little talk with him. He obeyed her gladly.

"Well, Willie," she said, "what would you like to be?"

Willie had just been helping to shoe a horse at the smithy, and, in fact, had driven one of the nails—an operation perilous to the horse. Full of the thing which had last occupied him, he answered without a moment's hesitation—

"I should like to be a blacksmith, grannie."

The old lady smiled. She had seen more black on Willie's hands than could have come from the coals, and judged from that and his answer that he had just come from the smithy.

An unwise grandmother, had she wished to turn him from the notion, would have started an objection at once—probably calling it a dirty trade, or a dangerous trade, or a trade that the son of a professional man could not be allowed to follow; but Willie's grandmother knew better, and went on talking about the thing in the quietest manner.

"It's a fine trade," she said; "thorough manly work, and healthy,

I believe, notwithstanding the heat. But why would you take to it,

Willie?"

Willie fell back on his principles, and thought for a minute.

"Of course, if I'm to be any good at all I must have a hand in what

Hector calls the general business of the universe, grannie."

"To be sure; and that, as a smith, you would have; but why should you choose to be a smith rather than anything else in the world?"

"Because—because—people can't get on without horse-shoes, and ploughs and harrows, and tires for cart-wheels, and locks, and all that. It would help people very much if I were a smith."

"I don't doubt it. But if you were a mason you could do quite as much to make them comfortable; you could build them houses."

"Yes, I could. It would be delightful to build houses for people. I should like that."

"It's very hard work," said his grandmother. "Only you wouldn't mind that, I know, Willie."

"No man minds hard work," said Willie. "I think I should like to be a mason; for then, you see, I should be able to look at what I had done. The ploughs and carts would go away out of sight, but the good houses would stand where I had built them, and I should be able to see how comfortable the people were in them. I should come nearer to the people themselves that way with my work. Yes, grannie, I would rather be a mason than a smith."

"A carpenter fits up the houses inside," said his grandmother. "Don't you think, with his work, he comes nearer the people that live in it than the mason does?"

"To be sure," cried Willie, laughing. "People hardly see the mason's work, except as they're coming up to the door. I know more about carpenter's work too. Yes, grannie, I have settled now; I'll be a carpenter—there!" cried Willie, jumping up from his seat. "If it hadn't been for Mr Spelman, I don't see how we could have had you with us, grannie. Think of that!"

"Only, if you had been a tailor or a shoemaker, you would have come still nearer to the people themselves."

"I don't know much about tailoring," returned Willie. "I could stitch well enough, but I couldn't cut out. I could soon be a shoemaker, though. I've done everything wanted in a shoe or a boot with my own hands already; Hector will tell you so. I could begin to be a shoemaker to-morrow. That is nearer than a carpenter. Yes."

"I was going to suggest," said his grannie, "that there's a kind of work that goes yet nearer to the people it helps than any of those. But, of course, if you've made up your mind"—

"Oh no, grannie! I don't mean it so much as that—if there's a better way, you know. Tell me what it is."

"I want you to think and find out."

Willie thought, looked puzzled, and said he couldn't tell what it was.

"Then you must think a little longer," said his grandmother. "And now go and wash your hands."

CHAPTER XVIX. A TALK WITH Mr SHEPHERD.

In a few minutes Willie came rushing back from his room, with his hands and face half wet and half dry.

"Grannie! grannie!" he panted—"what a stupid I am! How can a body be so stupid! Of course you mean a doctor's work! My father comes nearer to people to help them than anybody else can—and yet I never thought what you meant. How is it you can know a thing and not know it at the same moment?"

"Well, now you've found what I meant, what do you think of it?" said his grandmother.

"Why, of course, it's the best of all. When I was a little fellow, I used to think I should be a doctor some day, but I don't feel quite so sure of it now. Do you really think, grannie, I could be a doctor like papa? You see that wants such a good head—and—and—everything."

"Yes; it does want a good head and everything. But you've got a good enough head to begin with, and it depends on yourself to make it a better one. So long as people's hearts keep growing better, their heads do the same. I think you have every faculty for the making of a good doctor in you."

"Do you really think so, grannie?" cried Willie, delighted.

"I do indeed."

"Then I shall ask papa to teach me."

But Willie did not find his papa quite ready to take him in hand.

"No, Willie," he said. "You must learn a great many other things before it would be of much use for me to commence my part. I will teach you if you like, after school-hours, to compound certain medicines; but the important thing is to get on at school. You are quite old enough now to work at home too; and though I don't want to confine you to your lessons, I should like you to spend a couple of hours at them every evening. You can have the remainders of the evenings, all the mornings before breakfast, and the greater parts of your half-holidays, for whatever you like to do of another sort."

Willie never required any urging to what his father wished. He became at once more of a student, without becoming much less of a workman—for he found plenty of time to do all he wanted, by being more careful of his odd moments.

One lovely evening in spring, when the sun had gone down and left the air soft, and balmy, and full of the scents which rise from the earth after a shower, and the odours of the buds which were swelling and bursting in all directions, Willie was standing looking out of his open window into the parson's garden, when Mr Shepherd saw him and called to him—

"Come down here, Willie," he said. "I want to have a little talk with you."

Willie got on the wall from the top of his stair, dropped into the stable-yard, which served for the parson's pony as well as the Doctor's two horses, and thence passed into Mr Shepherd's garden, where the two began to walk up and down together.

The year was like a child waking up from a sleep into which he had fallen crying. Its life was returning to it, fresh and new. It was as if God were again drawing nigh to His world. All the winter through He had never left it, only had, as it were, been rolling it along the path before Him; but now had taken it up in His hand, and was carrying it for a while; and that was how its birds were singing so sweetly, and its buds were coming so blithely out of doors, and the wind blew so soft, and the rain fell so repentantly, and the earth sent up such a gracious odour.

"The year is coming to itself again, Willie—growing busy once more," Mr

Shepherd said.

"Yes," answered Willie. "It's been all but dead, and has come to life

116

again. It must have had the doctor to it."

"Eh? What doctor, Willie?"

"Well, you know, there is but One that could be doctor to this big world."

"Yes, surely," returned Mr Shepherd. "And that brings me to what I wanted to talk to you about. I hear your father means to make a doctor of you."

"Yes. Isn't it good of him?" said Willie.

"Then you would like it?"

"Yes; that I should!"

"Why would you like it?"

"Because I must have a hand in the general business."

"What do you mean by that?"

Willie set forth Hector Macallaster's way of thinking about such matters.

"Very good—very good indeed!" remarked Mr Shepherd. "But why, then, should you prefer being a doctor to being a shoemaker? Is it because you will get better paid for it?"

"I never thought of that," returned Willie. "Of course I should be better paid—for Hector couldn't keep a horse, and a horse I must have, else some of my patients would be dead before I could get to them. But that's not why I want to be a doctor. It's because I want to help people."

"What makes you want to help people?"

"Because it's the best thing you can do with yourself."

"Who told you that?"

"I don't know. It seems as if everybody and everything had been teaching me that, ever since I can remember."

"Well, it's no wonder it should seem as if everything taught you that, seeing that is what God is always doing—and what Jesus taught us as the law of His kingdom—which is the only real kingdom—namely, that the greatest man in it is he who gives himself the most to help other people. It was because Jesus Himself did so—giving Himself up utterly—that God has so highly exalted Him and given Him a name above every name. And, indeed, if you are a good doctor, you will be doing something of what Jesus did when He was in the world."

"Yes; but He didn't give people medicine to cure them."

"No; that wasn't necessary, because He was Himself the cure. But now that He is not present with His bodily presence—now, medicine and advice and other good things are just the packets in which He wraps up the healing He sends; and the wisest doctor is but the messenger who carries to the sick as much of healing and help as the Great Doctor sees fit to send. For He is so anxious to cure thoroughly that in many cases He will not cure all at once."

"How I should like to take His healing about!" cried Willie—"just as the doctors' boys take the medicines about in baskets: grannie tells me they do in the big towns. I should like to be the Great Doctor's boy!"

"You really think then," Mr Shepherd resumed, after a pause, "that a doctor's is the best way of helping people?"

"Yes, I do," answered Willie, decidedly. "A doctor, you see, comes nearest to them with his help. It's not the outside of a man's body he helps, but his inside health—how he feels, you know."

Mr Shepherd again thought for a few moments. At length he said—

"What's the difference between your father's work and mine?"

"A great difference, of course," replied Willie.

"Tell me then what it is?"

"I must think before I can do that," said Willie. "It's not so easy to put things in words!—You very often go to help the same people: that's something to start with."

"But not to give them the same help."

"No, not quite. And yet"—

"At least, I cannot write prescriptions or compound medicines for them, seeing I know nothing about such things," said Mr Shepherd. "But, on the other hand, though I can't give them medicine out of your papa's basket, your papa very often gives them medicine out of mine."

"That's a riddle, I suppose," said Willie.

"No, it's not. How is it your papa can come so near people to help them?"

"He gives them things that make them well again."

"What do they do with the things he gives them?"

"They take them."

"How?"

"Put them in their mouths and swallow them."

"Couldn't they take them at their ears?"

"No," answered Willie, laughing.

"Why not?"

"Because their ears aren't meant for taking them."

"Aren't their ears meant for taking anything, then?"

"Only words."

"Well, if one were to try, mightn't words be mixed so as to be medicine?"

"I don't see how."

"If you were to take a few strong words, a few persuasive words, and a few tender words, mightn't you mix them so—that is, so set them in order—

as to make them a good medicine for a sore heart, for instance?"

"Ah! I see, I see! Yes, the medicine for the heart must go in at the ears."

"Not necessarily. It might go in at the eyes. Jesus gave it at the eyes, for doubting hearts, when He said—Consider the lilies,—consider the ravens."

"At the ears, too, though," said Willie; "just as papa sometimes gives a medicine to be taken and to be rubbed in both."

"Only the ears could have done nothing with the words if the eyes hadn't taken in the things themselves first. But where does this medicine go to, Willie?"

"I suppose it must go to the heart, if that's the place wants healing."

"Does it go to what a doctor would call the heart, then?"

"No, no; it must go to what—to what a clergyman—to what you call the heart."

"And which heart is nearer to the person himself?"

Willie thought for a moment, then answered, merrily—the doctor's heart, to be sure!"

"No, Willie; you're wrong there," said Mr Shepherd, looking, as he felt, a little disappointed.

"Oh yes, please!" said Willie; "I'm almost sure I'm right this time."

"No, Willie; what the clergyman calls the heart is the nearest to the man himself."

"No, no," persisted Willie. "The heart you've got to do with is the man himself. So of course the doctor's heart is the nearer to the man."

Mr Shepherd laughed a low, pleasant laugh.

"You're quite right, Willie. You've got the best of it. I'm very pleased. But then, Willie, doesn't it strike you that after all there might be a closer way of helping men than the doctor's way?"

120

Again Willie thought a while.

"There would be," he said, at length, "if you could give them medicine to make them happy when they are miserable."

"Even the doctor can do a little at that," returned Mr Shepherd; "for when in good health people are much happier than when they are ill."

"If you could give them what would make them good when they are bad then," said Willie.

"Ah, there you have it!" rejoined Mr Shepherd. "That is the very closest way of helping men."

"But nobody can do that—nobody can make a bad man good—but God," said

Willie.

"Certainly. But He uses medicines; and He sends people about with them, just like the doctors' boys you were speaking of. What else am I here for? I've been carrying His medicines about for a good many years now."

"Then your work and not my father's comes nearest to people to help them after all! My father's work, I see, doesn't help the very man himself; it only helps his body—or at best his happiness: it doesn't go deep enough to touch himself. But yours helps the very man. Yours is the best after all."

"I don't know," returned Mr Shepherd, thoughtfully. "It depends, I think, on the kind of preparation gone through."

"Oh yes!" said Willie. "You had to go through the theological classes. I must of course take the medical."

"That's true, but it's not true enough," said Mr Shepherd. "That wouldn't make a fraction of the difference I mean. There's just one preparation essential for a man who would carry about the best sort of medicines. Can you think what it is? It's not necessary for the other sort."

"The man must be good," said Willie. "I suppose that's it."

"That doesn't make the difference exactly," returned Mr Shepherd. "It is as necessary for a doctor to be good as for a parson."

"Yes," said Willie; "but though the doctor were a bad man, his medicines might be good."

"Not by any means so likely to be!" said the parson. "You can never be sure that anything a bad man has to do with will be good. It may be, because no man is all bad; but you can't be sure of it. We are coming nearer it now. Mightn't the parson's medicines be good if he were bad just as well as the doctor's?"

"Less likely still, I think," said Willie. "The words might be all of the right sort, but they would be like medicines that had lain in his drawers or stood in his bottles till the good was all out of them."

"You're coming very near to the difference of preparation I wanted to point out to you," said Mr Shepherd. "It is this: that the physician of men's selves, commonly called souls, must have taken and must keep taking the medicine he carries about with him; while the less the doctor wants of his the better."

"I see, I see," cried Willie, whom a fitting phrase, or figure, or form of expressing a thing, pleased as much as a clever machine—"I see! It's all right! I understand now."

"But," Mr Shepherd went on, "your father carries about both sorts of medicines in his basket. He is such a healthy man that I believe he very seldom uses any of his own medicines; but he is always taking some of the other sort, and that's what makes him fit to carry them about. He does far more good among the sick than I can. Many who don't like my medicine, will yet take a little of it when your father mixes it with his, as he has a wonderful art in doing. I hope, when your turn comes, you will be able to help the very man himself, as your father does."

"Do you want me to be a doctor of your kind, Mr Shepherd?"

"No. It is a very wrong thing to take up that basket without being told by Him who makes the medicine. If He wants a man to do so, He will let him know—He will call him and tell him to do it. But everybody ought to take the medicine, for everybody needs it; and the happy thing is, that, as soon as anyone has found how good it is—food and wine and all upholding things in one—he becomes both able and anxious to give it to others. If you would help people as much as your father does, you must begin by taking some of the real medicine yourself."

This conversation gave Willie a good deal to think about. And he had much need to think about it, for soon after this he left his father's house for the first time in his life, and went to a great town, to receive there a little further preparation for college. The next year he gained a scholarship, or, as they call it there, a bursary, and was at once fully occupied with classics and mathematics, hoping, however, the next year, to combine with them certain scientific studies bearing less indirectly upon the duties of the medical man.

CHAPTER XX. HOW WILLIE DID HIS BEST TO MAKE A BIRD OF AGNES.

During the time he was at college, he did often think of what Mr Shepherd had said to him. When he was tempted to any self-indulgence, the thought would always rise that this was not the way to become able to help people, especially the real selves of them; and, when amongst the medical students, he could not help thinking how much better doctors some of them would make if they would but try the medicine of the other basket for themselves. He thought this especially when he saw that they cared nothing for their patients, neither had any desire to take a part in the general business for the work's sake, but only wanted a practice that they might make a living. For such are nearly as unfit to be healers of the body, as mere professional clergymen to be healers of broken hearts and wounded minds. To do a man good in any way, you must sympathise with him—that is, know what he feels, and reflect the feeling in your own mirror; and to be a good doctor, one must love to heal; must honour the art of the physician and rejoice in it; must give himself to it, that he may learn all of it that he can—from its root of love to its branches of theory, and its leaves and fruits of healing.

He always came home to Priory Leas for the summer intervals, when you may be sure there was great rejoicing—loudest on the part of Agnes, who was then his constant companion, as much so, at least, as she was allowed. Willie saw a good deal of Mona Shepherd also, who had long been set free from the oppressive charge of Janet, and was now under the care of a governess, a wise, elderly lady; and as she was a great friend of Mrs Macmichael, the two families were even more together now than they had been in former years.

Of course, while at college he had no time to work with his hands: all his labour there must be with his head; but when he came home he had plenty of time for both sorts. He spent a couple of hours before breakfast in the study of physiology; after breakfast, another hour or two either in the surgery, or in a part of the ruins which he had roughly fitted up for a laboratory with a bench, a few shelves, and a furnace. His father, however, did not favour his being in the latter for a long time together; for young experimenters are commonly careless, and will often neglect proper precautions—breathing, for instance, many gases they ought not to breathe. He was so careful over Agnes, however, that often he would not let her in at all; and when he did, he generally confined himself to her amusement. He would show her such lovely things!—for instance, liquids that changed from one gorgeous hue to another; bubbles that burst into flame, and ascended in rings of white revolving smoke; light so intense, that it seemed to darken the daylight. Sometimes Mona would be of the party, and nothing pleased Agnes or her better than such wonderful things as these; while Willie found it very amusing to hear Agnes, who was sharp enough to pick up not a few of the chemical names, dropping the big words from her lips as if she were on the most familiar terms with the things they signified—phosphuretted hydrogen, metaphosphoric acid, sesquiferrocyanide of iron, and such like.

Then he would give an hour to preparation for the studies of next term; after which, until their early dinner, he would work at his bench or turning-lathe, generally at something for his mother or grandmother; or he would do a little mason-work amongst the ruins, patching and strengthening, or even buttressing, where he thought there was most danger of further fall—for he had resolved that, if he could help it, not another stone should come to the ground.

In this, his first summer at home from college, he also fitted up a small forge—in a part of the ruins where there was a wide chimney, whose vent ran up a long way unbroken. Here he constructed a pair of great bellows, and set up an old anvil, which he bought for a trifle from Mr Willett; and here his father actually trusted him to shoe his horses; nor did he ever find a nail of Willie's driving require to be drawn before the shoe had to give place to a new one.

In the afternoon, he always read history, or tales, or poetry; and in the evening did whatever he felt inclined to do—which brings me to what occupied him the last hours of the daylight, for a good part of this first summer.

One lovely evening in June, he came upon Agnes, who was now eight years old, lying under the largest elm of a clump of great elms and Scotch firs at the bottom of the garden. They were the highest trees in all the neighbourhood, and his father was very fond of them. To look up into those elms in the summer time your eyes seemed to lose their way in a mist of leaves; whereas the firs had only great, bony, bare, gaunt arms, with a tuft of bristles here and there. But when a ray of the setting sun alighted upon one of these firs it shone like a flamingo. It seemed as if the surly old tree and the gracious sunset had some secret between them, which, as often as they met, broke out in ruddy flame.

Now Agnes was lying on the thin grass under this clump of trees, looking up into their mystery—and—what else do you think she was doing?—She was sucking her thumb—her custom always when she was thoughtful; and thoughtful she seemed now, for the tears were in her eyes.

"What is the matter with my pet?" said Willie.

But instead of jumping up and flinging her arms about him, she only looked at him, gave a little sigh, drew her thumb from her mouth, pointed with it up into the tree, and said, "I can't get up there! I wish I was a bird," and put her thumb in her mouth again.

"But if you were a bird, you wouldn't be a girl, you know, and you wouldn't like that," said Willie—"at least I shouldn't like it."

"I shouldn't mind. I would rather have wings and fly about in the trees."

"If you had wings you couldn't have arms."

"I'd rather have wings."

"If you were a bird up there, you would be sure to wish you were a girl down here. For if you were a bird you couldn't lie in the grass and look up into the tree."

"Oh yes, I could."

"What a comical little bird you would look then—lying on your little round feathery back, with wings spread out to keep you from rolling over, and little sparkling eyes, one on each side of such a long beak, staring up into the tree!—Miaw! Miaw! Here comes the cat to eat you up!"

Agnes sprang to her feet in terror, and rushed to Willie. She had so fully fancied herself a bird that the very mention of the cat had filled her with horror. Once more she took her thumb from her mouth to give a little scream, and did not put it in again.

"O Willie! you frightened me so!" she said—joining, however, in his laugh.

"Poor birdie!" said Willie. "Did the naughty puss frighten it? Stwoke its fedders den.—Stwoke it—stwoke it," he continued, smoothing down her hair.

"But wouldn't it be nice," persisted Agnes, "to be so tall as the birds can make themselves with their wings? Fancy having your head up there in the green leaves—so cool! and hearing them all whisper, whisper, about your ears, and being able to look down on people's heads, you know, Willie! I do wish I was a bird! I do!"

But with Willie to comfort and play with her, she soon forgot her soaring ambition. Willie, however, did not forget it. If Agnes wished to enjoy the privacy of the leaves up in the height of the trees, why shouldn't she? At least, why shouldn't she if he could help her to it. Certainly he couldn't change her arms into wings, or cover her with feathers, or make her bones hollow so that the air might get all through her, even into her quills; but he could get her up into the tree, and even something more, perhaps. He would see about it— that is, he would think about it, for how it was to be done he did not yet see.

Long ago, almost the moment he arrived, he had set his wheel in order, and got his waking-machine into working trim. And now more than ever he enjoyed being pulled out of bed in the middle of the night—especially in the fine weather; for then, in that hushed hour when the night is just melting into the morn, and the earth looks as if she were losing her dreams, yet had not begun to recognise her own thoughts, he would not unfrequently go out into the garden, and wander about for a few thoughtful minutes.

The same night, when his wheel pulled him, he rose and went out into the garden. The night was at odds with morning which was which. An occasional bat would flit like a doubtful shadow across his eyes, but a cool breath of air was roaming about as well, which was not of the night at all, but plainly belonged to the morning. He wandered to the bottom of the garden—to the clump of trees, lay down where Agnes had been lying the night before, and thought and thought until he felt in himself how the child had felt when she longed to be a bird. What could he do to content her? He knew every bough of the old trees himself, having scrambled over them like a squirrel scores of times; but even if he could get Agnes up the bare bole of an elm or fir, he could not trust her to go scrambling about the branches. On the other hand, wherever he could go, he could surely somehow help Agnes to go. Having gathered a thought or two, he went back to bed.

The very next evening he set to work and spent the whole of that and the following at his bench, planing, and shaping, and generally preparing for a construction, the plan of which was now clear in his head. At length, on the third evening, he carried half a dozen long poles, and wheeled several barrowfuls of short planks, measuring but a few inches over two feet, down to the clump of trees.

At the foot of the largest elm he began to dig, with the intention of inserting the thick end of one of the poles; but he soon found it impossible to get half deep enough, because of the tremendous roots of the tree, and giving it up, thought of a better plan.

He set off to the smithy, and bought of Mr Willett some fifteen feet of iron rod, with a dozen staples. Carrying them home to his small forge, he cut the rod into equal lengths of a little over two feet, and made a hook at both ends of each length. Then he carried them down to the elm, and drove six of the staples into the bole of the tree at equal distances all round it, a foot from the ground; the others he drove one into each of the six poles, a foot from the thick end; after which he connected the poles with the tree, each by a hooked rod and its corresponding staples, when the tops of the poles just reached to the first fork of the elm. Then he nailed a bracket to the tree, at the height of an easy step from the ground, and at the same height nailed a piece of wood

128

across between two of the poles. Resting on the bracket and this piece of wood, he laid the first step of a stair, and fastened it firmly to both. Another bracket a little higher, and another piece of wood nailed to two poles, raised the next step; and so he went round and round the tree in an ascending spiral, climbing on the steps already placed to fix others above them. Encircling the tree some four or five times, for he wanted the ascent easy for little feet, he was at length at its fork. There he laid a platform or landing-place, and paused to consider what to do next. This was on the third evening from the laying of the first step.

From the fork many boughs rose and spread—amongst them two very near each other, between which he saw how, by help of various inequalities, he might build a little straight staircase leading up into a perfect wilderness of leaves and branches. He set about it at once, and, although he found it more difficult than he had expected, succeeded at last in building a safe stair between the boughs, with a hand-rail of rope on each side.

But Willie had chosen to ascend in this direction for another reason as well: one of these boughs was in close contact with a bough belonging to one of the largest of the red firs. On this fir-bough he constructed a landing-place, upon which it was as easy as possible to step from the stair in the elm. Next, the bough being very large, he laid along it a plank steadied by blocks underneath—a level for the little feet. Then he began to weave a network of rope and string along each side of the bough, so that the child could not fall off; but finding this rather a long job, and thinking it a pity to balk her of so much pleasure merely for the sake of surprising her the more thoroughly, he resolved to reveal what he had already done, and permit her to enjoy it.

For, as I ought to have mentioned sooner, he had taken Mona into his confidence, and she had kept Agnes out of the way for now nearly a whole week of evenings. But she was finding it more and more difficult to restrain her from rushing off in search of Willie, and was very glad indeed when he told her that he was not going to keep the thing a secret any longer.

CHAPTER XXI. HOW AGNES LIKED BEING A BIRD.

But Willie began to think whether he might not give Agnes two surprises out of it, with a dream into the bargain, and thought over it until he saw how he could manage it.

She always went to bed at seven o'clock, so that by the time the other people in the house began to think of retiring, she was generally fast asleep. About ten o'clock, therefore, the next night, just as a great round moon was peering above the horizon, with a quantity of mackerel clouds ready to receive her when she rose a yard or two higher, Willie, taking a soft shawl of his mother's, went into Agnes's room, and having wrapped her in the shawl, with a corner of it over her head and face, carried her out into the garden, down to the trees, and up the stair into the midst of the great boughs and branches of the elm tree. It was a very warm night, with a soft breath of south wind blowing, and there was no risk of her taking cold. He uncovered her face, but did not wake her, leaving that to the change of her position and the freshness of the air.

Nor was he disappointed. In a few moments she began to stir, then half-opened her eyes, then shut them, then opened them again, then rubbed them, then drew a deep breath, and then began to lift her head from Willie's shoulder, and look about her. Through the thick leaves the moon was shining like a great white fire, and must have looked to her sleepy eyes almost within a yard of her. Even if she had not been half asleep, so beheld through the leaves, it would have taken her a while to make up her mind what the huge bright thing was. Then she heard a great fluttering as if the leaves were talking to her, and out of them came a soft wind that blew in her face, and felt very sweet and pleasant. She rubbed her eyes again, but could not get the sleep out of them. As last she said to Willie, who stood as still as a stone—but her tongue and her voice and her lips could hardly make the words she wanted them to utter:

"Am I awake? Am I dreaming? It's so nice!"

Willie did not answer her, and the little head sunk on his shoulder again. He drew the corner of the shawl over it, and carried her back to her bed. When he had laid her down, she opened her eyes wide, stared him in the face for a moment, as if she knew all about everything except just what she was looking at, put her thumb in her mouth, and was fast asleep.

The next morning at breakfast, her papa out, and her mamma not yet come down, she told Willie that she had had such a beautiful dream!—that an angel, with great red wings, came and took her in his arms, and flew up and up with her to a cloud that lay close by the moon, and there stopped. The cloud was made all of little birds that kept fluttering their wings and talking to each other, and the fluttering of their wings made a wind in her face, and the wind made her very happy, and the moon kept looking through the birds quite close to them, and smiling at her, and she saw the face of the man in the moon quite plain. But then it grew dark and began to thunder, and the angel went down very fast, and the thunder was the clapping of his big red wings, and he flew with her into her mamma's room, and laid her down in her crib, and when she looked at him he was so like Willie.

"Do you think the dream could have come of your wishing to be a bird,

Agnes?" asked Willie.

"I don't know. Perhaps," replied Agnes. "Are you angry with me for wishing I was a bird, Willie?"

"No, darling. What makes you ask such a question?"

"Because ever since then you won't let me go with you—when you are doing things, you know."

"Why, you were in the laboratory with me yesterday!" said Willie.

"Yes, but you wouldn't have me in the evening when you used to let me be with you always. What are you doing down amongst the trees always now?"

"If you will have patience and not go near them all day, I will show you in the evening."

Agnes promised; and Willie gave the whole day to getting things on a bit. Amongst other things he wove such a network along the bough of the Scotch fir, that it was quite safe for Agnes to walk on it down to the great red hole of the tree. There he was content to make a pause for the present, constructing first, however, a little chair of bough and branch and rope and twig in which she could safely sit.

Just as he had finished the chair, he heard her voice calling, in a tone that grew more and more pitiful.

"Willie!—Willie!—Willie!—Willie!"

He got down and ran to find her. She was at the window of his room, where she had gone to wait till he called her, but her patience had at last given way.

"I'm so tired, Willie! Mayn't I come yet?"

"Wait just one moment more," said Willie, and ran to the house for his mother's shawl.

As soon as he began to wrap it about her, Agnes said, thoughtfully—

"Somebody did that to me before—not long ago—I remember: it was the angel in my dream."

When Willie put the corner over her face, she said, "He did that too!" and when he took her in his arms, she said, "He did that too! How funny you should do just what the angel did in my dream!"

Willie ran about with her here and there through the ruins, into the house, up and down the stairs, and through the garden in many directions, until he was satisfied he must have thoroughly bewildered her as to whereabouts they were, and then at last sped with her up the stair to the fork of the elm-tree. There he threw back the shawl, and told her to look.

To see her first utterly bewildered expression—then the slow glimmering dawn of intelligence, as she began to understand where she was—next the gradual rise of light in her face as if it came there from some spring down below, until it broke out in a smile all over it, when at length she perceived that this was what he had been working at, and why he wouldn't have her with him—gave Willie all the pleasure he had hoped for—quite satisfied him, and made him count his labour well rewarded.

"O Willie! Willie! it was all for me!—Wasn't it now?"

"Yes, it was, pet," said Willie.

"It was all to make a bird of me—wasn't it?" she went on.

"Yes—as much of a bird as I could. I couldn't give you wings, you know, and I hadn't any of my own to fly up with you to the moon, as the angel in your dream did. The dream was much nicer—wasn't it?"

"I'm not sure about that—really I'm not. I think it is nicer to have a wind coming you don't know from where, and making all the leaves flutter about, than to have the wings of birdies making the wind. And I don't care about the man in the moon much. He's not so nice as you, Willie. And yon red ray of the sun through there on the fir-tree is as good nearly as the moon."

"Oh! but you may have the moon, if you wait a bit. She'll be too late to-night, though."

"But now I think of it, Willie," said Agnes, "I do believe it wasn't a dream at all."

"Do you think a real angel carried you really up to the moon, then?" asked Willie.

"No; but a real Willie carried me really up into this tree, and the moon shone through the leaves, and I thought they were birds. You're my angel, Willie, only better to me than twenty hundred angels."

And Agnes threw her arms round his neck and hugged and kissed him.

As soon as he could speak, that is, as soon as she ceased choking him, he said—

"You were up in this tree last night: and the wind was fluttering the

133

leaves; and the moon was shining through them"—

"And you carried me in this shawl, and that was the red wings of the angel," cried Agnes, dancing with delight.

"Yes, pet, I daresay it was. But aren't you sorry to lose your big angel?"

"The angel was only in a dream, and you're here, Willie. Besides, you'll be a big angel some day, Willie, and then you'll have wings, and be able to fly me about."

"But you'll have wings of your own then, and be able to fly without me."

"But I may fold them up sometimes—mayn't I? for it would be much nicer to be carried by your wings—sometimes, you know. Look, look, Willie! Look at the sunbeam on the trunk of the fir—how red it's got. I do wish I could have a peep at the sun. Where can he be? I should see him if I were to go into his beam there—shouldn't I?"

"He's shining past the end of the cottage," said Willie. "Go, and you'll see him."

"Go where?" asked Agnes.

"Into the red sunbeam on the fir-tree."

"I haven't got my wings yet, Willie."

"That's what people very often say when they're not inclined to try what they can do with their legs."

"But I can't go there, Willie."

"You haven't tried."

"How am I to try?"

"You're not even trying to try. You're standing talking, and saying you can't."

It was nearly all Agnes could do to keep from crying. But she felt she must do something more lest Willie should be vexed. There seemed but one way to get nearer to the sunbeam, and that was to go down this tree and run to the foot of the other. What if Willie had made a stair up it also? But as she turned to see how she was to go down, for she had been carried up blind, she caught sight of the straight staircase between the two boughs, and, with a shriek of delight, up she ran.

"Gently, gently! Don't bring the tree down with your tremendous weight," cried Willie, following her close behind.

At the end of the stairs she sprang upon the bough of the fir, and in a moment more was sitting in the full light of the sunset.

"O Willie! Willie! this is grand! How good, how kind of you! You have made a bird of me! What will papa and mamma say? Won't they be delighted? I must run and fetch Mona."

So saying she hurried across again, and down the stair, and away to look for Mona Shepherd, shouting with delight as she ran. In a few minutes her cries had gathered the whole house to the bottom of the garden, as well as Mr Shepherd and Mona and Mrs Hunter. Mr Macmichael and all of them went up into the tree, Mr Shepherd last and with some misgivings; for, having no mechanical faculty himself, he could not rightly value Willie's, and feared that he might not have made the stair safe. But Mr Macmichael soon satisfied him, showing him how strong and firm Willie had made every part of it.

The next evening, Willie went on with his plan, which was to make a way for Bird Agnes from one tree to another over the whole of the clump. It took him many evenings, however, to complete it, and a good many more to construct in the elm tree a thin wooden house cunningly perched upon several of the strongest boughs and branches. He called it Bird Agnes's Nest. It had doors and windows, and several stories in it, only the upper stories did not rest on the lower, but upon higher branches of the tree. To two of these he made stairs, and a rope-ladder to a third. When the house was finished, he put a little table in the largest room, and having got some light chairs from the house, asked his father and mother and grandmother to tea in Bird Agnes's Nest. But grannie declined to go up the tree. She said her climbing days were over long ago.

CHAPTER XXII. WILLIE'S PLANS BUD.

Either they were over, or were only beginning; for, the next winter, while Willie was at college, grannie was taken ill; and although they sent for him to come home at once, she had climbed higher ere he arrived. When they opened her will, they found that she had left everything to Willie. There was more than a hundred pounds in ready money, and property that brought in about fifty pounds a-year—not much to one who would have spent everything on himself, but a good deal to one who loved other people, and for their sakes would contrive that a little should go a long way.

So Willie was henceforth able to relieve his father by paying all his own college expenses. He laid by a little too, as his father wished him, until he should see how best to use it. His father always talked about using never about spending money.

When he came home the next summer, he moved again into his own old room, for Agnes slept in a little closet off her mother's, and much preferred that to a larger and more solitary room for herself. His mother especially was glad to have him under the same roof once more at night. But Willie felt that something ought to be done with the room he had left in the ruins, for nothing ought to be allowed to spoil by uselessness. He did not, however, see for some time to what he could turn it.

I need hardly say that he kept up all his old friendships. No day passed while he was at home without his going to see some one of his former companions—Mr Willett, or Mr Spelman, or Mr Wilson. For Hector, he went to see him oftenest of all, he being his favourite, and sickly, and therefore in most need of attention. But he greatly improved his acquaintance with William Webster; and although he had now so much to occupy him, would not be satisfied until he was able to drive the shuttle, and work the treadles and the batten, and, in short, turn out almost as good a bit of linen as William himself—only he wanted about twice as much time to it.

One day, going in to see Hector, he found him in bed and very poorly.

"My shoemaking is nearly over, Mr Willie," he said. "But I don't mind much; I'm sure to find a corner in the general business ready for me somewhere when I'm not wanted here any more."

"Have you been drinking the water lately?" asked Willie.

"No. I was very busy last week, and hadn't time, and it was rather cold for me to go out. But for that matter the wind blew in through door and window so dreadfully—and it's but a clay floor, and firing is dear—that I caught a cold, and a cold is the worst thing for me—that is for this poor rickety body of mine. And this cold is a bad one."

Here a great fit of coughing came on, accompanied by symptoms that Willie saw were dangerous, and he went home at once to get him some medicine.

On the way back a thought struck him, about which, however, he would say nothing to Hector until he should have talked to his father and mother about it, which he did that same evening at supper.

"I'll tell you what, Hector," he said, when he went to see him the next day—"you must come and occupy my room in the ruins. Since grannie went home I don't want it, and it's a pity to have it lying idle. It's a deal warmer than this, and I'll get a stove in before the winter. You won't have to work so hard when you've got no rent to pay, and you will have as much of the water as you like without the trouble of walking up the hill for it. Then there's the garden for you to walk in when you please—all on a level, and only the little stair to climb to get back to your own room."

"But I should be such a trouble to you all, Mr Willie!"

"You'd be no trouble—we've two servants now. If you like you can give the little one a shilling now and then, and she'll be glad enough to make your bed, and sweep out your room; and you know Tibby has a great regard for you, and will be very glad to do all the cooking you will want—it's not much, I know: your porridge and a cup of tea is about all. And then there's my father to look after your health, and Agnes to amuse you sometimes, and my mother to look after everything, and"—

Here poor Hector fairly broke down. When he recovered himself he said—

"But how could gentle folks like you bear to see a hump-backed creature like me crawling about the place?"

"They would only enjoy it the more that you enjoyed it," said Willie.

It was all arranged. As soon as Hector was able to be moved, he was carried up to the Ruins, and there nursed by everybody. Nothing could exceed his comfort now but his gratitude. He was soon able to work again, and as he was evidently happier when doing a little towards the general business, Mr Macmichael thought it best for him.

One day, Willie being at work in his laboratory, and getting himself half-stifled with a sudden fume of chlorine, opened the door for some air just as Hector had passed it. He stood at the door and followed him down the walk with his eyes, watching him as he went—now disappearing behind the blossoms of an apple-tree, now climbing one of the little mounds, and now getting up into the elm-tree, and looking about him on all sides, his sickly face absolutely shining with pleasure.

"But," said Willie all at once to himself, "why should Hector be the only invalid to have this pleasure?"

He found no answer to the question. I don't think he looked for one very hard though. And again, all at once, he said to himself—

"What if this is what my grannie's money was given me for?"

That night he had a dream. The two questions had no doubt a share in giving it him, and perhaps also a certain essay of Lord Bacon—"Of Building," namely—which he had been reading before he went to bed.

He dreamed that, being pulled up in the middle of the night by his wheel, he went down to go into the garden. But the moment he was out of the back door, he fancied there was something strange going on in his room in the ruins—he could not tell what, but he must go and see. When he climbed the stairs and opened the door, there was Hector Macallaster where

138

he ought to be, asleep in his bed. But there was something strange going on; for a stream, which came dashing over the side of the wooden spout, was flowing all round Hector's bed, and then away he knew not whither. Another strange thing was, that in the further wall was a door which was new to him. He opened it, and found himself in another chamber, like his own; and there also lay some one, he knew not who, in a bed, with a stream of water flowing all around it. There was also a second door, beyond which was a third room, and a third patient asleep, and a third stream flowing around the bed, and a third door beyond. He went from room to room, on and on, through about a hundred such, he thought, and at length came to a vaulted chamber, which seemed to be over the well. From the centre of the vault rose a great chimney, and under the chimney was a huge fire, and on the fire stood a mighty golden cauldron, up to which, through a large pipe, came the water of the well, and went pouring in with a great rushing, and hissing, and bubbling. From the other side of the cauldron, the water rushed away through another pipe into the trough that ran through all the chambers, and made the rivers that flowed the beds of the sleeping patients. And what was most wonderful of all—by the fire stood two angels, with grand lovely wings, and they made a great fanning with their wings, and so blew the fire up loud and strong about the golden cauldron. And when Willie looked into their faces, he saw that one of them was his father, and the other Mr Shepherd. And he gave a great cry of delight, and woke weeping.

CHAPTER XXIII. WILLIE'S PLANS BLOSSOM.

In the morning, Willie's head was full of his dream. How gladly would he have turned it into a reality! That was impossible—but might he not do something towards it? He had long ago seen that those who are doomed not to realise their ideal, are just those who will not take the first step towards it. "Oh! this is such a little thing to do, it can't be any use!" they say. "And it's such a distance off what I mean, and what I should give my life to have!" They think and they say that they would give their life for it, and yet they will not give a single hearty effort. Hence they just stop where they are, or rather go back and back until they do not care a bit for the thoughts they used to think so great that they cherished them for the glory of having thought them. But even the wretched people who set their hearts on making money, begin by saving the first penny they can, and then the next and the next. And they have their reward: they get the riches they want—with the loss of their souls to be sure, but that they did not think of. The people on the other hand who want to be noble and good, begin by taking the first thing that comes to their hand and doing that right, and so they go on from one thing to another, growing better and better.

In the same way, although it would have been absurd in Willie to rack his brain for some scheme by which to restore such a grand building as the Priory, he could yet bethink himself that the hundredth room did not come next the first, neither did the third; the one after the first was the second, and he might do something towards the existence of that.

He went out immediately after breakfast, and began peering about the ruins to see where the second room might be. To his delight he saw that, with a little contrivance, it could be built on the other side of the wall of Hector's room.

He had plenty of money for it, his grannie's legacy not being yet touched. He thought it all over himself, talked it all over with his father, and then consulted it all over with Spelman. The end was, that without nearly spending his little store, he had, before the time came for his return to the college, built another room.

As the garret was full of his grandmother's furniture, nothing was easier than to fit it up—and that very nicely too. It remained only to find an occupant for it. This would have been easy enough also without going far from the door, but both Willie and his father were practical men, and therefore could not be content with merely doing good: they wanted to do as much good as they could. It would not therefore satisfy them to put into their new room such a person—say, as Mrs Wilson, who could get on pretty well where she was, though she might have been made more comfortable. But suppose they could find the sickly mother of a large family, whom a few weeks of change, with the fine air from the hills and the wonderful water from the Prior's well, would restore to strength and cheerfulness, how much more good would they not be doing in that way—seeing that to help a mother with children is to help all the children as well, not to mention the husband and the friends of the family! There were plenty such to be found amongst the patients he had to attend while at college. The expense of living was not great at Priory Leas, and Mr MacMichael was willing to bear that, if only to test the influences of the water and climate upon strangers.

Although it was not by any means the best season for the experiment, it was yet thoroughly successful with the pale rheumatic mother of six, whom Willie first sent home to his father's care. She returned to her children at Christmas, comparatively a hale woman, capable of making them and everybody about her twice as happy as before. Another as nearly like her in bodily condition and circumstances as he could find, took her place,—with a like result; and before long the healing that hovered about Priory Leas began to be known and talked of amongst the professors of the college, and the medical men of the city.

CHAPTER XXIV. WILLIE'S PLANS BEAR FRUIT.

When his studies were finished, Willie returned to assist his father, for he had no desire to settle in a great city with the ambition of becoming a fashionable doctor getting large fees and growing rich. He regarded the end of life as being, in a large measure, just to take his share in the general business.

By this time the reputation of the Prior's Well had spread on all sides, and the country people had begun to visit the Leas, and stay for a week or ten days to drink of the water. Indeed so many kept coming and going at all hours through the garden, that the MacMichaels at length found it very troublesome, and had a small pipe laid to a little stone trough built into the garden wall on the outside, so that whoever would might come and drink with less trouble to all concerned.

But Willie had come home with a new idea in his head.

An old valetudinarian in the city, who knew every spa in Europe, wanted to try that of Priory Leas and had consulted him about it. Finding that there was no such accommodation to be had as he judged suitable, he seriously advised Willie to build a house fit for persons of position, as he called them, assuring him that they would soon make their fortunes if they did. Now although, as I have said, this was not the ambition of either father or son, for a fortune had never seemed to either worth taking trouble about, yet it suggested something that was better.

"Why," said Willie to his father, "shouldn't we restore a bit of the Priory in such a way that a man like Mr Yellowley could endure it for a little while? He would pay us well, and then we should be able to do more for those that can't pay us."

"We couldn't cook for a man like that," said his mother.

"He wouldn't want that," said his father. "He would be sure to bring his own servants."

The result was that Mr MacMichael thought the thing worth trying, and resolved to lay out all his little savings, as well as what Willie could add, on getting a kitchen and a few convenient rooms constructed in the ruins—of course keeping as much as possible to their plan and architectural character. He found, however, that it would want a good deal more than they could manage to scrape together between them, and was on the point of giving up the scheme, or at least altering it for one that would have been much longer in making them any return, when Mr Shepherd, who had become acquainted with their plans, and consequently with their difficulties, offered to join them with the little he had laid aside for a rainy day—which proved just sufficient to complete the sum necessary. Between the three the thing was effected, and Mr Yellowley was their first visitor.

I am sorry to say he grumbled a good deal at first at the proximity of the cobbler, and at having to meet him in his walks about the garden; but this was a point on which Mr MacMichael, who of course took the old man's complaints good-humouredly, would not budge, and he had to reconcile himself to it as he best might. Nor was it very difficult after he found he must. Before long they became excellent friends, for if you will only give time and opportunity, in an ordinarily good man nature will overcome in the end. Mr Yellowley was at heart good-natured, and the cobbler was well worth knowing. Before the former left, the two were often to be seen pacing the garden together, and talking happily.

It is quite unnecessary to recount all the gradations of growth by which room after room arose from the ruins of the Priory. When Mr Yellowley went away, after nearly six months' sojourn, during the latter part of which, so wonderfully was he restored by the air and the water and the medical care of Mr MacMichael, he enjoyed a little shooting on the hills, he paid him a hundred and fifty pounds for accommodation and medical attendance—no great sum, as money goes now-a-days, but a good return in six months for the outlay of a thousand pounds. This they laid by to accumulate for the next addition. And the Priory, having once taken to growing, went on with it. They cleared away mound after mound from the garden, turning them once more into solid walls, for they were formed mainly of excellent stones, which had just been waiting to be put up again. The only evil consequence was that the garden became a little less picturesque by their removal, although, on the other hand, a good deal more productive.

Yes, there was a second apparently bad consequence—the Priory spread as well as grew, until it encroached not a little upon the garden. But for this a remedy soon appeared.

The next house and garden, although called the Manse, because the clergyman of the parish lived there, were Mr Shepherd's own property. The ruins formed a great part of the boundary between the two, and it was plain to see that the Priory had extended a good way into what was now the other garden. Indeed Mr Shepherd's house, as well as Mr MacMichael's, had been built out of the ruins. Mr Shepherd offered to have the wall thrown down and the building extended on his side as well—so that it should stand in the middle of one large garden.

My readers need not put a question as to what would have become of it if the two proprietors had quarrelled; for it had become less likely than ever that such a thing should happen. Willie had told Mona that he loved her more that he could tell, and wanted to ask her a question, only he didn't know how; and Mona had told Willie that she would suppose his question if he would suppose her answer; and Willie had said, "May I suppose it to be the very answer I should like?" and Mona had answered "Yes" quite decidedly; and Willie had given her a kiss; and Mona had taken the kiss and given him another for it; and so it was all understood, and there was no fear of the wall having to be built up again between the gardens.

So the Priory grew and flourished and gained great reputation; and the fame of the two doctors, father and son, spread far and wide for the cures they wrought. And many people came and paid them large sums. But the more rich people that came, the more poor people they invited. For they never would allow the making of money to intrude upon the dignity of their high calling. How should avarice and cure go together? A greedy healer of men! What a marriage of words!

The Priory became quite a grand building. The chapel grew up again, and had windows of stained glass that shone like jewels; and Mr Shepherd, having preached in the parish church in the morning, always preached in the Priory chapel on the Sunday evening, and all the patients, and any one besides that pleased, went to hear him.

They built great baths, hot and cold, and of all kinds—from baths where people could swim, to baths where they were only showered on by a very sharp rain. It was a great and admirable place.

After the two fathers died, Mona had a picture of Willie's dream painted, with portraits of them as the two angels.

This is the story of Gutta Percha Willie.

PHANTASTES: A FAERIE ROMANCE FOR MEN AND WOMEN

PREFACE

For offering this new edition of my father's Phantastes, my reasons are three. The first is to rescue the work from an edition illustrated without the author's sanction, and so unsuitably that all lovers of the book must have experienced some real grief in turning its pages. With the copyright I secured also the whole of that edition and turned it into pulp.

My second reason is to pay a small tribute to my father by way of personal gratitude for this, his first prose work, which was published nearly fifty years ago. Though unknown to many lovers of his greater writings, none of these has exceeded it in imaginative insight and power of expression. To me it rings with the dominant chord of his life's purpose and work.

My third reason is that wider knowledge and love of the book should be made possible. To this end I have been most happy in the help of my father's old friend, who has illustrated the book. I know of no other living artist who is capable of portraying the spirit of Phantastes; and every reader of this edition will, I believe, feel that the illustrations are a part of the romance, and will gain through them some perception of the brotherhood between George MacDonald and Arthur Hughes.

GREVILLE MACDONALD.

September 1905.

PHANTASTES A FAERIE ROMANCE

"Phantastes from 'their fount' all shapes deriving,

In new habiliments can quickly dight."

FLETCHER'S Purple Island

Es lassen sich Erzählungen ohne Zusammenhang, jedoch mit

Association, wie Träume, denken; Gedichte, die bloss

wohlklingend und voll schöner Worte sind, aber auch ohne

allen Sinn und Zusammenhang, höchstens einzelne Strophen

verständlich, wie Bruchstücke aus den verschiedenartigsten

Dingen. Diese wahre Poesie kann höchstens einen

allegorischen Sinn in Grossen, und eine indirecte Wirkung,

wie Musik, haben. Darum ist die Natur so rein poetisch, wie

die Stube eines Zauberers, eines Physikers, eine

Kinderstube, eine Polter- und Vorrathskammer.

Ein Märchen ist wie ein Traumbild ohne Zusammenhang. Ein

Ensemble wunderbarer Dinge und Begebenheiten, z. B. eine

musikalische Phantasie, die harmonischen Folgen einer

Aeolsharfe, die Natur selbst...

In einem echten Märchen muss alles wunderbar, geheimnissvoll

und zusammenhängend sein; alles belebt, jeder auf eine

andere Art. Die ganze Natur muss wunderlich mit der ganzen

Geisterwelt gemischt sein; hier tritt die Zeit der Anarchie,

der Gesetzlosigkeit, Freiheit, der Naturstand der Natur, die

Zeit von der Welt ein . . . Die Welt des Märchens ist die,

der Welt der Wahrheit durchaus entgegengesetzte, und eben

darum ihr so durchaus ähnlich, wie das Chaos der vollendeten

Schöpfung ähnlich ist.--NOVALIS.

CHAPTER I

"A spirit . . .

. . . . . .

The undulating and silent well,

And rippling rivulet, and evening gloom,

Now deepening the dark shades, for speech assuming,

Held commune with him; as if he and it

Were all that was."

SHELLEY'S *Alastor.*

I awoke one morning with the usual perplexity of mind which accompanies the return of consciousness. As I lay and looked through the eastern window of my room, a faint streak of peach-colour, dividing a cloud that just rose above the low swell of the horizon, announced the approach of the sun. As my thoughts, which a deep and apparently dreamless sleep had dissolved, began again to assume crystalline forms, the strange events of the foregoing night presented themselves anew to my wondering consciousness. The day before had been my one-and-twentieth birthday. Among other ceremonies investing me with my legal rights, the keys of an old secretary, in which my father had kept his private papers, had been delivered up to me. As soon as I was left alone, I ordered lights in the chamber where the secretary stood, the first lights that had been there for many a year; for, since my father's death, the room had been left undisturbed. But, as if the darkness had been too long an inmate to be easily expelled, and had dyed with blackness the walls to which, bat-like, it had clung, these tapers served but ill to light up the gloomy hangings, and seemed to throw yet darker shadows into the hollows of the deep-wrought cornice. All the further portions of the room lay shrouded in a mystery whose deepest folds were gathered around the dark oak cabinet which I now approached with a strange mingling of reverence and curiosity. Perhaps, like a geologist, I was about to turn up to the light some of the buried strata of the human world, with its fossil remains charred by passion and petrified by tears. Perhaps I was to learn how my father, whose personal history was unknown to me, had woven his web of story; how he had found the world, and how the world had left him. Perhaps I was to find only the records of lands and money, how gotten and how secured; coming down from strange men, and through troublous times, to me, who knew little or nothing of them all. To solve my speculations, and to dispel the awe which was fast gathering around me as if the dead were drawing near, I approached the secretary; and having found the key that fitted the upper portion, I opened it with some difficulty, drew near it a heavy high-backed chair, and sat down before a multitude of little drawers and slides and pigeon-holes. But the door of a little cupboard in the centre especially attracted my interest, as if there lay the secret of this long-hidden world. Its key I found.

One of the rusty hinges cracked and broke as I opened the door: it revealed a number of small pigeon-holes. These, however, being but shallow compared with the depth of those around the little cupboard, the outer ones reaching to the back of the desk, I concluded that there must be some accessible space behind; and found, indeed, that they were formed in a separate framework, which admitted of the whole being pulled out in one piece. Behind, I found a sort of flexible portcullis of small bars of wood laid close together horizontally. After long search, and trying many ways to move it, I discovered at last a scarcely projecting point of steel on one side. I pressed this repeatedly and hard with the point of an old tool that was lying near, till at length it yielded inwards; and the little slide, flying up suddenly, disclosed a chamber—empty, except that in one corner lay a little heap of withered rose-leaves, whose long-lived scent had long since departed; and, in another, a small packet of papers, tied with a bit of ribbon, whose colour had gone with the rose-scent. Almost fearing to touch them, they witnessed so mutely to the law of oblivion, I leaned back in my chair, and regarded them for a moment; when suddenly there stood on the threshold of the little chamber, as though she had just emerged from its depth, a tiny woman-form, as perfect in shape as if she had been a small Greek statuette roused to life and motion. Her dress was of a kind that could never grow old-fashioned, because it was

152

simply natural: a robe plaited in a band around the neck, and confined by a belt about the waist, descended to her feet. It was only afterwards, however, that I took notice of her dress, although my surprise was by no means of so overpowering a degree as such an apparition might naturally be expected to excite. Seeing, however, as I suppose, some astonishment in my countenance, she came forward within a yard of me, and said, in a voice that strangely recalled a sensation of twilight, and reedy river banks, and a low wind, even in this deathly room:—

"Anodos, you never saw such a little creature before, did you?"

"No," said I; "and indeed I hardly believe I do now."

"Ah! that is always the way with you men; you believe nothing the first time; and it is foolish enough to let mere repetition convince you of what you consider in itself unbelievable. I am not going to argue with you, however, but to grant you a wish."

Here I could not help interrupting her with the foolish speech, of which, however, I had no cause to repent—

"How can such a very little creature as you grant or refuse anything?"

"Is that all the philosophy you have gained in one-and-twenty years?" said she. "Form is much, but size is nothing. It is a mere matter of relation. I suppose your six-foot lordship does not feel altogether insignificant, though to others you do look small beside your old Uncle Ralph, who rises above you a great half-foot at least. But size is of so little consequence with old me, that I may as well accommodate myself to your foolish prejudices."

So saying, she leapt from the desk upon the floor, where she stood a tall, gracious lady, with pale face and large blue eyes. Her dark hair flowed behind, wavy but uncurled, down to her waist, and against it her form stood clear in its robe of white.

"Now," said she, "you will believe me."

Overcome with the presence of a beauty which I could now perceive, and drawn towards her by an attraction irresistible as incomprehensible, I suppose I stretched out my arms towards her, for she drew back a step or two, and said—

"Foolish boy, if you could touch me, I should hurt you. Besides, I was two hundred and thirty-seven years old, last Midsummer eve; and a man must not fall in love with his grandmother, you know."

"But you are not my grandmother," said I.

"How do you know that?" she retorted. "I dare say you know something of your great-grandfathers a good deal further back than that; but you know very little about your great-grandmothers on either side. Now, to the point. Your little sister was reading a fairy-tale to you last night."

"She was."

"When she had finished, she said, as she closed the book, 'Is there a fairy-country, brother?' You replied with a sigh, 'I suppose there is, if one could find the way into it.'"

"I did; but I meant something quite different from what you seem to think."

"Never mind what I seem to think. You shall find the way into Fairy Land to-morrow. Now look in my eyes."

Eagerly I did so. They filled me with an unknown longing. I remembered somehow that my mother died when I was a baby. I looked deeper and deeper, till they spread around me like seas, and I sank in their waters. I forgot all the rest, till I found myself at the window, whose gloomy curtains were withdrawn, and where I stood gazing on a whole heaven of stars, small and sparkling in the moonlight. Below lay a sea, still as death and hoary in the moon, sweeping into bays and around capes and islands, away, away, I knew not whither. Alas! it was no sea, but a low bog burnished by the moon. "Surely there is such a sea somewhere!" said I to myself. A low sweet voice beside me replied—

"In Fairy Land, Anodos."

I turned, but saw no one. I closed the secretary, and went to my own room, and to bed.

All this I recalled as I lay with half-closed eyes. I was soon to find the truth of the lady's promise, that this day I should discover the road into Fairy Land.

CHAPTER II

"'Where is the stream?' cried he, with tears. 'Seest thou

its not in blue waves above us?' He looked up, and lo! the

blue stream was flowing gently over their heads."

—NOVALIS, *Heinrich von Ofterdingen.*

While these strange events were passing through my mind, I suddenly, as one awakes to the consciousness that the sea has been moaning by him for hours, or that the storm has been howling about his window all night, became aware of the sound of running water near me; and, looking out of bed, I saw that a large green marble basin, in which I was wont to wash, and which stood on a low pedestal of the same material in a corner of my room, was overflowing like a spring; and that a stream of clear water was running over the carpet, all the length of the room, finding its outlet I knew not where. And, stranger still, where this carpet, which I had myself designed to imitate a field of grass and daisies, bordered the course of the little stream, the grass-blades and daisies seemed to wave in a tiny breeze that followed the water's flow; while under the rivulet they bent and swayed with every motion of the changeful current, as if they were about to dissolve with it, and, forsaking their fixed form, become fluent as the waters.

My dressing-table was an old-fashioned piece of furniture of black oak, with drawers all down the front. These were elaborately carved in foliage, of which ivy formed the chief part. The nearer end of this table remained just as it had been, but on the further end a singular change had commenced. I happened to fix my eye on a little cluster of ivy-leaves. The first of these was evidently the work of the carver; the next looked curious; the third was unmistakable ivy; and just beyond it a tendril of clematis had twined itself about the gilt handle of one of the drawers. Hearing next a slight motion above me, I looked up, and saw that the branches and leaves designed upon the curtains of my bed were slightly in motion. Not knowing what change might follow next, I thought it high time to get up; and, springing from the bed, my bare feet alighted upon a cool green sward; and although I dressed in all haste, I found myself completing my toilet under the boughs of a great tree, whose top waved in the golden stream of the sunrise with many interchanging lights, and with shadows of leaf and branch gliding over leaf and branch, as the cool morning wind swung it to and fro, like a sinking sea-wave.

After washing as well as I could in the clear stream, I rose and looked around me. The tree under which I seemed to have lain all night was one of the advanced guard of a dense forest, towards which the rivulet ran. Faint traces of a footpath, much overgrown with grass and moss, and with here and there a pimpernel even, were discernible along the right bank. "This," thought I, "must surely be the path into Fairy Land, which the lady of last night promised I should so soon find." I crossed the rivulet, and accompanied it, keeping the footpath on its right bank, until it led me, as I expected, into the wood. Here I left it, without any good reason: and with a vague feeling that I ought to have followed its course, I took a more southerly direction.

CHAPTER III

"Man doth usurp all space,

Stares thee, in rock, bush, river, in

the face.

Never thine eyes behold a tree;

'Tis no sea thou seest in the sea,

'Tis but a disguised humanity.

To avoid thy fellow, vain thy plan;

All that interests a man, is man."

HENRY SUTTON.

The trees, which were far apart where I entered, giving free passage to the level rays of the sun, closed rapidly as I advanced, so that ere long their crowded stems barred the sunlight out, forming as it were a thick grating between me and the East. I seemed to be advancing towards a second midnight. In the midst of the intervening twilight, however, before I entered what appeared to be the darkest portion of the forest, I saw a country maiden coming towards me from its very depths. She did not seem to observe me, for she was apparently intent upon a bunch of wild flowers which she carried in her hand. I could hardly see her face; for, though she came direct towards me, she never looked up. But when we met, instead of passing, she turned and walked alongside of me for a few yards, still keeping her face downwards, and busied with her flowers. She spoke rapidly, however, all the time, in a low tone, as if talking to herself, but evidently addressing the purport of her words to me.

She seemed afraid of being observed by some lurking foe. "Trust the Oak," said she; "trust the Oak, and the Elm, and the great Beech. Take care of the Birch, for though she is honest, she is too young not to be changeable.

But shun the Ash and the Alder; for the Ash is an ogre,—you will know him by his thick fingers; and the Alder will smother you with her web of hair, if you let her near you at night." All this was uttered without pause or alteration of tone. Then she turned suddenly and left me, walking still with the same unchanging gait. I could not conjecture what she meant, but satisfied myself with thinking that it would be time enough to find out her meaning when there was need to make use of her warning, and that the occasion would reveal the admonition. I concluded from the flowers that she carried, that the forest could not be everywhere so dense as it appeared from where I was now walking; and I was right in this conclusion. For soon I came to a more open part, and by-and-by crossed a wide grassy glade, on which were several circles of brighter green. But even here I was struck with the utter stillness. No bird sang. No insect hummed. Not a living creature crossed my way. Yet somehow the whole environment seemed only asleep, and to wear even in sleep an air of expectation. The trees seemed all to have an expression of conscious mystery, as if they said to themselves, "we could, an' if we would." They had all a meaning look about them. Then I remembered that night is the fairies' day, and the moon their sun; and I thought—Everything sleeps and dreams now: when the night comes, it will be different. At the same time I, being a man and a child of the day, felt some anxiety as to how I should fare among the elves and other children of the night who wake when mortals dream, and find their common life in those wondrous hours that flow noiselessly over the moveless death-like forms of men and women and children, lying strewn and parted beneath the weight of the heavy waves of night, which flow on and beat them down, and hold them drowned and senseless, until the ebbtide comes, and the waves sink away, back into the ocean of the dark. But I took courage and went on. Soon, however, I became again anxious, though from another cause. I had eaten nothing that day, and for an hour past had been feeling the want of food. So I grew afraid lest I should find nothing to meet my human necessities in this strange place; but once more I comforted myself with hope and went on.

Before noon, I fancied I saw a thin blue smoke rising amongst the stems of larger trees in front of me; and soon I came to an open spot of ground in which stood a little cottage, so built that the stems of four great trees formed its corners, while their branches met and intertwined over its roof, heaping a great cloud of leaves over it, up towards the heavens. I wondered at finding a human dwelling in this neighbourhood; and yet it did not look altogether human, though sufficiently so to encourage me to expect to find some sort of food. Seeing no door, I went round to the other side, and there I found one, wide open. A woman sat beside it, preparing some vegetables for dinner. This was homely and comforting. As I came near, she looked up, and seeing me, showed no surprise, but bent her head again over her work, and said in a low tone:

"Did you see my daughter?"

"I believe I did," said I. "Can you give me something to eat, for I am very hungry?" "With pleasure," she replied, in the same tone; "but do not say anything more, till you come into the house, for the Ash is watching us."

Having said this, she rose and led the way into the cottage; which, I now saw, was built of the stems of small trees set closely together, and was furnished with rough chairs and tables, from which even the bark had not been removed. As soon as she had shut the door and set a chair—

"You have fairy blood in you," said she, looking hard at me.

"How do you know that?"

"You could not have got so far into this wood if it were not so; and I am trying to find out some trace of it in your countenance. I think I see it."

"What do you see?"

"Oh, never mind: I may be mistaken in that."

"But how then do you come to live here?"

"Because I too have fairy blood in me."

Here I, in my turn, looked hard at her, and thought I could perceive, notwithstanding the coarseness of her features, and especially the heaviness of her eyebrows, a something unusual—I could hardly call it grace, and yet it was an expression that strangely contrasted with the form of her features. I noticed too that her hands were delicately formed, though brown with work and exposure.

"I should be ill," she continued, "if I did not live on the borders of the fairies' country, and now and then eat of their food. And I see by your eyes that you are not quite free of the same need; though, from your education and the activity of your mind, you have felt it less than I. You may be further removed too from the fairy race."

I remembered what the lady had said about my grandmothers.

Here she placed some bread and some milk before me, with a kindly apology for the homeliness of the fare, with which, however, I was in no humour to quarrel. I now thought it time to try to get some explanation of the strange words both of her daughter and herself.

"What did you mean by speaking so about the Ash?"

She rose and looked out of the little window. My eyes followed her; but as the window was too small to allow anything to be seen from where I was sitting, I rose and looked over her shoulder. I had just time to see, across the open space, on the edge of the denser forest, a single large ash-tree, whose foliage showed bluish, amidst the truer green of the other trees around it; when she pushed me back with an expression of impatience and terror, and then almost shut out the light from the window by setting up a large old book in it.

"In general," said she, recovering her composure, "there is no danger in the daytime, for then he is sound asleep; but there is something unusual going on in the woods; there must be some solemnity among the fairies to-night, for all the trees are restless, and although they cannot come awake, they see and hear in their sleep."

"But what danger is to be dreaded from him?"

Instead of answering the question, she went again to the window and looked out, saying she feared the fairies would be interrupted by foul weather, for a storm was brewing in the west.

"And the sooner it grows dark, the sooner the Ash will be awake," added she.

I asked her how she knew that there was any unusual excitement in the woods. She replied—

"Besides the look of the trees, the dog there is unhappy; and the eyes and ears of the white rabbit are redder than usual, and he frisks about as if he expected some fun. If the cat were at home, she would have her back up; for the young fairies pull the sparks out of her tail with bramble thorns, and she knows when they are coming. So do I, in another way."

At this instant, a grey cat rushed in like a demon, and disappeared in a hole in the wall.

"There, I told you!" said the woman.

"But what of the ash-tree?" said I, returning once more to the subject. Here, however, the young woman, whom I had met in the morning, entered. A smile passed between the mother and daughter; and then the latter began to help her mother in little household duties.

"I should like to stay here till the evening," I said; "and then go on my journey, if you will allow me."

"You are welcome to do as you please; only it might be better to stay all night, than risk the dangers of the wood then. Where are you going?"

"Nay, that I do not know," I replied, "but I wish to see all that is to be seen, and therefore I should like to start just at sundown." "You are a bold youth, if you have any idea of what you are daring; but a rash one, if you know nothing about it; and, excuse me, you do not seem very well informed about the country and its manners. However, no one comes here but for some reason, either known to himself or to those who have charge of him; so you shall do just as you wish."

Accordingly I sat down, and feeling rather tired, and disinclined for further talk, I asked leave to look at the old book which still screened the window. The woman brought it to me directly, but not before taking another look towards the forest, and then drawing a white blind over the window. I sat down opposite to it by the table, on which I laid the great old volume, and read. It contained many wondrous tales of Fairy Land, and olden times, and the Knights of King Arthur's table. I read on and on, till the shades of the afternoon began to deepen; for in the midst of the forest it gloomed earlier than in the open country. At length I came to this passage—

"Here it chanced, that upon their quest, Sir Galahad and Sir Percivale rencountered in the depths of a great forest. Now, Sir Galahad was dight all in harness of silver, clear and shining; the which is a delight to look upon, but full hasty to tarnish, and withouten the labour of a ready squire, uneath to be kept fair and clean. And yet withouten squire or page, Sir Galahad's armour shone like the moon. And he rode a great white mare, whose bases and other housings were black, but all besprent with fair lilys of silver sheen. Whereas Sir Percivale bestrode a red horse, with a tawny mane and tail; whose trappings were all to-smirched with mud and mire; and his armour was wondrous rosty to behold, ne could he by any art furbish it again; so that as the sun in his going down shone twixt the bare trunks of the trees, full upon the knights twain, the one did seem all shining with light, and the other all to glow with ruddy fire. Now it came about in this wise. For Sir Percivale, after his escape from the demon lady, whenas the cross on the handle of his sword smote him to the heart, and he rove himself through the thigh, and escaped away, he came to a great wood; and, in nowise cured of his fault, yet bemoaning the same, the damosel of the alder tree encountered him, right fair to see; and with her fair words and false countenance she comforted him and beguiled him, until he followed her where she led him to a—"

Here a low hurried cry from my hostess caused me to look up from the book, and I read no more.

"Look there!" she said; "look at his fingers!"

Just as I had been reading in the book, the setting sun was shining through a cleft in the clouds piled up in the west; and a shadow as of a large distorted hand, with thick knobs and humps on the fingers, so that it was much wider across the fingers than across the undivided part of the hand, passed slowly over the little blind, and then as slowly returned in the opposite direction.

"He is almost awake, mother; and greedier than usual to-night."

"Hush, child; you need not make him more angry with us than he is; for you do not know how soon something may happen to oblige us to be in the forest after nightfall."

"But you are in the forest," said I; "how is it that you are safe here?"

"He dares not come nearer than he is now," she replied; "for any of those four oaks, at the corners of our cottage, would tear him to pieces; they are our friends. But he stands there and makes awful faces at us sometimes, and stretches out his long arms and fingers, and tries to kill us with fright; for, indeed, that is his favourite way of doing. Pray, keep out of his way to-night."

"Shall I be able to see these things?" said I.

"That I cannot tell yet, not knowing how much of the fairy nature there is in you. But we shall soon see whether you can discern the fairies in my little garden, and that will be some guide to us."

"Are the trees fairies too, as well as the flowers?" I asked.

"They are of the same race," she replied; "though those you call fairies in your country are chiefly the young children of the flower fairies. They are very fond of having fun with the thick people, as they call you; for, like most children, they like fun better than anything else."

"Why do you have flowers so near you then? Do they not annoy you?"

"Oh, no, they are very amusing, with their mimicries of grown people, and mock solemnities. Sometimes they will act a whole play through before my eyes, with perfect composure and assurance, for they are not afraid of me. Only, as soon as they have done, they burst into peals of tiny laughter, as if it was such a joke to have been serious over anything. These I speak of, however, are the fairies of the garden. They are more staid and educated than those of the fields and woods. Of course they have near relations amongst the wild flowers, but they patronise them, and treat them as country cousins, who know nothing of life, and very little of manners. Now and then, however, they are compelled to envy the grace and simplicity of the natural flowers."

"Do they live in the flowers?" I said.

"I cannot tell," she replied. "There is something in it I do not understand. Sometimes they disappear altogether, even from me, though I know they are near. They seem to die always with the flowers they resemble, and by whose names they are called; but whether they return to life with the fresh flowers, or, whether it be new flowers, new fairies, I cannot tell. They have as many sorts of dispositions as men and women, while their moods are yet more variable; twenty different expressions will cross their little faces in half a minute. I often amuse myself with watching them, but I have never been able to make personal acquaintance with any of them. If I speak to one, he or she looks up in my face, as if I were not worth heeding, gives a little laugh, and runs away." Here the woman started, as if suddenly recollecting herself, and said in a low voice to her daughter, "Make haste—go and watch him, and see in what direction he goes."

I may as well mention here, that the conclusion I arrived at from the observations I was afterwards able to make, was, that the flowers die because the fairies go away; not that the fairies disappear because the flowers die. The flowers seem a sort of houses for them, or outer bodies, which they can put on or off when they please. Just as you could form some idea of the nature of a man from the kind of house he built, if he followed his own taste, so you could, without seeing the fairies, tell what any one of them is like, by looking at the flower till you feel that you understand it. For just what the flower says to you, would the face and form of the fairy say; only so much more plainly as a face and human figure can express more than a flower. For the house or the clothes, though like the inhabitant or the wearer, cannot be wrought into an equal power of utterance. Yet you would see a strange resemblance, almost oneness, between the flower and the fairy, which you could not describe, but which described itself to you. Whether all the flowers have fairies, I cannot determine, any more than I can be sure whether all men and women have souls.

The woman and I continued the conversation for a few minutes longer. I was much interested by the information she gave me, and astonished at the language in which she was able to convey it. It seemed that intercourse with the fairies was no bad education in itself. But now the daughter returned with the news, that the Ash had just gone away in a south-westerly direction; and, as my course seemed to lie eastward, she hoped I should be in no danger of meeting him if I departed at once. I looked out of the little window, and there stood the ash-tree, to my eyes the same as before; but I believed that they knew better than I did, and prepared to go. I pulled out my purse, but to my dismay there was nothing in it. The woman with a smile begged me not to trouble myself, for money was not of the slightest use there; and as I might meet with people in my journeys whom I could not recognise to be fairies, it was well I had no money to offer, for nothing offended them so much.

"They would think," she added, "that you were making game of them; and that is their peculiar privilege with regard to us." So we went together into the little garden which sloped down towards a lower part of the wood.

Here, to my great pleasure, all was life and bustle. There was still light enough from the day to see a little; and the pale half-moon, halfway to the zenith, was reviving every moment. The whole garden was like a carnival, with tiny, gaily decorated forms, in groups, assemblies, processions, pairs or trios, moving stately on, running about wildly, or sauntering hither or thither. From the cups or bells of tall flowers, as from balconies, some looked down on the masses below, now bursting with laughter, now grave as owls; but even in their deepest solemnity, seeming only to be waiting for the arrival of the next laugh. Some were launched on a little marshy stream at the bottom, in boats chosen from the heaps of last year's leaves that lay about, curled and withered. These soon sank with them; whereupon they swam ashore and got others. Those who took fresh rose-leaves for their boats floated the longest; but for these they had to fight; for the fairy of the rose-tree complained bitterly that they were stealing her clothes, and defended her property bravely.

"You can't wear half you've got," said some.

"Never you mind; I don't choose you to have them: they are my property."

"All for the good of the community!" said one, and ran off with a great hollow leaf. But the rose-fairy sprang after him (what a beauty she was! only too like a drawing-room young lady), knocked him heels-over-head as he ran, and recovered her great red leaf. But in the meantime twenty had hurried off in different directions with others just as good; and the little creature sat down and cried, and then, in a pet, sent a perfect pink snowstorm of petals from her tree, leaping from branch to branch, and stamping and shaking and pulling. At last, after another good cry, she chose the biggest she could find, and ran away laughing, to launch her boat amongst the rest.

But my attention was first and chiefly attracted by a group of fairies near the cottage, who were talking together around what seemed a last dying primrose. They talked singing, and their talk made a song, something like this:

> "*Sister Snowdrop died*
>> *Before we were born.*"
> "*She came like a bride*
>> *In a snowy morn.*"
> "*What's a bride?*"
>> "*What is snow?*"
> "*Never tried.*"
>> "*Do not know.*"
> "*Who told you about her?*"
>> "*Little Primrose there*
> *Cannot do without her.*"
>> "*Oh, so sweetly fair!*"
> "*Never fear,*
>> *She will come,*

Primrose dear.”

“Is she dumb?”

“She’ll come by-and-by.”

“You will never see her.”

“She went home to dies,

“Till the new year.”

“Snowdrop!” “‘Tis no good

To invite her.”

“Primrose is very rude,

“I will bite her.”

“Oh, you naughty Pocket!

“Look, she drops her head.”

“She deserved it, Rocket,

“And she was nearly dead.”

“To your hammock—off with you!”

“And swing alone.”

“No one will laugh with you.”

“No, not one.”

“Now let us moan.”

“And cover her o’er.”

“Primrose is gone.”

“All but the flower.”

"Here is a leaf."

"Lay her upon it."

"Follow in grief."

"Pocket has done it."

"Deeper, poor creature!

Winter may come."

"He cannot reach her—

That is a hum."

"She is buried, the beauty!"

"Now she is done."

"That was the duty."

"Now for the fun."

And with a wild laugh they sprang away, most of them towards the cottage. During the latter part of the song-talk, they had formed themselves into a funeral procession, two of them bearing poor Primrose, whose death Pocket had hastened by biting her stalk, upon one of her own great leaves. They bore her solemnly along some distance, and then buried her under a tree. Although I say her I saw nothing but the withered primrose-flower on its long stalk. Pocket, who had been expelled from the company by common consent, went sulkily away towards her hammock, for she was the fairy of the calceolaria, and looked rather wicked. When she reached its stem, she stopped and looked round. I could not help speaking to her, for I stood near her. I said, "Pocket, how could you be so naughty?"

"I am never naughty," she said, half-crossly, half-defiantly; "only if you come near my hammock, I will bite you, and then you will go away."

"Why did you bite poor Primrose?"

"Because she said we should never see Snowdrop; as if we were not good enough to look at her, and she was, the proud thing!—served her right!"

169

"Oh, Pocket, Pocket," said I; but by this time the party which had gone towards the house, rushed out again, shouting and screaming with laughter. Half of them were on the cat's back, and half held on by her fur and tail, or ran beside her; till, more coming to their help, the furious cat was held fast; and they proceeded to pick the sparks out of her with thorns and pins, which they handled like harpoons. Indeed, there were more instruments at work about her than there could have been sparks in her. One little fellow who held on hard by the tip of the tail, with his feet planted on the ground at an angle of forty-five degrees, helping to keep her fast, administered a continuous flow of admonitions to Pussy.

"Now, Pussy, be patient. You know quite well it is all for your good. You cannot be comfortable with all those sparks in you; and, indeed, I am charitably disposed to believe" (here he became very pompous) "that they are the cause of all your bad temper; so we must have them all out, every one; else we shall be reduced to the painful necessity of cutting your claws, and pulling out your eye-teeth. Quiet! Pussy, quiet!"

But with a perfect hurricane of feline curses, the poor animal broke loose, and dashed across the garden and through the hedge, faster than even the fairies could follow. "Never mind, never mind, we shall find her again; and by that time she will have laid in a fresh stock of sparks. Hooray!" And off they set, after some new mischief.

But I will not linger to enlarge on the amusing display of these frolicsome creatures. Their manners and habits are now so well known to the world, having been so often described by eyewitnesses, that it would be only indulging self-conceit, to add my account in full to the rest. I cannot help wishing, however, that my readers could see them for themselves. Especially do I desire that they should see the fairy of the daisy; a little, chubby, round-eyed child, with such innocent trust in his look! Even the most mischievous of the fairies would not tease him, although he did not belong to their set at all, but was quite a little country bumpkin. He wandered about alone, and looked at everything, with his hands in his little pockets, and a white night-cap on, the darling! He was not so beautiful as many other wild flowers I saw afterwards, but so dear and loving in his looks and little confident ways.

170

CHAPTER IV

"When bale is att hyest, boote is nyest."

Ballad of Sir Aldingar.

By this time, my hostess was quite anxious that I should be gone. So, with warm thanks for their hospitality, I took my leave, and went my way through the little garden towards the forest. Some of the garden flowers had wandered into the wood, and were growing here and there along the path, but the trees soon became too thick and shadowy for them. I particularly noticed some tall lilies, which grew on both sides of the way, with large dazzlingly white flowers, set off by the universal green. It was now dark enough for me to see that every flower was shining with a light of its own. Indeed it was by this light that I saw them, an internal, peculiar light, proceeding from each, and not reflected from a common source of light as in the daytime. This light sufficed only for the plant itself, and was not strong enough to cast any but the faintest shadows around it, or to illuminate any of the neighbouring objects with other than the faintest tinge of its own individual hue. From the lilies above mentioned, from the campanulas, from the foxgloves, and every bell-shaped flower, curious little figures shot up their heads, peeped at me, and drew back. They seemed to inhabit them, as snails their shells but I was sure some of them were intruders, and belonged to the gnomes or goblin-fairies, who inhabit the ground and earthy creeping plants. From the cups of Arum lilies, creatures with great heads and grotesque faces shot up like Jack-in-the-box, and made grimaces at me; or rose slowly and slily over the edge of the cup, and spouted water at me, slipping suddenly back, like those little soldier-crabs that inhabit the shells of sea-snails. Passing a row of tall thistles, I saw them crowded with little faces, which peeped every one from behind its flower, and drew back as quickly; and I heard them saying to each other, evidently intending me to hear, but the speaker always hiding behind his tuft, when I looked in his direction, "Look at him! Look at him! He has begun a story without a beginning, and it will never have any end. He! he! he! Look at him!"

But as I went further into the wood, these sights and sounds became fewer, giving way to others of a different character. A little forest of wild hyacinths was alive with exquisite creatures, who stood nearly motionless, with drooping necks, holding each by the stem of her flower, and swaying gently with it, whenever a low breath of wind swung the crowded floral belfry. In like manner, though differing of course in form and meaning, stood a group of harebells, like little angels waiting, ready, till they were wanted to go on some yet unknown message. In darker nooks, by the mossy roots of the trees, or in little tufts of grass, each dwelling in a globe of its own green light, weaving a network of grass and its shadows, glowed the glowworms.

They were just like the glowworms of our own land, for they are fairies everywhere; worms in the day, and glowworms at night, when their own can appear, and they can be themselves to others as well as themselves. But they had their enemies here. For I saw great strong-armed beetles, hurrying about with most unwieldy haste, awkward as elephant-calves, looking apparently for glowworms; for the moment a beetle espied one, through what to it was a forest of grass, or an underwood of moss, it pounced upon it, and bore it away, in spite of its feeble resistance. Wondering what their object could be, I watched one of the beetles, and then I discovered a thing I could not account for. But it is no use trying to account for things in Fairy Land; and one who travels there soon learns to forget the very idea of doing so, and takes everything as it comes; like a child, who, being in a chronic condition of wonder, is surprised at nothing. What I saw was this. Everywhere, here and there over the ground, lay little, dark-looking lumps of something more like earth than anything else, and about the size of a chestnut. The beetles hunted in couples for these; and having found one, one of them stayed to watch it, while the other hurried to find a glowworm. By signals, I presume, between them, the latter soon found his companion again: they then took the glowworm and held its luminous tail to the dark earthly pellet; when lo, it shot up into the air like a sky-rocket, seldom, however, reaching the height of the highest tree. Just like a rocket too, it burst in the air, and fell in a shower of the most gorgeously coloured sparks of every variety of hue; golden and red, and purple and green, and blue and rosy fires crossed and inter-crossed each other, beneath the shadowy heads, and between the columnar stems of the forest trees. They never used the same glowworm twice, I observed; but let him go, apparently uninjured by the use they had made of him.

In other parts, the whole of the immediately surrounding foliage was illuminated by the interwoven dances in the air of splendidly coloured fire-flies, which sped hither and thither, turned, twisted, crossed, and recrossed, entwining every complexity of intervolved motion. Here and there, whole mighty trees glowed with an emitted phosphorescent light. You could trace the very course of the great roots in the earth by the faint light that came through; and every twig, and every vein on every leaf was a streak of pale fire.

All this time, as I went through the wood, I was haunted with the feeling that other shapes, more like my own size and mien, were moving about at a little distance on all sides of me. But as yet I could discern none of them, although the moon was high enough to send a great many of her rays down between the trees, and these rays were unusually bright, and sight-giving, notwithstanding she was only a half-moon. I constantly imagined, however, that forms were visible in all directions except that to which my gaze was turned; and that they only became invisible, or resolved themselves into other woodland shapes, the moment my looks were directed towards them. However this may have been, except for this feeling of presence, the woods seemed utterly bare of anything like human companionship, although my glance often fell on some object which I fancied to be a human form; for I soon found that I was quite deceived; as, the moment I fixed my regard on it, it showed plainly that it was a bush, or a tree, or a rock.

Soon a vague sense of discomfort possessed me. With variations of relief, this gradually increased; as if some evil thing were wandering about in my neighbourhood, sometimes nearer and sometimes further off, but still approaching. The feeling continued and deepened, until all my pleasure in the shows of various kinds that everywhere betokened the presence of the merry fairies vanished by degrees, and left me full of anxiety and fear, which I was unable to associate with any definite object whatever. At length the thought crossed my mind with horror: "Can it be possible that the Ash is looking for me? or that, in his nightly wanderings, his path is gradually verging towards mine?" I comforted myself, however, by remembering that he had started quite in another direction; one that would lead him, if he kept it, far apart from me; especially as, for the last two or three hours, I had been diligently journeying eastward. I kept on my way, therefore, striving by direct effort of the will against the encroaching fear; and to this end occupying my mind, as much as I could, with other thoughts. I was so far successful that, although I was conscious, if I yielded for a moment, I should be almost overwhelmed with horror, I was yet able to walk right on for an hour or more. What I feared I could not tell. Indeed, I was left in a state of the vaguest uncertainty as regarded the nature of my enemy, and knew not the mode or object of his attacks; for, somehow or other, none of my questions had succeeded in drawing a definite answer from the dame in the cottage. How then to defend myself I knew not; nor even by what sign I might with certainty recognise the presence of my foe; for as yet this vague though powerful fear was all the indication of danger I had. To add to my distress, the clouds in the west had risen nearly to the top of the skies, and they and the moon were travelling slowly towards each other. Indeed, some of their advanced guard had already met her, and she had begun to wade through a filmy vapour that gradually deepened.

At length she was for a moment almost entirely obscured. When she shone out again, with a brilliancy increased by the contrast, I saw plainly on the path before me—from around which at this spot the trees receded, leaving a small space of green sward—the shadow of a large hand, with knotty joints and protuberances here and there. Especially I remarked, even in the midst of my fear, the bulbous points of the fingers. I looked hurriedly all around, but could see nothing from which such a shadow should fall. Now, however, that I had a direction, however undetermined, in which to project my apprehension, the very sense of danger and need of action overcame that stifling which is the worst property of fear. I reflected in a moment, that if this were indeed a shadow, it was useless to look for the object that cast it in any other direction than between the shadow and the moon. I looked, and peered, and intensified my vision, all to no purpose. I could see nothing of that kind, not even an ash-tree in the neighbourhood. Still the shadow remained; not steady, but moving to and fro, and once I saw the fingers close, and grind themselves close, like the claws of a wild animal, as if in uncontrollable longing for some anticipated prey. There seemed but one mode left of discovering the substance of this shadow. I went forward boldly, though with an inward shudder which I would not heed, to the spot where the shadow lay, threw myself on the ground, laid my head within the form of the hand, and turned my eyes towards the moon Good heavens! what did I see? I wonder that ever I arose, and that the very shadow of the hand did not hold me where I lay until fear had frozen my brain. I saw the strangest figure; vague, shadowy, almost transparent, in the central parts, and gradually deepening in substance towards the outside, until it ended in extremities capable of casting such a shadow as fell from the hand, through the awful fingers of which I now saw the moon. The hand was uplifted in the attitude of a paw about to strike its prey. But the face, which throbbed with fluctuating and pulsatory visibility—not from changes in the light it reflected, but from changes in its own conditions of reflecting power, the alterations being from within, not from without—it was horrible. I do not know how to describe it. It caused a new sensation. Just as one cannot translate a horrible odour, or a ghastly pain, or a fearful sound, into words, so I cannot describe this new form of awful hideousness. I can only try to describe something that is not it, but seems somewhat parallel to it; or at least is suggested by it. It reminded me of what I had heard of vampires; for the face resembled that of a corpse more than anything else I can think of; especially when I can conceive such a face in motion, but not suggesting any life as the source of the motion. The features were rather handsome than otherwise, except the mouth, which had scarcely a curve in it. The lips were of equal thickness; but the thickness was not at all remarkable, even although they looked slightly swollen. They seemed fixedly open, but were not wide apart. Of course I did not remark these lineaments at the time: I was too horrified for that. I noted them afterwards, when the form returned on my inward sight with a vividness too intense to admit of my doubting the accuracy of the reflex. But the most awful of the features were the eyes. These were alive, yet not with life.

They seemed lighted up with an infinite greed. A gnawing voracity, which devoured the devourer, seemed to be the indwelling and propelling power of the whole ghostly apparition. I lay for a few moments simply imbruted with terror; when another cloud, obscuring the moon, delivered me from the immediately paralysing effects of the presence to the vision of the object of horror, while it added the force of imagination to the power of fear within me; inasmuch as, knowing far worse cause for apprehension than before, I remained equally ignorant from what I had to defend myself, or how to take any precautions: he might be upon me in the darkness any moment. I sprang to my feet, and sped I knew not whither, only away from the spectre. I thought no longer of the path, and often narrowly escaped dashing myself against a tree, in my headlong flight of fear.

Great drops of rain began to patter on the leaves. Thunder began to mutter, then growl in the distance. I ran on. The rain fell heavier. At length the thick leaves could hold it up no longer; and, like a second firmament, they poured their torrents on the earth. I was soon drenched, but that was nothing. I came to a small swollen stream that rushed through the woods. I had a vague hope that if I crossed this stream, I should be in safety from my pursuer; but I soon found that my hope was as false as it was vague. I dashed across the stream, ascended a rising ground, and reached a more open space, where stood only great trees. Through them I directed my way, holding eastward as nearly as I could guess, but not at all certain that I was not moving in an opposite direction. My mind was just reviving a little from its extreme terror, when, suddenly, a flash of lightning, or rather a cataract of successive flashes, behind me, seemed to throw on the ground in front of me, but far more faintly than before, from the extent of the source of the light, the shadow of the same horrible hand. I sprang forward, stung to yet wilder speed; but had not run many steps before my foot slipped, and, vainly attempting to recover myself, I fell at the foot of one of the large trees. Half-stunned, I yet raised myself, and almost involuntarily looked back. All I saw was the hand within three feet of my face. But, at the same moment, I felt two large soft arms thrown round me from behind; and a voice like a woman's said: "Do not fear the goblin; he dares not hurt you now." With that, the hand was suddenly withdrawn as from a fire, and disappeared in the darkness and the rain. Overcome with the mingling of terror and joy, I lay for some time almost insensible. The first thing I remember is the sound of a voice above me, full and low, and strangely reminding me of the sound of a gentle wind amidst the leaves of a great tree. It murmured over and over again: "I may love him, I may love him; for he is a man, and I am only a beech-tree." I found I was seated on the ground, leaning against a human form, and supported still by the arms around me, which I knew to be those of a woman who must be rather above the human size, and largely proportioned. I turned my head, but without moving otherwise, for I feared lest the arms should untwine themselves; and clear, somewhat mournful eyes met mine. At least that is how they impressed me; but I could see very little of colour or outline as we sat in the dark and rainy shadow of the tree. The face seemed very lovely, and solemn from its stillness; with the aspect of one who is quite content, but waiting for something. I saw my conjecture from her arms was correct: she was above the human scale throughout, but not greatly.

"Why do you call yourself a beech-tree?" I said.

"Because I am one," she replied, in the same low, musical, murmuring voice.

"You are a woman," I returned.

"Do you think so? Am I very like a woman then?"

"You are a very beautiful woman. Is it possible you should not know it?"

"I am very glad you think so. I fancy I feel like a woman sometimes. I do so to-night—and always when the rain drips from my hair. For there is an old prophecy in our woods that one day we shall all be men and women like you. Do you know anything about it in your region? Shall I be very happy when I am a woman? I fear not, for it is always in nights like these that I feel like one. But I long to be a woman for all that."

I had let her talk on, for her voice was like a solution of all musical sounds. I now told her that I could hardly say whether women were happy or not. I knew one who had not been happy; and for my part, I had often longed for Fairy Land, as she now longed for the world of men. But then neither of us had lived long, and perhaps people grew happier as they grew older. Only I doubted it.

I could not help sighing. She felt the sigh, for her arms were still round me. She asked me how old I was.

"Twenty-one," said I.

"Why, you baby!" said she, and kissed me with the sweetest kiss of winds and odours. There was a cool faithfulness in the kiss that revived my heart wonderfully. I felt that I feared the dreadful Ash no more.

"What did the horrible Ash want with me?" I said.

"I am not quite sure, but I think he wants to bury you at the foot of his tree. But he shall not touch you, my child."

"Are all the ash-trees as dreadful as he?"

"Oh, no. They are all disagreeable selfish creatures—(what horrid men they will make, if it be true!)—but this one has a hole in his heart that nobody knows of but one or two; and he is always trying to fill it up, but he cannot. That must be what he wanted you for. I wonder if he will ever be a man. If he is, I hope they will kill him."

"How kind of you to save me from him!"

"I will take care that he shall not come near you again. But there are some in the wood more like me, from whom, alas! I cannot protect you. Only if you see any of them very beautiful, try to walk round them."

"What then?"

"I cannot tell you more. But now I must tie some of my hair about you, and then the Ash will not touch you. Here, cut some off. You men have strange cutting things about you."

She shook her long hair loose over me, never moving her arms.

"I cannot cut your beautiful hair. It would be a shame."

"Not cut my hair! It will have grown long enough before any is wanted again in this wild forest. Perhaps it may never be of any use again—not till I am a woman." And she sighed.

As gently as I could, I cut with a knife a long tress of flowing, dark hair, she hanging her beautiful head over me. When I had finished, she shuddered and breathed deep, as one does when an acute pain, steadfastly endured without sign of suffering, is at length relaxed. She then took the hair and tied it round me, singing a strange, sweet song, which I could not understand, but which left in me a feeling like this—

> *"I saw thee ne'er before;*
>
> *I see thee never more;*
>
> *But love, and help, and pain, beautiful one,*
>
> *Have made thee mine, till all my years are done."*

I cannot put more of it into words. She closed her arms about me again, and went on singing. The rain in the leaves, and a light wind that had arisen, kept her song company. I was wrapt in a trance of still delight. It told me the secret of the woods, and the flowers, and the birds. At one time I felt as if I was wandering in childhood through sunny spring forests, over carpets of primroses, anemones, and little white starry things—I had almost said creatures, and finding new wonderful flowers at every turn. At another, I lay half dreaming in the hot summer noon, with a book of old tales beside me, beneath a great beech; or, in autumn, grew sad because I trod on the leaves that had sheltered me, and received their last blessing in the sweet odours of decay; or, in a winter evening, frozen still, looked up, as I went home to a warm fireside, through the netted boughs and twigs to the cold, snowy moon, with her opal zone around her. At last I had fallen asleep; for I know nothing more that passed till I found myself lying under a superb beech-tree, in the clear light of the morning, just before sunrise. Around me was a girdle of fresh beech-leaves. Alas! I brought nothing with me out of Fairy Land, but memories—memories. The great boughs of the beech hung drooping around me. At my head rose its smooth stem, with its great sweeps of curving surface that swelled like undeveloped limbs. The leaves and branches above kept on the song which had sung me asleep; only now, to my mind, it sounded like a farewell and a speedwell. I sat a long time, unwilling to go; but my unfinished story urged me on. I must act and wander. With the sun well risen, I rose, and put my arms as far as they would reach around the beech-tree, and kissed it, and said good-bye. A trembling went through the leaves; a few of the last drops of the night's rain fell from off them at my feet; and as I walked slowly away, I seemed to hear in a whisper once more the words: "I may love him, I may love him; for he is a man, and I am only a beech-tree."

CHAPTER V

"And she was smooth and full, as if one gush

Of life had washed her, or as if a sleep

Lay on her eyelid, easier to sweep

Than bee from daisy."

BEDDOIS' *Pygmalion.*

"Sche was as whyt as lylye yn May,

Or snow that sneweth yn wynterys day."

Romance of Sir Launfal.

I walked on, in the fresh morning air, as if new-born. The only thing that damped my pleasure was a cloud of something between sorrow and delight that crossed my mind with the frequently returning thought of my last night's hostess. "But then," thought I, "if she is sorry, I could not help it; and she has all the pleasures she ever had. Such a day as this is surely a joy to her, as much at least as to me. And her life will perhaps be the richer, for holding now within it the memory of what came, but could not stay. And if ever she is a woman, who knows but we may meet somewhere? there is plenty of room for meeting in the universe." Comforting myself thus, yet with a vague compunction, as if I ought not to have left her, I went on. There was little to distinguish the woods to-day from those of my own land; except that all the wild things, rabbits, birds, squirrels, mice, and the numberless other inhabitants, were very tame; that is, they did not run away from me, but gazed at me as I passed, frequently coming nearer, as if to examine me more closely. Whether this came from utter ignorance, or from familiarity with the human appearance of beings who never hurt them, I could not tell. As I stood once, looking up to the splendid flower of a parasite, which hung from the branch of a tree over my head, a large white rabbit cantered slowly up, put one of its little feet on one of mine, and looked up at me with its red eyes, just as I had been looking up at the flower above me. I stooped and stroked it; but when I attempted to lift it, it banged the ground with its hind feet and scampered off at a great rate, turning, however, to look at me several times before I lost sight of it. Now and then, too, a dim human figure would appear and disappear, at some distance, amongst the trees, moving like a sleep-walker. But no one ever came near me.

This day I found plenty of food in the forest—strange nuts and fruits I had never seen before. I hesitated to eat them; but argued that, if I could live on the air of Fairy Land, I could live on its food also. I found my reasoning correct, and the result was better than I had hoped; for it not only satisfied my hunger, but operated in such a way upon my senses that I was brought into far more complete relationship with the things around me. The human forms appeared much more dense and defined; more tangibly visible, if I may say so. I seemed to know better which direction to choose when any doubt arose. I began to feel in some degree what the birds meant in their songs, though I could not express it in words, any more than you can some landscapes. At times, to my surprise, I found myself listening attentively, and as if it were no unusual thing with me, to a conversation between two squirrels or monkeys. The subjects were not very interesting, except as associated with the individual life and necessities of the little creatures: where the best nuts were to be found in the neighbourhood, and who could crack them best, or who had most laid up for the winter, and such like; only they never said where the store was. There was no great difference in kind between their talk and our ordinary human conversation. Some of the creatures I never heard speak at all, and believe they never do so, except under the impulse of some great excitement. The mice talked; but the hedgehogs seemed very phlegmatic; and though I met a couple of moles above ground several times, they never said a word to each other in my hearing. There were no wild beasts in the forest; at least, I did not see one larger than a wild cat. There were plenty of snakes, however, and I do not think they were all harmless; but none ever bit me.

Soon after mid-day I arrived at a bare rocky hill, of no great size, but very steep; and having no trees—scarcely even a bush—upon it, entirely exposed

182

to the heat of the sun. Over this my way seemed to lie, and I immediately began the ascent. On reaching the top, hot and weary, I looked around me, and saw that the forest still stretched as far as the sight could reach on every side of me. I observed that the trees, in the direction in which I was about to descend, did not come so near the foot of the hill as on the other side, and was especially regretting the unexpected postponement of shelter, because this side of the hill seemed more difficult to descend than the other had been to climb, when my eye caught the appearance of a natural path, winding down through broken rocks and along the course of a tiny stream, which I hoped would lead me more easily to the foot. I tried it, and found the descent not at all laborious; nevertheless, when I reached the bottom, I was very tired and exhausted with the heat. But just where the path seemed to end, rose a great rock, quite overgrown with shrubs and creeping plants, some of them in full and splendid blossom: these almost concealed an opening in the rock, into which the path appeared to lead. I entered, thirsting for the shade which it promised. What was my delight to find a rocky cell, all the angles rounded away with rich moss, and every ledge and projection crowded with lovely ferns, the variety of whose forms, and groupings, and shades wrought in me like a poem; for such a harmony could not exist, except they all consented to some one end! A little well of the clearest water filled a mossy hollow in one corner. I drank, and felt as if I knew what the elixir of life must be; then threw myself on a mossy mound that lay like a couch along the inner end. Here I lay in a delicious reverie for some time; during which all lovely forms, and colours, and sounds seemed to use my brain as a common hall, where they could come and go, unbidden and unexcused. I had never imagined that such capacity for simple happiness lay in me, as was now awakened by this assembly of forms and spiritual sensations, which yet were far too vague to admit of being translated into any shape common to my own and another mind. I had lain for an hour, I should suppose, though it may have been far longer, when, the harmonious tumult in my mind having somewhat relaxed, I became aware that my eyes were fixed on a strange, time-worn bas-relief on the rock opposite to me. This, after some pondering, I concluded to represent Pygmalion, as he awaited the quickening of his statue. The sculptor sat more rigid than the figure to which his eyes were turned. That seemed about to step from its pedestal and embrace the man, who waited rather than expected.

"A lovely story," I said to myself. "This cave, now, with the bushes cut away from the entrance to let the light in, might be such a place as he would choose, withdrawn from the notice of men, to set up his block of marble, and mould into a visible body the thought already clothed with form in the unseen hall of the sculptor's brain. And, indeed, if I mistake not," I said, starting up, as a sudden ray of light arrived at that moment through a crevice in the roof, and lighted up a small portion of the rock, bare of vegetation, "this very rock is marble, white enough and delicate enough for any statue, even if destined to become an ideal woman in the arms of the sculptor."

I took my knife and removed the moss from a part of the block on which I had been lying; when, to my surprise, I found it more like alabaster than ordinary marble, and soft to the edge of the knife. In fact, it was alabaster. By an inexplicable, though by no means unusual kind of impulse, I went on removing the moss from the surface of the stone; and soon saw that it was polished, or at least smooth, throughout. I continued my labour; and after clearing a space of about a couple of square feet, I observed what caused me to prosecute the work with more interest and care than before. For the ray of sunlight had now reached the spot I had cleared, and under its lustre the alabaster revealed its usual slight transparency when polished, except where my knife had scratched the surface; and I observed that the transparency seemed to have a definite limit, and to end upon an opaque body like the more solid, white marble. I was careful to scratch no more. And first, a vague anticipation gave way to a startling sense of possibility; then, as I proceeded, one revelation after another produced the entrancing conviction, that under the crust of alabaster lay a dimly visible form in marble, but whether of man or woman I could not yet tell. I worked on as rapidly as the necessary care would permit; and when I had uncovered the whole mass, and rising from my knees, had retreated a little way, so that the effect of the whole might fall on me, I saw before me with sufficient plainness—though at the same time with considerable indistinctness, arising from the limited amount of light the place admitted, as well as from the nature of the object itself—a block of pure alabaster enclosing the form, apparently in marble, of a reposing woman. She lay on one side, with her hand under her cheek, and her face towards me; but her hair had fallen partly over her face, so that I could not see the expression of the whole. What I did see appeared to me perfectly lovely; more near the face that had been born with me in my soul, than anything I had seen before in nature or art. The actual outlines of the rest of the form were so indistinct, that the more than semi-opacity of the alabaster seemed insufficient to account for the fact; and I conjectured that a light robe added its obscurity. Numberless histories passed through my mind of change of substance from enchantment and other causes, and of imprisonments such as this before me. I thought of the Prince of the Enchanted City, half marble and half a man; of Ariel; of Niobe; of the Sleeping Beauty in the Wood; of the bleeding trees; and many other histories. Even my adventure of the preceding evening with the lady of the beech-tree contributed to arouse the wild hope, that by some means life might be given to this form also, and that, breaking from her alabaster tomb, she might glorify my eyes with her presence. "For," I argued, "who can tell but this cave may be the home of Marble, and this, essential Marble—that spirit of marble which, present throughout, makes it capable of being moulded into any form? Then if she should awake! But how to awake her? A kiss awoke the Sleeping Beauty! a kiss cannot reach her through the incrusting alabaster." I kneeled, however, and kissed the pale coffin; but she slept on. I bethought me of Orpheus, and the following stones—that trees should follow his music seemed nothing surprising now. Might not a song awake this form, that the glory of motion might for a time displace the loveliness of rest? Sweet sounds can go where kisses may not enter. I sat and thought. Now, although always delighting in music, I had never been gifted with the power of song, until I entered the fairy forest. I had a voice, and I had a true sense of sound; but when I tried to sing, the one would not content the other, and so I remained silent. This morning, however, I had found myself, ere I was aware, rejoicing in a song; but whether it was before or after I had eaten of the fruits of the forest, I could not satisfy myself. I concluded it was after, however; and that the increased impulse to sing I now felt, was in part owing to having drunk of the little well, which shone like a brilliant eye in a corner of the cave. I sat down on the ground by the "antenatal tomb," leaned upon it with my face towards the head of the figure within, and sang—the words and tones coming together, and inseparably connected, as if word and tone formed one thing; or, as if each word could be uttered only in that tone, and was incapable of distinction from it, except in idea, by an acute analysis. I sang something like this: but the words are only a dull representation of a state whose very elevation precluded the possibility of remembrance; and in which I presume the words really employed were as far above these, as that state transcended this wherein I recall it:

"Marble woman, vainly sleeping

In the very death of dreams!

Wilt thou—slumber from thee sweeping,

All but what with vision teems—

Hear my voice come through the golden

Mist of memory and hope;

And with shadowy smile embolden

Me with primal Death to cope?

"Thee the sculptors all pursuing,

Have embodied but their own;

Round their visions, form enduring,

Marble vestments thou hast thrown;

But thyself, in silence winding,

Thou hast kept eternally;

Thee they found not, many finding—

I have found thee: wake for me."

As I sang, I looked earnestly at the face so vaguely revealed before me. I fancied, yet believed it to be but fancy, that through the dim veil of the

186

alabaster, I saw a motion of the head as if caused by a sinking sigh. I gazed more earnestly, and concluded that it was but fancy. Neverthless I could not help singing again—

> "Rest is now filled full of beauty,
>
> And can give thee up, I ween;
>
> Come thou forth, for other duty
>
> Motion pineth for her queen.
>
> "Or, if needing years to wake thee
>
> From thy slumbrous solitudes,
>
> Come, sleep-walking, and betake thee
>
> To the friendly, sleeping woods.
>
> Sweeter dreams are in the forest,
>
> Round thee storms would never rave;
>
> And when need of rest is sorest,
>
> Glide thou then into thy cave.
>
> "Or, if still thou choosest rather
>
> Marble, be its spell on me;
>
> Let thy slumber round me gather,
>
> Let another dream with thee!"

Again I paused, and gazed through the stony shroud, as if, by very force of penetrative sight, I would clear every lineament of the lovely face. And now I thought the hand that had lain under the cheek, had slipped a little downward. But then I could not be sure that I had at first observed its position accurately. So I sang again; for the longing had grown into a

187

passionate need of seeing her alive—

> *"Or art thou Death, O woman? for since I*
>
> *Have set me singing by thy side,*
>
> *Life hath forsook the upper sky,*
>
> *And all the outer world hath died.*
>
> *"Yea, I am dead; for thou hast drawn*
>
> *My life all downward unto thee.*
>
> *Dead moon of love! let twilight dawn:*
>
> *Awake! and let the darkness flee.*
>
> *"Cold lady of the lovely stone!*
>
> *Awake! or I shall perish here;*
>
> *And thou be never more alone,*
>
> *My form and I for ages near.*
>
> *"But words are vain; reject them all—*
>
> *They utter but a feeble part:*
>
> *Hear thou the depths from which they call,*
>
> *The voiceless longing of my heart."*

There arose a slightly crashing sound. Like a sudden apparition that comes and is gone, a white form, veiled in a light robe of whiteness, burst upwards from the stone, stood, glided forth, and gleamed away towards the woods. For I followed to the mouth of the cave, as soon as the amazement and concentration of delight permitted the nerves of motion again to act; and saw the white form amidst the trees, as it crossed a little glade on the edge of the forest where the sunlight fell full, seeming to gather with intenser radiance on the one object that floated rather than flitted through its lake of beams. I gazed after her in a kind of despair; found, freed, lost! It seemed useless to follow, yet follow I must. I marked the direction she took; and without once looking round to the forsaken cave, I hastened towards the forest.

CHAPTER VI

"Ah, let a man beware, when his wishes, fulfilled, rain down

upon him, and his happiness is unbounded."

—FOUQUE, Der Zauberring.

"Thy red lips, like worms,

Travel over my cheek."

—MOTHERWELL.

But as I crossed the space between the foot of the hill and the forest, a vision of another kind delayed my steps. Through an opening to the westward flowed, like a stream, the rays of the setting sun, and overflowed with a ruddy splendour the open space where I was. And riding as it were down this stream towards me, came a horseman in what appeared red armour. From frontlet to tail, the horse likewise shone red in the sunset. I felt as if I must have seen the knight before; but as he drew near, I could recall no feature of his countenance. Ere he came up to me, however, I remembered the legend of Sir Percival in the rusty armour, which I had left unfinished in the old book in the cottage: it was of Sir Percival that he reminded me. And no wonder; for when he came close up to me, I saw that, from crest to heel, the whole surface of his armour was covered with a light rust. The golden spurs shone, but the iron greaves glowed in the sunlight. The morning star, which hung from his wrist, glittered and glowed with its silver and bronze. His whole appearance was terrible; but his face did not answer to this appearance. It was sad, even to gloominess; and something of shame seemed to cover it. Yet it was noble and high, though thus beclouded; and the form looked lofty, although the head drooped, and the whole frame was bowed as with an inward grief. The horse seemed to share in his master's dejection, and walked spiritless and slow. I noticed, too, that the white plume on his helmet was discoloured and drooping. "He has fallen in a joust with spears," I said to myself; "yet it becomes not a noble knight to be conquered in spirit because his body hath fallen." He appeared not to observe me, for he was riding past without looking up, and started into a warlike attitude the moment the first sound of my voice reached him. Then a flush, as of shame, covered all of his face that the lifted beaver disclosed. He returned my greeting with distant courtesy, and passed on. But suddenly, he reined up, sat a moment still, and then turning his horse, rode back to where I stood looking after him.

"I am ashamed," he said, "to appear a knight, and in such a guise; but it behoves me to tell you to take warning from me, lest the same evil, in his kind, overtake the singer that has befallen the knight. Hast thou ever read the story of Sir Percival and the"—(here he shuddered, that his armour rang)—"Maiden of the Alder-tree?"

"In part, I have," said I; "for yesterday, at the entrance of this forest, I found in a cottage the volume wherein it is recorded." "Then take heed," he rejoined; "for, see my armour—I put it off; and as it befell to him, so has it befallen to me. I that was proud am humble now. Yet is she terribly beautiful—beware. Never," he added, raising his head, "shall this armour be furbished, but by the blows of knightly encounter, until the last speck has disappeared from every spot where the battle-axe and sword of evil-doers, or noble foes, might fall; when I shall again lift my head, and say to my squire, 'Do thy duty once more, and make this armour shine.'"

Before I could inquire further, he had struck spurs into his horse and galloped away, shrouded from my voice in the noise of his armour. For I called after him, anxious to know more about this fearful enchantress; but in vain— he heard me not. "Yet," I said to myself, "I have now been often warned; surely I shall be well on my guard; and I am fully resolved I shall not be ensnared by any beauty, however beautiful. Doubtless, some one man may escape, and I shall be he." So I went on into the wood, still hoping to find, in some one of its mysterious recesses, my lost lady of the marble. The sunny afternoon died into the loveliest twilight. Great bats began to flit about with their own noiseless flight, seemingly purposeless, because its objects are unseen. The monotonous music of the owl issued from all unexpected quarters in the half-darkness around me. The glow-worm was alight here and there, burning out into the great universe. The night-hawk heightened all the harmony and stillness with his oft-recurring, discordant jar. Numberless unknown sounds came out of the unknown dusk; but all were of twilight-kind, oppressing the heart as with a condensed atmosphere of dreamy undefined love and longing. The odours of night arose, and bathed me in that luxurious mournfulness peculiar to them, as if the plants whence they floated had been watered with bygone tears. Earth drew me towards her bosom; I felt as if I could fall down and kiss her. I forgot I was in Fairy Land, and seemed to be walking in a perfect night of our own old nursing earth. Great stems rose about me, uplifting a thick multitudinous roof above me of branches, and twigs, and leaves—the bird and insect world uplifted over mine, with its own landscapes, its own thickets, and paths, and glades, and dwellings; its own bird-ways and insect-delights. Great boughs crossed my path; great roots based the tree-columns, and mightily clasped the earth, strong to lift and strong to uphold. It seemed an old, old forest, perfect in forest ways and pleasures. And when, in the midst of this ecstacy, I remembered that under some close canopy of leaves, by some giant stem, or in some mossy cave, or beside some leafy well, sat the lady of the marble, whom my songs had called forth into the outer world, waiting (might it not be?) to meet and thank her deliverer in a twilight which would veil her confusion, the whole night became one dream-realm of joy, the central form of which was everywhere present, although unbeheld. Then, remembering how my songs seemed to have called her from the marble, piercing through the pearly shroud of alabaster—"Why," thought I, "should not my voice reach her now, through the ebon night that inwraps her." My voice burst into song so spontaneously that it seemed involuntarily.

> *"Not a sound*
>
> *But, echoing in me,*
>
> *Vibrates all around*
>
> *With a blind delight,*
>
> *Till it breaks on Thee,*
>
> *Queen of Night!*

Every tree,

O'ershadowing with gloom,

Seems to cover thee

Secret, dark, love-still'd,

In a holy room

Silence-filled.

"Let no moon

Creep up the heaven to-night;

I in darksome noon

Walking hopefully,

Seek my shrouded light—

Grope for thee!

"Darker grow

The borders of the dark!

Through the branches glow,

From the roof above,

Star and diamond-sparks

Light for love."

Scarcely had the last sounds floated away from the hearing of my own ears, when I heard instead a low delicious laugh near me. It was not the laugh of one who would not be heard, but the laugh of one who has just received something long and patiently desired—a laugh that ends in a low musical moan. I started, and, turning sideways, saw a dim white figure seated beside an intertwining thicket of smaller trees and underwood.

"It is my white lady!" I said, and flung myself on the ground beside her; striving, through the gathering darkness, to get a glimpse of the form which had broken its marble prison at my call.

"It is your white lady!" said the sweetest voice, in reply, sending a thrill of speechless delight through a heart which all the love-charms of the preceding day and evening had been tempering for this culminating hour. Yet, if I would have confessed it, there was something either in the sound of the voice, although it seemed sweetness itself, or else in this yielding which awaited no gradation of gentle approaches, that did not vibrate harmoniously with the beat of my inward music. And likewise, when, taking her hand in mine, I drew closer to her, looking for the beauty of her face, which, indeed, I found too plenteously, a cold shiver ran through me; but "it is the marble," I said to myself, and heeded it not.

She withdrew her hand from mine, and after that would scarce allow me to touch her. It seemed strange, after the fulness of her first greeting, that she could not trust me to come close to her. Though her words were those of a lover, she kept herself withdrawn as if a mile of space interposed between us.

"Why did you run away from me when you woke in the cave?" I said.

"Did I?" she returned. "That was very unkind of me; but I did not know better."

"I wish I could see you. The night is very dark."

"So it is. Come to my grotto. There is light there."

"Have you another cave, then?"

"Come and see."

But she did not move until I rose first, and then she was on her feet before I could offer my hand to help her. She came close to my side, and conducted me through the wood. But once or twice, when, involuntarily almost, I was about to put my arm around her as we walked on through the warm gloom, she sprang away several paces, always keeping her face full towards me, and then stood looking at me, slightly stooping, in the attitude of one who fears

194

some half-seen enemy. It was too dark to discern the expression of her face. Then she would return and walk close beside me again, as if nothing had happened. I thought this strange; but, besides that I had almost, as I said before, given up the attempt to account for appearances in Fairy Land, I judged that it would be very unfair to expect from one who had slept so long and had been so suddenly awakened, a behaviour correspondent to what I might unreflectingly look for. I knew not what she might have been dreaming about. Besides, it was possible that, while her words were free, her sense of touch might be exquisitely delicate.

At length, after walking a long way in the woods, we arrived at another thicket, through the intertexture of which was glimmering a pale rosy light.

"Push aside the branches," she said, "and make room for us to enter."

I did as she told me.

"Go in," she said; "I will follow you."

I did as she desired, and found myself in a little cave, not very unlike the marble cave. It was festooned and draperied with all kinds of green that cling to shady rocks. In the furthest corner, half-hidden in leaves, through which it glowed, mingling lovely shadows between them, burned a bright rosy flame on a little earthen lamp. The lady glided round by the wall from behind me, still keeping her face towards me, and seated herself in the furthest corner, with her back to the lamp, which she hid completely from my view. I then saw indeed a form of perfect loveliness before me. Almost it seemed as if the light of the rose-lamp shone through her (for it could not be reflected from her); such a delicate shade of pink seemed to shadow what in itself must be a marbly whiteness of hue. I discovered afterwards, however, that there was one thing in it I did not like; which was, that the white part of the eye was tinged with the same slight roseate hue as the rest of the form. It is strange that I cannot recall her features; but they, as well as her somewhat girlish figure, left on me simply and only the impression of intense loveliness. I lay down at her feet, and gazed up into her face as I lay. She began, and told me a strange tale, which, likewise, I cannot recollect; but which, at every turn and every pause, somehow or other fixed my eyes and thoughts upon her extreme beauty;

seeming always to culminate in something that had a relation, revealed or hidden, but always operative, with her own loveliness. I lay entranced. It was a tale which brings back a feeling as of snows and tempests; torrents and water-sprites; lovers parted for long, and meeting at last; with a gorgeous summer night to close up the whole. I listened till she and I were blended with the tale; till she and I were the whole history. And we had met at last in this same cave of greenery, while the summer night hung round us heavy with love, and the odours that crept through the silence from the sleeping woods were the only signs of an outer world that invaded our solitude. What followed I cannot clearly remember. The succeeding horror almost obliterated it. I woke as a grey dawn stole into the cave. The damsel had disappeared; but in the shrubbery, at the mouth of the cave, stood a strange horrible object. It looked like an open coffin set up on one end; only that the part for the head and neck was defined from the shoulder-part. In fact, it was a rough representation of the human frame, only hollow, as if made of decaying bark torn from a tree.

It had arms, which were only slightly seamed, down from the shoulder-blade by the elbow, as if the bark had healed again from the cut of a knife. But the arms moved, and the hand and the fingers were tearing asunder a long silky tress of hair. The thing turned round—it had for a face and front those of my enchantress, but now of a pale greenish hue in the light of the morning, and with dead lustreless eyes. In the horror of the moment, another fear invaded me. I put my hand to my waist, and found indeed that my girdle of beech-leaves was gone. Hair again in her hands, she was tearing it fiercely. Once more, as she turned, she laughed a low laugh, but now full of scorn and derision; and then she said, as if to a companion with whom she had been talking while I slept, "There he is; you can take him now." I lay still, petrified with dismay and fear; for I now saw another figure beside her, which, although vague and indistinct, I yet recognised but too well. It was the Ash-tree. My beauty was the Maid of the Alder! and she was giving me, spoiled of my only availing defence, into the hands of my awful foe. The Ash bent his Gorgon-head, and entered the cave. I could not stir. He drew near me. His ghoul-eyes and his ghastly face fascinated me. He came stooping, with the hideous hand outstretched, like a beast of prey. I had given myself up to a death of unfathomable horror, when, suddenly, and just as he was on the point of seizing me, the dull, heavy blow of an axe echoed through the wood, followed by others in quick repetition. The Ash shuddered and groaned, withdrew the outstretched hand, retreated backwards to the mouth of the cave, then turned and disappeared amongst the trees. The other walking Death looked at me once, with a careless dislike on her beautifully moulded features; then, heedless any more to conceal her hollow deformity, turned her frightful back and likewise vanished amid the green obscurity without. I lay and wept. The Maid of the Alder-tree had befooled me—nearly slain me—in spite of all the warnings I had received from those who knew my danger.

CHAPTER VII

"Fight on, my men, Sir Andrew sayes,

A little I am hurt, but yett not slaine;

I'le but lye downe and bleede awhile,

And then I'le rise and fight againe."

Ballad of Sir Andrew Barton.

But I could not remain where I was any longer, though the daylight was hateful to me, and the thought of the great, innocent, bold sunrise unendurable. Here there was no well to cool my face, smarting with the bitterness of my own tears. Nor would I have washed in the well of that grotto, had it flowed clear as the rivers of Paradise. I rose, and feebly left the sepulchral cave. I took my way I knew not whither, but still towards the sunrise. The birds were singing; but not for me. All the creatures spoke a language of their own, with which I had nothing to do, and to which I cared not to find the key any more.

I walked listlessly along. What distressed me most—more even than my own folly—was the perplexing question, How can beauty and ugliness dwell so near? Even with her altered complexion and her face of dislike; disenchanted of the belief that clung around her; known for a living, walking sepulchre, faithless, deluding, traitorous; I felt notwithstanding all this, that she was beautiful. Upon this I pondered with undiminished perplexity, though not without some gain. Then I began to make surmises as to the mode of my deliverance; and concluded that some hero, wandering in search of adventure, had heard how the forest was infested; and, knowing it was useless to attack the evil thing in person, had assailed with his battle-axe the body in which he dwelt, and on which he was dependent for his power of mischief in the wood. "Very likely," I thought, "the repentant-knight, who warned me of the evil which has befallen me, was busy retrieving his lost honour, while I was sinking into the same sorrow with himself; and, hearing of the dangerous and mysterious being, arrived at his tree in time to save me from being dragged to its roots, and buried like carrion, to nourish him for yet deeper insatiableness." I found afterwards that my conjecture was correct. I wondered how he had fared when his blows recalled the Ash himself, and that too I learned afterwards.

I walked on the whole day, with intervals of rest, but without food; for I could not have eaten, had any been offered me; till, in the afternoon, I seemed to approach the outskirts of the forest, and at length arrived at a farm-house. An unspeakable joy arose in my heart at beholding an abode of human beings once more, and I hastened up to the door, and knocked. A kind-looking, matronly woman, still handsome, made her appearance; who, as soon as she saw me, said kindly, "Ah, my poor boy, you have come from the wood! Were you in it last night?"

I should have ill endured, the day before, to be called boy; but now the motherly kindness of the word went to my heart; and, like a boy indeed, I burst into tears. She soothed me right gently; and, leading me into a room, made me lie down on a settle, while she went to find me some refreshment. She soon returned with food, but I could not eat. She almost compelled me to swallow some wine, when I revived sufficiently to be able to answer some of her questions. I told her the whole story.

"It is just as I feared," she said; "but you are now for the night beyond the reach of any of these dreadful creatures. It is no wonder they could delude a child like you. But I must beg you, when my husband comes in, not to say a word about these things; for he thinks me even half crazy for believing anything of the sort. But I must believe my senses, as he cannot believe beyond his, which give him no intimations of this kind. I think he could spend the whole of Midsummer-eve in the wood and come back with the report that he saw nothing worse than himself. Indeed, good man, he would hardly find anything better than himself, if he had seven more senses given him."

"But tell me how it is that she could be so beautiful without any heart at all—without any place even for a heart to live in."

"I cannot quite tell," she said; "but I am sure she would not look so beautiful if she did not take means to make herself look more beautiful than she is. And then, you know, you began by being in love with her before you saw her beauty, mistaking her for the lady of the marble—another kind altogether, I should think. But the chief thing that makes her beautiful is this: that, although she loves no man, she loves the love of any man; and when she finds one in her power, her desire to bewitch him and gain his love (not for the sake of his love either, but that she may be conscious anew of her own beauty, through the admiration he manifests), makes her very lovely—with a self-destructive beauty, though; for it is that which is constantly wearing her away within, till, at last, the decay will reach her face, and her whole front, when all the lovely mask of nothing will fall to pieces, and she be vanished for ever. So a wise man, whom she met in the wood some years ago, and who, I think, for all his wisdom, fared no better than you, told me, when, like you, he spent the next night here, and recounted to me his adventures."

I thanked her very warmly for her solution, though it was but partial; wondering much that in her, as in woman I met on my first entering the forest, there should be such superiority to her apparent condition. Here she left me to take some rest; though, indeed, I was too much agitated to rest in any other way than by simply ceasing to move.

In half an hour, I heard a heavy step approach and enter the house. A jolly voice, whose slight huskiness appeared to proceed from overmuch laughter, called out "Betsy, the pigs' trough is quite empty, and that is a pity. Let them swill, lass! They're of no use but to get fat. Ha! ha! ha! Gluttony is not forbidden in their commandments. Ha! ha! ha!" The very voice, kind and jovial, seemed to disrobe the room of the strange look which all new places wear—to disenchant it out of the realm of the ideal into that of the actual. It began to look as if I had known every corner of it for twenty years; and when, soon after, the dame came and fetched me to partake of their early supper, the grasp of his great hand, and the harvest-moon of his benevolent face, which was needed to light up the rotundity of the globe beneath it, produced such a reaction in me, that, for a moment, I could hardly believe that there was a Fairy Land; and that all I had passed through since I left home, had not been the wandering dream of a diseased imagination, operating on a too mobile frame, not merely causing me indeed to travel, but peopling for me with vague phantoms the regions through which my actual steps had led me. But the next moment my eye fell upon a little girl who was sitting in the chimney-corner, with a little book open on her knee, from which she had apparently just looked up to fix great inquiring eyes upon me. I believed in Fairy Land again. She went on with her reading, as soon as she saw that I observed her looking at me. I went near, and peeping over her shoulder, saw that she was reading The History of Graciosa and Percinet.

"Very improving book, sir," remarked the old farmer, with a good-humoured laugh. "We are in the very hottest corner of Fairy Land here. Ha! ha! Stormy night, last night, sir."

"Was it, indeed?" I rejoined. "It was not so with me. A lovelier night I never saw." "Indeed! Where were you last night?"

"I spent it in the forest. I had lost my way."

"Ah! then, perhaps, you will be able to convince my good woman, that there is nothing very remarkable about the forest; for, to tell the truth, it bears but a bad name in these parts. I dare say you saw nothing worse than yourself there?"

"I hope I did," was my inward reply; but, for an audible one, I contented myself with saying, "Why, I certainly did see some appearances I could hardly account for; but that is nothing to be wondered at in an unknown wild forest, and with the uncertain light of the moon alone to go by."

"Very true! you speak like a sensible man, sir. We have but few sensible folks round about us. Now, you would hardly credit it, but my wife believes every fairy-tale that ever was written. I cannot account for it. She is a most sensible woman in everything else."

"But should not that make you treat her belief with something of respect, though you cannot share in it yourself?"

"Yes, that is all very well in theory; but when you come to live every day in the midst of absurdity, it is far less easy to behave respectfully to it. Why, my wife actually believes the story of the 'White Cat.' You know it, I dare say."

"I read all these tales when a child, and know that one especially well."

"But, father," interposed the little girl in the chimney-corner, "you know quite well that mother is descended from that very princess who was changed by the wicked fairy into a white cat. Mother has told me so a many times, and you ought to believe everything she says."

"I can easily believe that," rejoined the farmer, with another fit of laughter; "for, the other night, a mouse came gnawing and scratching beneath the floor, and would not let us go to sleep. Your mother sprang out of bed, and going as near it as she could, mewed so infernally like a great cat, that the noise ceased instantly. I believe the poor mouse died of the fright, for we have never heard it again. Ha! ha! ha!"

The son, an ill-looking youth, who had entered during the conversation, joined in his father's laugh; but his laugh was very different from the old man's: it was polluted with a sneer. I watched him, and saw that, as soon as it was over, he looked scared, as if he dreaded some evil consequences to follow his presumption. The woman stood near, waiting till we should seat ourselves at the table, and listening to it all with an amused air, which had something in it of the look with which one listens to the sententious remarks of a pompous child. We sat down to supper, and I ate heartily. My bygone distresses began already to look far off.

"In what direction are you going?" asked the old man.

"Eastward," I replied; nor could I have given a more definite answer. "Does the forest extend much further in that direction?"

"Oh! for miles and miles; I do not know how far. For although I have lived on the borders of it all my life, I have been too busy to make journeys of discovery into it. Nor do I see what I could discover. It is only trees and trees, till one is sick of them. By the way, if you follow the eastward track from here, you will pass close to what the children say is the very house of the ogre that Hop-o'-my-Thumb visited, and ate his little daughters with the crowns of gold."

"Oh, father! ate his little daughters! No; he only changed their gold crowns for nightcaps; and the great long-toothed ogre killed them in mistake; but I do not think even he ate them, for you know they were his own little ogresses."

"Well, well, child; you know all about it a great deal better than I do. However, the house has, of course, in such a foolish neighbourhood as this, a bad enough name; and I must confess there is a woman living in it, with teeth long enough, and white enough too, for the lineal descendant of the greatest ogre that ever was made. I think you had better not go near her."

In such talk as this the night wore on. When supper was finished, which lasted some time, my hostess conducted me to my chamber.

"If you had not had enough of it already," she said, "I would have put you in another room, which looks towards the forest; and where you would most likely have seen something more of its inhabitants. For they frequently pass the window, and even enter the room sometimes. Strange creatures spend whole nights in it, at certain seasons of the year. I am used to it, and do not mind it. No more does my little girl, who sleeps in it always. But this room looks southward towards the open country, and they never show themselves here; at least I never saw any."

I was somewhat sorry not to gather any experience that I might have, of the inhabitants of Fairy Land; but the effect of the farmer's company, and of my own later adventures, was such, that I chose rather an undisturbed night in my more human quarters; which, with their clean white curtains and white linen, were very inviting to my weariness.

In the morning I awoke refreshed, after a profound and dreamless sleep. The sun was high, when I looked out of the window, shining over a wide, undulating, cultivated country. Various garden-vegetables were growing beneath my window. Everything was radiant with clear sunlight. The dew-drops were sparkling their busiest; the cows in a near-by field were eating as if they had not been at it all day yesterday; the maids were singing at their work as they passed to and fro between the out-houses: I did not believe in Fairy Land. I went down, and found the family already at breakfast. But before I entered the room where they sat, the little girl came to me, and looked up in my face, as though she wanted to say something to me. I stooped towards her; she put her arms round my neck, and her mouth to my ear, and whispered—

"A white lady has been flitting about the house all night."

"No whispering behind doors!" cried the farmer; and we entered together. "Well, how have you slept? No bogies, eh?"

"Not one, thank you; I slept uncommonly well."

"I am glad to hear it. Come and breakfast."

After breakfast, the farmer and his son went out; and I was left alone with the mother and daughter.

"When I looked out of the window this morning," I said, "I felt almost certain that Fairy Land was all a delusion of my brain; but whenever I come near you or your little daughter, I feel differently. Yet I could persuade myself, after my last adventures, to go back, and have nothing more to do with such strange beings."

"How will you go back?" said the woman.

"Nay, that I do not know."

"Because I have heard, that, for those who enter Fairy Land, there is no way of going back. They must go on, and go through it. How, I do not in the least know."

"That is quite the impression on my own mind. Something compels me to go on, as if my only path was onward, but I feel less inclined this morning to continue my adventures."

"Will you come and see my little child's room? She sleeps in the one I told you of, looking towards the forest."

"Willingly," I said.

So we went together, the little girl running before to open the door for us. It was a large room, full of old-fashioned furniture, that seemed to have once belonged to some great house.

The window was built with a low arch, and filled with lozenge-shaped panes. The wall was very thick, and built of solid stone. I could see that part of the house had been erected against the remains of some old castle or abbey, or other great building; the fallen stones of which had probably served to complete it. But as soon as I looked out of the window, a gush of wonderment and longing flowed over my soul like the tide of a great sea. Fairy Land lay before me, and drew me towards it with an irresistible attraction. The trees bathed their great heads in the waves of the morning, while their roots were planted deep in gloom; save where on the borders the sunshine broke against their stems, or swept in long streams through their avenues, washing with brighter hue all the leaves over which it flowed; revealing the rich brown of the decayed leaves and fallen pine-cones, and the delicate greens of the long grasses and tiny forests of moss that covered the channel over which it passed in motionless rivers of light. I turned hurriedly to bid my hostess farewell without further delay. She smiled at my haste, but with an anxious look.

"You had better not go near the house of the ogre, I think. My son will show you into another path, which will join the first beyond it."

Not wishing to be headstrong or too confident any more, I agreed; and having taken leave of my kind entertainers, went into the wood, accompanied by the youth. He scarcely spoke as we went along; but he led me through the trees till we struck upon a path. He told me to follow it, and, with a muttered "good morning" left me.

CHAPTER VIII

"I am a part of the part, which at first was the whole."

GOETHE.—Mephistopheles in Faust.

My spirits rose as I went deeper; into the forest; but I could not regain my former elasticity of mind. I found cheerfulness to be like life itself—not to be created by any argument. Afterwards I learned, that the best way to manage some kinds of pain filled thoughts, is to dare them to do their worst; to let them lie and gnaw at your heart till they are tired; and you find you still have a residue of life they cannot kill. So, better and worse, I went on, till I came to a little clearing in the forest. In the middle of this clearing stood a long, low hut, built with one end against a single tall cypress, which rose like a spire to the building. A vague misgiving crossed my mind when I saw it; but I must needs go closer, and look through a little half-open door, near the opposite end from the cypress. Window I saw none. On peeping in, and looking towards the further end, I saw a lamp burning, with a dim, reddish flame, and the head of a woman, bent downwards, as if reading by its light. I could see nothing more for a few moments. At length, as my eyes got used to the dimness of the place, I saw that the part of the rude building near me was used for household purposes; for several rough utensils lay here and there, and a bed stood in the corner.

An irresistible attraction caused me to enter. The woman never raised her face, the upper part of which alone I could see distinctly; but, as soon as I stepped within the threshold, she began to read aloud, in a low and not altogether unpleasing voice, from an ancient little volume which she held open with one hand on the table upon which stood the lamp. What she read was something like this:

"So, then, as darkness had no beginning, neither will it ever have an end. So, then, is it eternal. The negation of aught else, is its affirmation. Where the light cannot come, there abideth the darkness. The light doth but hollow a mine out of the infinite extension of the darkness. And ever upon the steps of the light treadeth the darkness; yea, springeth in fountains and wells amidst it, from the secret channels of its mighty sea. Truly, man is but a passing flame, moving unquietly amid the surrounding rest of night; without which he yet could not be, and whereof he is in part compounded."

As I drew nearer, and she read on, she moved a little to turn a leaf of the dark old volume, and I saw that her face was sallow and slightly forbidding. Her forehead was high, and her black eyes repressedly quiet. But she took no notice of me. This end of the cottage, if cottage it could be called, was destitute of furniture, except the table with the lamp, and the chair on which the woman sat. In one corner was a door, apparently of a cupboard in the wall, but which might lead to a room beyond. Still the irresistible desire which had made me enter the building urged me: I must open that door, and see what was beyond it. I approached, and laid my hand on the rude latch. Then the woman spoke, but without lifting her head or looking at me: "You had better not open that door." This was uttered quite quietly; and she went on with her reading, partly in silence, partly aloud; but both modes seemed equally intended for herself alone. The prohibition, however, only increased my desire to see; and as she took no further notice, I gently opened the door to its full width, and looked in. At first, I saw nothing worthy of attention. It seemed a common closet, with shelves on each hand, on which stood various little necessaries for the humble uses of a cottage. In one corner stood one or two brooms, in another a hatchet and other common tools; showing that it was in use every hour of the day for household purposes. But, as I looked, I saw that there were no shelves at the back, and that an empty space went in further; its termination appearing to be a faintly glimmering wall or curtain, somewhat less, however, than the width and height of the doorway where I stood. But, as I continued looking, for a few seconds, towards this faintly luminous limit, my eyes came into true relation with their object. All at once, with such a shiver as when one is suddenly conscious of the presence of another in a room where he has, for hours, considered himself alone, I saw that the seemingly luminous extremity was a sky, as of night, beheld through the long perspective of a narrow, dark passage, through what, or built of what, I could not tell. As I gazed, I clearly discerned two or three stars glimmering

207

faintly in the distant blue. But, suddenly, and as if it had been running fast from a far distance for this very point, and had turned the corner without abating its swiftness, a dark figure sped into and along the passage from the blue opening at the remote end. I started back and shuddered, but kept looking, for I could not help it. On and on it came, with a speedy approach but delayed arrival; till, at last, through the many gradations of approach, it seemed to come within the sphere of myself, rushed up to me, and passed me into the cottage. All I could tell of its appearance was, that it seemed to be a dark human figure. Its motion was entirely noiseless, and might be called a gliding, were it not that it appeared that of a runner, but with ghostly feet. I had moved back yet a little to let him pass me, and looked round after him instantly. I could not see him.

"Where is he?" I said, in some alarm, to the woman, who still sat reading.

"There, on the floor, behind you," she said, pointing with her arm half-outstretched, but not lifting her eyes. I turned and looked, but saw nothing. Then with a feeling that there was yet something behind me, I looked round over my shoulder; and there, on the ground, lay a black shadow, the size of a man. It was so dark, that I could see it in the dim light of the lamp, which shone full upon it, apparently without thinning at all the intensity of its hue.

"I told you," said the woman, "you had better not look into that closet."

"What is it?" I said, with a growing sense of horror.

"It is only your shadow that has found you," she replied. "Everybody's shadow is ranging up and down looking for him. I believe you call it by a different name in your world: yours has found you, as every person's is almost certain to do who looks into that closet, especially after meeting one in the forest, whom I dare say you have met."

Here, for the first time, she lifted her head, and looked full at me: her mouth was full of long, white, shining teeth; and I knew that I was in the house of the ogre. I could not speak, but turned and left the house, with the shadow at my heels. "A nice sort of valet to have," I said to myself bitterly, as I stepped into the sunshine, and, looking over my shoulder, saw that it lay yet blacker in the full blaze of the sunlight. Indeed, only when I stood between it and the sun, was the blackness at all diminished. I was so bewildered—stunned—both by the event itself and its suddenness, that I could not at all realise to myself what it would be to have such a constant and strange attendance; but with a dim conviction that my present dislike would soon grow to loathing, I took my dreary way through the wood.

CHAPTER IX

"O lady! we receive but what we give,

And in our life alone does nature live:

Ours is her wedding garments ours her shrorwd!

. . . . .

Ah! from the soul itself must issue forth,

A light, a glory, a fair luminous cloud,

Enveloping the Earth—

And from the soul itself must there be sent

A sweet and potent voice of its own birth,

Of all sweet sounds the life and element!"

COLERIDGE.

From this time, until I arrived at the palace of Fairy Land, I can attempt no consecutive account of my wanderings and adventures. Everything, henceforward, existed for me in its relation to my attendant. What influence he exercised upon everything into contact with which I was brought, may be understood from a few detached instances. To begin with this very day on which he first joined me: after I had walked heartlessly along for two or three hours, I was very weary, and lay down to rest in a most delightful part of the forest, carpeted with wild flowers. I lay for half an hour in a dull repose, and then got up to pursue my way. The flowers on the spot where I had lain were crushed to the earth: but I saw that they would soon lift their heads and rejoice again in the sun and air. Not so those on which my shadow had lain. The very outline of it could be traced in the withered lifeless grass, and the scorched and shrivelled flowers which stood there, dead, and hopeless of any resurrection. I shuddered, and hastened away with sad forebodings.

In a few days, I had reason to dread an extension of its baleful influences from the fact, that it was no longer confined to one position in regard to myself. Hitherto, when seized with an irresistible desire to look on my evil demon (which longing would unaccountably seize me at any moment, returning at longer or shorter intervals, sometimes every minute), I had to turn my head backwards, and look over my shoulder; in which position, as long as I could retain it, I was fascinated. But one day, having come out on a clear grassy hill, which commanded a glorious prospect, though of what I cannot now tell, my shadow moved round, and came in front of me. And, presently, a new manifestation increased my distress. For it began to coruscate, and shoot out on all sides a radiation of dim shadow. These rays of gloom issued from the central shadow as from a black sun, lengthening and shortening with continual change. But wherever a ray struck, that part of earth, or sea, or sky, became void, and desert, and sad to my heart. On this, the first development of its new power, one ray shot out beyond the rest, seeming to lengthen infinitely, until it smote the great sun on the face, which withered and darkened beneath the blow. I turned away and went on. The shadow retreated to its former position; and when I looked again, it had drawn in all its spears of darkness, and followed like a dog at my heels.

Once, as I passed by a cottage, there came out a lovely fairy child, with two wondrous toys, one in each hand. The one was the tube through which the fairy-gifted poet looks when he beholds the same thing everywhere; the other that through which he looks when he combines into new forms of loveliness those images of beauty which his own choice has gathered from all regions wherein he has travelled. Round the child's head was an aureole of emanating rays. As I looked at him in wonder and delight, round crept from behind me the something dark, and the child stood in my shadow. Straightway he was a commonplace boy, with a rough broad-brimmed straw hat, through which brim the sun shone from behind. The toys he carried were a multiplying-glass and a kaleidoscope. I sighed and departed.

One evening, as a great silent flood of western gold flowed through an avenue in the woods, down the stream, just as when I saw him first, came the sad knight, riding on his chestnut steed.

But his armour did not shine half so red as when I saw him first.

Many a blow of mighty sword and axe, turned aside by the strength of his mail, and glancing adown the surface, had swept from its path the fretted rust, and the glorious steel had answered the kindly blow with the thanks of returning light. These streaks and spots made his armour look like the floor of a forest in the sunlight. His forehead was higher than before, for the contracting wrinkles were nearly gone; and the sadness that remained on his face was the sadness of a dewy summer twilight, not that of a frosty autumn morn. He, too, had met the Alder-maiden as I, but he had plunged into the torrent of mighty deeds, and the stain was nearly washed away. No shadow followed him. He had not entered the dark house; he had not had time to open the closet door. "Will he ever look in?" I said to myself. "Must his shadow find him some day?" But I could not answer my own questions.

We travelled together for two days, and I began to love him. It was plain that he suspected my story in some degree; and I saw him once or twice looking curiously and anxiously at my attendant gloom, which all this time had remained very obsequiously behind me; but I offered no explanation, and he asked none. Shame at my neglect of his warning, and a horror which shrunk from even alluding to its cause, kept me silent; till, on the evening of the second day, some noble words from my companion roused all my heart; and I was at the point of falling on his neck, and telling him the whole story; seeking, if not for helpful advice, for of that I was hopeless, yet for the comfort of sympathy—when round slid the shadow and inwrapt my friend; and I could not trust him.

The glory of his brow vanished; the light of his eye grew cold; and I held my peace. The next morning we parted.

But the most dreadful thing of all was, that I now began to feel something like satisfaction in the presence of the shadow. I began to be rather vain of my attendant, saying to myself, "In a land like this, with so many illusions everywhere, I need his aid to disenchant the things around me. He does away with all appearances, and shows me things in their true colour and form. And I am not one to be fooled with the vanities of the common crowd. I will not see beauty where there is none. I will dare to behold things as they are. And if I live in a waste instead of a paradise, I will live knowing where I live." But of this a certain exercise of his power which soon followed quite cured me, turning my feelings towards him once more into loathing and distrust. It was thus:

One bright noon, a little maiden joined me, coming through the wood in a direction at right angles to my path. She came along singing and dancing, happy as a child, though she seemed almost a woman. In her hands—now in one, now in another—she carried a small globe, bright and clear as the purest crystal. This seemed at once her plaything and her greatest treasure. At one moment, you would have thought her utterly careless of it, and at another, overwhelmed with anxiety for its safety. But I believe she was taking care of it all the time, perhaps not least when least occupied about it. She stopped by me with a smile, and bade me good day with the sweetest voice. I felt a wonderful liking to the child—for she produced on me more the impression of a child, though my understanding told me differently. We talked a little, and then walked on together in the direction I had been pursuing. I asked her about the globe she carried, but getting no definite answer, I held out my hand to take it. She drew back, and said, but smiling almost invitingly the while, "You must not touch it;"—then, after a moment's pause—"Or if you do, it must be very gently." I touched it with a finger. A slight vibratory motion arose in it, accompanied, or perhaps manifested, by a faint sweet sound. I touched it again, and the sound increased. I touched it the third time: a tiny torrent of harmony rolled out of the little globe. She would not let me touch it any more.

We travelled on together all that day. She left me when twilight came on; but next day, at noon, she met me as before, and again we travelled till evening. The third day she came once more at noon, and we walked on together. Now, though we had talked about a great many things connected with Fairy Land, and the life she had led hitherto, I had never been able to learn anything about the globe. This day, however, as we went on, the shadow glided round and inwrapt the maiden. It could not change her. But my desire to know about the globe, which in his gloom began to waver as

213

with an inward light, and to shoot out flashes of many-coloured flame, grew irresistible. I put out both my hands and laid hold of it. It began to sound as before. The sound rapidly increased, till it grew a low tempest of harmony, and the globe trembled, and quivered, and throbbed between my hands. I had not the heart to pull it away from the maiden, though I held it in spite of her attempts to take it from me; yes, I shame to say, in spite of her prayers, and, at last, her tears. The music went on growing in, intensity and complication of tones, and the globe vibrated and heaved; till at last it burst in our hands, and a black vapour broke upwards from out of it; then turned, as if blown sideways, and enveloped the maiden, hiding even the shadow in its blackness. She held fast the fragments, which I abandoned, and fled from me into the forest in the direction whence she had come, wailing like a child, and crying, "You have broken my globe; my globe is broken—my globe is broken!" I followed her, in the hope of comforting her; but had not pursued her far, before a sudden cold gust of wind bowed the tree-tops above us, and swept through their stems around us; a great cloud overspread the day, and a fierce tempest came on, in which I lost sight of her. It lies heavy on my heart to this hour. At night, ere I fall asleep, often, whatever I may be thinking about, I suddenly hear her voice, crying out, "You have broken my globe; my globe is broken; ah, my globe!"

Here I will mention one more strange thing; but whether this peculiarity was owing to my shadow at all, I am not able to assure myself. I came to a village, the inhabitants of which could not at first sight be distinguished from the dwellers in our land. They rather avoided than sought my company, though they were very pleasant when I addressed them. But at last I observed, that whenever I came within a certain distance of any one of them, which distance, however, varied with different individuals, the whole appearance of the person began to change; and this change increased in degree as I approached. When I receded to the former distance, the former appearance was restored. The nature of the change was grotesque, following no fixed rule. The nearest resemblance to it that I know, is the distortion produced in your countenance when you look at it as reflected in a concave or convex surface—say, either side of a bright spoon. Of this phenomenon I first became aware in rather a ludicrous way. My host's daughter was a very pleasant pretty girl, who made herself more agreeable to me than most of those about me. For some days my companion-shadow had been less obtrusive than usual; and such was the reaction of spirits occasioned by the simple mitigation of torment, that, although I had cause enough besides to be gloomy, I felt light and comparatively happy. My impression is, that she was quite aware of the law of appearances that existed between the people of the place and myself, and had resolved to amuse herself at my expense; for one evening, after some jesting and raillery, she, somehow or other, provoked me to attempt to kiss her. But she was well defended from any assault of the kind. Her countenance became, of a sudden, absurdly hideous; the pretty mouth was elongated and otherwise amplified sufficiently to have allowed of six simultaneous kisses. I started back in bewildered dismay; she burst into the merriest fit of laughter, and ran from the room. I soon found that the same undefinable law of change operated between me and all the other villagers; and that, to feel I was in pleasant company, it was absolutely necessary for me to discover and observe the right focal distance between myself and each one with whom I had to do. This done, all went pleasantly enough. Whether, when I happened to neglect this precaution, I presented to them an equally ridiculous appearance, I did not ascertain; but I presume that the alteration was common to the approximating parties. I was likewise unable to determine whether I was a necessary party to the production of this strange transformation, or whether it took place as well, under the given circumstances, between the inhabitants themselves.

CHAPTER X

"From Eden's bowers the full-fed rivers flow,

To guide the outcasts to the land of woe:

Our Earth one little toiling streamlet yields.

To guide the wanderers to the happy fields."

After leaving this village, where I had rested for nearly a week, I travelled through a desert region of dry sand and glittering rocks, peopled principally by goblin-fairies. When I first entered their domains, and, indeed, whenever I fell in with another tribe of them, they began mocking me with offered handfuls of gold and jewels, making hideous grimaces at me, and performing the most antic homage, as if they thought I expected reverence, and meant to humour me like a maniac. But ever, as soon as one cast his eyes on the shadow behind me, he made a wry face, partly of pity, partly of contempt, and looked ashamed, as if he had been caught doing something inhuman; then, throwing down his handful of gold, and ceasing all his grimaces, he stood aside to let me pass in peace, and made signs to his companions to do the like. I had no inclination to observe them much, for the shadow was in my heart as well as at my heels. I walked listlessly and almost hopelessly along, till I arrived one day at a small spring; which, bursting cool from the heart of a sun-heated rock, flowed somewhat southwards from the direction I had been taking. I drank of this spring, and found myself wonderfully refreshed. A kind of love to the cheerful little stream arose in my heart. It was born in a desert; but it seemed to say to itself, "I will flow, and sing, and lave my banks, till I make my desert a paradise." I thought I could not do better than follow it, and see what it made of it. So down with the stream I went, over rocky lands, burning with sunbeams. But the rivulet flowed not far, before a few blades of grass appeared on its banks, and then, here and there, a stunted bush. Sometimes it disappeared altogether under ground; and after I had wandered some distance, as near as I could guess, in the direction it seemed to take, I would suddenly hear it again, singing, sometimes far away to my right or left, amongst new rocks, over which it made new cataracts of watery melodies. The verdure on its banks increased as it flowed; other streams joined it; and at last, after many days' travel, I found myself, one gorgeous summer evening, resting by the side of a broad river, with a glorious horse-chestnut tree towering above me, and dropping its blossoms, milk-white and rosy-red, all about me. As I sat, a gush of joy sprang forth in my heart, and over flowed at my eyes.

Through my tears, the whole landscape glimmered in such bewildering loveliness, that I felt as if I were entering Fairy Land for the first time, and some loving hand were waiting to cool my head, and a loving word to warm my heart. Roses, wild roses, everywhere! So plentiful were they, they not only perfumed the air, they seemed to dye it a faint rose-hue. The colour floated abroad with the scent, and clomb, and spread, until the whole west blushed and glowed with the gathered incense of roses. And my heart fainted with longing in my bosom.

Could I but see the Spirit of the Earth, as I saw once the in dwelling woman of the beech-tree, and my beauty of the pale marble, I should be content. Content!—Oh, how gladly would I die of the light of her eyes! Yea, I would cease to be, if that would bring me one word of love from the one mouth. The twilight sank around, and infolded me with sleep. I slept as I had not slept for months. I did not awake till late in the morning; when, refreshed in body and mind, I rose as from the death that wipes out the sadness of life, and then dies itself in the new morrow. Again I followed the stream; now climbing a steep rocky bank that hemmed it in; now wading through long grasses and wild flowers in its path; now through meadows; and anon through woods that crowded down to the very lip of the water.

At length, in a nook of the river, gloomy with the weight of overhanging foliage, and still and deep as a soul in which the torrent eddies of pain have hollowed a great gulf, and then, subsiding in violence, have left it full of a motionless, fathomless sorrow—I saw a little boat lying. So still was the water here, that the boat needed no fastening. It lay as if some one had just stepped ashore, and would in a moment return. But as there were no signs of presence, and no track through the thick bushes; and, moreover, as I was in

217

Fairy Land where one does very much as he pleases, I forced my way to the brink, stepped into the boat, pushed it, with the help of the tree-branches, out into the stream, lay down in the bottom, and let my boat and me float whither the stream would carry us. I seemed to lose myself in the great flow of sky above me unbroken in its infinitude, except when now and then, coming nearer the shore at a bend in the river, a tree would sweep its mighty head silently above mine, and glide away back into the past, never more to fling its shadow over me. I fell asleep in this cradle, in which mother Nature was rocking her weary child; and while I slept, the sun slept not, but went round his arched way. When I awoke, he slept in the waters, and I went on my silent path beneath a round silvery moon. And a pale moon looked up from the floor of the great blue cave that lay in the abysmal silence beneath.

Why are all reflections lovelier than what we call the reality?—not so grand or so strong, it may be, but always lovelier? Fair as is the gliding sloop on the shining sea, the wavering, trembling, unresting sail below is fairer still. Yea, the reflecting ocean itself, reflected in the mirror, has a wondrousness about its waters that somewhat vanishes when I turn towards itself. All mirrors are magic mirrors. The commonest room is a room in a poem when I turn to the glass. (And this reminds me, while I write, of a strange story which I read in the fairy palace, and of which I will try to make a feeble memorial in its place.) In whatever way it may be accounted for, of one thing we may be sure, that this feeling is no cheat; for there is no cheating in nature and the simple unsought feelings of the soul. There must be a truth involved in it, though we may but in part lay hold of the meaning. Even the memories of past pain are beautiful; and past delights, though beheld only through clefts in the grey clouds of sorrow, are lovely as Fairy Land. But how have I wandered into the deeper fairyland of the soul, while as yet I only float towards the fairy palace of Fairy Land! The moon, which is the lovelier memory or reflex of the down-gone sun, the joyous day seen in the faint mirror of the brooding night, had rapt me away.

I sat up in the boat. Gigantic forest trees were about me; through which, like a silver snake, twisted and twined the great river. The little waves, when I moved in the boat, heaved and fell with a plash as of molten silver, breaking the image of the moon into a thousand morsels, fusing again into one, as the ripples of laughter die into the still face of joy. The sleeping woods, in undefined massiveness; the water that flowed in its sleep; and, above all, the enchantress moon, which had cast them all, with her pale eye, into the charmed slumber, sank into my soul, and I felt as if I had died in a dream, and should never more awake.

From this I was partly aroused by a glimmering of white, that, through the trees on the left, vaguely crossed my vision, as I gazed upwards. But the trees again hid the object; and at the moment, some strange melodious bird took up its song, and sang, not an ordinary bird-song, with constant repetitions of the same melody, but what sounded like a continuous strain, in which one thought was expressed, deepening in intensity as evolved in progress. It sounded like a welcome already overshadowed with the coming farewell. As in all sweetest music, a tinge of sadness was in every note. Nor do we know how much of the pleasures even of life we owe to the intermingled sorrows. Joy cannot unfold the deepest truths, although deepest truth must be deepest joy. Cometh white-robed Sorrow, stooping and wan, and flingeth wide the doors she may not enter. Almost we linger with Sorrow for very love.

As the song concluded the stream bore my little boat with a gentle sweep round a bend of the river; and lo! on a broad lawn, which rose from the water's edge with a long green slope to a clear elevation from which the trees receded on all sides, stood a stately palace glimmering ghostly in the moonshine: it seemed to be built throughout of the whitest marble. There was no reflection of moonlight from windows—there seemed to be none; so there was no cold glitter; only, as I said, a ghostly shimmer. Numberless shadows tempered the shine, from column and balcony and tower. For everywhere galleries ran along the face of the buildings; wings were extended in many directions; and numberless openings, through which the moonbeams vanished into the interior, and which served both for doors and windows, had their separate balconies in front, communicating with a common gallery that rose on its own pillars. Of course, I did not discover all this from the river, and in the moonlight. But, though I was there for many days, I did not succeed in mastering the inner topography of the building, so extensive and complicated

219

was it.

Here I wished to land, but the boat had no oars on board. However, I found that a plank, serving for a seat, was unfastened, and with that I brought the boat to the bank and scrambled on shore. Deep soft turf sank beneath my feet, as I went up the ascent towards the palace.

When I reached it, I saw that it stood on a great platform of marble, with an ascent, by broad stairs of the same, all round it. Arrived on the platform, I found there was an extensive outlook over the forest, which, however, was rather veiled than revealed by the moonlight.

Entering by a wide gateway, but without gates, into an inner court, surrounded on all sides by great marble pillars supporting galleries above, I saw a large fountain of porphyry in the middle, throwing up a lofty column of water, which fell, with a noise as of the fusion of all sweet sounds, into a basin beneath; overflowing which, it ran into a single channel towards the interior of the building. Although the moon was by this time so low in the west, that not a ray of her light fell into the court, over the height of the surrounding buildings; yet was the court lighted by a second reflex from the sun of other lands. For the top of the column of water, just as it spread to fall, caught the moonbeams, and like a great pale lamp, hung high in the night air, threw a dim memory of light (as it were) over the court below. This court was paved in diamonds of white and red marble. According to my custom since I entered Fairy Land, of taking for a guide whatever I first found moving in any direction, I followed the stream from the basin of the fountain. It led me to a great open door, beneath the ascending steps of which it ran through a low arch and disappeared. Entering here, I found myself in a great hall, surrounded with white pillars, and paved with black and white. This I could see by the moonlight, which, from the other side, streamed through open windows into the hall.

Its height I could not distinctly see. As soon as I entered, I had the feeling so common to me in the woods, that there were others there besides myself, though I could see no one, and heard no sound to indicate a presence. Since my visit to the Church of Darkness, my power of seeing the fairies of the higher orders had gradually diminished, until it had almost ceased. But I could frequently believe in their presence while unable to see them. Still, although I had company, and doubtless of a safe kind, it seemed rather dreary to spend the night in an empty marble hall, however beautiful, especially as the moon was near the going down, and it would soon be dark. So I began at the place where I entered, and walked round the hall, looking for some door or passage that might lead me to a more hospitable chamber. As I walked, I was deliciously haunted with the feeling that behind some one of the seemingly innumerable pillars, one who loved me was waiting for me. Then I thought she was following me from pillar to pillar as I went along; but no arms came out of the faint moonlight, and no sigh assured me of her presence.

At length I came to an open corridor, into which I turned; notwithstanding that, in doing so, I left the light behind. Along this I walked with outstretched hands, groping my way, till, arriving at another corridor, which seemed to strike off at right angles to that in which I was, I saw at the end a faintly glimmering light, too pale even for moonshine, resembling rather a stray phosphorescence. However, where everything was white, a little light went a great way. So I walked on to the end, and a long corridor it was. When I came up to the light, I found that it proceeded from what looked like silver letters upon a door of ebony; and, to my surprise even in the home of wonder itself, the letters formed the words, The Chamber of Sir Anodos. Although I had as yet no right to the honours of a knight, I ventured to conclude that the chamber was indeed intended for me; and, opening the door without hesitation, I entered. Any doubt as to whether I was right in so doing, was soon dispelled. What to my dark eyes seemed a blaze of light, burst upon me. A fire of large pieces of some sweet-scented wood, supported by dogs of silver, was burning on the hearth, and a bright lamp stood on a table, in the midst of a plentiful meal, apparently awaiting my arrival. But what surprised me more than all, was, that the room was in every respect a copy of my own room, the room whence the little stream from my basin had led me into Fairy Land. There was the very carpet of grass and moss and daisies, which I had myself designed; the curtains of pale blue silk, that fell like a cataract over the windows; the old-fashioned bed, with the chintz furniture, on which I had

221

slept from boyhood. "Now I shall sleep," I said to myself. "My shadow dares not come here."

I sat down to the table, and began to help myself to the good things before me with confidence. And now I found, as in many instances before, how true the fairy tales are; for I was waited on, all the time of my meal, by invisible hands. I had scarcely to do more than look towards anything I wanted, when it was brought me, just as if it had come to me of itself. My glass was kept filled with the wine I had chosen, until I looked towards another bottle or decanter; when a fresh glass was substituted, and the other wine supplied. When I had eaten and drank more heartily and joyfully than ever since I entered Fairy Land, the whole was removed by several attendants, of whom some were male and some female, as I thought I could distinguish from the way the dishes were lifted from the table, and the motion with which they were carried out of the room. As soon as they were all taken away, I heard a sound as of the shutting of a door, and knew that I was left alone. I sat long by the fire, meditating, and wondering how it would all end; and when at length, wearied with thinking, I betook myself to my own bed, it was half with a hope that, when I awoke in the morning, I should awake not only in my own room, but in my own castle also; and that I should walk, out upon my own native soil, and find that Fairy Land was, after all, only a vision of the night. The sound of the falling waters of the fountain floated me into oblivion.

CHAPTER XI

"A wilderness of building, sinking far

And self-withdrawn into a wondrous depth,

Far sinking into splendour—without end:

Fabric it seemed of diamond and of gold,

With alabaster domes, and silver spires,

And blazing terrace upon terrace, high

Uplifted."

WORDSWORTH.

But when, after a sleep, which, although dreamless, yet left behind it a sense of past blessedness, I awoke in the full morning, I found, indeed, that the room was still my own; but that it looked abroad upon an unknown landscape of forest and hill and dale on the one side—and on the other, upon the marble court, with the great fountain, the crest of which now flashed glorious in the sun, and cast on the pavement beneath a shower of faint shadows from the waters that fell from it into the marble basin below.

Agreeably to all authentic accounts of the treatment of travellers in Fairy Land, I found by my bedside a complete suit of fresh clothing, just such as I was in the habit of wearing; for, though varied sufficiently from the one removed, it was yet in complete accordance with my tastes. I dressed myself in this, and went out. The whole palace shone like silver in the sun. The marble was partly dull and partly polished; and every pinnacle, dome, and turret ended in a ball, or cone, or cusp of silver. It was like frost-work, and too dazzling, in the sun, for earthly eyes like mine.

I will not attempt to describe the environs, save by saying, that all the pleasures to be found in the most varied and artistic arrangement of wood and river, lawn and wild forest, garden and shrubbery, rocky hill and luxurious vale; in living creatures wild and tame, in gorgeous birds, scattered fountains, little streams, and reedy lakes—all were here. Some parts of the palace itself I shall have occasion to describe more minutely.

For this whole morning I never thought of my demon shadow; and not till the weariness which supervened on delight brought it again to my memory, did I look round to see if it was behind me: it was scarcely discernible. But its presence, however faintly revealed, sent a pang to my heart, for the pain of which, not all the beauties around me could compensate. It was followed, however, by the comforting reflection that, peradventure, I might here find the magic word of power to banish the demon and set me free, so that I should no longer be a man beside myself. The Queen of Fairy Land, thought I, must dwell here: surely she will put forth her power to deliver me, and send me singing through the further gates of her country back to my own land. "Shadow of me!" I said; "which art not me, but which representest thyself to me as me; here I may find a shadow of light which will devour thee, the shadow of darkness! Here I may find a blessing which will fall on thee as a curse, and damn thee to the blackness whence thou hast emerged unbidden." I said this, stretched at length on the slope of the lawn above the river; and as the hope arose within me, the sun came forth from a light fleecy cloud that swept across his face; and hill and dale, and the great river winding on through the still mysterious forest, flashed back his rays as with a silent shout of joy; all nature lived and glowed; the very earth grew warm beneath me; a magnificent dragon-fly went past me like an arrow from a bow, and a whole concert of birds burst into choral song.

The heat of the sun soon became too intense even for passive support. I therefore rose, and sought the shelter of one of the arcades. Wandering along from one to another of these, wherever my heedless steps led me, and wondering everywhere at the simple magnificence of the building, I arrived at another hall, the roof of which was of a pale blue, spangled with constellations of silver stars, and supported by porphyry pillars of a paler red than ordinary.—In this house (I may remark in passing), silver seemed everywhere preferred to gold; and such was the purity of the air, that it showed nowhere signs of tarnishing.—The whole of the floor of this hall, except a narrow path behind the pillars, paved with black, was hollowed into a huge basin, many feet deep, and filled with the purest, most liquid and radiant water. The sides of the basin were white marble, and the bottom was paved with all kinds of refulgent stones, of every shape and hue.

In their arrangement, you would have supposed, at first sight, that there was no design, for they seemed to lie as if cast there from careless and playful hands; but it was a most harmonious confusion; and as I looked at the play of their colours, especially when the waters were in motion, I came at last to feel as if not one little pebble could be displaced, without injuring the effect of the whole. Beneath this floor of the water, lay the reflection of the blue inverted roof, fretted with its silver stars, like a second deeper sea, clasping and upholding the first. The fairy bath was probably fed from the fountain in the court. Led by an irresistible desire, I undressed, and plunged into the water. It clothed me as with a new sense and its object both in one. The waters lay so close to me, they seemed to enter and revive my heart. I rose to the surface, shook the water from my hair, and swam as in a rainbow, amid the coruscations of the gems below seen through the agitation caused by my motion. Then, with open eyes, I dived, and swam beneath the surface. And here was a new wonder. For the basin, thus beheld, appeared to extend on all sides like a sea, with here and there groups as of ocean rocks, hollowed by ceaseless billows into wondrous caves and grotesque pinnacles. Around the caves grew sea-weeds of all hues, and the corals glowed between; while far off, I saw the glimmer of what seemed to be creatures of human form at home in the waters. I thought I had been enchanted; and that when I rose to the surface, I should find myself miles from land, swimming alone upon a heaving sea; but when my eyes emerged from the waters, I saw above me the blue spangled vault, and the red pillars around. I dived again, and found myself once more in the heart of a great sea. I then arose, and swam to the edge, where I got out easily, for the water reached the very brim, and, as I drew near washed in tiny waves over the black marble border. I dressed, and went out, deeply refreshed.

And now I began to discern faint, gracious forms, here and there throughout the building. Some walked together in earnest conversation.

Others strayed alone. Some stood in groups, as if looking at and talking about a picture or a statue. None of them heeded me. Nor were they plainly visible to my eyes. Sometimes a group, or single individual, would fade entirely out of the realm of my vision as I gazed. When evening came, and the moon arose, clear as a round of a horizon-sea when the sun hangs over it in the west, I began to see them all more plainly; especially when they came between me and the moon; and yet more especially, when I myself was in the shade. But, even then, I sometimes saw only the passing wave of a white robe; or a lovely arm or neck gleamed by in the moonshine; or white feet went walking alone over the moony sward. Nor, I grieve to say, did I ever come much nearer to these glorious beings, or ever look upon the Queen of the Fairies herself. My destiny ordered otherwise.

In this palace of marble and silver, and fountains and moonshine, I spent many days; waited upon constantly in my room with everything desirable, and bathing daily in the fairy bath. All this time I was little troubled with my demon shadow I had a vague feeling that he was somewhere about the palace; but it seemed as if the hope that I should in this place be finally freed from his hated presence, had sufficed to banish him for a time. How and where I found him, I shall soon have to relate.

The third day after my arrival, I found the library of the palace; and here, all the time I remained, I spent most of the middle of the day. For it was, not to mention far greater attractions, a luxurious retreat from the noontide sun. During the mornings and afternoons, I wandered about the lovely neighbourhood, or lay, lost in delicious day-dreams, beneath some mighty tree on the open lawn. My evenings were by-and-by spent in a part of the palace, the account of which, and of my adventures in connection with it, I must yet postpone for a little.

The library was a mighty hall, lighted from the roof, which was formed of something like glass, vaulted over in a single piece, and stained throughout with a great mysterious picture in gorgeous colouring.

The walls were lined from floor to roof with books and books: most of them in ancient bindings, but some in strange new fashions which I had never seen, and which, were I to make the attempt, I could ill describe. All around the walls, in front of the books, ran galleries in rows, communicating by stairs. These galleries were built of all kinds of coloured stones; all sorts of marble and granite, with porphyry, jasper, lapis lazuli, agate, and various others, were ranged in wonderful melody of successive colours. Although the material, then, of which these galleries and stairs were built, rendered necessary a certain degree of massiveness in the construction, yet such was the size of the place, that they seemed to run along the walls like cords.

Over some parts of the library, descended curtains of silk of various dyes, none of which I ever saw lifted while I was there; and I felt somehow that it would be presumptuous in me to venture to look within them. But the use of the other books seemed free; and day after day I came to the library, threw myself on one of the many sumptuous eastern carpets, which lay here and there on the floor, and read, and read, until weary; if that can be designated as weariness, which was rather the faintness of rapturous delight; or until, sometimes, the failing of the light invited me to go abroad, in the hope that a cool gentle breeze might have arisen to bathe, with an airy invigorating bath, the limbs which the glow of the burning spirit within had withered no less than the glow of the blazing sun without.

One peculiarity of these books, or at least most of those I looked into, I must make a somewhat vain attempt to describe.

If, for instance, it was a book of metaphysics I opened, I had scarcely read two pages before I seemed to myself to be pondering over discovered truth, and constructing the intellectual machine whereby to communicate the discovery to my fellow men. With some books, however, of this nature, it seemed rather as if the process was removed yet a great way further back; and I was trying to find the root of a manifestation, the spiritual truth whence a material vision sprang; or to combine two propositions, both apparently true, either at once or in different remembered moods, and to find the point in which their invisibly converging lines would unite in one, revealing a truth higher than either and differing from both; though so far from being opposed to either, that it was that whence each derived its life and power. Or if the book was one of travels, I found myself the traveller. New lands, fresh experiences, novel customs, rose around me. I walked, I discovered, I fought, I suffered, I rejoiced in my success. Was it a history? I was the chief actor therein. I suffered my own blame; I was glad in my own praise. With a fiction it was the same. Mine was the whole story. For I took the place of the character who was most like myself, and his story was mine; until, grown weary with the life of years condensed in an hour, or arrived at my deathbed, or the end of the volume, I would awake, with a sudden bewilderment, to the consciousness of my present life, recognising the walls and roof around me, and finding I joyed or sorrowed only in a book. If the book was a poem, the words disappeared, or took the subordinate position of an accompaniment to the succession of forms and images that rose and vanished with a soundless rhythm, and a hidden rime.

In one, with a mystical title, which I cannot recall, I read of a world that is not like ours. The wondrous account, in such a feeble, fragmentary way as is possible to me, I would willingly impart. Whether or not it was all a poem, I cannot tell; but, from the impulse I felt, when I first contemplated writing it, to break into rime, to which impulse I shall give way if it comes upon me again, I think it must have been, partly at least, in verse.

CHAPTER XII

"Chained is the Spring. The night-wind bold

Blows over the hard earth;

Time is not more confused and cold,

Nor keeps more wintry mirth.

"Yet blow, and roll the world about;

Blow, Time—blow, winter's Wind!

Through chinks of Time, heaven peepeth out,

And Spring the frost behind."

G. E. M.

They who believe in the influences of the stars over the fates of men, are, in feeling at least, nearer the truth than they who regard the heavenly bodies as related to them merely by a common obedience to an external law. All that man sees has to do with man. Worlds cannot be without an intermundane relationship. The community of the centre of all creation suggests an interradiating connection and dependence of the parts. Else a grander idea is conceivable than that which is already imbodied. The blank, which is only a forgotten life, lying behind the consciousness, and the misty splendour, which is an undeveloped life, lying before it, may be full of mysterious revelations of other connexions with the worlds around us, than those of science and poetry. No shining belt or gleaming moon, no red and green glory in a self-encircling twin-star, but has a relation with the hidden things of a man's soul, and, it may be, with the secret history of his body as well. They are portions of the living house wherein he abides.

Through the realms of the monarch Sun

Creeps a world, whose course had begun,

On a weary path with a weary pace,

Before the Earth sprang forth on her race:

But many a time the Earth had sped

Around the path she still must tread,

Ere the elder planet, on leaden wing,

Once circled the court of the planet's king.

There, in that lonely and distant star,

The seasons are not as our seasons are;

But many a year hath Autumn to dress

The trees in their matron loveliness;

As long hath old Winter in triumph to go

O'er beauties dead in his vaults below;

And many a year the Spring doth wear

Combing the icicles from her hair;

And Summer, dear Summer, hath years of June,

With large white clouds, and cool showers at noon:

And a beauty that grows to a weight like grief,

Till a burst of tears is the heart's relief.

Children, born when Winter is king,

May never rejoice in the hoping Spring;

Though their own heart-buds are bursting with joy,

And the child hath grown to the girl or boy;

But may die with cold and icy hours

Watching them ever in place of flowers.

And some who awake from their primal sleep,

When the sighs of Summer through forests creep,

Live, and love, and are loved again;

Seek for pleasure, and find its pain;

Sink to their last, their forsaken sleeping,

With the same sweet odours around them creeping.

Now the children, there, are not born as the children are born in worlds nearer to the sun. For they arrive no one knows how. A maiden, walking alone, hears a cry: for even there a cry is the first utterance; and searching about, she findeth, under an overhanging rock, or within a clump of bushes, or, it may be, betwixt gray stones on the side of a hill, or in any other sheltered and unexpected spot, a little child. This she taketh tenderly, and beareth home with joy, calling out, "Mother, mother"—if so be that her mother lives—"I have got a baby—I have found a child!" All the household gathers round to see;—"Where is it? What is it like? Where did you find it?" and such-like questions, abounding. And thereupon she relates the whole story of the discovery; for by the circumstances, such as season of the year, time of the day, condition of the air, and such like, and, especially, the peculiar and never-repeated aspect of the heavens and earth at the time, and the nature of the place of shelter wherein it is found, is determined, or at least indicated, the nature of the child thus discovered. Therefore, at certain seasons, and in certain states of the weather, according, in part, to their own fancy, the young women go out to look for children. They generally avoid seeking them, though they cannot help sometimes finding them, in places and with circumstances uncongenial to their peculiar likings. But no sooner is a child found, than its claim for protection and nurture obliterates all feeling of choice in the matter. Chiefly, however, in the season of summer, which lasts so long, coming as it does after such long intervals; and mostly in the warm evenings, about the middle of twilight; and principally in the woods and along the river banks, do the maidens go looking for children just as children look for flowers. And

231

ever as the child grows, yea, more and more as he advances in years, will his face indicate to those who understand the spirit of Nature, and her utterances in the face of the world, the nature of the place of his birth, and the other circumstances thereof; whether a clear morning sun guided his mother to the nook whence issued the boy's low cry; or at eve the lonely maiden (for the same woman never finds a second, at least while the first lives) discovers the girl by the glimmer of her white skin, lying in a nest like that of the lark, amid long encircling grasses, and the upward-gazing eyes of the lowly daisies; whether the storm bowed the forest trees around, or the still frost fixed in silence the else flowing and babbling stream.

After they grow up, the men and women are but little together. There is this peculiar difference between them, which likewise distinguishes the women from those of the earth. The men alone have arms; the women have only wings. Resplendent wings are they, wherein they can shroud themselves from head to foot in a panoply of glistering glory. By these wings alone, it may frequently be judged in what seasons, and under what aspects, they were born. From those that came in winter, go great white wings, white as snow; the edge of every feather shining like the sheen of silver, so that they flash and glitter like frost in the sun. But underneath, they are tinged with a faint pink or rose-colour. Those born in spring have wings of a brilliant green, green as grass; and towards the edges the feathers are enamelled like the surface of the grass-blades. These again are white within. Those that are born in summer have wings of a deep rose-colour, lined with pale gold. And those born in autumn have purple wings, with a rich brown on the inside. But these colours are modified and altered in all varieties, corresponding to the mood of the day and hour, as well as the season of the year; and sometimes I found the various colours so intermingled, that I could not determine even the season, though doubtless the hieroglyphic could be deciphered by more experienced eyes. One splendour, in particular, I remember—wings of deep carmine, with an inner down of warm gray, around a form of brilliant whiteness.

She had been found as the sun went down through a low sea-fog, casting crimson along a broad sea-path into a little cave on the shore, where a bathing maiden saw her lying.

But though I speak of sun and fog, and sea and shore, the world there is in some respects very different from the earth whereon men live. For instance, the waters reflect no forms. To the unaccustomed eye they appear, if undisturbed, like the surface of a dark metal, only that the latter would reflect indistinctly, whereas they reflect not at all, except light which falls immediately upon them. This has a great effect in causing the landscapes to differ from those on the earth. On the stillest evening, no tall ship on the sea sends a long wavering reflection almost to the feet of him on shore; the face of no maiden brightens at its own beauty in a still forest-well. The sun and moon alone make a glitter on the surface. The sea is like a sea of death, ready to ingulf and never to reveal: a visible shadow of oblivion. Yet the women sport in its waters like gorgeous sea-birds. The men more rarely enter them. But, on the contrary, the sky reflects everything beneath it, as if it were built of water like ours. Of course, from its concavity there is some distortion of the reflected objects; yet wondrous combinations of form are often to be seen in the overhanging depth. And then it is not shaped so much like a round dome as the sky of the earth, but, more of an egg-shape, rises to a great towering height in the middle, appearing far more lofty than the other. When the stars come out at night, it shows a mighty cupola, "fretted with golden fires," wherein there is room for all tempests to rush and rave.

One evening in early summer, I stood with a group of men and women on a steep rock that overhung the sea. They were all questioning me about my world and the ways thereof. In making reply to one of their questions, I was compelled to say that children are not born in the Earth as with them. Upon this I was assailed with a whole battery of inquiries, which at first I tried to avoid; but, at last, I was compelled, in the vaguest manner I could invent, to make some approach to the subject in question. Immediately a dim notion of what I meant, seemed to dawn in the minds of most of the women. Some of them folded their great wings all around them, as they generally do when in the least offended, and stood erect and motionless. One spread out her rosy pinions, and flashed from the promontory into the gulf at its foot. A great light shone in the eyes of one maiden, who turned and walked slowly away, with her purple and white wings half dispread behind her. She was found, the next morning, dead beneath a withered tree on a bare hill-side, some miles inland. They buried her where she lay, as is their custom; for, before they die, they instinctively search for a spot like the place of their birth, and having found one that satisfies them, they lie down, fold their wings around them, if they be women, or cross their arms over their breasts, if they are men, just as if they were going to sleep; and so sleep indeed. The sign or cause of coming death is an indescribable longing for something, they know not what, which seizes them, and drives them into solitude, consuming them within, till the body fails. When a youth and a maiden look too deep into each other's eyes, this longing seizes and possesses them; but instead of drawing nearer to each other, they wander away, each alone, into solitary places, and die of their desire. But it seems to me, that thereafter they are born babes upon our earth: where, if, when grown, they find each other, it goes well with them; if not, it will seem to go ill. But of this I know nothing. When I told them that the women on the Earth had not wings like them, but arms, they stared, and said how bold and masculine they must look; not knowing that their wings, glorious as they are, are but undeveloped arms.

But see the power of this book, that, while recounting what I can recall of its contents, I write as if myself had visited the far-off planet, learned its ways and appearances, and conversed with its men and women. And so, while writing, it seemed to me that I had.

The book goes on with the story of a maiden, who, born at the close of autumn, and living in a long, to her endless winter, set out at last to find the regions of spring; for, as in our earth, the seasons are divided over the globe. It begins something like this:

She watched them dying for many a day,

Dropping from off the old trees away,

One by one; or else in a shower

Crowding over the withered flower

For as if they had done some grievous wrong,

The sun, that had nursed them and loved them so long,

Grew weary of loving, and, turning back,

Hastened away on his southern track;

And helplessly hung each shrivelled leaf,

Faded away with an idle grief.

And the gusts of wind, sad Autumn's sighs,

Mournfully swept through their families;

Casting away with a helpless moan

All that he yet might call his own,

As the child, when his bird is gone for ever,

Flingeth the cage on the wandering river.

And the giant trees, as bare as Death,

Slowly bowed to the great Wind's breath;

And groaned with trying to keep from groaning

Amidst the young trees bending and moaning.

And the ancient planet's mighty sea

Was heaving and falling most restlessly,

And the tops of the waves were broken and white,

Tossing about to ease their might;

And the river was striving to reach the main,

And the ripple was hurrying back again.

Nature lived in sadness now;

Sadness lived on the maiden's brow,

As she watched, with a fixed, half-conscious eye,

One lonely leaf that trembled on high,

Till it dropped at last from the desolate bough—

Sorrow, oh, sorrow! 'tis winter now.

And her tears gushed forth, though it was but a leaf,

For little will loose the swollen fountain of grief:

When up to the lip the water goes,

It needs but a drop, and it overflows.

Oh! many and many a dreary year

Must pass away ere the buds appear:

Many a night of darksome sorrow

Yield to the light of a joyless morrow,

Ere birds again, on the clothed trees,

Shall fill the branches with melodies.

She will dream of meadows with wakeful streams;

Of wavy grass in the sunny beams;

Of hidden wells that soundless spring,

Hoarding their joy as a holy thing;

Of founts that tell it all day long

To the listening woods, with exultant song;

She will dream of evenings that die into nights,

Where each sense is filled with its own delights,

And the soul is still as the vaulted sky,

Lulled with an inner harmony;

And the flowers give out to the dewy night,

Changed into perfume, the gathered light;

And the darkness sinks upon all their host,

Till the sun sail up on the eastern coast—

She will wake and see the branches bare,

Weaving a net in the frozen air.

The story goes on to tell how, at last, weary with wintriness, she travelled towards the southern regions of her globe, to meet the spring on its slow way northwards; and how, after many sad adventures, many disappointed hopes, and many tears, bitter and fruitless, she found at last, one stormy afternoon, in a leafless forest, a single snowdrop growing betwixt the borders of the winter and spring. She lay down beside it and died. I almost believe that a child, pale and peaceful as a snowdrop, was born in the Earth within a fixed season from that stormy afternoon.

CHAPTER XIII

"I saw a ship sailing upon the sea

Deeply laden as ship could be;

But not so deep as in love I am

For I care not whether I sink or swim."

Old Ballad.

"But Love is such a Mystery

I cannot find it out:

For when I think I'm best resolv'd,

I then am in most doubt."

SIR JOHN SUCKLING.

One story I will try to reproduce. But, alas! it is like trying to reconstruct a forest out of broken branches and withered leaves. In the fairy book, everything was just as it should be, though whether in words or something else, I cannot tell. It glowed and flashed the thoughts upon the soul, with such a power that the medium disappeared from the consciousness, and it was occupied only with the things themselves. My representation of it must resemble a translation from a rich and powerful language, capable of embodying the thoughts of a splendidly developed people, into the meagre and half-articulate speech of a savage tribe. Of course, while I read it, I was Cosmo, and his history was mine. Yet, all the time, I seemed to have a kind of double consciousness, and the story a double meaning. Sometimes it seemed only to represent a simple story of ordinary life, perhaps almost of universal life; wherein two souls, loving each other and longing to come nearer, do, after all, but behold each other as in a glass darkly.

As through the hard rock go the branching silver veins; as into the solid land run the creeks and gulfs from the unresting sea; as the lights and influences of the upper worlds sink silently through the earth's atmosphere; so doth Faerie invade the world of men, and sometimes startle the common eye with an association as of cause and effect, when between the two no connecting links can be traced.

Cosmo von Wehrstahl was a student at the University of Prague. Though of a noble family, he was poor, and prided himself upon the independence that poverty gives; for what will not a man pride himself upon, when he cannot get rid of it? A favourite with his fellow students, he yet had no companions; and none of them had ever crossed the threshold of his lodging in the top of one of the highest houses in the old town. Indeed, the secret of much of that complaisance which recommended him to his fellows, was the thought of his unknown retreat, whither in the evening he could betake himself and indulge undisturbed in his own studies and reveries. These studies, besides those subjects necessary to his course at the University, embraced some less commonly known and approved; for in a secret drawer lay the works of Albertus Magnus and Cornelius Agrippa, along with others less read and more abstruse. As yet, however, he had followed these researches only from curiosity, and had turned them to no practical purpose.

His lodging consisted of one large low-ceiled room, singularly bare of furniture; for besides a couple of wooden chairs, a couch which served for dreaming on both by day and night, and a great press of black oak, there was very little in the room that could be called furniture.

But curious instruments were heaped in the corners; and in one stood a skeleton, half-leaning against the wall, half-supported by a string about its neck. One of its hands, all of fingers, rested on the heavy pommel of a great sword that stood beside it.

Various weapons were scattered about over the floor. The walls were utterly bare of adornment; for the few strange things, such as a large dried bat with wings dispread, the skin of a porcupine, and a stuffed sea-mouse, could hardly be reckoned as such. But although his fancy delighted in vagaries like these, he indulged his imagination with far different fare. His mind had never yet been filled with an absorbing passion; but it lay like a still twilight open to any wind, whether the low breath that wafts but odours, or the storm that bows the great trees till they strain and creak. He saw everything as through a rose-coloured glass. When he looked from his window on the street below, not a maiden passed but she moved as in a story, and drew his thoughts after her till she disappeared in the vista. When he walked in the streets, he always felt as if reading a tale, into which he sought to weave every face of interest that went by; and every sweet voice swept his soul as with the wing of a passing angel. He was in fact a poet without words; the more absorbed and endangered, that the springing-waters were dammed back into his soul, where, finding no utterance, they grew, and swelled, and undermined. He used to lie on his hard couch, and read a tale or a poem, till the book dropped from his hand; but he dreamed on, he knew not whether awake or asleep, until the opposite roof grew upon his sense, and turned golden in the sunrise. Then he arose too; and the impulses of vigorous youth kept him ever active, either in study or in sport, until again the close of the day left him free; and the world of night, which had lain drowned in the cataract of the day, rose up in his soul, with all its stars, and dim-seen phantom shapes. But this could hardly last long. Some one form must sooner or later step within the charmed circle, enter the house of life, and compel the bewildered magician to kneel and worship.

One afternoon, towards dusk, he was wandering dreamily in one of the principal streets, when a fellow student roused him by a slap on the shoulder, and asked him to accompany him into a little back alley to look at some old armour which he had taken a fancy to possess. Cosmo was considered an authority in every matter pertaining to arms, ancient or modern. In the use of weapons, none of the students could come near him; and his practical acquaintance with some had principally contributed to establish his authority in reference to all. He accompanied him willingly.

They entered a narrow alley, and thence a dirty little court, where a low arched door admitted them into a heterogeneous assemblage of everything musty, and dusty, and old, that could well be imagined. His verdict on the armour was satisfactory, and his companion at once concluded the purchase.

As they were leaving the place, Cosmo's eye was attracted by an old mirror of an elliptical shape, which leaned against the wall, covered with dust. Around it was some curious carving, which he could see but very indistinctly by the glimmering light which the owner of the shop carried in his hand. It was this carving that attracted his attention; at least so it appeared to him. He left the place, however, with his friend, taking no further notice of it. They walked together to the main street, where they parted and took opposite directions.

No sooner was Cosmo left alone, than the thought of the curious old mirror returned to him. A strong desire to see it more plainly arose within him, and he directed his steps once more towards the shop. The owner opened the door when he knocked, as if he had expected him. He was a little, old, withered man, with a hooked nose, and burning eyes constantly in a slow restless motion, and looking here and there as if after something that eluded them. Pretending to examine several other articles, Cosmo at last approached the mirror, and requested to have it taken down.

"Take it down yourself, master; I cannot reach it," said the old man.

Cosmo took it down carefully, when he saw that the carving was indeed delicate and costly, being both of admirable design and execution; containing withal many devices which seemed to embody some meaning to which he had no clue. This, naturally, in one of his tastes and temperament, increased the interest he felt in the old mirror; so much, indeed, that he now longed to possess it, in order to study its frame at his leisure. He pretended, however, to want it only for use; and saying he feared the plate could be of little service, as it was rather old, he brushed away a little of the dust from its face, expecting to see a dull reflection within. His surprise was great when he found the reflection brilliant, revealing a glass not only uninjured by age, but wondrously clear and perfect (should the whole correspond to this part) even for one newly from the hands of the maker. He asked carelessly what the owner wanted for the thing. The old man replied by mentioning a sum of money far beyond the reach of poor Cosmo, who proceeded to replace the mirror where it had stood before.

"You think the price too high?" said the old man.

"I do not know that it is too much for you to ask," replied Cosmo; "but it is far too much for me to give."

The old man held up his light towards Cosmo's face. "I like your look," said he.

Cosmo could not return the compliment. In fact, now he looked closely at him for the first time, he felt a kind of repugnance to him, mingled with a strange feeling of doubt whether a man or a woman stood before him.

"What is your name?" he continued.

"Cosmo von Wehrstahl."

"Ah, ah! I thought as much. I see your father in you. I knew your father very well, young sir. I dare say in some odd corners of my house, you might find some old things with his crest and cipher upon them still. Well, I like you: you shall have the mirror at the fourth part of what I asked for it; but upon one condition."

"What is that?" said Cosmo; for, although the price was still a great deal for him to give, he could just manage it; and the desire to possess the mirror had increased to an altogether unaccountable degree, since it had seemed beyond his reach.

"That if you should ever want to get rid of it again, you will let me have the first offer."

"Certainly," replied Cosmo, with a smile; adding, "a moderate condition indeed."

"On your honour?" insisted the seller.

"On my honour," said the buyer; and the bargain was concluded.

"I will carry it home for you," said the old man, as Cosmo took it in his hands.

"No, no; I will carry it myself," said he; for he had a peculiar dislike to revealing his residence to any one, and more especially to this person, to whom he felt every moment a greater antipathy. "Just as you please," said the old creature, and muttered to himself as he held his light at the door to show him out of the court: "Sold for the sixth time! I wonder what will be the upshot of it this time. I should think my lady had enough of it by now!"

Cosmo carried his prize carefully home. But all the way he had an uncomfortable feeling that he was watched and dogged. Repeatedly he looked about, but saw nothing to justify his suspicions. Indeed, the streets were too crowded and too ill lighted to expose very readily a careful spy, if such there should be at his heels. He reached his lodging in safety, and leaned his purchase against the wall, rather relieved, strong as he was, to be rid of its weight; then, lighting his pipe, threw himself on the couch, and was soon lapt in the folds of one of his haunting dreams.

He returned home earlier than usual the next day, and fixed the mirror to the wall, over the hearth, at one end of his long room.

He then carefully wiped away the dust from its face, and, clear as the water of a sunny spring, the mirror shone out from beneath the envious covering. But his interest was chiefly occupied with the curious carving of the frame. This he cleaned as well as he could with a brush; and then he proceeded to a minute examination of its various parts, in the hope of discovering some index to the intention of the carver. In this, however, he was unsuccessful; and, at length, pausing with some weariness and disappointment, he gazed vacantly for a few moments into the depth of the reflected room. But ere long he said, half aloud: "What a strange thing a mirror is! and what a wondrous affinity exists between it and a man's imagination! For this room of mine, as I behold it in the glass, is the same, and yet not the same. It is not the mere representation of the room I live in, but it looks just as if I were reading about it in a story I like. All its commonness has disappeared. The mirror has lifted it out of the region of fact into the realm of art; and the very representing of it to me has clothed with interest that which was otherwise hard and bare; just as one sees with delight upon the stage the representation of a character from which one would escape in life as from something unendurably wearisome. But is it not rather that art rescues nature from the weary and sated regards of our senses, and the degrading injustice of our anxious everyday life, and, appealing to the imagination, which dwells apart, reveals Nature in some degree as she really is, and as she represents herself to the eye of the child, whose every-day life, fearless and unambitious, meets the true import of the wonder-teeming world around him, and rejoices therein without questioning? That skeleton, now—I almost fear it, standing there so still, with eyes only for the unseen, like a watch-tower looking across all the waste of this busy world into the quiet regions of rest beyond. And yet I know every bone and every joint in it as well as my own fist. And that old battle-axe looks as if any moment it might be caught up by a mailed hand, and, borne forth by the mighty arm, go crashing through casque, and skull, and brain, invading the Unknown with yet another bewildered ghost. I should like to live in that room if I could only get into it."

Scarcely had the half-moulded words floated from him, as he stood gazing into the mirror, when, striking him as with a flash of amazement that fixed him in his posture, noiseless and unannounced, glided suddenly through the door into the reflected room, with stately motion, yet reluctant and faltering step, the graceful form of a woman, clothed all in white. Her back only was visible as she walked slowly up to the couch in the further end of the room, on which she laid herself wearily, turning towards him a face of unutterable loveliness, in which suffering, and dislike, and a sense of compulsion, strangely mingled with the beauty. He stood without the power of motion for some moments, with his eyes irrecoverably fixed upon her; and even after he was conscious of the ability to move, he could not summon up courage to turn and look on her, face to face, in the veritable chamber in which he stood. At length, with a sudden effort, in which the exercise of the will was so pure, that it seemed involuntary, he turned his face to the couch. It was vacant. In bewilderment, mingled with terror, he turned again to the mirror: there, on the reflected couch, lay the exquisite lady-form. She lay with closed eyes, whence two large tears were just welling from beneath the veiling lids; still as death, save for the convulsive motion of her bosom.

Cosmo himself could not have described what he felt. His emotions were of a kind that destroyed consciousness, and could never be clearly recalled. He could not help standing yet by the mirror, and keeping his eyes fixed on the lady, though he was painfully aware of his rudeness, and feared every moment that she would open hers, and meet his fixed regard. But he was, ere long, a little relieved; for, after a while, her eyelids slowly rose, and her eyes remained uncovered, but unemployed for a time; and when, at length, they began to wander about the room, as if languidly seeking to make some acquaintance with her environment, they were never directed towards him: it seemed nothing but what was in the mirror could affect her vision; and, therefore, if she saw him at all, it could only be his back, which, of necessity, was turned towards her in the glass. The two figures in the mirror could not meet face to face, except he turned and looked at her, present in his room; and, as she was not there, he concluded that if he were to turn towards the part in his room corresponding to that in which she lay, his reflection would either be invisible to her altogether, or at least it must appear to her to gaze vacantly towards her, and no meeting of the eyes would produce the impression of spiritual proximity. By-and-by her eyes fell upon the skeleton, and he saw her shudder and close them. She did not open them again, but signs of repugnance continued evident on her countenance. Cosmo would have removed the obnoxious thing at once, but he feared to discompose her yet more by the assertion of his presence which the act would involve. So he stood and watched her. The eyelids yet shrouded the eyes, as a costly case the jewels within; the troubled expression gradually faded from the countenance, leaving only a faint sorrow behind; the features settled into an unchanging expression of rest; and by these signs, and the slow regular motion of her breathing, Cosmo knew that she slept. He could now gaze on her without embarrassment. He saw that her figure, dressed in the simplest robe of white, was worthy of her face; and so harmonious, that either the delicately moulded foot, or any finger of the equally delicate hand, was an index to the whole. As she lay, her whole form manifested the relaxation of perfect repose. He gazed till he was weary, and at last seated himself near the new-found shrine, and mechanically took up a book, like one who watches by a sick-bed. But his eyes gathered no thoughts from the page before him. His intellect had been stunned by the bold contradiction, to its face, of all its experience, and now lay passive, without assertion, or speculation, or even conscious astonishment; while his imagination sent one wild dream of blessedness after another coursing through his soul. How long he sat he knew not; but at length he roused himself, rose, and, trembling in every portion of his frame, looked again into the mirror. She was gone. The mirror reflected faithfully what his room presented, and nothing more. It stood there like a golden setting whence the central jewel has been stolen away—like a night-sky without the glory of its stars. She had carried with her all the strangeness of the reflected room. It had sunk to the level of the one without.

But when the first pangs of his disappointment had passed, Cosmo began to comfort himself with the hope that she might return, perhaps the next evening, at the same hour. Resolving that if she did, she should not at least be scared by the hateful skeleton, he removed that and several other articles of questionable appearance into a recess by the side of the hearth, whence they could not possibly cast any reflection into the mirror; and having made his poor room as tidy as he could, sought the solace of the open sky and of a night wind that had begun to blow, for he could not rest where he was. When he returned, somewhat composed, he could hardly prevail with himself to lie down on his bed; for he could not help feeling as if she had lain upon it; and for him to lie there now would be something like sacrilege. However, weariness prevailed; and laying himself on the couch, dressed as he was, he slept till day.

With a beating heart, beating till he could hardly breathe, he stood in dumb hope before the mirror, on the following evening. Again the reflected room shone as through a purple vapour in the gathering twilight. Everything seemed waiting like himself for a coming splendour to glorify its poor earthliness with the presence of a heavenly joy. And just as the room vibrated with the strokes of the neighbouring church bell, announcing the hour of six, in glided the pale beauty, and again laid herself on the couch. Poor Cosmo nearly lost his senses with delight. She was there once more! Her eyes sought the corner where the skeleton had stood, and a faint gleam of satisfaction crossed her face, apparently at seeing it empty. She looked suffering still, but there was less of discomfort expressed in her countenance than there had been the night before. She took more notice of the things about her, and seemed to gaze with some curiosity on the strange apparatus standing here and there in her room. At length, however, drowsiness seemed to overtake her, and again she fell asleep. Resolved not to lose sight of her this time, Cosmo watched the sleeping form. Her slumber was so deep and absorbing that a fascinating repose seemed to pass contagiously from her to him as he gazed upon her; and he started as if from a dream, when the lady moved, and, without opening her eyes, rose, and passed from the room with the gait of a somnambulist.

Cosmo was now in a state of extravagant delight. Most men have a secret treasure somewhere. The miser has his golden hoard; the virtuoso his pet ring; the student his rare book; the poet his favourite haunt; the lover his secret drawer; but Cosmo had a mirror with a lovely lady in it. And now that he knew by the skeleton, that she was affected by the things around her, he had a new object in life: he would turn the bare chamber in the mirror into a room such as no lady need disdain to call her own. This he could effect only by furnishing and adorning his. And Cosmo was poor. Yet he possessed accomplishments that could be turned to account; although, hitherto, he had preferred living on his slender allowance, to increasing his means by what his pride considered unworthy of his rank. He was the best swordsman in the University; and now he offered to give lessons in fencing and similar exercises, to such as chose to pay him well for the trouble. His proposal was heard with surprise by the students; but it was eagerly accepted by many; and soon his instructions were not confined to the richer students, but were anxiously sought by many of the young nobility of Prague and its neighbourhood. So that very soon he had a good deal of money at his command. The first thing he did was to remove his apparatus and oddities into a closet in the room. Then he placed his bed and a few other necessaries on each side of the hearth, and parted them from the rest of the room by two screens of Indian fabric. Then he put an elegant couch for the lady to lie upon, in the corner where his bed had formerly stood; and, by degrees, every day adding some article of luxury, converted it, at length, into a rich boudoir.

Every night, about the same time, the lady entered. The first time she saw the new couch, she started with a half-smile; then her face grew very sad, the tears came to her eyes, and she laid herself upon the couch, and pressed her face into the silken cushions, as if to hide from everything. She

247

took notice of each addition and each change as the work proceeded; and a look of acknowledgment, as if she knew that some one was ministering to her, and was grateful for it, mingled with the constant look of suffering. At length, after she had lain down as usual one evening, her eyes fell upon some paintings with which Cosmo had just finished adorning the walls. She rose, and to his great delight, walked across the room, and proceeded to examine them carefully, testifying much pleasure in her looks as she did so. But again the sorrowful, tearful expression returned, and again she buried her face in the pillows of her couch. Gradually, however, her countenance had grown more composed; much of the suffering manifest on her first appearance had vanished, and a kind of quiet, hopeful expression had taken its place; which, however, frequently gave way to an anxious, troubled look, mingled with something of sympathetic pity.

Meantime, how fared Cosmo? As might be expected in one of his temperament, his interest had blossomed into love, and his love—shall I call it ripened, or—withered into passion. But, alas! he loved a shadow. He could not come near her, could not speak to her, could not hear a sound from those sweet lips, to which his longing eyes would cling like bees to their honey-founts. Ever and anon he sang to himself:

"I shall die for love of the maiden;"

and ever he looked again, and died not, though his heart seemed ready to break with intensity of life and longing. And the more he did for her, the more he loved her; and he hoped that, although she never appeared to see him, yet she was pleased to think that one unknown would give his life to her. He tried to comfort himself over his separation from her, by thinking that perhaps some day she would see him and make signs to him, and that would satisfy him; "for," thought he, "is not this all that a loving soul can do to enter into communion with another? Nay, how many who love never come nearer than to behold each other as in a mirror; seem to know and yet never know the inward life; never enter the other soul; and part at last, with but the vaguest notion of the universe on the borders of which they have been hovering for years? If I could but speak to her, and knew that she heard me, I should be satisfied." Once he contemplated painting a picture on the

248

wall, which should, of necessity, convey to the lady a thought of himself; but, though he had some skill with the pencil, he found his hand tremble so much when he began the attempt, that he was forced to give it up. . . . . .

"Who lives, he dies; who dies, he is alive."

One evening, as he stood gazing on his treasure, he thought he saw a faint expression of self-consciousness on her countenance, as if she surmised that passionate eyes were fixed upon her. This grew; till at last the red blood rose over her neck, and cheek, and brow. Cosmo's longing to approach her became almost delirious. This night she was dressed in an evening costume, resplendent with diamonds. This could add nothing to her beauty, but it presented it in a new aspect; enabled her loveliness to make a new manifestation of itself in a new embodiment. For essential beauty is infinite; and, as the soul of Nature needs an endless succession of varied forms to embody her loveliness, countless faces of beauty springing forth, not any two the same, at any one of her heart-throbs; so the individual form needs an infinite change of its environments, to enable it to uncover all the phases of its loveliness. Diamonds glittered from amidst her hair, half hidden in its luxuriance, like stars through dark rain-clouds; and the bracelets on her white arms flashed all the colours of a rainbow of lightnings, as she lifted her snowy hands to cover her burning face. But her beauty shone down all its adornment. "If I might have but one of her feet to kiss," thought Cosmo, "I should be content." Alas! he deceived himself, for passion is never content. Nor did he know that there are two ways out of her enchanted house. But, suddenly, as if the pang had been driven into his heart from without, revealing itself first in pain, and afterwards in definite form, the thought darted into his mind, "She has a lover somewhere. Remembered words of his bring the colour on her face now. I am nowhere to her. She lives in another world all day, and all night, after she leaves me. Why does she come and make me love her, till I, a strong man, am too faint to look upon her more?" He looked again, and her face was pale as a lily. A sorrowful compassion seemed to rebuke the glitter of the restless jewels, and the slow tears rose in her eyes. She left her room sooner this evening than was her wont. Cosmo remained alone, with a feeling as if his bosom had been suddenly left empty and hollow, and the weight of the whole world was crushing in its walls. The next evening, for the first time since she began to come, she came not.

And now Cosmo was in wretched plight. Since the thought of a rival had occurred to him, he could not rest for a moment. More than ever he longed to see the lady face to face. He persuaded himself that if he but knew the worst he would be satisfied; for then he could abandon Prague, and find that relief in constant motion, which is the hope of all active minds when invaded by distress. Meantime he waited with unspeakable anxiety for the next night, hoping she would return: but she did not appear. And now he fell really ill. Rallied by his fellow students on his wretched looks, he ceased to attend the lectures. His engagements were neglected. He cared for nothing. The sky, with the great sun in it, was to him a heartless, burning desert. The men and women in the streets were mere puppets, without motives in themselves, or interest to him. He saw them all as on the ever-changing field of a camera obscura. She—she alone and altogether—was his universe, his well of life, his incarnate good. For six evenings she came not. Let his absorbing passion, and the slow fever that was consuming his brain, be his excuse for the resolution which he had taken and begun to execute, before that time had expired.

Reasoning with himself, that it must be by some enchantment connected with the mirror, that the form of the lady was to be seen in it, he determined to attempt to turn to account what he had hitherto studied principally from curiosity. "For," said he to himself, "if a spell can force her presence in that glass (and she came unwillingly at first), may not a stronger spell, such as I know, especially with the aid of her half-presence in the mirror, if ever she appears again, compel her living form to come to me here? If I do her wrong, let love be my excuse. I want only to know my doom from her own lips." He never doubted, all the time, that she was a real earthly woman; or, rather, that there was a woman, who, somehow or other, threw this reflection of her form into the magic mirror.

He opened his secret drawer, took out his books of magic, lighted his lamp, and read and made notes from midnight till three in the morning, for three successive nights. Then he replaced his books; and the next night went out in quest of the materials necessary for the conjuration. These were not easy to find; for, in love-charms and all incantations of this nature, ingredients are employed scarcely fit to be mentioned, and for the thought even of which, in connexion with her, he could only excuse himself on the score of his bitter need. At length he succeeded in procuring all he required; and on the seventh evening from that on which she had last appeared, he found himself prepared for the exercise of unlawful and tyrannical power.

He cleared the centre of the room; stooped and drew a circle of red on the floor, around the spot where he stood; wrote in the four quarters mystical signs, and numbers which were all powers of seven or nine; examined the whole ring carefully, to see that no smallest break had occurred in the circumference; and then rose from his bending posture. As he rose, the church clock struck seven; and, just as she had appeared the first time, reluctant, slow, and stately, glided in the lady. Cosmo trembled; and when, turning, she revealed a countenance worn and wan, as with sickness or inward trouble, he grew faint, and felt as if he dared not proceed. But as he gazed on the face and form, which now possessed his whole soul, to the exclusion of all other joys and griefs, the longing to speak to her, to know that she heard him, to hear from her one word in return, became so unendurable, that he suddenly and hastily resumed his preparations. Stepping carefully from the circle, he put a small brazier into its centre. He then set fire to its contents of charcoal, and while it burned up, opened his window and seated himself, waiting, beside it.

It was a sultry evening. The air was full of thunder. A sense of luxurious depression filled the brain. The sky seemed to have grown heavy, and to compress the air beneath it. A kind of purplish tinge pervaded the atmosphere, and through the open window came the scents of the distant fields, which all the vapours of the city could not quench. Soon the charcoal glowed. Cosmo sprinkled upon it the incense and other substances which he had compounded, and, stepping within the circle, turned his face from the brazier and towards the mirror. Then, fixing his eyes upon the face of the lady, he began with a trembling voice to repeat a powerful incantation. He had not gone far, before the lady grew pale; and then, like a returning wave, the blood washed all its banks with its crimson tide, and she hid her face in her hands. Then he passed to a conjuration stronger yet.

The lady rose and walked uneasily to and fro in her room. Another spell; and she seemed seeking with her eyes for some object on which they wished to rest. At length it seemed as if she suddenly espied him; for her eyes fixed themselves full and wide upon his, and she drew gradually, and somewhat unwillingly, close to her side of the mirror, just as if his eyes had fascinated her. Cosmo had never seen her so near before. Now at least, eyes met eyes; but he could not quite understand the expression of hers. They were full of tender entreaty, but there was something more that he could not interpret. Though his heart seemed to labour in his throat, he would allow no delight or agitation to turn him from his task. Looking still in her face, he passed on to the mightiest charm he knew. Suddenly the lady turned and walked out of the door of her reflected chamber. A moment after she entered his room with veritable presence; and, forgetting all his precautions, he sprang from the charmed circle, and knelt before her. There she stood, the living lady of his passionate visions, alone beside him, in a thundery twilight, and the glow of a magic fire.

"Why," said the lady, with a trembling voice, "didst thou bring a poor maiden through the rainy streets alone?"

"Because I am dying for love of thee; but I only brought thee from the mirror there."

"Ah, the mirror!" and she looked up at it, and shuddered. "Alas! I am but a slave, while that mirror exists. But do not think it was the power of thy spells that drew me; it was thy longing desire to see me, that beat at the door of my heart, till I was forced to yield."

"Canst thou love me then?" said Cosmo, in a voice calm as death, but almost inarticulate with emotion.

"I do not know," she replied sadly; "that I cannot tell, so long as I am bewildered with enchantments. It were indeed a joy too great, to lay my head on thy bosom and weep to death; for I think thou lovest me, though I do not know;—but——"

Cosmo rose from his knees.

"I love thee as—nay, I know not what—for since I have loved thee, there is nothing else."

He seized her hand: she withdrew it.

"No, better not; I am in thy power, and therefore I may not."

She burst into tears, and kneeling before him in her turn, said—

"Cosmo, if thou lovest me, set me free, even from thyself; break the mirror."

"And shall I see thyself instead?"

"That I cannot tell, I will not deceive thee; we may never meet again."

A fierce struggle arose in Cosmo's bosom. Now she was in his power. She did not dislike him at least; and he could see her when he would. To break the mirror would be to destroy his very life to banish out of his universe the only glory it possessed. The whole world would be but a prison, if he annihilated the one window that looked into the paradise of love. Not yet pure in love, he hesitated.

With a wail of sorrow the lady rose to her feet. "Ah! he loves me not; he loves me not even as I love him; and alas! I care more for his love than even for the freedom I ask."

"I will not wait to be willing," cried Cosmo; and sprang to the corner where the great sword stood.

Meantime it had grown very dark; only the embers cast a red glow through the room. He seized the sword by the steel scabbard, and stood before the mirror; but as he heaved a great blow at it with the heavy pommel, the blade slipped half-way out of the scabbard, and the pommel struck the wall above the mirror. At that moment, a terrible clap of thunder seemed to burst in the very room beside them; and ere Cosmo could repeat the blow, he fell senseless on the hearth. When he came to himself, he found that the lady and the mirror had both disappeared. He was seized with a brain fever, which kept him to his couch for weeks.

When he recovered his reason, he began to think what could have become of the mirror. For the lady, he hoped she had found her way back as she came; but as the mirror involved her fate with its own, he was more immediately anxious about that. He could not think she had carried it away. It was much too heavy, even if it had not been too firmly fixed in the wall, for her to remove it. Then again, he remembered the thunder; which made him believe that it was not the lightning, but some other blow that had struck him down. He concluded that, either by supernatural agency, he having exposed himself to the vengeance of the demons in leaving the circle of safety, or in some other mode, the mirror had probably found its way back to its former owner; and, horrible to think of, might have been by this time once more disposed of, delivering up the lady into the power of another man; who, if he used his power no worse than he himself had done, might yet give Cosmo abundant cause to curse the selfish indecision which prevented him from shattering the mirror at once. Indeed, to think that she whom he loved, and who had prayed to him for freedom, should be still at the mercy, in some degree, of the possessor of the mirror, and was at least exposed to his constant observation, was in itself enough to madden a chary lover.

Anxiety to be well retarded his recovery; but at length he was able to creep abroad. He first made his way to the old broker's, pretending to be in search of something else. A laughing sneer on the creature's face convinced him that he knew all about it; but he could not see it amongst his furniture, or get any information out of him as to what had become of it. He expressed the utmost surprise at hearing it had been stolen, a surprise which Cosmo saw at once to be counterfeited; while, at the same time, he fancied that the old wretch was not at all anxious to have it mistaken for genuine. Full of distress, which he concealed as well as he could, he made many searches, but with no avail. Of course he could ask no questions; but he kept his ears awake for any remotest hint that might set him in a direction of search. He never went out without a short heavy hammer of steel about him, that he might shatter the mirror the moment he was made happy by the sight of his lost treasure, if ever that blessed moment should arrive. Whether he should see the lady again, was now a thought altogether secondary, and postponed to the achievement of her freedom. He wandered here and there, like an anxious ghost, pale and haggard; gnawed ever at the heart, by the thought of what she might be suffering—all from his fault.

One night, he mingled with a crowd that filled the rooms of one of the most distinguished mansions in the city; for he accepted every invitation, that he might lose no chance, however poor, of obtaining some information that might expedite his discovery. Here he wandered about, listening to every stray word that he could catch, in the hope of a revelation. As he approached some ladies who were talking quietly in a corner, one said to another:

"Have you heard of the strange illness of the Princess von Hohenweiss?"

"Yes; she has been ill for more than a year now. It is very sad for so fine a creature to have such a terrible malady. She was better for some weeks lately, but within the last few days the same attacks have returned, apparently accompanied with more suffering than ever. It is altogether an inexplicable story."

"Is there a story connected with her illness?"

"I have only heard imperfect reports of it; but it is said that she gave offence some eighteen months ago to an old woman who had held an office of trust in the family, and who, after some incoherent threats, disappeared. This peculiar affection followed soon after. But the strangest part of the story is its association with the loss of an antique mirror, which stood in her dressing-room, and of which she constantly made use."

Here the speaker's voice sank to a whisper; and Cosmo, although his very soul sat listening in his ears, could hear no more. He trembled too much to dare to address the ladies, even if it had been advisable to expose himself to their curiosity. The name of the Princess was well known to him, but he had never seen her; except indeed it was she, which now he hardly doubted, who had knelt before him on that dreadful night. Fearful of attracting attention, for, from the weak state of his health, he could not recover an appearance of calmness, he made his way to the open air, and reached his lodgings; glad in this, that he at least knew where she lived, although he never dreamed of approaching her openly, even if he should be happy enough to free her from her hateful bondage. He hoped, too, that as he had unexpectedly learned so much, the other and far more important part might be revealed to him ere long.

"Have you seen Steinwald lately?"

"No, I have not seen him for some time. He is almost a match for me at the rapier, and I suppose he thinks he needs no more lessons."

"I wonder what has become of him. I want to see him very much. Let me see; the last time I saw him he was coming out of that old broker's den, to which, if you remember, you accompanied me once, to look at some armour. That is fully three weeks ago."

This hint was enough for Cosmo. Von Steinwald was a man of influence in the court, well known for his reckless habits and fierce passions. The very possibility that the mirror should be in his possession was hell itself to Cosmo. But violent or hasty measures of any sort were most unlikely to succeed. All that he wanted was an opportunity of breaking the fatal glass; and to obtain this he must bide his time. He revolved many plans in his mind, but without being able to fix upon any.

At length, one evening, as he was passing the house of Von Steinwald, he saw the windows more than usually brilliant. He watched for a while, and seeing that company began to arrive, hastened home, and dressed as richly as he could, in the hope of mingling with the guests unquestioned: in effecting which, there could be no difficulty for a man of his carriage.

In a lofty, silent chamber, in another part of the city, lay a form more like marble than a living woman. The loveliness of death seemed frozen upon her face, for her lips were rigid, and her eyelids closed. Her long white hands were crossed over her breast, and no breathing disturbed their repose. Beside the dead, men speak in whispers, as if the deepest rest of all could be broken by the sound of a living voice. Just so, though the soul was evidently beyond the reach of all intimations from the senses, the two ladies, who sat beside her, spoke in the gentlest tones of subdued sorrow. "She has lain so for an hour."

"This cannot last long, I fear."

"How much thinner she has grown within the last few weeks! If she would only speak, and explain what she suffers, it would be better for her. I think she has visions in her trances, but nothing can induce her to refer to them when she is awake."

"Does she ever speak in these trances?"

"I have never heard her; but they say she walks sometimes, and once put the whole household in a terrible fright by disappearing for a whole hour, and returning drenched with rain, and almost dead with exhaustion and fright. But even then she would give no account of what had happened."

A scarce audible murmur from the yet motionless lips of the lady here startled her attendants. After several ineffectual attempts at articulation, the word "Cosmo!" burst from her. Then she lay still as before; but only for a moment. With a wild cry, she sprang from the couch erect on the floor, flung her arms above her head, with clasped and straining hands, and, her wide eyes flashing with light, called aloud, with a voice exultant as that of a spirit bursting from a sepulchre, "I am free! I am free! I thank thee!" Then she flung herself on the couch, and sobbed; then rose, and paced wildly up and down the room, with gestures of mingled delight and anxiety. Then turning to her motionless attendants—"Quick, Lisa, my cloak and hood!" Then lower—"I must go to him. Make haste, Lisa! You may come with me, if you will."

In another moment they were in the street, hurrying along towards one of the bridges over the Moldau. The moon was near the zenith, and the streets were almost empty. The Princess soon outstripped her attendant, and was half-way over the bridge, before the other reached it.

"Are you free, lady? The mirror is broken: are you free?"

The words were spoken close beside her, as she hurried on. She turned; and there, leaning on the parapet in a recess of the bridge, stood Cosmo, in a splendid dress, but with a white and quivering face.

"Cosmo!—I am free—and thy servant for ever. I was coming to you now."

"And I to you, for Death made me bold; but I could get no further.

257

Have I atoned at all? Do I love you a little—truly?"

"Ah, I know now that you love me, my Cosmo; but what do you say about death?"

He did not reply. His hand was pressed against his side. She looked more closely: the blood was welling from between the fingers. She flung her arms around him with a faint bitter wail.

When Lisa came up, she found her mistress kneeling above a wan dead face, which smiled on in the spectral moonbeams.

And now I will say no more about these wondrous volumes; though I could tell many a tale out of them, and could, perhaps, vaguely represent some entrancing thoughts of a deeper kind which I found within them. From many a sultry noon till twilight, did I sit in that grand hall, buried and risen again in these old books. And I trust I have carried away in my soul some of the exhalations of their undying leaves. In after hours of deserved or needful sorrow, portions of what I read there have often come to me again, with an unexpected comforting; which was not fruitless, even though the comfort might seem in itself groundless and vain.

CHAPTER XIV

"Your gallery

Ha we pass'd through, not without much content

In many singularities; but we saw not

That which my daughter came to look upon,

The state of her mother."

Winter's Tale.

It seemed to me strange, that all this time I had heard no music in the fairy palace. I was convinced there must be music in it, but that my sense was as yet too gross to receive the influence of those mysterious motions that beget sound. Sometimes I felt sure, from the way the few figures of which I got such transitory glimpses passed me, or glided into vacancy before me, that they were moving to the law of music; and, in fact, several times I fancied for a moment that I heard a few wondrous tones coming I knew not whence. But they did not last long enough to convince me that I had heard them with the bodily sense. Such as they were, however, they took strange liberties with me, causing me to burst suddenly into tears, of which there was no presence to make me ashamed, or casting me into a kind of trance of speechless delight, which, passing as suddenly, left me faint and longing for more.

Now, on an evening, before I had been a week in the palace, I was wandering through one lighted arcade and corridor after another. At length I arrived, through a door that closed behind me, in another vast hall of the palace. It was filled with a subdued crimson light; by which I saw that slender pillars of black, built close to walls of white marble, rose to a great height, and then, dividing into innumerable divergent arches, supported a roof, like the walls, of white marble, upon which the arches intersected intricately, forming a fretting of black upon the white, like the network of a skeleton-leaf. The floor was black.

Between several pairs of the pillars upon every side, the place of the wall behind was occupied by a crimson curtain of thick silk, hanging in heavy and rich folds. Behind each of these curtains burned a powerful light, and these were the sources of the glow that filled the hall. A peculiar delicious odour pervaded the place. As soon as I entered, the old inspiration seemed to return to me, for I felt a strong impulse to sing; or rather, it seemed as if some one else was singing a song in my soul, which wanted to come forth at my lips, imbodied in my breath. But I kept silence; and feeling somewhat overcome by the red light and the perfume, as well as by the emotion within me, and seeing at one end of the hall a great crimson chair, more like a throne than a chair, beside a table of white marble, I went to it, and, throwing myself in it, gave myself up to a succession of images of bewildering beauty, which passed before my inward eye, in a long and occasionally crowded train. Here I sat for hours, I suppose; till, returning somewhat to myself, I saw that the red light had paled away, and felt a cool gentle breath gliding over my forehead. I rose and left the hall with unsteady steps, finding my way with some difficulty to my own chamber, and faintly remembering, as I went, that only in the marble cave, before I found the sleeping statue, had I ever had a similar experience.

After this, I repaired every morning to the same hall; where I sometimes sat in the chair and dreamed deliciously, and sometimes walked up and down over the black floor. Sometimes I acted within myself a whole drama, during one of these perambulations; sometimes walked deliberately through the whole epic of a tale; sometimes ventured to sing a song, though with a shrinking fear of I knew not what. I was astonished at the beauty of my own voice as it rang through the place, or rather crept undulating, like a serpent of sound, along the walls and roof of this superb music-hall. Entrancing verses arose within me as of their own accord, chanting themselves to their own melodies, and requiring no addition of music to satisfy the inward sense. But, ever in the pauses of these, when the singing mood was upon me, I seemed to hear something like the distant sound of multitudes of dancers, and felt as if it was the unheard music, moving their rhythmic motion, that within me blossomed in verse and song. I felt, too, that could I but see the dance, I should, from the harmony of complicated movements, not of the dancers in relation to each other merely, but of each dancer individually in the manifested plastic power that moved the consenting harmonious form, understand the whole of the music on the billows of which they floated and swung.

At length, one night, suddenly, when this feeling of dancing came upon me, I bethought me of lifting one of the crimson curtains, and looking if, perchance, behind it there might not be hid some other mystery, which might at least remove a step further the bewilderment of the present one. Nor was I altogether disappointed. I walked to one of the magnificent draperies, lifted a corner, and peeped in. There, burned a great, crimson, globe-shaped light, high in the cubical centre of another hall, which might be larger or less than that in which I stood, for its dimensions were not easily perceived, seeing that floor and roof and walls were entirely of black marble.

The roof was supported by the same arrangement of pillars radiating in arches, as that of the first hall; only, here, the pillars and arches were of dark red. But what absorbed my delighted gaze, was an innumerable assembly of white marble statues, of every form, and in multitudinous posture, filling the hall throughout. These stood, in the ruddy glow of the great lamp, upon pedestals of jet black. Around the lamp shone in golden letters, plainly legible from where I stood, the two words—

TOUCH NOT!

There was in all this, however, no solution to the sound of dancing; and now I was aware that the influence on my mind had ceased. I did not go in that evening, for I was weary and faint, but I hoarded up the expectation of entering, as of a great coming joy.

Next night I walked, as on the preceding, through the hall. My mind was filled with pictures and songs, and therewith so much absorbed, that I did not for some time think of looking within the curtain I had last night lifted. When the thought of doing so occurred to me first, I happened to be within a few yards of it. I became conscious, at the same moment, that the sound of dancing had been for some time in my ears. I approached the curtain quickly, and, lifting it, entered the black hall. Everything was still as death. I should have concluded that the sound must have proceeded from some other more distant quarter, which conclusion its faintness would, in ordinary circumstances, have necessitated from the first; but there was a something about the statues that caused me still to remain in doubt. As I said, each stood perfectly still upon its black pedestal: but there was about every one a certain air, not of motion, but as if it had just ceased from movement; as if the rest were not altogether of the marbly stillness of thousands of years. It was as if the peculiar atmosphere of each had yet a kind of invisible tremulousness; as if its agitated wavelets had not yet subsided into a perfect calm. I had the suspicion that they had anticipated my appearance, and had sprung, each, from the living joy of the dance, to the death-silence and blackness of its isolated pedestal, just before I entered. I walked across the central hall to the curtain opposite the one I had lifted, and, entering there, found all the appearances similar; only that the statues were different, and differently grouped. Neither did they produce on my mind that impression—of motion just expired, which I had experienced from the others. I found that behind every one of the crimson curtains was a similar hall, similarly lighted, and similarly occupied.

The next night, I did not allow my thoughts to be absorbed as before with inward images, but crept stealthily along to the furthest curtain in the hall, from behind which, likewise, I had formerly seemed to hear the sound of dancing. I drew aside its edge as suddenly as I could, and, looking in, saw that the utmost stillness pervaded the vast place. I walked in, and passed through it to the other end.

There I found that it communicated with a circular corridor, divided from it only by two rows of red columns. This corridor, which was black, with red niches holding statues, ran entirely about the statue-halls, forming a communication between the further ends of them all; further, that is, as regards the central hall of white whence they all diverged like radii, finding their circumference in the corridor.

Round this corridor I now went, entering all the halls, of which there were twelve, and finding them all similarly constructed, but filled with quite various statues, of what seemed both ancient and modern sculpture. After I had simply walked through them, I found myself sufficiently tired to long for rest, and went to my own room.

In the night I dreamed that, walking close by one of the curtains, I was suddenly seized with the desire to enter, and darted in. This time I was too quick for them. All the statues were in motion, statues no longer, but men and women—all shapes of beauty that ever sprang from the brain of the sculptor, mingled in the convolutions of a complicated dance. Passing through them to the further end, I almost started from my sleep on beholding, not taking part in the dance with the others, nor seemingly endued with life like them, but standing in marble coldness and rigidity upon a black pedestal in the extreme left corner—my lady of the cave; the marble beauty who sprang from her tomb or her cradle at the call of my songs. While I gazed in speechless astonishment and admiration, a dark shadow, descending from above like the curtain of a stage, gradually hid her entirely from my view. I felt with a shudder that this shadow was perchance my missing demon, whom I had not seen for days. I awoke with a stifled cry.

Of course, the next evening I began my journey through the halls (for I knew not to which my dream had carried me), in the hope of proving the dream to be a true one, by discovering my marble beauty upon her black pedestal. At length, on reaching the tenth hall, I thought I recognised some of the forms I had seen dancing in my dream; and to my bewilderment, when I arrived at the extreme corner on the left, there stood, the only one I had yet seen, a vacant pedestal. It was exactly in the position occupied, in my dream, by the pedestal on which the white lady stood. Hope beat violently in my heart.

"Now," said I to myself, "if yet another part of the dream would but come true, and I should succeed in surprising these forms in their nightly dance; it might be the rest would follow, and I should see on the pedestal my marble queen. Then surely if my songs sufficed to give her life before, when she lay in the bonds of alabaster, much more would they be sufficient then to give her volition and motion, when she alone of assembled crowds of marble forms, would be standing rigid and cold."

But the difficulty was, to surprise the dancers. I had found that a premeditated attempt at surprise, though executed with the utmost care and rapidity, was of no avail. And, in my dream, it was effected by a sudden thought suddenly executed. I saw, therefore, that there was no plan of operation offering any probability of success, but this: to allow my mind to be occupied with other thoughts, as I wandered around the great centre-hall; and so wait till the impulse to enter one of the others should happen to arise in me just at the moment when I was close to one of the crimson curtains. For I hoped that if I entered any one of the twelve halls at the right moment, that would as it were give me the right of entrance to all the others, seeing they all had communication behind. I would not diminish the hope of the right chance, by supposing it necessary that a desire to enter should awake within me, precisely when I was close to the curtains of the tenth hall.

At first the impulses to see recurred so continually, in spite of the crowded imagery that kept passing through my mind, that they formed too nearly a continuous chain, for the hope that any one of them would succeed as a surprise. But as I persisted in banishing them, they recurred less and less often; and after two or three, at considerable intervals, had come when the spot where I happened to be was unsuitable, the hope strengthened, that soon one might arise just at the right moment; namely, when, in walking round the hall, I should be close to one of the curtains.

At length the right moment and the impulse coincided. I darted into the ninth hall. It was full of the most exquisite moving forms. The whole space wavered and swam with the involutions of an intricate dance. It seemed to break suddenly as I entered, and all made one or two bounds towards their pedestals; but, apparently on finding that they were thoroughly overtaken, they returned to their employment (for it seemed with them earnest enough to be called such) without further heeding me. Somewhat impeded by the floating crowd, I made what haste I could towards the bottom of the hall; whence, entering the corridor, I turned towards the tenth. I soon arrived at the corner I wanted to reach, for the corridor was comparatively empty; but, although the dancers here, after a little confusion, altogether disregarded my presence, I was dismayed at beholding, even yet, a vacant pedestal. But I had a conviction that she was near me. And as I looked at the pedestal, I thought

264

I saw upon it, vaguely revealed as if through overlapping folds of drapery, the indistinct outlines of white feet. Yet there was no sign of drapery or concealing shadow whatever. But I remembered the descending shadow in my dream. And I hoped still in the power of my songs; thinking that what could dispel alabaster, might likewise be capable of dispelling what concealed my beauty now, even if it were the demon whose darkness had overshadowed all my life.

CHAPTER XV

"Alexander. 'When will you finish Campaspe?'

Apelles. 'Never finish: for always in absolute

beauty there is somewhat above art.'"

LYLY'S Campaspe.

And now, what song should I sing to unveil my Isis, if indeed she was present unseen? I hurried away to the white hall of Phantasy, heedless of the innumerable forms of beauty that crowded my way: these might cross my eyes, but the unseen filled my brain. I wandered long, up and down the silent space: no songs came. My soul was not still enough for songs. Only in the silence and darkness of the soul's night, do those stars of the inward firmament sink to its lower surface from the singing realms beyond, and shine upon the conscious spirit. Here all effort was unavailing. If they came not, they could not be found.

Next night, it was just the same. I walked through the red glimmer of the silent hall; but lonely as there I walked, as lonely trod my soul up and down the halls of the brain. At last I entered one of the statue-halls. The dance had just commenced, and I was delighted to find that I was free of their assembly. I walked on till I came to the sacred corner. There I found the pedestal just as I had left it, with the faint glimmer as of white feet still resting on the dead black. As soon as I saw it, I seemed to feel a presence which longed to become visible; and, as it were, called to me to gift it with self-manifestation, that it might shine on me. The power of song came to me. But the moment my voice, though I sang low and soft, stirred the air of the hall, the dancers started; the quick interweaving crowd shook, lost its form, divided; each figure sprang to its pedestal, and stood, a self-evolving life no more, but a rigid, life-like, marble shape, with the whole form composed into the expression of a single state or act. Silence rolled like a spiritual thunder through the grand space. My song had ceased, scared at its own influences. But I saw in the hand of one of the statues close by me, a harp whose chords yet quivered. I remembered that as she bounded past me, her harp had brushed against my arm; so the spell of the marble had not infolded it. I sprang to her, and with a gesture of entreaty, laid my hand on the harp. The marble hand, probably from its contact with the uncharmed harp, had strength enough to relax its hold, and yield the harp to me. No other motion indicated life. Instinctively I struck the chords and sang. And not to break upon the record of my song, I mention here, that as I sang the first four lines, the loveliest feet became clear upon the black pedestal; and ever as I sang, it was as if a veil were being lifted up from before the form, but an invisible veil, so that the statue appeared to grow before me, not so much by evolution, as by infinitesimal degrees of added height. And, while I sang, I did not feel that I stood by a statue, as indeed it appeared to be, but that a real woman-soul was revealing itself by successive stages of imbodiment, and consequent manifestatlon and expression.

> Feet of beauty, firmly planting
>
>> Arches white on rosy heel!
>
> Whence the life-spring, throbbing, panting,
>
>> Pulses upward to reveal!
>
> Fairest things know least despising;
>
>> Foot and earth meet tenderly:
>
> 'Tis the woman, resting, rising
>
>> Upward to sublimity,
>
> Rise the limbs, sedately sloping,
>
>> Strong and gentle, full and free;
>
> Soft and slow, like certain hoping,
>
>> Drawing nigh the broad firm knee.
>
> Up to speech! As up to roses
>
>> Pants the life from leaf to flower,

So each blending change discloses,

    Nearer still, expression's power.

Lo! fair sweeps, white surges, twining

    Up and outward fearlessly!

Temple columns, close combining,

    Lift a holy mystery.

Heart of mine! what strange surprises

    Mount aloft on such a stair!

Some great vision upward rises,

    Curving, bending, floating fair.

Bands and sweeps, and hill and hollow

    Lead my fascinated eye;

Some apocalypse will follow,

    Some new world of deity.

Zoned unseen, and outward swelling,

    With new thoughts and wonders rife,

Queenly majesty foretelling,

    See the expanding house of life!

Sudden heaving, unforbidden

    Sighs eternal, still the same—

Mounts of snow have summits hidden

    In the mists of uttered flame.

But the spirit, dawning nearly

  Finds no speech for earnest pain;

Finds a soundless sighing merely—

  Builds its stairs, and mounts again.

Heart, the queen, with secret hoping,

  Sendeth out her waiting pair;

Hands, blind hands, half blindly groping,

  Half inclasping visions rare;

And the great arms, heartways bending;

  Might of Beauty, drawing home

There returning, and re-blending,

  Where from roots of love they roam.

Build thy slopes of radiance beamy

  Spirit, fair with womanhood!

Tower thy precipice, white-gleamy,

  Climb unto the hour of good.

Dumb space will be rent asunder,

  Now the shining column stands

Ready to be crowned with wonder

  By the builder's joyous hands.

All the lines abroad are spreading,

  Like a fountain's falling race.

Lo, the chin, first feature, treading,

    Airy foot to rest the face!

Speech is nigh; oh, see the blushing,

    Sweet approach of lip and breath!

Round the mouth dim silence, hushing,

    Waits to die ecstatic death.

Span across in treble curving,

    Bow of promise, upper lip!

Set them free, with gracious swerving;

    Let the wing-words float and dip.

Dumb art thou? O Love immortal,

    More than words thy speech must be;

Childless yet the tender portal

    Of the home of melody.

Now the nostrils open fearless,

    Proud in calm unconsciousness,

Sure it must be something peerless

    That the great Pan would express!

Deepens, crowds some meaning tender,

    In the pure, dear lady-face.

Lo, a blinding burst of splendour!—

    'Tis the free soul's issuing grace.

Two calm lakes of molten glory

   Circling round unfathomed deeps!

Lightning-flashes, transitory,

   Cross the gulfs where darkness sleeps.

This the gate, at last, of gladness,

   To the outward striving me:

In a rain of light and sadness,

   Out its loves and longings flee!

With a presence I am smitten

   Dumb, with a foreknown surprise;

Presence greater yet than written

   Even in the glorious eyes.

Through the gulfs, with inward gazes,

   I may look till I am lost;

Wandering deep in spirit-mazes,

   In a sea without a coast.

Windows open to the glorious!

   Time and space, oh, far beyond!

Woman, ah! thou art victorious,

   And I perish, overfond.

Springs aloft the yet Unspoken

   In the forehead's endless grace,

Full of silences unbroken;

 Infinite, unfeatured face.

Domes above, the mount of wonder;

 Height and hollow wrapt in night;

Hiding in its caverns under

 Woman-nations in their might.

Passing forms, the highest Human

 Faints away to the Divine

Features none, of man or woman,

 Can unveil the holiest shine.

Sideways, grooved porches only

 Visible to passing eye,

Stand the silent, doorless, lonely

 Entrance-gates of melody.

But all sounds fly in as boldly,

 Groan and song, and kiss and cry

At their galleries, lifted coldly,

 Darkly, 'twixt the earth and sky.

Beauty, thou art spent, thou knowest

 So, in faint, half-glad despair,

From the summit thou o'erflowest

 In a fall of torrent hair;

Hiding what thou hast created

In a half-transparent shroud:

Thus, with glory soft-abated,

Shines the moon through vapoury cloud.

CHAPTER XVI

"Ev'n the Styx, which ninefold her infoldeth

Hems not Ceres' daughter in its flow;

But she grasps the apple—ever holdeth

Her, sad Orcus, down below."

SCHILLER, *Das Ideal und das Leben.*

Ever as I sang, the veil was uplifted; ever as I sang, the signs of life grew; till, when the eyes dawned upon me, it was with that sunrise of splendour which my feeble song attempted to re-imbody.

The wonder is, that I was not altogether overcome, but was able to complete my song as the unseen veil continued to rise. This ability came solely from the state of mental elevation in which I found myself. Only because uplifted in song, was I able to endure the blaze of the dawn. But I cannot tell whether she looked more of statue or more of woman; she seemed removed into that region of phantasy where all is intensely vivid, but nothing clearly defined. At last, as I sang of her descending hair, the glow of soul faded away, like a dying sunset. A lamp within had been extinguished, and the house of life shone blank in a winter morn. She was a statue once more—but visible, and that was much gained. Yet the revulsion from hope and fruition was such, that, unable to restrain myself, I sprang to her, and, in defiance of the law of the place, flung my arms around her, as if I would tear her from the grasp of a visible Death, and lifted her from the pedestal down to my heart. But no sooner had her feet ceased to be in contact with the black pedestal, than she shuddered and trembled all over; then, writhing from my arms, before I could tighten their hold, she sprang into the corridor, with the reproachful cry, "You should not have touched me!" darted behind one of the exterior pillars of the circle, and disappeared. I followed almost as fast; but ere I could reach the pillar, the sound of a closing door, the saddest of all sounds sometimes, fell on my ear; and, arriving at the spot where she had vanished, I saw, lighted by a pale yellow lamp which hung above it, a heavy, rough door, altogether unlike any others I had seen in the palace; for they were all of ebony, or ivory, or covered with silver-plates, or of some odorous wood, and very ornate; whereas this seemed of old oak, with heavy nails and iron studs. Notwithstanding the precipitation of my pursuit, I could not help reading, in silver letters beneath the lamp: "No one enters here without the leave of the Queen." But what was the Queen to me, when I followed my white lady? I dashed the door to the wall and sprang through. Lo! I stood on a waste windy hill. Great stones like tombstones stood all about me. No door, no palace was to be seen. A white figure gleamed past me, wringing her hands, and crying, "Ah! you should have sung to me; you should have sung to me!" and disappeared behind one of the stones. I followed. A cold gust of wind met me from behind the stone; and when I looked, I saw nothing but a great hole in the earth, into which I could find no way of entering. Had she fallen in? I could not tell. I must wait for the daylight. I sat down and wept, for there was no help.

CHAPTER XVII

"First, I thought, almost despairing,

This must crush my spirit now;

Yet I bore it, and am bearing—

Only do not ask me how."

HEINE.

When the daylight came, it brought the possibility of action, but with it little of consolation. With the first visible increase of light, I gazed into the chasm, but could not, for more than an hour, see sufficiently well to discover its nature. At last I saw it was almost a perpendicular opening, like a roughly excavated well, only very large. I could perceive no bottom; and it was not till the sun actually rose, that I discovered a sort of natural staircase, in many parts little more than suggested, which led round and round the gulf, descending spirally into its abyss. I saw at once that this was my path; and without a moment's hesitation, glad to quit the sunlight, which stared at me most heartlessly, I commenced my tortuous descent. It was very difficult. In some parts I had to cling to the rocks like a bat. In one place, I dropped from the track down upon the next returning spire of the stair; which being broad in this particular portion, and standing out from the wall at right angles, received me upon my feet safe, though somewhat stupefied by the shock. After descending a great way, I found the stair ended at a narrow opening which entered the rock horizontally. Into this I crept, and, having entered, had just room to turn round. I put my head out into the shaft by which I had come down, and surveyed the course of my descent. Looking up, I saw the stars; although the sun must by this time have been high in the heavens. Looking below, I saw that the sides of the shaft went sheer down, smooth as glass; and far beneath me, I saw the reflection of the same stars I had seen in the heavens when I looked up. I turned again, and crept inwards some distance, when the passage widened, and I was at length able to stand and walk upright. Wider and loftier grew the way; new paths branched off on every side; great open halls appeared; till at last I found myself wandering on through an underground country, in which the sky was of rock, and instead of trees and flowers, there were only fantastic rocks and stones. And ever as I went, darker grew my thoughts, till at last I had no hope whatever of finding the white lady: I no longer called her to myself my white lady. Whenever a choice was necessary, I always chose the path which seemed to lead downwards.

At length I began to find that these regions were inhabited. From behind a rock a peal of harsh grating laughter, full of evil humour, rang through my ears, and, looking round, I saw a queer, goblin creature, with a great head and ridiculous features, just such as those described, in German histories and travels, as Kobolds. "What do you want with me?" I said. He pointed at me with a long forefinger, very thick at the root, and sharpened to a point, and answered, "He! he! he! what do you want here?" Then, changing his tone, he continued, with mock humility—"Honoured sir, vouchsafe to withdraw from thy slaves the lustre of thy august presence, for thy slaves cannot support its brightness." A second appeared, and struck in: "You are so big, you keep the sun from us. We can't see for you, and we're so cold." Thereupon arose, on all sides, the most terrific uproar of laughter, from voices like those of children in volume, but scrannel and harsh as those of decrepit age, though, unfortunately, without its weakness. The whole pandemonium of fairy devils, of all varieties of fantastic ugliness, both in form and feature, and of all sizes from one to four feet, seemed to have suddenly assembled about me. At length, after a great babble of talk among themselves, in a language unknown to me, and after seemingly endless gesticulation, consultation, elbow-nudging, and unmitigated peals of laughter, they formed into a circle about one of their number, who scrambled upon a stone, and, much to my surprise, and somewhat to my dismay, began to sing, in a voice corresponding in its nature to his talking one, from beginning to end, the song with which I had brought the light into the eyes of the white lady. He sang the same air too; and, all the time, maintained a face of mock entreaty and worship; accompanying the song with the travestied gestures of one playing on the lute. The whole assembly kept silence, except at the close of every verse, when they roared, and danced, and shouted with laughter, and flung themselves on the ground, in real or pretended convulsions of delight. When he had finished, the singer threw himself from the top of the stone, turning heels over head several times in his descent; and when he did alight, it was on the top of his head, on which he hopped about, making the most grotesque gesticulations with his legs in the air. Inexpressible laughter followed, which broke up in a shower of tiny stones from innumerable hands. They could not materially injure me, although they cut me on the head and face. I attempted to run away, but they all rushed upon me, and, laying hold of every part that afforded a grasp, held me tight. Crowding about me like bees, they shouted an insect-swarm of exasperating speeches up into my face, among which the most frequently recurring were—"You shan't have her; you shan't have her; he! he! he! She's for a better man; how he'll kiss her! how he'll kiss her!"

The galvanic torrent of this battery of malevolence stung to life within me a spark of nobleness, and I said aloud, "Well, if he is a better man, let him have her."

They instantly let go their hold of me, and fell back a step or two, with a whole broadside of grunts and humphs, as of unexpected and disappointed approbation. I made a step or two forward, and a lane was instantly opened for me through the midst of the grinning little antics, who bowed most politely to me on every side as I passed. After I had gone a few yards, I looked back, and saw them all standing quite still, looking after me, like a great school of boys; till suddenly one turned round, and with a loud whoop, rushed into the midst of the others. In an instant, the whole was one writhing and tumbling heap of contortion, reminding me of the live pyramids of intertwined snakes of which travellers make report. As soon as one was worked out of the mass, he bounded off a few paces, and then, with a somersault and a run, threw himself gyrating into the air, and descended with all his weight on the summit of the heaving and struggling chaos of fantastic figures. I left them still busy at this fierce and apparently aimless amusement. And as I went, I sang—

> If a nobler waits for thee,
>
> I will weep aside;

It is well that thou should'st be,

Of the nobler, bride.

For if love builds up the home,

Where the heart is free,

Homeless yet the heart must roam,

That has not found thee.

One must suffer: I, for her

Yield in her my part

Take her, thou art worthier—

Still I be still, my heart!

Gift ungotten! largess high

Of a frustrate will!

But to yield it lovingly

Is a something still.

Then a little song arose of itself in my soul; and I felt for the moment, while it sank sadly within me, as if I was once more walking up and down the white hall of Phantasy in the Fairy Palace. But this lasted no longer than the song; as will be seen.

Do not vex thy violet

Perfume to afford:

Else no odour thou wilt get

From its little hoard.

In thy lady's gracious eyes

Look not thou too long;

Else from them the glory flies,

And thou dost her wrong.

Come not thou too near the maid,

Clasp her not too wild;

Else the splendour is allayed,

And thy heart beguiled.

A crash of laughter, more discordant and deriding than any I had yet heard, invaded my ears. Looking on in the direction of the sound, I saw a little elderly woman, much taller, however, than the goblins I had just left, seated upon a stone by the side of the path. She rose, as I drew near, and came forward to meet me.

She was very plain and commonplace in appearance, without being hideously ugly. Looking up in my face with a stupid sneer, she said: "Isn't it a pity you haven't a pretty girl to walk all alone with you through this sweet country? How different everything would look? wouldn't it? Strange that one can never have what one would like best! How the roses would bloom and all that, even in this infernal hole! wouldn't they, Anodos? Her eyes would light up the old cave, wouldn't they?"

"That depends on who the pretty girl should be," replied I.

"Not so very much matter that," she answered; "look here."

I had turned to go away as I gave my reply, but now I stopped and looked at her. As a rough unsightly bud might suddenly blossom into the most lovely flower; or rather, as a sunbeam bursts through a shapeless cloud, and transfigures the earth; so burst a face of resplendent beauty, as it were through the unsightly visage of the woman, destroying it with light as it dawned through it. A summer sky rose above me, gray with heat; across a shining slumberous landscape, looked from afar the peaks of snow-capped mountains; and down from a great rock beside me fell a sheet of water mad with its own delight.

"Stay with me," she said, lifting up her exquisite face, and looking full in mine.

I drew back. Again the infernal laugh grated upon my ears; again the rocks closed in around me, and the ugly woman looked at me with wicked, mocking hazel eyes.

"You shall have your reward," said she. "You shall see your white lady again."

"That lies not with you," I replied, and turned and left her.

She followed me with shriek upon shriek of laughter, as I went on my way.

I may mention here, that although there was always light enough to see my path and a few yards on every side of me, I never could find out the source of this sad sepulchral illumination.

CHAPTER XVIII

"In the wind's uproar, the sea's raging grim,

And the sighs that are born in him."

HEINE.

"From dreams of bliss shall men awake

One day, but not to weep:

The dreams remain; they only break

The mirror of the sleep."

JEAN PAUL, Hesperus.

How I got through this dreary part of my travels, I do not know. I do not think I was upheld by the hope that any moment the light might break in upon me; for I scarcely thought about that. I went on with a dull endurance, varied by moments of uncontrollable sadness; for more and more the conviction grew upon me that I should never see the white lady again. It may seem strange that one with whom I had held so little communion should have so engrossed my thoughts; but benefits conferred awaken love in some minds, as surely as benefits received in others. Besides being delighted and proud that my songs had called the beautiful creature to life, the same fact caused me to feel a tenderness unspeakable for her, accompanied with a kind of feeling of property in her; for so the goblin Selfishness would reward the angel Love. When to all this is added, an overpowering sense of her beauty, and an unquestioning conviction that this was a true index to inward loveliness, it may be understood how it came to pass that my imagination filled my whole soul with the play of its own multitudinous colours and harmonies around the form which yet stood, a gracious marble radiance, in the midst of its white hall of phantasy. The time passed by unheeded; for my thoughts were busy. Perhaps this was also in part the cause of my needing no food, and never thinking how I should find any, during this subterraneous part of my travels. How long they endured I could not tell, for I had no means of measuring time; and when I looked back, there was such a discrepancy between the decisions of my imagination and my judgment, as to the length of time that had passed, that I was bewildered, and gave up all attempts to arrive at any conclusion on the point.

A gray mist continually gathered behind me. When I looked back towards the past, this mist was the medium through which my eyes had to strain for a vision of what had gone by; and the form of the white lady had receded into an unknown region. At length the country of rock began to close again around me, gradually and slowly narrowing, till I found myself walking in a gallery of rock once more, both sides of which I could touch with my outstretched hands. It narrowed yet, until I was forced to move carefully, in order to avoid striking against the projecting pieces of rock. The roof sank lower and lower, until I was compelled, first to stoop, and then to creep on my hands and knees. It recalled terrible dreams of childhood; but I was not much afraid, because I felt sure that this was my path, and my only hope of leaving Fairy Land, of which I was now almost weary.

At length, on getting past an abrupt turn in the passage, through which I had to force myself, I saw, a few yards ahead of me, the long-forgotten daylight shining through a small opening, to which the path, if path it could now be called, led me. With great difficulty I accomplished these last few yards, and came forth to the day. I stood on the shore of a wintry sea, with a wintry sun just a few feet above its horizon-edge. It was bare, and waste, and gray. Hundreds of hopeless waves rushed constantly shorewards, falling exhausted upon a beach of great loose stones, that seemed to stretch miles and miles in both directions. There was nothing for the eye but mingling shades of gray; nothing for the ear but the rush of the coming, the roar of the breaking, and the moan of the retreating wave. No rock lifted up a sheltering severity above the dreariness around; even that from which I had myself emerged rose scarcely a foot above the opening by which I had reached the dismal day, more dismal even than the tomb I had left. A cold, death-like wind swept across the shore, seeming to issue from a pale mouth of cloud upon the horizon. Sign of life was nowhere visible. I wandered over the stones, up and down the beach, a human imbodiment of the nature around me. The wind increased; its keen waves flowed through my soul; the foam rushed higher up the stones; a few dead stars began to gleam in the east; the sound of the waves grew louder and yet more despairing. A dark curtain of cloud was lifted up, and a pale blue rent shone between its foot and the edge of the sea, out from which rushed an icy storm of frozen wind, that tore the waters into spray as it passed, and flung the billows in raving heaps upon the desolate shore. I could bear it no longer.

"I will not be tortured to death," I cried; "I will meet it half-way. The life within me is yet enough to bear me up to the face of Death, and then I die unconquered."

Before it had grown so dark, I had observed, though without any particular interest, that on one part of the shore a low platform of rock seemed to run out far into the midst of the breaking waters.

Towards this I now went, scrambling over smooth stones, to which scarce even a particle of sea-weed clung; and having found it, I got on it, and followed its direction, as near as I could guess, out into the tumbling chaos. I could hardly keep my feet against the wind and sea. The waves repeatedly all but swept me off my path; but I kept on my way, till I reached the end of the low promontory, which, in the fall of the waves, rose a good many feet above the surface, and, in their rise, was covered with their waters. I stood one moment and gazed into the heaving abyss beneath me; then plunged headlong into the mounting wave below. A blessing, like the kiss of a mother, seemed to alight on my soul; a calm, deeper than that which accompanies a hope deferred, bathed my spirit. I sank far into the waters, and sought not to return. I felt as if once more the great arms of the beech-tree were around me, soothing me after the miseries I had passed through, and telling me, like a little sick child, that I should be better to-morrow. The waters of themselves lifted me, as with loving arms, to the surface. I breathed again, but did not unclose my eyes. I would not look on the wintry sea, and the pitiless gray sky. Thus I floated, till something gently touched me. It was a little boat floating beside me. How it came there I could not tell; but it rose and sank on the waters, and kept touching me in its fall, as if with a human will to let me know that help was by me. It was a little gay-coloured boat, seemingly covered with glistering scales like those of a fish, all of brilliant rainbow hues. I scrambled into it, and lay down in the bottom, with a sense of exquisite repose.

Then I drew over me a rich, heavy, purple cloth that was beside me; and, lying still, knew, by the sound of the waters, that my little bark was fleeting rapidly onwards. Finding, however, none of that stormy motion which the sea had manifested when I beheld it from the shore, I opened my eyes; and, looking first up, saw above me the deep violet sky of a warm southern night; and then, lifting my head, saw that I was sailing fast upon a summer sea, in the last border of a southern twilight. The aureole of the sun yet shot the extreme faint tips of its longest rays above the horizon-waves, and withdrew them not. It was a perpetual twilight. The stars, great and earnest, like children's eyes, bent down lovingly towards the waters; and the reflected stars within seemed to float up, as if longing to meet their embraces. But when I looked down, a new wonder met my view. For, vaguely revealed beneath the wave, I floated above my whole Past. The fields of my childhood flitted by; the halls of my youthful labours; the streets of great cities where I had dwelt; and the assemblies of men and women wherein I had wearied myself seeking for rest. But so indistinct were the visions, that sometimes I thought I was sailing on a shallow sea, and that strange rocks and forests of sea-plants beguiled my eye, sufficiently to be transformed, by the magic of the phantasy, into well-known objects and regions. Yet, at times, a beloved form seemed to lie close beneath me in sleep; and the eyelids would tremble as if about to forsake the conscious eye; and the arms would heave upwards, as if in dreams they sought for a satisfying presence. But these motions might come only from the heaving of the waters between those forms and me. Soon I fell asleep, overcome with fatigue and delight. In dreams of unspeakable joy—of restored friendships; of revived embraces; of love which said it had never died; of faces that had vanished long ago, yet said with smiling lips that they knew nothing of the grave; of pardons implored, and granted with such bursting floods of love, that I was almost glad I had sinned—thus I passed through this wondrous twilight. I awoke with the feeling that I had been kissed and loved to my heart's content; and found that my boat was floating motionless by the grassy shore of a little island.

CHAPTER XIX

"In still rest, in changeless simplicity, I bear,

uninterrupted, the consciousness of the whole of Humanity

within me."—SCHLEIERMACHERS, Monologen.

"... such a sweetness, such a grace,

In all thy speech appear,

That what to th'eye a beauteous face,

That thy tongue is to the ear."

—COWLEY.

The water was deep to the very edge; and I sprang from the little boat upon a soft grassy turf. The island seemed rich with a profusion of all grasses and low flowers. All delicate lowly things were most plentiful; but no trees rose skywards, not even a bush overtopped the tall grasses, except in one place near the cottage I am about to describe, where a few plants of the gum-cistus, which drops every night all the blossoms that the day brings forth, formed a kind of natural arbour. The whole island lay open to the sky and sea. It rose nowhere more than a few feet above the level of the waters, which flowed deep all around its border. Here there seemed to be neither tide nor storm. A sense of persistent calm and fulness arose in the mind at the sight of the slow, pulse-like rise and fall of the deep, clear, unrippled waters against the bank of the island, for shore it could hardly be called, being so much more like the edge of a full, solemn river. As I walked over the grass towards the cottage, which stood at a little distance from the bank, all the flowers of childhood looked at me with perfect child-eyes out of the grass. My heart, softened by the dreams through which it had passed, overflowed in a sad, tender love towards them. They looked to me like children impregnably fortified in a helpless confidence. The sun stood half-way down the western sky, shining very soft and golden; and there grew a second world of shadows amidst the world of grasses and wild flowers.

The cottage was square, with low walls, and a high pyramidal roof thatched with long reeds, of which the withered blossoms hung over all the eaves. It is noticeable that most of the buildings I saw in Fairy Land were cottages. There was no path to a door, nor, indeed, was there any track worn by footsteps in the island.

The cottage rose right out of the smooth turf. It had no windows that I could see; but there was a door in the centre of the side facing me, up to which I went. I knocked, and the sweetest voice I had ever heard said, "Come in." I entered. A bright fire was burning on a hearth in the centre of the earthern floor, and the smoke found its way out at an opening in the centre of the pyramidal roof. Over the fire hung a little pot, and over the pot bent a woman-face, the most wonderful, I thought, that I had ever beheld. For it was older than any countenance I had ever looked upon. There was not a spot in which a wrinkle could lie, where a wrinkle lay not. And the skin was ancient and brown, like old parchment. The woman's form was tall and spare: and when she stood up to welcome me, I saw that she was straight as an arrow. Could that voice of sweetness have issued from those lips of age? Mild as they were, could they be the portals whence flowed such melody? But the moment I saw her eyes, I no longer wondered at her voice: they were absolutely young—those of a woman of five-and-twenty, large, and of a clear gray. Wrinkles had beset them all about; the eyelids themselves were old, and heavy, and worn; but the eyes were very incarnations of soft light. She held out her hand to me, and the voice of sweetness again greeted me, with the single word, "Welcome." She set an old wooden chair for me, near the fire, and went on with her cooking. A wondrous sense of refuge and repose came upon me. I felt like a boy who has got home from school, miles across the hills, through a heavy storm of wind and snow. Almost, as I gazed on her, I sprang from my seat to kiss those old lips. And when, having finished her cooking, she brought some of the dish she had prepared, and set it on a little table by me, covered with a snow-white cloth, I could not help laying my head on her bosom, and bursting into happy tears. She put her arms round me, saying, "Poor child; poor child!"

As I continued to weep, she gently disengaged herself, and, taking a spoon, put some of the food (I did not know what it was) to my lips, entreating me most endearingly to swallow it. To please her, I made an effort, and succeeded. She went on feeding me like a baby, with one arm round me, till I looked up in her face and smiled: then she gave me the spoon and told me to eat, for it would do me good. I obeyed her, and found myself wonderfully refreshed. Then she drew near the fire an old-fashioned couch that was in the cottage, and making me lie down upon it, sat at my feet, and began to sing. Amazing store of old ballads rippled from her lips, over the pebbles of ancient tunes; and the voice that sang was sweet as the voice of a tuneful maiden that singeth ever from very fulness of song. The songs were almost all sad, but with a sound of comfort. One I can faintly recall. It was something like this:

> *Sir Aglovaile through the churchyard rode;*
>
> *Sing, All alone I lie:*
>
> *Little recked he where'er he yode,*
>
> *All alone, up in the sky.*
>
> *Swerved his courser, and plunged with fear*
>
> *All alone i lie:*
>
> *His cry might have wakened the dead men near,*
>
> *All alone, up in the sky.*
>
> *The very dead that lay at his feet,*
>
> *Lapt in the mouldy winding-sheet.*
>
> *But he curbed him and spurred him, until he stood*
>
> *Still in his place, like a horse of wood,*

288

With nostrils uplift, and eyes wide and wan;
  But the sweat in streams from his fetlocks ran.

A ghost grew out of the shadowy air,
  And sat in the midst of her moony hair.

In her gleamy hair she sat and wept;
  In the dreamful moon they lay and slept;

The shadows above, and the bodies below,
  Lay and slept in the moonbeams slow.

And she sang, like the moan of an autumn wind
  Over the stubble left behind:

  Alas, how easily things go wrong!
    A sigh too much, or a kiss too long,
  And there follows a mist and a weeping rain,
    And life is never the same again.

  Alas, how hardly things go right!
    'Tis hard to watch on a summer night,
  For the sigh will come and the kiss will stay,
    And the summer night is a winter day.

"Oh, lovely ghosts my heart is woes
  To see thee weeping and wailing so.

Oh, lovely ghost," said the fearless knight,

"Can the sword of a warrior set it right?

Or prayer of bedesman, praying mild,

As a cup of water a feverish child,

Sooth thee at last, in dreamless mood

To sleep the sleep a dead lady should?

Thine eyes they fill me with longing sore,

As if I had known thee for evermore.

Oh, lovely ghost, I could leave the day

To sit with thee in the moon away

If thou wouldst trust me, and lay thy head

To rest on a bosom that is not dead."

The lady sprang up with a strange ghost-cry,

And she flung her white ghost-arms on high:

And she laughed a laugh that was not gay,

And it lengthened out till it died away;

And the dead beneath turned and moaned,

And the yew-trees above they shuddered and groaned.

"Will he love me twice with a love that is vain?

Will he kill the poor ghost yet again?

I thought thou wert good; but I said, and wept:

'Can I have dreamed who have not slept?'

And I knew, alas! or ever I would,
Whether I dreamed, or thou wert good.

When my baby died, my brain grew wild.
I awoke, and found I was with my child."

"If thou art the ghost of my Adelaide,
How is it? Thou wert but a village maid,

And thou seemest an angel lady white,
Though thin, and wan, and past delight."

The lady smiled a flickering smile,
And she pressed her temples hard the while.

"Thou seest that Death for a woman can
Do more than knighthood for a man."

"But show me the child thou callest mine,
Is she out to-night in the ghost's sunshine?"

"In St. Peter's Church she is playing on,
At hide-and-seek, with Apostle John.

When the moonbeams right through the window go,
Where the twelve are standing in glorious show,

She says the rest of them do not stir,

But one comes down to play with her.

Then I can go where I list, and weep,
For good St. John my child will keep."

"Thy beauty filleth the very air,
Never saw I a woman so fair."

"Come, if thou darest, and sit by my side;
But do not touch me, or woe will betide.

Alas, I am weak: I might well know
This gladness betokens some further woe.

Yet come. It will come. I will bear it. I can.
For thou lovest me yet—though but as a man."

The knight dismounted in earnest speed;
Away through the tombstones thundered the steed,

And fell by the outer wall, and died.
But the knight he kneeled by the lady's side;

Kneeled beside her in wondrous bliss,
Rapt in an everlasting kiss:

Though never his lips come the lady nigh,
And his eyes alone on her beauty lie.

All the night long, till the cock crew loud,

He kneeled by the lady, lapt in her shroud.

And what they said, I may not say:
Dead night was sweeter than living day.

How she made him so blissful glad
Who made her and found her so ghostly sad,

I may not tell; but it needs no touch
To make them blessed who love so much.

"Come every night, my ghost, to me;
And one night I will come to thee.

'Tis good to have a ghostly wife:
She will not tremble at clang of strife;

She will only hearken, amid the din,
Behind the door, if he cometh in."

And this is how Sir Aglovaile
Often walked in the moonlight pale.

And oft when the crescent but thinned the gloom,
Full orbed moonlight filled his room;

And through beneath his chamber door,
Fell a ghostly gleam on the outer floor;

And they that passed, in fear averred

That murmured words they often heard.

'Twas then that the eastern crescent shone
Through the chancel window, and good St. John

Played with the ghost-child all the night,
And the mother was free till the morning light,

And sped through the dawning night, to stay
With Aglovaile till the break of day.

And their love was a rapture, lone and high,
And dumb as the moon in the topmost sky.

One night Sir Aglovaile, weary, slept
And dreamed a dream wherein he wept.

A warrior he was, not often wept he,
But this night he wept full bitterly.

He woke—beside him the ghost-girl shone
Out of the dark: 'twas the eve of St. John.

He had dreamed a dream of a still, dark wood,
Where the maiden of old beside him stood;

But a mist came down, and caught her away,
And he sought her in vain through the pathless day,

Till he wept with the grief that can do no more,

And thought he had dreamt the dream before.

From bursting heart the weeping flowed on;
And lo! beside him the ghost-girl shone;

Shone like the light on a harbour's breast,
Over the sea of his dream's unrest;

Shone like the wondrous, nameless boon,
That the heart seeks ever, night or noon:

Warnings forgotten, when needed most,
He clasped to his bosom the radiant ghost.

She wailed aloud, and faded, and sank.
With upturn'd white face, cold and blank,

In his arms lay the corpse of the maiden pale,
And she came no more to Sir Aglovaile.

Only a voice, when winds were wild,
Sobbed and wailed like a chidden child.

Alas, how easily things go wrong!
A sigh too much, or a kiss too long,
And there follows a mist and a weeping rain,
And life is never the same again.

This was one of the simplest of her songs, which, perhaps, is the cause of my being able to remember it better than most of the others. While she sung, I was in Elysium, with the sense of a rich soul upholding, embracing, and overhanging mine, full of all plenty and bounty. I felt as if she could give me everything I wanted; as if I should never wish to leave her, but would be content to be sung to and fed by her, day after day, as years rolled by. At last I fell asleep while she sang.

When I awoke, I knew not whether it was night or day. The fire had sunk to a few red embers, which just gave light enough to show me the woman standing a few feet from me, with her back towards me, facing the door by which I had entered. She was weeping, but very gently and plentifully. The tears seemed to come freely from her heart. Thus she stood for a few minutes; then, slowly turning at right angles to her former position, she faced another of the four sides of the cottage. I now observed, for the first time, that here was a door likewise; and that, indeed, there was one in the centre of every side of the cottage.

When she looked towards the second door, her tears ceased to flow, but sighs took their place. She often closed her eyes as she stood; and every time she closed her eyes, a gentle sigh seemed to be born in her heart, and to escape at her lips. But when her eyes were open, her sighs were deep and very sad, and shook her whole frame. Then she turned towards the third door, and a cry as of fear or suppressed pain broke from her; but she seemed to hearten herself against the dismay, and to front it steadily; for, although I often heard a slight cry, and sometimes a moan, yet she never moved or bent her head, and I felt sure that her eyes never closed. Then she turned to the fourth door, and I saw her shudder, and then stand still as a statue; till at last she turned towards me and approached the fire. I saw that her face was white as death. But she gave one look upwards, and smiled the sweetest, most child-innocent smile; then heaped fresh wood on the fire, and, sitting down by the blaze, drew her wheel near her, and began to spin. While she spun, she murmured a low strange song, to which the hum of the wheel made a kind of infinite symphony. At length she paused in her spinning and singing, and glanced towards me, like a mother who looks whether or not her child gives signs of waking. She smiled when she saw that my eyes were open. I asked her whether it was day yet. She answered, "It is always day here, so long as I keep my fire burning."

I felt wonderfully refreshed; and a great desire to see more of the island awoke within me. I rose, and saying that I wished to look about me, went towards the door by which I had entered.

"Stay a moment," said my hostess, with some trepidation in her voice. "Listen to me. You will not see what you expect when you go out of that door. Only remember this: whenever you wish to come back to me, enter wherever you see this mark."

She held up her left hand between me and the fire. Upon the palm, which appeared almost transparent, I saw, in dark red, a mark like this —> which I took care to fix in my mind.

She then kissed me, and bade me good-bye with a solemnity that awed me; and bewildered me too, seeing I was only going out for a little ramble in an island, which I did not believe larger than could easily be compassed in a few hours' walk at most. As I went she resumed her spinning.

I opened the door, and stepped out. The moment my foot touched the smooth sward, I seemed to issue from the door of an old barn on my father's estate, where, in the hot afternoons, I used to go and lie amongst the straw, and read. It seemed to me now that I had been asleep there. At a little distance in the field, I saw two of my brothers at play. The moment they caught sight of me, they called out to me to come and join them, which I did; and we played together as we had done years ago, till the red sun went down in the west, and the gray fog began to rise from the river. Then we went home together with a strange happiness. As we went, we heard the continually renewed larum of a landrail in the long grass. One of my brothers and I separated to a little distance, and each commenced running towards the part whence the sound appeared to come, in the hope of approaching the spot where the bird was, and so getting at least a sight of it, if we should not be able to capture the little creature. My father's voice recalled us from trampling down the rich long grass, soon to be cut down and laid aside for the winter. I had quite forgotten all about Fairy Land, and the wonderful old woman, and the curious red mark.

My favourite brother and I shared the same bed. Some childish dispute arose between us; and our last words, ere we fell asleep, were not of kindness, notwithstanding the pleasures of the day. When I woke in the morning, I missed him. He had risen early, and had gone to bathe in the river. In another hour, he was brought home drowned. Alas! alas! if we had only gone to sleep as usual, the one with his arm about the other! Amidst the horror of the moment, a strange conviction flashed across my mind, that I had gone through the very same once before.

I rushed out of the house, I knew not why, sobbing and crying bitterly. I ran through the fields in aimless distress, till, passing the old barn, I caught sight of a red mark on the door. The merest trifles sometimes rivet the attention in the deepest misery; the intellect has so little to do with grief. I went up to look at this mark, which I did not remember ever to have seen before. As I looked at it, I thought I would go in and lie down amongst the straw, for I was very weary with running about and weeping. I opened the door; and there in the cottage sat the old woman as I had left her, at her spinning-wheel.

"I did not expect you quite so soon," she said, as I shut the door behind me. I went up to the couch, and threw myself on it with that fatigue wherewith one awakes from a feverish dream of hopeless grief.

The old woman sang:

> *The great sun, benighted,*
>> *May faint from the sky;*
> *But love, once uplighted,*
>> *Will never more die.*

> *Form, with its brightness,*
>> *From eyes will depart:*
> *It walketh, in whiteness,*
>> *The halls of the heart.*

Ere she had ceased singing, my courage had returned. I started from the couch, and, without taking leave of the old woman, opened the door of Sighs, and sprang into what should appear.

I stood in a lordly hall, where, by a blazing fire on the hearth, sat a lady, waiting, I knew, for some one long desired. A mirror was near me, but I saw that my form had no place within its depths, so I feared not that I should be seen. The lady wonderfully resembled my marble lady, but was altogether of the daughters of men, and I could not tell whether or not it was she.

It was not for me she waited. The tramp of a great horse rang through the court without. It ceased, and the clang of armour told that his rider alighted, and the sound of his ringing heels approached the hall. The door opened; but the lady waited, for she would meet her lord alone. He strode in: she flew like a home-bound dove into his arms, and nestled on the hard steel. It was the knight of the soiled armour. But now the armour shone like polished glass; and strange to tell, though the mirror reflected not my form, I saw a dim shadow of myself in the shining steel.

"O my beloved, thou art come, and I am blessed."

Her soft fingers speedily overcame the hard clasp of his helmet; one by one she undid the buckles of his armour; and she toiled under the weight of the mail, as she would carry it aside. Then she unclasped his greaves, and unbuckled his spurs; and once more she sprang into his arms, and laid her head where she could now feel the beating of his heart. Then she disengaged herself from his embrace, and, moving back a step or two, gazed at him. He stood there a mighty form, crowned with a noble head, where all sadness had disappeared, or had been absorbed in solemn purpose. Yet I suppose that he looked more thoughtful than the lady had expected to see him, for she did not renew her caresses, although his face glowed with love, and the few words he spoke were as mighty deeds for strength; but she led him towards the hearth, and seated him in an ancient chair, and set wine before him, and sat at his feet.

"I am sad," he said, "when I think of the youth whom I met twice in the forests of Fairy Land; and who, you say, twice, with his songs, roused you from the death-sleep of an evil enchantment. There was something noble in him, but it was a nobleness of thought, and not of deed. He may yet perish of vile fear."

"Ah!" returned the lady, "you saved him once, and for that I thank you; for may I not say that I somewhat loved him? But tell me how you fared, when you struck your battle-axe into the ash-tree, and he came and found you; for so much of the story you had told me, when the beggar-child came and took you away."

"As soon as I saw him," rejoined the knight, "I knew that earthly arms availed not against such as he; and that my soul must meet him in its naked strength. So I unclasped my helm, and flung it on the ground; and, holding my good axe yet in my hand, gazed at him with steady eyes. On he came, a horror indeed, but I did not flinch. Endurance must conquer, where force could not reach. He came nearer and nearer, till the ghastly face was close to mine. A shudder as of death ran through me; but I think I did not move, for he seemed to quail, and retreated. As soon as he gave back, I struck one more sturdy blow on the stem of his tree, that the forest rang; and then looked at him again. He writhed and grinned with rage and apparent pain, and again approached me, but retreated sooner than before. I heeded him no more, but hewed with a will at the tree, till the trunk creaked, and the head bowed, and with a crash it fell to the earth. Then I looked up from my labour, and lo! the spectre had vanished, and I saw him no more; nor ever in my wanderings have I heard of him again."

"Well struck! well withstood! my hero," said the lady.

"But," said the knight, somewhat troubled, "dost thou love the youth still?"

"Ah!" she replied, "how can I help it? He woke me from worse than death; he loved me. I had never been for thee, if he had not sought me first. But I love him not as I love thee. He was but the moon of my night; thou art the sun of my day, O beloved."

"Thou art right," returned the noble man. "It were hard, indeed, not to have some love in return for such a gift as he hath given thee. I, too, owe him more than words can speak."

Humbled before them, with an aching and desolate heart, I yet could not restrain my words:

"Let me, then, be the moon of thy night still, O woman! And when thy day is beclouded, as the fairest days will be, let some song of mine comfort thee, as an old, withered, half-forgotten thing, that belongs to an ancient mournful hour of uncompleted birth, which yet was beautiful in its time."

They sat silent, and I almost thought they were listening. The colour of the lady's eyes grew deeper and deeper; the slow tears grew, and filled them, and overflowed. They rose, and passed, hand in hand, close to where I stood; and each looked towards me in passing. Then they disappeared through a door which closed behind them; but, ere it closed, I saw that the room into which it opened was a rich chamber, hung with gorgeous arras. I stood with an ocean of sighs frozen in my bosom. I could remain no longer. She was near me, and I could not see her; near me in the arms of one loved better than I, and I would not see her, and I would not be by her. But how to escape from the nearness of the best beloved? I had not this time forgotten the mark; for the fact that I could not enter the sphere of these living beings kept me aware that, for me, I moved in a vision, while they moved in life. I looked all about for the mark, but could see it nowhere; for I avoided looking just where it was. There the dull red cipher glowed, on the very door of their secret chamber. Struck with agony, I dashed it open, and fell at the feet of the ancient woman, who still spun on, the whole dissolved ocean of my sighs bursting from me in a storm of tearless sobs. Whether I fainted or slept, I do not know; but, as I returned to consciousness, before I seemed to have power to move, I heard the woman singing, and could distinguish the words:

> *O light of dead and of dying days!*
>
> *O Love! in thy glory go,*
>
> *In a rosy mist and a moony maze,*
>
> *O'er the pathless peaks of snow.*

> *But what is left for the cold gray soul,*
>
> *That moans like a wounded dove?*
>
> *One wine is left in the broken bowl!—*
>
> *'Tis—To love, and love and love.*

Now I could weep. When she saw me weeping, she sang:

> *Better to sit at the waters' birth,*
>
> *Than a sea of waves to win;*
>
> *To live in the love that floweth forth,*
>
> *Than the love that cometh in.*
>
> *Be thy heart a well of love, my child,*
>
> *Flowing, and free, and sure;*
>
> *For a cistern of love, though undefiled,*
>
> *Keeps not the spirit pure.*

I rose from the earth, loving the white lady as I had never loved her before.

Then I walked up to the door of Dismay, and opened it, and went out. And lo! I came forth upon a crowded street, where men and women went to and fro in multitudes. I knew it well; and, turning to one hand, walked sadly along the pavement. Suddenly I saw approaching me, a little way off, a form well known to me (well-known!—alas, how weak the word!) in the years when I thought my boyhood was left behind, and shortly before I entered the realm of Fairy Land. Wrong and Sorrow had gone together, hand-in-hand as it is well they do.

Unchangeably dear was that face. It lay in my heart as a child lies in its own white bed; but I could not meet her.

"Anything but that," I said, and, turning aside, sprang up the steps to a door, on which I fancied I saw the mystic sign. I entered—not the mysterious cottage, but her home. I rushed wildly on, and stood by the door of her room.

"She is out," I said, "I will see the old room once more."

I opened the door gently, and stood in a great solemn church. A deep-toned bell, whose sounds throbbed and echoed and swam through the empty building, struck the hour of midnight. The moon shone through the windows of the clerestory, and enough of the ghostly radiance was diffused through the church to let me see, walking with a stately, yet somewhat trailing and stumbling step, down the opposite aisle, for I stood in one of the transepts, a figure dressed in a white robe, whether for the night, or for that longer night which lies too deep for the day, I could not tell. Was it she? and was this her chamber? I crossed the church, and followed. The figure stopped, seemed to ascend as it were a high bed, and lay down. I reached the place where it lay, glimmering white. The bed was a tomb. The light was too ghostly to see clearly, but I passed my hand over the face and the hands and the feet, which were all bare. They were cold—they were marble, but I knew them. It grew dark. I turned to retrace my steps, but found, ere long, that I had wandered into what seemed a little chapel. I groped about, seeking the door. Everything I touched belonged to the dead. My hands fell on the cold effigy of a knight who lay with his legs crossed and his sword broken beside him. He lay in his noble rest, and I lived on in ignoble strife. I felt for the left hand and a certain finger; I found there the ring I knew: he was one of my own ancestors. I was in the chapel over the burial-vault of my race. I called aloud: "If any of the dead are moving here, let them take pity upon me, for I, alas! am still alive; and let some dead woman comfort me, for I am a stranger in the land of the dead, and see no light." A warm kiss alighted on my lips through the dark. And I said, "The dead kiss well; I will not be afraid." And a great hand was reached out of the dark, and grasped mine for a moment, mightily and tenderly. I said to myself: "The veil between, though very dark, is very thin."

Groping my way further, I stumbled over the heavy stone that covered the entrance of the vault: and, in stumbling, descried upon the stone the mark, glowing in red fire. I caught the great ring. All my effort could not have moved the huge slab; but it opened the door of the cottage, and I threw myself once more, pale and speechless, on the couch beside the ancient dame. She sang once more:

> Thou dreamest: on a rock thou art,
>> High o'er the broken wave;
> Thou fallest with a fearful start
>> But not into thy grave;
> For, waking in the morning's light,
>> Thou smilest at the vanished night
>
> So wilt thou sink, all pale and dumb,
>> Into the fainting gloom;
> But ere the coming terrors come,
>> Thou wak'st—where is the tomb?
> Thou wak'st—the dead ones smile above,
>> With hovering arms of sleepless love.

She paused; then sang again:

> We weep for gladness, weep for grief;
>> The tears they are the same;
> We sigh for longing, and relief;
>> The sighs have but one name,
>
> And mingled in the dying strife,
>> Are moans that are not sad
> The pangs of death are throbs of life,
>> Its sighs are sometimes glad.

The face is very strange and white:

It is Earth's only spot

That feebly flickers back the light

The living seeth not.

I fell asleep, and slept a dreamless sleep, for I know not how long. When I awoke, I found that my hostess had moved from where she had been sitting, and now sat between me and the fourth door.

I guessed that her design was to prevent my entering there. I sprang from the couch, and darted past her to the door. I opened it at once and went out. All I remember is a cry of distress from the woman: "Don't go there, my child! Don't go there!" But I was gone.

I knew nothing more; or, if I did, I had forgot it all when I awoke to consciousness, lying on the floor of the cottage, with my head in the lap of the woman, who was weeping over me, and stroking my hair with both hands, talking to me as a mother might talk to a sick and sleeping, or a dead child. As soon as I looked up and saw her, she smiled through her tears; smiled with withered face and young eyes, till her countenance was irradiated with the light of the smile. Then she bathed my head and face and hands in an icy cold, colourless liquid, which smelt a little of damp earth. Immediately I was able to sit up. She rose and put some food before me. When I had eaten, she said: "Listen to me, my child. You must leave me directly!"

"Leave you!" I said. "I am so happy with you. I never was so happy in my life."

"But you must go," she rejoined sadly. "Listen! What do you hear?"

"I hear the sound as of a great throbbing of water."

"Ah! you do hear it? Well, I had to go through that door—the door of the Timeless" (and she shuddered as she pointed to the fourth door)—"to find you; for if I had not gone, you would never have entered again; and because I went, the waters around my cottage will rise and rise, and flow and come, till they build a great firmament of waters over my dwelling. But as long as I keep my fire burning, they cannot enter. I have fuel enough for years; and after one year they will sink away again, and be just as they were before you came. I have not been buried for a hundred years now." And she smiled and wept.

"Alas! alas!" I cried. "I have brought this evil on the best and kindest of friends, who has filled my heart with great gifts."

"Do not think of that," she rejoined. "I can bear it very well. You will come back to me some day, I know. But I beg you, for my sake, my dear child, to do one thing. In whatever sorrow you may be, however inconsolable and irremediable it may appear, believe me that the old woman in the cottage, with the young eyes" (and she smiled), "knows something, though she must not always tell it, that would quite satisfy you about it, even in the worst moments of your distress. Now you must go."

"But how can I go, if the waters are all about, and if the doors all lead into other regions and other worlds?"

"This is not an island," she replied; "but is joined to the land by a narrow neck; and for the door, I will lead you myself through the right one."

She took my hand, and led me through the third door; whereupon I found myself standing in the deep grassy turf on which I had landed from the little boat, but upon the opposite side of the cottage. She pointed out the direction I must take, to find the isthmus and escape the rising waters.

Then putting her arms around me, she held me to her bosom; and as I kissed her, I felt as if I were leaving my mother for the first time, and could not help weeping bitterly. At length she gently pushed me away, and with the words, "Go, my son, and do something worth doing," turned back, and, entering the cottage, closed the door behind her. I felt very desolate as I went.

306

CHAPTER XX

"Thou hadst no fame; that which thou didst like good

Was but thy appetite that swayed thy blood

For that time to the best; for as a blast

That through a house comes, usually doth cast

Things out of order, yet by chance may come

And blow some one thing to his proper room,

So did thy appetite, and not thy zeal,

Sway thee by chance to do some one thing well."

FLETCHER'S *Faithful Shepherdess.*

"The noble hart that harbours vertuous thought

And is with childe of glorious great intent,

Can never rest, until it forth have brought

Th' eternall brood of glorie excellent."

SPENSER, *The Faerie Queene.*

I had not gone very far before I felt that the turf beneath my feet was soaked with the rising waters. But I reached the isthmus in safety. It was rocky, and so much higher than the level of the peninsula, that I had plenty of time to cross. I saw on each side of me the water rising rapidly, altogether without wind, or violent motion, or broken waves, but as if a slow strong fire were glowing beneath it. Ascending a steep acclivity, I found myself at last in an open, rocky country. After travelling for some hours, as nearly in a straight line as I could, I arrived at a lonely tower, built on the top of a little hill, which overlooked the whole neighbouring country. As I approached,

I heard the clang of an anvil; and so rapid were the blows, that I despaired of making myself heard till a pause in the work should ensue. It was some minutes before a cessation took place; but when it did, I knocked loudly, and had not long to wait; for, a moment after, the door was partly opened by a noble-looking youth, half-undressed, glowing with heat, and begrimed with the blackness of the forge. In one hand he held a sword, so lately from the furnace that it yet shone with a dull fire. As soon as he saw me, he threw the door wide open, and standing aside, invited me very cordially to enter. I did so; when he shut and bolted the door most carefully, and then led the way inwards. He brought me into a rude hall, which seemed to occupy almost the whole of the ground floor of the little tower, and which I saw was now being used as a workshop. A huge fire roared on the hearth, beside which was an anvil. By the anvil stood, in similar undress, and in a waiting attitude, hammer in hand, a second youth, tall as the former, but far more slightly built. Reversing the usual course of perception in such meetings, I thought them, at first sight, very unlike; and at the second glance, knew that they were brothers. The former, and apparently the elder, was muscular and dark, with curling hair, and large hazel eyes, which sometimes grew wondrously soft. The second was slender and fair, yet with a countenance like an eagle, and an eye which, though pale blue, shone with an almost fierce expression. He stood erect, as if looking from a lofty mountain crag, over a vast plain outstretched below. As soon as we entered the hall, the elder turned to me, and I saw that a glow of satisfaction shone on both their faces. To my surprise and great pleasure, he addressed me thus:

"Brother, will you sit by the fire and rest, till we finish this part of our work?"

I signified my assent; and, resolved to await any disclosure they might be inclined to make, seated myself in silence near the hearth.

The elder brother then laid the sword in the fire, covered it well over, and when it had attained a sufficient degree of heat, drew it out and laid it on the anvil, moving it carefully about, while the younger, with a succession of quick smart blows, appeared either to be welding it, or hammering one part of it to a consenting shape with the rest. Having finished, they laid it carefully in the fire; and, when it was very hot indeed, plunged it into a vessel full of some liquid, whence a blue flame sprang upwards, as the glowing steel entered.

There they left it; and drawing two stools to the fire, sat down, one on each side of me.

"We are very glad to see you, brother. We have been expecting you for some days," said the dark-haired youth.

"I am proud to be called your brother," I rejoined; "and you will not think I refuse the name, if I desire to know why you honour me with it?"

"Ah! then he does not know about it," said the younger. "We thought you had known of the bond betwixt us, and the work we have to do together. You must tell him, brother, from the first."

So the elder began:

"Our father is king of this country. Before we were born, three giant brothers had appeared in the land. No one knew exactly when, and no one had the least idea whence they came. They took possession of a ruined castle that had stood unchanged and unoccupied within the memory of any of the country people. The vaults of this castle had remained uninjured by time, and these, I presume, they made use of at first. They were rarely seen, and never offered the least injury to any one; so that they were regarded in the neighbourhood as at least perfectly harmless, if not rather benevolent beings. But it began to be observed, that the old castle had assumed somehow or other, no one knew when or how, a somewhat different look from what it used to have. Not only were several breaches in the lower part of the walls built up, but actually some of the battlements which yet stood, had been repaired, apparently to prevent them from falling into worse decay, while the more important parts were being restored. Of course, every one supposed the giants must have a hand in the work, but no one ever saw them engaged in it. The peasants became yet more uneasy, after one, who had concealed himself, and watched all night, in the neighbourhood of the castle, reported that he had seen, in full moonlight, the three huge giants working with might and main, all night long, restoring to their former position some massive stones, formerly steps of a grand turnpike stair, a great portion of which had long since fallen, along with part of the wall of the round tower in which it had been built. This wall they were completing, foot by foot, along with the stair. But the people said they had no just pretext for interfering: although the real reason for letting the giants alone was, that everybody was far too much afraid of them to interrupt them.

"At length, with the help of a neighbouring quarry, the whole of the external wall of the castle was finished. And now the country folks were in greater fear than before. But for several years the giants remained very peaceful. The reason of this was afterwards supposed to be the fact, that they were distantly related to several good people in the country; for, as long as these lived, they remained quiet; but as soon as they were all dead the real nature of the giants broke out. Having completed the outside of their castle, they proceeded, by spoiling the country houses around them, to make a quiet luxurious provision for their comfort within. Affairs reached such a pass, that the news of their robberies came to my father's ears; but he, alas! was so crippled in his resources, by a war he was carrying on with a neighbouring prince, that he could only spare a very few men, to attempt the capture of their stronghold. Upon these the giants issued in the night, and slew every man of them. And now, grown bolder by success and impunity, they no longer confined their depredations to property, but began to seize the persons of their distinguished neighbours, knights and ladies, and hold them in durance, the misery of which was heightened by all manner of indignity, until they were redeemed by their friends, at an exorbitant ransom. Many knights have adventured their overthrow, but to their own instead; for they have all been slain, or captured, or forced to make a hasty retreat. To crown their enormities, if any man now attempts their destruction, they, immediately upon his defeat, put one or more of their captives to a shameful death, on a turret in sight of all passers-by; so that they have been much less molested of late; and we, although we have burned, for years, to attack these demons and destroy them, dared not, for the sake of their captives, risk the adventure, before we should have reached at least our earliest manhood. Now, however, we are preparing for the attempt; and the grounds of this preparation are

310

these. Having only the resolution, and not the experience necessary for the undertaking, we went and consulted a lonely woman of wisdom, who lives not very far from here, in the direction of the quarter from which you have come. She received us most kindly, and gave us what seems to us the best of advice. She first inquired what experience we had had in arms. We told her we had been well exercised from our boyhood, and for some years had kept ourselves in constant practice, with a view to this necessity.

"'But you have not actually fought for life and death?' said she.

"We were forced to confess we had not.

"'So much the better in some respects,' she replied. 'Now listen to me. Go first and work with an armourer, for as long time as you find needful to obtain a knowledge of his craft; which will not be long, seeing your hearts will be all in the work. Then go to some lonely tower, you two alone. Receive no visits from man or woman. There forge for yourselves every piece of armour that you wish to wear, or to use, in your coming encounter. And keep up your exercises. As, however, two of you can be no match for the three giants, I will find you, if I can, a third brother, who will take on himself the third share of the fight, and the preparation. Indeed, I have already seen one who will, I think, be the very man for your fellowship, but it will be some time before he comes to me. He is wandering now without an aim. I will show him to you in a glass, and, when he comes, you will know him at once. If he will share your endeavours, you must teach him all you know, and he will repay you well, in present song, and in future deeds.'

"She opened the door of a curious old cabinet that stood in the room. On the inside of this door was an oval convex mirror. Looking in it for some time, we at length saw reflected the place where we stood, and the old dame seated in her chair. Our forms were not reflected. But at the feet of the dame lay a young man, yourself, weeping.

"'Surely this youth will not serve our ends,' said I, 'for he weeps.'

"The old woman smiled. 'Past tears are present strength,' said she.

"'Oh!' said my brother, 'I saw you weep once over an eagle you shot.'

311

"'That was because it was so like you, brother,' I replied; 'but indeed, this youth may have better cause for tears than that—I was wrong.'

"'Wait a while,' said the woman; 'if I mistake not, he will make you weep till your tears are dry for ever. Tears are the only cure for weeping. And you may have need of the cure, before you go forth to fight the giants. You must wait for him, in your tower, till he comes.'

"Now if you will join us, we will soon teach you to make your armour; and we will fight together, and work together, and love each other as never three loved before. And you will sing to us, will you not?"

"That I will, when I can," I answered; "but it is only at times that the power of song comes upon me. For that I must wait; but I have a feeling that if I work well, song will not be far off to enliven the labour."

This was all the compact made: the brothers required nothing more, and I did not think of giving anything more. I rose, and threw off my upper garments.

"I know the uses of the sword," I said. "I am ashamed of my white hands beside yours so nobly soiled and hard; but that shame will soon be wiped away."

"No, no; we will not work to-day. Rest is as needful as toil. Bring the wine, brother; it is your turn to serve to-day."

The younger brother soon covered a table with rough viands, but good wine; and we ate and drank heartily, beside our work. Before the meal was over, I had learned all their story. Each had something in his heart which made the conviction, that he would victoriously perish in the coming conflict, a real sorrow to him. Otherwise they thought they would have lived enough. The causes of their trouble were respectively these:

While they wrought with an armourer, in a city famed for workmanship in steel and silver, the elder had fallen in love with a lady as far beneath him in real rank, as she was above the station he had as apprentice to an armourer. Nor did he seek to further his suit by discovering himself; but there was simply so much manhood about him, that no one ever thought of rank when in his company. This is what his brother said about it. The lady could not help loving him in return. He told her when he left her, that he had a perilous adventure before him, and that when it was achieved, she would either see him return to claim her, or hear that he had died with honour. The younger brother's grief arose from the fact, that, if they were both slain, his old father, the king, would be childless. His love for his father was so exceeding, that to one unable to sympathise with it, it would have appeared extravagant. Both loved him equally at heart; but the love of the younger had been more developed, because his thoughts and anxieties had not been otherwise occupied. When at home, he had been his constant companion; and, of late, had ministered to the infirmities of his growing age. The youth was never weary of listening to the tales of his sire's youthful adventures; and had not yet in the smallest degree lost the conviction, that his father was the greatest man in the world. The grandest triumph possible to his conception was, to return to his father, laden with the spoils of one of the hated giants. But they both were in some dread, lest the thought of the loneliness of these two might occur to them, in the moment when decision was most necessary, and disturb, in some degree, the self-possession requisite for the success of their attempt. For, as I have said, they were yet untried in actual conflict. "Now," thought I, "I see to what the powers of my gift must minister." For my own part, I did not dread death, for I had nothing to care to live for; but I dreaded the encounter because of the responsibility connected with it. I resolved however to work hard, and thus grow cool, and quick, and forceful.

The time passed away in work and song, in talk and ramble, in friendly fight and brotherly aid. I would not forge for myself armour of heavy mail like theirs, for I was not so powerful as they, and depended more for any success I might secure, upon nimbleness of motion, certainty of eye, and ready response of hand. Therefore I began to make for myself a shirt of steel plates and rings; which work, while more troublesome, was better suited to me than the heavier labour. Much assistance did the brothers give me, even after, by their instructions, I was able to make some progress alone. Their work was in a moment abandoned, to render any required aid to mine. As the old woman had promised, I tried to repay them with song; and many were the tears they both shed over my ballads and dirges. The songs they liked best to hear were two which I made for them. They were not half so good as many others I knew, especially some I had learned from the wise woman in the cottage; but what comes nearest to our needs we like the best.

I   *The king sat on his throne*

       Glowing in gold and red;

   The crown in his right hand shone,

      And the gray hairs crowned his head.

    His only son walks in,

      And in walls of steel he stands:

   Make me, O father, strong to win,

     With the blessing of holy hands."

    He knelt before his sire,

      Who blessed him with feeble smile

   His eyes shone out with a kingly fire,

     But his old lips quivered the while.

  "Go to the fight, my son,

     Bring back the giant's head;

And the crown with which my brows have done,

    Shall glitter on thine instead."

  "My father, I seek no crowns,

    But unspoken praise from thee;

  For thy people's good, and thy renown,

I will die to set them free."

The king sat down and waited there,
    And rose not, night nor day;
Till a sound of shouting filled the air,
    And cries of a sore dismay.

Then like a king he sat once more,
    With the crown upon his head;
And up to the throne the people bore
    A mighty giant dead.

And up to the throne the people bore
    A pale and lifeless boy.
The king rose up like a prophet of yore,
    In a lofty, deathlike joy.

He put the crown on the chilly brow:
    "Thou should'st have reigned with me
But Death is the king of both, and now
    I go to obey with thee.

"Surely some good in me there lay,
    To beget the noble one."
The old man smiled like a winter day,
    And fell beside his son.

II   "O lady, thy lover is dead," they cried;

"He is dead, but hath slain the foe;

He hath left his name to be magnified

In a song of wonder and woe."

"Alas! I am well repaid," said she,

"With a pain that stings like joy:

For I feared, from his tenderness to me,

That he was but a feeble boy.

"Now I shall hold my head on high,

The queen among my kind;

If ye hear a sound, 'tis only a sigh

For a glory left behind."

The first three times I sang these songs they both wept passionately. But after the third time, they wept no more. Their eyes shone, and their faces grew pale, but they never wept at any of my songs again.

CHAPTER XXI

"I put my life in my hands."—*The Book of Judges.*

At length, with much toil and equal delight, our armour was finished. We armed each other, and tested the strength of the defence, with many blows of loving force. I was inferior in strength to both my brothers, but a little more agile than either; and upon this agility, joined to precision in hitting with the point of my weapon, I grounded my hopes of success in the ensuing combat. I likewise laboured to develop yet more the keenness of sight with which I was naturally gifted; and, from the remarks of my companions, I soon learned that my endeavours were not in vain.

The morning arrived on which we had determined to make the attempt, and succeed or perish—perhaps both. We had resolved to fight on foot; knowing that the mishap of many of the knights who had made the attempt, had resulted from the fright of their horses at the appearance of the giants; and believing with Sir Gawain, that, though mare's sons might be false to us, the earth would never prove a traitor. But most of our preparations were, in their immediate aim at least, frustrated.

We rose, that fatal morning, by daybreak. We had rested from all labour the day before, and now were fresh as the lark. We bathed in cold spring water, and dressed ourselves in clean garments, with a sense of preparation, as for a solemn festivity. When we had broken our fast, I took an old lyre, which I had found in the tower and had myself repaired, and sung for the last time the two ballads of which I have said so much already. I followed them with this, for a closing song:

> *Oh, well for him who breaks his dream*
>
> *With the blow that ends the strife*
>
> *And, waking, knows the peace that flows*
>
> *Around the pain of life!*

We are dead, my brothers! Our bodies clasp,

As an armour, our souls about;

This hand is the battle-axe I grasp,

And this my hammer stout.

Fear not, my brothers, for we are dead;

No noise can break our rest;

The calm of the grave is about the head,

And the heart heaves not the breast.

And our life we throw to our people back,

To live with, a further store;

We leave it them, that there be no lack

In the land where we live no more.

Oh, well for him who breaks his dream

With the blow that ends the strife

And, waking, knows the peace that flows

Around the noise of life!

As the last few tones of the instrument were following, like a dirge, the death of the song, we all sprang to our feet. For, through one of the little windows of the tower, towards which I had looked as I sang, I saw, suddenly rising over the edge of the slope on which our tower stood, three enormous heads. The brothers knew at once, by my looks, what caused my sudden movement. We were utterly unarmed, and there was no time to arm.

But we seemed to adopt the same resolution simultaneously; for each caught up his favourite weapon, and, leaving his defence behind, sprang to the door. I snatched up a long rapier, abruptly, but very finely pointed, in my sword-hand, and in the other a sabre; the elder brother seized his heavy battle-axe; and the younger, a great, two-handed sword, which he wielded in one hand like a feather. We had just time to get clear of the tower, embrace and say good-bye, and part to some little distance, that we might not encumber each other's motions, ere the triple giant-brotherhood drew near to attack us. They were about twice our height, and armed to the teeth. Through the visors of their helmets their monstrous eyes shone with a horrible ferocity. I was in the middle position, and the middle giant approached me. My eyes were busy with his armour, and I was not a moment in settling my mode of attack. I saw that his body-armour was somewhat clumsily made, and that the overlappings in the lower part had more play than necessary; and I hoped that, in a fortunate moment, some joint would open a little, in a visible and accessible part. I stood till he came near enough to aim a blow at me with the mace, which has been, in all ages, the favourite weapon of giants, when, of course, I leaped aside, and let the blow fall upon the spot where I had been standing. I expected this would strain the joints of his armour yet more. Full of fury, he made at me again; but I kept him busy, constantly eluding his blows, and hoping thus to fatigue him. He did not seem to fear any assault from me, and I attempted none as yet; but while I watched his motions in order to avoid his blows, I, at the same time, kept equal watch upon those joints of his armour, through some one of which I hoped to reach his life. At length, as if somewhat fatigued, he paused a moment, and drew himself slightly up; I bounded forward, foot and hand, ran my rapier right through to the armour of his back, let go the hilt, and passing under his right arm, turned as he fell, and flew at him with my sabre. At one happy blow I divided the band of his helmet, which fell off, and allowed me, with a second cut across the eyes, to blind him quite; after which I clove his head, and turned, uninjured, to see how my brothers had fared. Both the giants were down, but so were my brothers. I flew first to the one and then to the other couple. Both pairs of combatants were dead, and yet locked together, as in the death-struggle. The elder had buried his battle-axe in the body of his foe, and had fallen beneath him as he fell. The giant had strangled him in his own death-agonies. The younger had nearly hewn off the left leg of his enemy;

and, grappled with in the act, had, while they rolled together on the earth, found for his dagger a passage betwixt the gorget and cuirass of the giant, and stabbed him mortally in the throat. The blood from the giant's throat was yet pouring over the hand of his foe, which still grasped the hilt of the dagger sheathed in the wound. They lay silent. I, the least worthy, remained the sole survivor in the lists.

As I stood exhausted amidst the dead, after the first worthy deed of my life, I suddenly looked behind me, and there lay the Shadow, black in the sunshine. I went into the lonely tower, and there lay the useless armour of the noble youths—supine as they.

Ah, how sad it looked! It was a glorious death, but it was death. My songs could not comfort me now. I was almost ashamed that I was alive, when they, the true-hearted, were no more. And yet I breathed freer to think that I had gone through the trial, and had not failed. And perhaps I may be forgiven, if some feelings of pride arose in my bosom, when I looked down on the mighty form that lay dead by my hand.

"After all, however," I said to myself, and my heart sank, "it was only skill. Your giant was but a blunderer."

I left the bodies of friends and foes, peaceful enough when the death-fight was over, and, hastening to the country below, roused the peasants. They came with shouting and gladness, bringing waggons to carry the bodies. I resolved to take the princes home to their father, each as he lay, in the arms of his country's foe. But first I searched the giants, and found the keys of their castle, to which I repaired, followed by a great company of the people. It was a place of wonderful strength. I released the prisoners, knights and ladies, all in a sad condition, from the cruelties and neglects of the giants. It humbled me to see them crowding round me with thanks, when in truth the glorious brothers, lying dead by their lonely tower, were those to whom the thanks belonged. I had but aided in carrying out the thought born in their brain, and uttered in visible form before ever I laid hold thereupon. Yet I did count myself happy to have been chosen for their brother in this great deed.

After a few hours spent in refreshing and clothing the prisoners, we all commenced our journey towards the capital. This was slow at first; but, as the strength and spirits of the prisoners returned, it became more rapid; and in three days we reached the palace of the king. As we entered the city gates, with the huge bulks lying each on a waggon drawn by horses, and two of them inextricably intertwined with the dead bodies of their princes, the people raised a shout and then a cry, and followed in multitudes the solemn procession.

I will not attempt to describe the behaviour of the grand old king. Joy and pride in his sons overcame his sorrow at their loss. On me he heaped every kindness that heart could devise or hand execute. He used to sit and question me, night after night, about everything that was in any way connected with them and their preparations. Our mode of life, and relation to each other, during the time we spent together, was a constant theme. He entered into the minutest details of the construction of the armour, even to a peculiar mode of riveting some of the plates, with unwearying interest. This armour I had intended to beg of the king, as my sole memorials of the contest; but, when I saw the delight he took in contemplating it, and the consolation it appeared to afford him in his sorrow, I could not ask for it; but, at his request, left my own, weapons and all, to be joined with theirs in a trophy, erected in the grand square of the palace. The king, with gorgeous ceremony, dubbed me knight with his own old hand, in which trembled the sword of his youth.

During the short time I remained, my company was, naturally, much courted by the young nobles. I was in a constant round of gaiety and diversion, notwithstanding that the court was in mourning. For the country was so rejoiced at the death of the giants, and so many of their lost friends had been restored to the nobility and men of wealth, that the gladness surpassed the grief. "Ye have indeed left your lives to your people, my great brothers!" I said.

But I was ever and ever haunted by the old shadow, which I had not seen all the time that I was at work in the tower. Even in the society of the ladies of the court, who seemed to think it only their duty to make my stay there as pleasant to me as possible, I could not help being conscious of its presence, although it might not be annoying me at the time. At length, somewhat weary of uninterrupted pleasure, and nowise strengthened thereby, either in body

321

or mind, I put on a splendid suit of armour of steel inlaid with silver, which the old king had given me, and, mounting the horse on which it had been brought to me, took my leave of the palace, to visit the distant city in which the lady dwelt, whom the elder prince had loved. I anticipated a sore task, in conveying to her the news of his glorious fate: but this trial was spared me, in a manner as strange as anything that had happened to me in Fairy Land.

CHAPTER XXII

"No one has my form but the I."

Schoppe, in JEAN PAUL'S Titan.

"Joy's a subtil elf.

I think man's happiest when he forgets himself."

CYRIL TOURNEUR, The Revenger's Tragedy.

On the third day of my journey, I was riding gently along a road, apparently little frequented, to judge from the grass that grew upon it. I was approaching a forest. Everywhere in Fairy Land forests are the places where one may most certainly expect adventures. As I drew near, a youth, unarmed, gentle, and beautiful, who had just cut a branch from a yew growing on the skirts of the wood, evidently to make himself a bow, met me, and thus accosted me:

"Sir knight, be careful as thou ridest through this forest; for it is said to be strangely enchanted, in a sort which even those who have been witnesses of its enchantment can hardly describe."

I thanked him for his advice, which I promised to follow, and rode on. But the moment I entered the wood, it seemed to me that, if enchantment there was, it must be of a good kind; for the Shadow, which had been more than usually dark and distressing, since I had set out on this journey, suddenly disappeared. I felt a wonderful elevation of spirits, and began to reflect on my past life, and especially on my combat with the giants, with such satisfaction, that I had actually to remind myself, that I had only killed one of them; and that, but for the brothers, I should never have had the idea of attacking them, not to mention the smallest power of standing to it. Still I rejoiced, and counted myself amongst the glorious knights of old; having even the unspeakable presumption—my shame and self-condemnation at the memory of it are such, that I write it as the only and sorest penance I can perform—to think of myself (will the world believe it?) as side by side with Sir Galahad! Scarcely had the thought been born in my mind, when, approaching me from the left, through the trees, I espied a resplendent knight, of mighty size, whose armour seemed to shine of itself, without the sun. When he drew near, I was astonished to see that this armour was like my own; nay, I could trace, line for line, the correspondence of the inlaid silver to the device on my own. His horse, too, was like mine in colour, form, and motion; save that, like his rider, he was greater and fiercer than his counterpart. The knight rode with beaver up. As he halted right opposite to me in the narrow path, barring my way, I saw the reflection of my countenance in the centre plate of shining steel on his breastplate. Above it rose the same face—his face—only, as I have said, larger and fiercer. I was bewildered. I could not help feeling some admiration of him, but it was mingled with a dim conviction that he was evil, and that I ought to fight with him.

"Let me pass," I said.

"When I will," he replied.

Something within me said: "Spear in rest, and ride at him! else thou art for ever a slave."

I tried, but my arm trembled so much, that I could not couch my lance. To tell the truth, I, who had overcome the giant, shook like a coward before this knight. He gave a scornful laugh, that echoed through the wood, turned his horse, and said, without looking round, "Follow me."

I obeyed, abashed and stupefied. How long he led, and how long I followed, I cannot tell. "I never knew misery before," I said to myself. "Would that I had at least struck him, and had had my death-blow in return! Why, then, do I not call to him to wheel and defend himself? Alas! I know not why, but I cannot. One look from him would cow me like a beaten hound." I followed, and was silent.

At length we came to a dreary square tower, in the middle of a dense forest. It looked as if scarce a tree had been cut down to make room for it. Across the very door, diagonally, grew the stem of a tree, so large that there was just room to squeeze past it in order to enter. One miserable square hole in the roof was the only visible suggestion of a window. Turret or battlement, or projecting masonry of any kind, it had none. Clear and smooth and massy, it rose from its base, and ended with a line straight and unbroken. The roof, carried to a centre from each of the four walls, rose slightly to the point where the rafters met. Round the base lay several little heaps of either bits of broken branches, withered and peeled, or half-whitened bones; I could not distinguish which. As I approached, the ground sounded hollow beneath my horse's hoofs. The knight took a great key from his pocket, and reaching past the stem of the tree, with some difficulty opened the door. "Dismount," he commanded. I obeyed. He turned my horse's head away from the tower, gave him a terrible blow with the flat side of his sword, and sent him madly tearing through the forest.

"Now," said he, "enter, and take your companion with you."

I looked round: knight and horse had vanished, and behind me lay the horrible shadow. I entered, for I could not help myself; and the shadow followed me. I had a terrible conviction that the knight and he were one. The door closed behind me.

Now I was indeed in pitiful plight. There was literally nothing in the tower but my shadow and me. The walls rose right up to the roof; in which, as I had seen from without, there was one little square opening. This I now knew to be the only window the tower possessed. I sat down on the floor, in listless wretchedness. I think I must have fallen asleep, and have slept for hours; for I suddenly became aware of existence, in observing that the moon was shining through the hole in the roof. As she rose higher and higher, her light crept down the wall over me, till at last it shone right upon my head. Instantaneously the walls of the tower seemed to vanish away like a mist. I sat beneath a beech, on the edge of a forest, and the open country lay, in the moonlight, for miles and miles around me, spotted with glimmering houses and spires and towers. I thought with myself, "Oh, joy! it was only a dream; the horrible narrow waste is gone, and I wake beneath a beech-tree, perhaps one that loves me, and I can go where I will." I rose, as I thought, and walked about, and did what I would, but ever kept near the tree; for always, and, of course, since my meeting with the woman of the beech-tree far more than ever, I loved that tree. So the night wore on. I waited for the sun to rise, before I could venture to renew my journey. But as soon as the first faint light of the dawn appeared, instead of shining upon me from the eye of the morning, it stole like a fainting ghost through the little square hole above my head; and the walls came out as the light grew, and the glorious night was swallowed up of the hateful day. The long dreary day passed. My shadow lay black on the floor. I felt no hunger, no need of food. The night came. The moon shone. I watched her light slowly descending the wall, as I might have watched, adown the sky, the long, swift approach of a helping angel. Her rays touched me, and I was free. Thus night after night passed away. I should have died but for this. Every night the conviction returned, that I was free. Every morning I sat wretchedly disconsolate. At length, when the course of the moon no longer permitted her beams to touch me, the night was dreary as the day.

When I slept, I was somewhat consoled by my dreams; but all the time I dreamed, I knew that I was only dreaming. But one night, at length, the moon, a mere shred of pallor, scattered a few thin ghostly rays upon me; and I think I fell asleep and dreamed. I sat in an autumn night before the vintage, on a hill overlooking my own castle. My heart sprang with joy. Oh, to be a child again, innocent, fearless, without shame or desire! I walked down to the castle. All were in consternation at my absence. My sisters were weeping for my loss. They sprang up and clung to me, with incoherent cries, as I entered. My old friends came flocking round me. A gray light shone on the roof of the hall. It was the light of the dawn shining through the square window of my tower. More earnestly than ever, I longed for freedom after this dream; more drearily than ever, crept on the next wretched day. I measured by the sunbeams, caught through the little window in the trap of my tower, how it went by, waiting only for the dreams of the night.

About noon, I started as if something foreign to all my senses and all my experience, had suddenly invaded me; yet it was only the voice of a woman singing. My whole frame quivered with joy, surprise, and the sensation of the unforeseen. Like a living soul, like an incarnation of Nature, the song entered my prison-house. Each tone folded its wings, and laid itself, like a caressing bird, upon my heart. It bathed me like a sea; inwrapt me like an odorous vapour; entered my soul like a long draught of clear spring-water; shone upon me like essential sunlight; soothed me like a mother's voice and hand. Yet, as the clearest forest-well tastes sometimes of the bitterness of decayed leaves, so to my weary, prisoned heart, its cheerfulness had a sting of cold, and its tenderness unmanned me with the faintness of long-departed joys. I wept half-bitterly, half-luxuriously; but not long. I dashed away the tears, ashamed of a weakness which I thought I had abandoned. Ere I knew, I had walked to the door, and seated myself with my ears against it, in order to catch every syllable of the revelation from the unseen outer world. And now I heard each word distinctly. The singer seemed to be standing or sitting near the tower, for the sounds indicated no change of place. The song was something like this:

> *The sun, like a golden knot on high,*
>
> *Gathers the glories of the sky,*
>
> *And binds them into a shining tent,*
>
> *Roofing the world with the firmament.*
>
> *And through the pavilion the rich winds blow,*
>
> *And through the pavilion the waters go.*
>
> *And the birds for joy, and the trees for prayer,*
>
> *Bowing their heads in the sunny air,*
>
> *And for thoughts, the gently talking springs,*
>
> *That come from the centre with secret things—*
>
> *All make a music, gentle and strong,*
>
> *Bound by the heart into one sweet song.*
>
> *And amidst them all, the mother Earth*
>
> *Sits with the children of her birth;*
>
> *She tendeth them all, as a mother hen*

Her little ones round her, twelve or ten:

Oft she sitteth, with hands on knee,

Idle with love for her family.

Go forth to her from the dark and the dust,

And weep beside her, if weep thou must;

If she may not hold thee to her breast,

Like a weary infant, that cries for rest

At least she will press thee to her knee,

And tell a low, sweet tale to thee,

Till the hue to thy cheeky and the light to thine eye,

Strength to thy limbs, and courage high

To thy fainting heart, return amain,

And away to work thou goest again.

From the narrow desert, O man of pride,

Come into the house, so high and wide.

Hardly knowing what I did, I opened the door. Why had I not done so before? I do not know.

At first I could see no one; but when I had forced myself past the tree which grew across the entrance, I saw, seated on the ground, and leaning against the tree, with her back to my prison, a beautiful woman. Her countenance seemed known to me, and yet unknown. She looked at me and smiled, when I made my appearance.

"Ah! were you the prisoner there? I am very glad I have wiled you out."

"Do you know me then?" "Do you not know me? But you hurt me, and that, I suppose, makes it easy for a man to forget. You broke my globe. Yet I

328

thank you. Perhaps I owe you many thanks for breaking it. I took the pieces, all black, and wet with crying over them, to the Fairy Queen. There was no music and no light in them now. But she took them from me, and laid them aside; and made me go to sleep in a great hall of white, with black pillars, and many red curtains. When I woke in the morning, I went to her, hoping to have my globe again, whole and sound; but she sent me away without it, and I have not seen it since. Nor do I care for it now. I have something so much better. I do not need the globe to play to me; for I can sing. I could not sing at all before. Now I go about everywhere through Fairy Land, singing till my heart is like to break, just like my globe, for very joy at my own songs. And wherever I go, my songs do good, and deliver people. And now I have delivered you, and I am so happy."

She ceased, and the tears came into her eyes.

All this time, I had been gazing at her; and now fully recognised the face of the child, glorified in the countenance of the woman.

I was ashamed and humbled before her; but a great weight was lifted from my thoughts. I knelt before her, and thanked her, and begged her to forgive me.

"Rise, rise," she said; "I have nothing to forgive; I thank you. But now I must be gone, for I do not know how many may be waiting for me, here and there, through the dark forests; and they cannot come out till I come."

She rose, and with a smile and a farewell, turned and left me. I dared not ask her to stay; in fact, I could hardly speak to her. Between her and me, there was a great gulf. She was uplifted, by sorrow and well-doing, into a region I could hardly hope ever to enter. I watched her departure, as one watches a sunset. She went like a radiance through the dark wood, which was henceforth bright to me, from simply knowing that such a creature was in it.

She was bearing the sun to the unsunned spots. The light and the music of her broken globe were now in her heart and her brain. As she went, she sang; and I caught these few words of her song; and the tones seemed to linger and wind about the trees after she had disappeared:

Thou goest thine, and I go mine—

Many ways we wend;

Many days, and many ways,

Ending in one end.

Many a wrong, and its curing song;

Many a road, and many an inn;

Room to roam, but only one home

For all the world to win.

And so she vanished. With a sad heart, soothed by humility, and the knowledge of her peace and gladness, I bethought me what now I should do. First, I must leave the tower far behind me, lest, in some evil moment, I might be once more caged within its horrible walls. But it was ill walking in my heavy armour; and besides I had now no right to the golden spurs and the resplendent mail, fitly dulled with long neglect. I might do for a squire; but I honoured knighthood too highly, to call myself any longer one of the noble brotherhood. I stripped off all my armour, piled it under the tree, just where the lady had been seated, and took my unknown way, eastward through the woods. Of all my weapons, I carried only a short axe in my hand.

Then first I knew the delight of being lowly; of saying to myself, "I am what I am, nothing more." "I have failed," I said, "I have lost myself—would it had been my shadow." I looked round: the shadow was nowhere to be seen. Ere long, I learned that it was not myself, but only my shadow, that I had lost. I learned that it is better, a thousand-fold, for a proud man to fall and be humbled, than to hold up his head in his pride and fancied innocence. I learned that he that will be a hero, will barely be a man; that he that will be nothing but a doer of his work, is sure of his manhood. In nothing was my ideal lowered, or dimmed, or grown less precious; I only saw it too plainly, to set myself for a moment beside it. Indeed, my ideal soon became my life; whereas, formerly, my life had consisted in a vain attempt to behold, if not my ideal in myself, at least myself in my ideal. Now, however, I took, at first, what perhaps was a mistaken pleasure, in despising and degrading myself. Another self seemed to arise, like a white spirit from a dead man, from the dumb and trampled self of the past. Doubtless, this self must again die and be buried, and again, from its tomb, spring a winged child; but of this my history as yet bears not the record.

Self will come to life even in the slaying of self; but there is ever something deeper and stronger than it, which will emerge at last from the unknown abysses of the soul: will it be as a solemn gloom, burning with eyes? or a clear morning after the rain? or a smiling child, that finds itself nowhere, and everywhere?

CHAPTER XXIII

"High erected thought, seated in a heart of courtesy."

SIR PHILIP SIDNEY.

"A sweet attractive kinde of grace,

A full assurance given by lookes,

Continuall comfort in a face,

The lineaments of Gospel bookes."

MATTHEW ROYDON, on Sir Philip Sidney.

I had not gone far, for I had but just lost sight of the hated tower, when a voice of another sort, sounding near or far, as the trees permitted or intercepted its passage, reached me. It was a full, deep, manly voice, but withal clear and melodious. Now it burst on the ear with a sudden swell, and anon, dying away as suddenly, seemed to come to me across a great space. Nevertheless, it drew nearer; till, at last, I could distinguish the words of the song, and get transient glimpses of the singer, between the columns of the trees. He came nearer, dawning upon me like a growing thought. He was a knight, armed from head to heel, mounted upon a strange-looking beast, whose form I could not understand. The words which I heard him sing were like these:

Heart be stout,

And eye be true;

Good blade out!

And ill shall rue.

Courage, horse!

Thou lackst no skill;

Well thy force

Hath matched my will.

For the foe

With fiery breath,

At a blow,

Is still in death.

Gently, horse!

Tread fearlessly;

'Tis his corse

That burdens thee.

The sun's eye

Is fierce at noon;

Thou and I

Will rest full soon.

And new strength

New work will meet;

Till, at length,

Long rest is sweet.

And now horse and rider had arrived near enough for me to see, fastened by the long neck to the hinder part of the saddle, and trailing its hideous length on the ground behind, the body of a great dragon. It was no wonder that, with such a drag at his heels, the horse could make but slow progress, notwithstanding his evident dismay. The horrid, serpent-like head, with its black tongue, forked with red, hanging out of its jaws, dangled against the horse's side. Its neck was covered with long blue hair, its sides with scales of green and gold. Its back was of corrugated skin, of a purple hue. Its belly was similar in nature, but its colour was leaden, dashed with blotches of livid blue. Its skinny, bat-like wings and its tail were of a dull gray. It was strange to see how so many gorgeous colours, so many curving lines, and such beautiful things as wings and hair and scales, combined to form the horrible creature, intense in ugliness.

The knight was passing me with a salutation; but, as I walked towards him, he reined up, and I stood by his stirrup. When I came near him, I saw to my surprise and pleasure likewise, although a sudden pain, like a birth of fire, sprang up in my heart, that it was the knight of the soiled armour, whom I knew before, and whom I had seen in the vision, with the lady of the marble. But I could have thrown my arms around him, because she loved him. This discovery only strengthened the resolution I had formed, before I recognised him, of offering myself to the knight, to wait upon him as a squire, for he seemed to be unattended. I made my request in as few words as possible. He hesitated for a moment, and looked at me thoughtfully. I saw that he suspected who I was, but that he continued uncertain of his suspicion. No doubt he was soon convinced of its truth; but all the time I was with him, not a word crossed his lips with reference to what he evidently concluded I wished to leave unnoticed, if not to keep concealed.

"Squire and knight should be friends," said he: "can you take me by the hand?" And he held out the great gauntleted right hand. I grasped it willingly and strongly. Not a word more was said. The knight gave the sign to his horse, which again began its slow march, and I walked beside and a little behind.

We had not gone very far before we arrived at a little cottage; from which, as we drew near, a woman rushed out with the cry:

"My child! my child! have you found my child?"

"I have found her," replied the knight, "but she is sorely hurt. I was forced to leave her with the hermit, as I returned. You will find her there, and

I think she will get better. You see I have brought you a present. This wretch will not hurt you again." And he undid the creature's neck, and flung the frightful burden down by the cottage door.

The woman was now almost out of sight in the wood; but the husband stood at the door, with speechless thanks in his face.

"You must bury the monster," said the knight. "If I had arrived a moment later, I should have been too late. But now you need not fear, for such a creature as this very rarely appears, in the same part, twice during a lifetime."

"Will you not dismount and rest you, Sir Knight?" said the peasant, who had, by this time, recovered himself a little.

"That I will, thankfully," said he; and, dismounting, he gave the reins to me, and told me to unbridle the horse, and lead him into the shade. "You need not tie him up," he added; "he will not run away."

When I returned, after obeying his orders, and entered the cottage, I saw the knight seated, without his helmet, and talking most familiarly with the simple host. I stood at the open door for a moment, and, gazing at him, inwardly justified the white lady in preferring him to me. A nobler countenance I never saw. Loving-kindness beamed from every line of his face. It seemed as if he would repay himself for the late arduous combat, by indulging in all the gentleness of a womanly heart. But when the talk ceased for a moment, he seemed to fall into a reverie. Then the exquisite curves of the upper lip vanished. The lip was lengthened and compressed at the same moment. You could have told that, within the lips, the teeth were firmly closed. The whole face grew stern and determined, all but fierce; only the eyes burned on like a holy sacrifice, uplift on a granite rock.

The woman entered, with her mangled child in her arms. She was pale as her little burden. She gazed, with a wild love and despairing tenderness, on the still, all but dead face, white and clear from loss of blood and terror.

The knight rose. The light that had been confined to his eyes, now shone from his whole countenance. He took the little thing in his arms, and, with the mother's help, undressed her, and looked to her wounds. The tears flowed down his face as he did so. With tender hands he bound them up, kissed the pale cheek, and gave her back to her mother. When he went home, all his tale would be of the grief and joy of the parents; while to me, who had looked on, the gracious countenance of the armed man, beaming from the panoply of steel, over the seemingly dead child, while the powerful hands turned it and shifted it, and bound it, if possible even more gently than the mother's, formed the centre of the story.

After we had partaken of the best they could give us, the knight took his leave, with a few parting instructions to the mother as to how she should treat the child.

I brought the knight his steed, held the stirrup while he mounted, and then followed him through the wood. The horse, delighted to be free of his hideous load, bounded beneath the weight of man and armour, and could hardly be restrained from galloping on. But the knight made him time his powers to mine, and so we went on for an hour or two. Then the knight dismounted, and compelled me to get into the saddle, saying: "Knight and squire must share the labour."

Holding by the stirrup, he walked along by my side, heavily clad as he was, with apparent ease. As we went, he led a conversation, in which I took what humble part my sense of my condition would permit me.

"Somehow or other," said he, "notwithstanding the beauty of this country of Faerie, in which we are, there is much that is wrong in it. If there are great splendours, there are corresponding horrors; heights and depths; beautiful women and awful fiends; noble men and weaklings. All a man has to do, is to better what he can. And if he will settle it with himself, that even renown and success are in themselves of no great value, and be content to be defeated, if so be that the fault is not his; and so go to his work with a cool brain and a strong will, he will get it done; and fare none the worse in the end, that he was not burdened with provision and precaution."

"But he will not always come off well," I ventured to say.

"Perhaps not," rejoined the knight, "in the individual act; but the result of his lifetime will content him."

"So it will fare with you, doubtless," thought I; "but for me——"

Venturing to resume the conversation after a pause, I said, hesitatingly:

"May I ask for what the little beggar-girl wanted your aid, when she came to your castle to find you?"

He looked at me for a moment in silence, and then said—

"I cannot help wondering how you know of that; but there is something about you quite strange enough to entitle you to the privilege of the country; namely, to go unquestioned. I, however, being only a man, such as you see me, am ready to tell you anything you like to ask me, as far as I can. The little beggar-girl came into the hall where I was sitting, and told me a very curious story, which I can only recollect very vaguely, it was so peculiar. What I can recall is, that she was sent to gather wings. As soon as she had gathered a pair of wings for herself, she was to fly away, she said, to the country she came from; but where that was, she could give no information.

"She said she had to beg her wings from the butterflies and moths; and wherever she begged, no one refused her. But she needed a great many of the wings of butterflies and moths to make a pair for her; and so she had to wander about day after day, looking for butterflies, and night after night, looking for moths; and then she begged for their wings. But the day before, she had come into a part of the forest, she said, where there were multitudes of splendid butterflies flitting about, with wings which were just fit to make the eyes in the shoulders of hers; and she knew she could have as many of them as she liked for the asking; but as soon as she began to beg, there came a great creature right up to her, and threw her down, and walked over her. When she got up, she saw the wood was full of these beings stalking about, and seeming to have nothing to do with each other. As soon as ever she began to beg, one of them walked over her; till at last in dismay, and in growing horror of the senseless creatures, she had run away to look for somebody to help her. I asked her what they were like. She said, like great men, made of wood, without knee-or elbow-joints, and without any noses or mouths or eyes in their faces. I laughed at the little maiden, thinking she was making child's game of me; but, although she burst out laughing too, she persisted in asserting the truth of her story."

"'Only come, knight, come and see; I will lead you.'

"So I armed myself, to be ready for anything that might happen, and followed the child; for, though I could make nothing of her story, I could see she was a little human being in need of some help or other. As she walked before me, I looked attentively at her. Whether or not it was from being so often knocked down and walked over, I could not tell, but her clothes were very much torn, and in several places her white skin was peeping through. I thought she was hump-backed; but on looking more closely, I saw, through the tatters of her frock—do not laugh at me—a bunch on each shoulder, of the most gorgeous colours. Looking yet more closely, I saw that they were of the shape of folded wings, and were made of all kinds of butterfly-wings and moth-wings, crowded together like the feathers on the individual butterfly pinion; but, like them, most beautifully arranged, and producing a perfect harmony of colour and shade. I could now more easily believe the rest of her story; especially as I saw, every now and then, a certain heaving motion in the wings, as if they longed to be uplifted and outspread. But beneath her scanty garments complete wings could not be concealed, and indeed, from her own story, they were yet unfinished.

"After walking for two or three hours (how the little girl found her way, I could not imagine), we came to a part of the forest, the very air of which was quivering with the motions of multitudes of resplendent butterflies; as gorgeous in colour, as if the eyes of peacocks' feathers had taken to flight, but of infinite variety of hue and form, only that the appearance of some kind of eye on each wing predominated. 'There they are, there they are!' cried the child, in a tone of victory mingled with terror. Except for this tone, I should have thought she referred to the butterflies, for I could see nothing else. But at that moment an enormous butterfly, whose wings had great eyes of blue surrounded by confused cloudy heaps of more dingy colouring, just like a break in the clouds on a stormy day towards evening, settled near us. The child instantly began murmuring: 'Butterfly, butterfly, give me your wings';

when, the moment after, she fell to the ground, and began crying as if hurt. I drew my sword and heaved a great blow in the direction in which the child had fallen. It struck something, and instantly the most grotesque imitation of a man became visible. You see this Fairy Land is full of oddities and all sorts of incredibly ridiculous things, which a man is compelled to meet and treat as real existences, although all the time he feels foolish for doing so. This being, if being it could be called, was like a block of wood roughly hewn into the mere outlines of a man; and hardly so, for it had but head, body, legs, and arms— the head without a face, and the limbs utterly formless. I had hewn off one of its legs, but the two portions moved on as best they could, quite independent of each other; so that I had done no good. I ran after it, and clove it in twain from the head downwards; but it could not be convinced that its vocation was not to walk over people; for, as soon as the little girl began her begging again, all three parts came bustling up; and if I had not interposed my weight between her and them, she would have been trampled again under them. I saw that something else must be done. If the wood was full of the creatures, it would be an endless work to chop them so small that they could do no injury; and then, besides, the parts would be so numerous, that the butterflies would be in danger from the drift of flying chips. I served this one so, however; and then told the girl to beg again, and point out the direction in which one was coming. I was glad to find, however, that I could now see him myself, and wondered how they could have been invisible before. I would not allow him to walk over the child; but while I kept him off, and she began begging again, another appeared; and it was all I could do, from the weight of my armour, to protect her from the stupid, persevering efforts of the two. But suddenly the right plan occurred to me. I tripped one of them up, and, taking him by the legs, set him up on his head, with his heels against a tree. I was delighted to find he could not move. Meantime the poor child was walked over by the other, but it was for the last time. Whenever one appeared, I followed the same plan—tripped him up and set him on his head; and so the little beggar was able to gather her wings without any trouble, which occupation she continued for several hours in my company."

"What became of her?" I asked.

"I took her home with me to my castle, and she told me all her story;

but it seemed to me, all the time, as if I were hearing a child talk in its sleep. I could not arrange her story in my mind at all, although it seemed to leave hers in some certain order of its own. My wife——"

Here the knight checked himself, and said no more. Neither did I urge the conversation farther.

Thus we journeyed for several days, resting at night in such shelter as we could get; and when no better was to be had, lying in the forest under some tree, on a couch of old leaves.

I loved the knight more and more. I believe never squire served his master with more care and joyfulness than I. I tended his horse; I cleaned his armour; my skill in the craft enabled me to repair it when necessary; I watched his needs; and was well repaid for all by the love itself which I bore him.

"This," I said to myself, "is a true man. I will serve him, and give him all worship, seeing in him the imbodiment of what I would fain become. If I cannot be noble myself, I will yet be servant to his nobleness." He, in return, soon showed me such signs of friendship and respect, as made my heart glad; and I felt that, after all, mine would be no lost life, if I might wait on him to the world's end, although no smile but his should greet me, and no one but him should say, "Well done! he was a good servant!" at last. But I burned to do something more for him than the ordinary routine of a squire's duty permitted.

One afternoon, we began to observe an appearance of roads in the wood. Branches had been cut down, and openings made, where footsteps had worn no path below. These indications increased as we passed on, till, at length, we came into a long, narrow avenue, formed by felling the trees in its line, as the remaining roots evidenced. At some little distance, on both hands, we observed signs of similar avenues, which appeared to converge with ours, towards one spot. Along these we indistinctly saw several forms moving, which seemed, with ourselves, to approach the common centre. Our path brought us, at last, up to a wall of yew-trees, growing close together, and intertwining their branches so, that nothing could be seen beyond it. An opening was cut in it like a door, and all the wall was trimmed smooth and perpendicular. The knight dismounted, and waited till I had provided for his horse's comfort; upon which we entered the place together.

It was a great space, bare of trees, and enclosed by four walls of yew, similar to that through which we had entered. These trees grew to a very great height, and did not divide from each other till close to the top, where their summits formed a row of conical battlements all around the walls. The space contained was a parallelogram of great length. Along each of the two longer sides of the interior, were ranged three ranks of men, in white robes, standing silent and solemn, each with a sword by his side, although the rest of his costume and bearing was more priestly than soldierly. For some distance inwards, the space between these opposite rows was filled with a company of men and women and children, in holiday attire. The looks of all were directed inwards, towards the further end. Far beyond the crowd, in a long avenue, seeming to narrow in the distance, went the long rows of the white-robed men. On what the attention of the multitude was fixed, we could not tell, for the sun had set before we arrived, and it was growing dark within. It grew darker and darker. The multitude waited in silence. The stars began to shine down into the enclosure, and they grew brighter and larger every moment. A wind arose, and swayed the pinnacles of the tree-tops; and made a strange sound, half like music, half like moaning, through the close branches and leaves of the tree-walls. A young girl who stood beside me, clothed in the same dress as the priests, bowed her head, and grew pale with awe.

The knight whispered to me, "How solemn it is! Surely they wait to hear the voice of a prophet. There is something good near!"

But I, though somewhat shaken by the feeling expressed by my master, yet had an unaccountable conviction that here was something bad. So I resolved to be keenly on the watch for what should follow.

Suddenly a great star, like a sun, appeared high in the air over the temple, illuminating it throughout; and a great song arose from the men in white, which went rolling round and round the building, now receding to the end, and now approaching, down the other side, the place where we stood. For some of the singers were regularly ceasing, and the next to them as regularly taking up the song, so that it crept onwards with gradations produced by changes which could not themselves be detected, for only a few of those who were singing ceased at the same moment. The song paused; and I saw a company of six of the white-robed men walk up the centre of the human avenue, surrounding a youth gorgeously attired beneath his robe of white, and wearing a chaplet of flowers on his head. I followed them closely, with my keenest observation; and, by accompanying their slow progress with my eyes, I was able to perceive more clearly what took place when they arrived at the other end. I knew that my sight was so much more keen than that of most people, that I had good reason to suppose I should see more than the rest could, at such a distance. At the farther end a throne stood upon a platform, high above the heads of the surrounding priests. To this platform I saw the company begin to ascend, apparently by an inclined plane or gentle slope. The throne itself was elevated again, on a kind of square pedestal, to the top of which led a flight of steps. On the throne sat a majestic-looking figure, whose posture seemed to indicate a mixture of pride and benignity, as he looked down on the multitude below. The company ascended to the foot of the throne, where they all kneeled for some minutes; then they rose and passed round to the side of the pedestal upon which the throne stood. Here they crowded close behind the youth, putting him in the foremost place, and one of them opened a door in the pedestal, for the youth to enter. I was sure I saw him shrink back, and those crowding behind pushed him in. Then, again, arose a burst of song from the multitude in white, which lasted some time. When it ceased, a new company of seven commenced its march up the centre. As they advanced, I looked up at my master: his noble countenance was full of reverence and awe. Incapable of evil himself, he could scarcely suspect it in another, much less in a multitude such as this, and surrounded with such appearances of solemnity. I was certain it was the really grand accompaniments that overcame him; that the stars overhead, the dark towering tops of the yew-trees, and the wind that, like an unseen spirit, sighed through their branches, bowed his spirit to the belief, that in all these ceremonies lay some great mystical meaning which, his humility told him, his ignorance prevented him from understanding.

342

More convinced than before, that there was evil here, I could not endure that my master should be deceived; that one like him, so pure and noble, should respect what, if my suspicions were true, was worse than the ordinary deceptions of priestcraft. I could not tell how far he might be led to countenance, and otherwise support their doings, before he should find cause to repent bitterly of his error. I watched the new procession yet more keenly, if possible, than the former. This time, the central figure was a girl; and, at the close, I observed, yet more indubitably, the shrinking back, and the crowding push. What happened to the victims, I never learned; but I had learned enough, and I could bear it no longer. I stooped, and whispered to the young girl who stood by me, to lend me her white garment. I wanted it, that I might not be entirely out of keeping with the solemnity, but might have at least this help to passing unquestioned. She looked up, half-amused and half-bewildered, as if doubting whether I was in earnest or not. But in her perplexity, she permitted me to unfasten it, and slip it down from her shoulders.

I easily got possession of it; and, sinking down on my knees in the crowd, I rose apparently in the habit of one of the worshippers.

Giving my battle-axe to the girl, to hold in pledge for the return of her stole, for I wished to test the matter unarmed, and, if it was a man that sat upon the throne, to attack him with hands bare, as I supposed his must be, I made my way through the crowd to the front, while the singing yet continued, desirous of reaching the platform while it was unoccupied by any of the priests. I was permitted to walk up the long avenue of white robes unmolested, though I saw questioning looks in many of the faces as I passed. I presume my coolness aided my passage; for I felt quite indifferent as to my own fate; not feeling, after the late events of my history, that I was at all worth taking care of; and enjoying, perhaps, something of an evil satisfaction, in the revenge I was thus taking upon the self which had fooled me so long. When I arrived on the platform, the song had just ceased, and I felt as if all were looking towards me. But instead of kneeling at its foot, I walked right up the stairs to the throne, laid hold of a great wooden image that seemed to sit upon it, and tried to hurl it from its seat. In this I failed at first, for I found it firmly fixed. But in dread lest, the first shock of amazement passing away, the guards would rush upon me before I had effected my purpose, I strained with all my might; and, with a noise as of the cracking, and breaking, and tearing of rotten wood, something gave way, and I hurled the image down the steps. Its displacement revealed a great hole in the throne, like the hollow of a decayed tree, going down apparently a great way. But I had no time to examine it, for, as I looked into it, up out of it rushed a great brute, like a wolf, but twice the size, and tumbled me headlong with itself, down the steps of the throne. As we fell, however, I caught it by the throat, and the moment we reached the platform, a struggle commenced, in which I soon got uppermost, with my hand upon its throat, and knee upon its heart. But now arose a wild cry of wrath and revenge and rescue. A universal hiss of steel, as every sword was swept from its scabbard, seemed to tear the very air in shreds. I heard the rush of hundreds towards the platform on which I knelt. I only tightened my grasp of the brute's throat. His eyes were already starting from his head, and his tongue was hanging out. My anxious hope was, that, even after they had killed me, they would be unable to undo my gripe of his throat, before the monster was past breathing. I therefore threw all my will, and force, and purpose, into the grasping hand. I remember no blow. A faintness came over me, and my consciousness departed.

344

CHAPTER XXIV

"We are ne'er like angels till our passions die."

DEKKER.

"This wretched Inn, where we scarce stay to bait,

    We call our Dwelling-Place:

    We call one Step a Race:

But angels in their full enlightened state,

Angels, who Live, and know what 'tis to Be,

Who all the nonsense of our language see,

Who speak things, and our words, their ill-drawn

    pictures, scorn,

    When we, by a foolish figure, say,

    Behold an old man dead! then they

Speak properly, and cry, Behold a man-child born!"

COWLEY.

I was dead, and right content. I lay in my coffin, with my hands folded in peace. The knight, and the lady I loved, wept over me.

Her tears fell on my face.

"Ah!" said the knight, "I rushed amongst them like a madman. I hewed them down like brushwood. Their swords battered on me like hail, but hurt me not. I cut a lane through to my friend. He was dead. But he had throttled the monster, and I had to cut the handful out of its throat, before I could disengage and carry off his body. They dared not molest me as I brought him back."

"He has died well," said the lady.

My spirit rejoiced. They left me to my repose. I felt as if a cool hand had been laid upon my heart, and had stilled it. My soul was like a summer evening, after a heavy fall of rain, when the drops are yet glistening on the trees in the last rays of the down-going sun, and the wind of the twilight has begun to blow. The hot fever of life had gone by, and I breathed the clear mountain-air of the land of Death. I had never dreamed of such blessedness. It was not that I had in any way ceased to be what I had been. The very fact that anything can die, implies the existence of something that cannot die; which must either take to itself another form, as when the seed that is sown dies, and arises again; or, in conscious existence, may, perhaps, continue to lead a purely spiritual life. If my passions were dead, the souls of the passions, those essential mysteries of the spirit which had imbodied themselves in the passions, and had given to them all their glory and wonderment, yet lived, yet glowed, with a pure, undying fire. They rose above their vanishing earthly garments, and disclosed themselves angels of light. But oh, how beautiful beyond the old form! I lay thus for a time, and lived as it were an unradiating existence; my soul a motionless lake, that received all things and gave nothing back; satisfied in still contemplation, and spiritual consciousness.

Ere long, they bore me to my grave. Never tired child lay down in his white bed, and heard the sound of his playthings being laid aside for the night, with a more luxurious satisfaction of repose than I knew, when I felt the coffin settle on the firm earth, and heard the sound of the falling mould upon its lid. It has not the same hollow rattle within the coffin, that it sends up to the edge of the grave. They buried me in no graveyard. They loved me too much for that, I thank them; but they laid me in the grounds of their own castle, amid many trees; where, as it was spring-time, were growing primroses, and blue-bells, and all the families of the woods

Now that I lay in her bosom, the whole earth, and each of her many births, was as a body to me, at my will. I seemed to feel the great heart of the mother beating into mine, and feeding me with her own life, her own

346

essential being and nature. I heard the footsteps of my friends above, and they sent a thrill through my heart. I knew that the helpers had gone, and that the knight and the lady remained, and spoke low, gentle, tearful words of him who lay beneath the yet wounded sod. I rose into a single large primrose that grew by the edge of the grave, and from the window of its humble, trusting face, looked full in the countenance of the lady. I felt that I could manifest myself in the primrose; that it said a part of what I wanted to say; just as in the old time, I had used to betake myself to a song for the same end. The flower caught her eye. She stooped and plucked it, saying, "Oh, you beautiful creature!" and, lightly kissing it, put it in her bosom. It was the first kiss she had ever given me. But the flower soon began to wither, and I forsook it.

It was evening. The sun was below the horizon; but his rosy beams yet illuminated a feathery cloud, that floated high above the world. I arose, I reached the cloud; and, throwing myself upon it, floated with it in sight of the sinking sun. He sank, and the cloud grew gray; but the grayness touched not my heart. It carried its rose-hue within; for now I could love without needing to be loved again. The moon came gliding up with all the past in her wan face. She changed my couch into a ghostly pallor, and threw all the earth below as to the bottom of a pale sea of dreams. But she could not make me sad. I knew now, that it is by loving, and not by being loved, that one can come nearest the soul of another; yea, that, where two love, it is the loving of each other, and not the being loved by each other, that originates and perfects and assures their blessedness. I knew that love gives to him that loveth, power over any soul beloved, even if that soul know him not, bringing him inwardly close to that spirit; a power that cannot be but for good; for in proportion as selfishness intrudes, the love ceases, and the power which springs therefrom dies. Yet all love will, one day, meet with its return. All true love will, one day, behold its own image in the eyes of the beloved, and be humbly glad. This is possible in the realms of lofty Death. "Ah! my friends," thought I, "how I will tend you, and wait upon you, and haunt you with my love."

"My floating chariot bore me over a great city. Its faint dull sound steamed up into the air—a sound—how composed?" How many hopeless cries," thought I, "and how many mad shouts go to make up the tumult, here so faint where I float in eternal peace, knowing that they will one day be stilled in the surrounding calm, and that despair dies into infinite hope, and the seeming impossible there, is the law here!

"But, O pale-faced women, and gloomy-browed men, and forgotten children, how I will wait on you, and minister to you, and, putting my arms about you in the dark, think hope into your hearts, when you fancy no one is near! Soon as my senses have all come back, and have grown accustomed to this new blessed life, I will be among you with the love that healeth."

With this, a pang and a terrible shudder went through me; a writhing as of death convulsed me; and I became once again conscious of a more limited, even a bodily and earthly life.

CHAPTER XXV

"Our life is no dream; but it ought to become one,

and perhaps will."—NOVALIS.

"And on the ground, which is my modres gate,

I knocke with my staf, erlich and late,

And say to hire, Leve mother, let me in."

CHAUCER, *The Pardoneres Tale.*

Sinking from such a state of ideal bliss, into the world of shadows which again closed around and infolded me, my first dread was, not unnaturally, that my own shadow had found me again, and that my torture had commenced anew. It was a sad revulsion of feeling. This, indeed, seemed to correspond to what we think death is, before we die. Yet I felt within me a power of calm endurance to which I had hitherto been a stranger. For, in truth, that I should be able if only to think such things as I had been thinking, was an unspeakable delight. An hour of such peace made the turmoil of a lifetime worth striving through.

I found myself lying in the open air, in the early morning, before sunrise. Over me rose the summer heaven, expectant of the sun. The clouds already saw him, coming from afar; and soon every dewdrop would rejoice in his individual presence within it.

I lay motionless for a few minutes; and then slowly rose and looked about me. I was on the summit of a little hill; a valley lay beneath, and a range of mountains closed up the view upon that side. But, to my horror, across the valley, and up the height of the opposing mountains, stretched, from my very feet, a hugely expanding shade. There it lay, long and large, dark and mighty. I turned away with a sick despair; when lo! I beheld the sun just lifting his head above the eastern hill, and the shadow that fell from me, lay only where his beams fell not. I danced for joy. It was only the natural shadow, that goes with every man who walks in the sun. As he arose, higher and higher, the shadow-head sank down the side of the opposite hill, and crept in across the valley towards my feet.

Now that I was so joyously delivered from this fear, I saw and recognised the country around me. In the valley below, lay my own castle, and the haunts of my childhood were all about me hastened home. My sisters received me with unspeakable joy; but I suppose they observed some change in me, for a kind of respect, with a slight touch of awe in it, mingled with their joy, and made me ashamed. They had been in great distress about me. On the morning of my disappearance, they had found the floor of my room flooded; and, all that day, a wondrous and nearly impervious mist had hung about the castle and grounds. I had been gone, they told me, twenty-one days. To me it seemed twenty-one years. Nor could I yet feel quite secure in my new experiences. When, at night, I lay down once more in my own bed, I did not feel at all sure that when I awoke, I should not find myself in some mysterious region of Fairy Land. My dreams were incessant and perturbed; but when I did awake, I saw clearly that I was in my own home.

My mind soon grew calm; and I began the duties of my new position, somewhat instructed, I hoped, by the adventures that had befallen me in Fairy Land. Could I translate the experience of my travels there, into common life? This was the question. Or must I live it all over again, and learn it all over again, in the other forms that belong to the world of men, whose experience yet runs parallel to that of Fairy Land? These questions I cannot answer yet. But I fear.

Even yet, I find myself looking round sometimes with anxiety, to see whether my shadow falls right away from the sun or no. I have never yet discovered any inclination to either side. And if I am not unfrequently sad, I yet cast no more of a shade on the earth, than most men who have lived in it as long as I. I have a strange feeling sometimes, that I am a ghost, sent into the world to minister to my fellow men, or, rather, to repair the wrongs I have already done.

May the world be brighter for me, at least in those portions of it, where my darkness falls not.

Thus I, who set out to find my Ideal, came back rejoicing that I had lost my Shadow.

When the thought of the blessedness I experienced, after my death in Fairy Land, is too high for me to lay hold upon it and hope in it, I often think of the wise woman in the cottage, and of her solemn assurance that she knew something too good to be told. When I am oppressed by any sorrow or real perplexity, I often feel as if I had only left her cottage for a time, and would soon return out of the vision, into it again. Sometimes, on such occasions, I find myself, unconsciously almost, looking about for the mystic mark of red, with the vague hope of entering her door, and being comforted by her wise tenderness. I then console myself by saying: "I have come through the door of Dismay; and the way back from the world into which that has led me, is through my tomb. Upon that the red sign lies, and I shall find it one day, and be glad."

I will end my story with the relation of an incident which befell me a few days ago. I had been with my reapers, and, when they ceased their work at noon, I had lain down under the shadow of a great, ancient beech-tree, that stood on the edge of the field. As I lay, with my eyes closed, I began to listen to the sound of the leaves overhead. At first, they made sweet inarticulate music alone; but, by-and-by, the sound seemed to begin to take shape, and to be gradually moulding itself into words; till, at last, I seemed able to distinguish these, half-dissolved in a little ocean of circumfluent tones: "A great good is coming—is coming—is coming to thee, Anodos;" and so over and over again. I fancied that the sound reminded me of the voice of the ancient woman, in the cottage that was four-square. I opened my eyes, and, for a moment, almost believed that I saw her face, with its many wrinkles and its young eyes, looking at me from between two hoary branches of the beech overhead. But when I looked more keenly, I saw only twigs and leaves, and the infinite sky, in tiny spots, gazing through between. Yet I know that good is coming to me—that good is always coming; though few have at all times the simplicity and the courage to believe it. What we call evil, is the only and best shape, which, for the person and his condition at the time, could be assumed by the best good. And so, Farewell.

About Author

Elizabeth Yates wrote of Sir Gibbie, "It moved me the way books did when, as a child, the great gates of literature began to open and first encounters with noble thoughts and utterances were unspeakably thrilling."

Even Mark Twain, who initially disliked MacDonald, became friends with him, and there is some evidence that Twain was influenced by him. The Christian author Oswald Chambers wrote in his "Christian Disciplines" that "it is a striking indication of the trend and shallowness of the modern reading public that George MacDonald's books have been so neglected".

Early life

George MacDonald was born on 10 December 1824 at Huntly, Aberdeenshire, Scotland. His father, a farmer, was one of the MacDonalds of Glen Coe and a direct descendant of one of the families that suffered in the massacre of 1692.

MacDonald grew up in an unusually literate environment: one of his maternal uncles was a notable Celtic scholar, editor of the Gaelic Highland Dictionary and collector of fairy tales and Celtic poetry. His paternal grandfather had supported the publication of an Ossian edition, the controversial Celtic text believed by some to have contributed to the starting of European Romanticism. MacDonald's step-uncle was a Shakespeare scholar, and his paternal cousin another Celtic academic. Both his parents were readers, his father harbouring predilections for Newton, Burns, Cowper, Chalmers, Coleridge, and Darwin, to quote a few, while his mother had received a classical education which included multiple languages.

An account cited how the young George suffered lapses in health in his early years and was subject to problems with his lungs such as asthma, bronchitis and even a bout of tuberculosis. This last illness was considered a family disease and two of MacDonald's brothers, his mother, and later three of his own children actually died from the ailment. Even in his adult life, he was constantly travelling in search of purer air for his lungs.

MacDonald grew up in the Congregational Church, with an atmosphere of Calvinism. However, his family was atypical, with his paternal grandfather a Catholic-born, fiddle-playing, Presbyterian elder; his paternal grandmother an Independent church rebel; his mother was a sister to the Gallic-speaking radical who became moderator of the disrupting Free Church, while his step-mother, to whom he was also very close, was the daughter of a Scottish Episcopalian priest.

MacDonald graduated from the University of Aberdeen in 1845 with a master's degree in chemistry and physics. He spent the next several years struggling with matters of faith and deciding what to do with his life. His son, biographer Greville MacDonald stated that his father could have pursued a career in the medical field but he speculated that lack of money put an end to this prospect. It was only in 1848 when MacDonald began theological training at Highbury College for the Congregational ministry.

Early career

MacDonald was appointed minister of Trinity Congregational Church, Arundel, in 1850, after briefly serving as a locum minister in Ireland. However, his sermons—which preached God's universal love and that everyone was capable of redemption —met with little favour and his salary was cut in half. In May 1853, MacDonald tendered his resignation from his pastoral duties at Arundel. Later he was engaged in ministerial work in Manchester, leaving that because of poor health. An account cited the role of Lady Byron in convincing MacDonald to travel to Algiers in 1856 with the hope that the sojourn would help turn his health around. When he got back, he settled in London and taught for some time at the University of London. MacDonald was also for a time editor of Good Words for the Young.

Writing Career

MacDonald's first novel David Elginbrod was published in 1863.

George MacDonald is often regarded as the founding father of modern fantasy writing. George MacDonald's best-known works are Phantastes, The Princess and the Goblin, At the Back of the North Wind, and Lilith (1895), all fantasy novels, and fairy tales such as "The Light Princess", "The Golden Key", and "The Wise Woman". "I write, not for children," he wrote, "but for the child-like, whether they be of five, or fifty, or seventy-five." MacDonald also published some volumes of sermons, the pulpit not having proved an unreservedly successful venue.

After his literary success, MacDonald went on to do a lecture tour in the United States in 1872–1873, after being invited to do so by a lecture company, the Boston Lyceum Bureau. On the tour, MacDonald lectured about other poets such as Robert Burns, Shakespeare, and Tom Hood. He performed this lecture to great acclaim, speaking in Boston to crowds in the neighborhood of three thousand people.

MacDonald served as a mentor to Lewis Carroll (the pen-name of Charles Lutwidge Dodgson); it was MacDonald's advice, and the enthusiastic reception of Alice by MacDonald's many sons and daughters, that convinced Carroll to submit Alice for publication. Carroll, one of the finest Victorian photographers, also created photographic portraits of several of the MacDonald children. MacDonald was also friends with John Ruskin, and served as a go-between in Ruskin's long courtship with Rose La Touche. While in America he was befriended by Longfellow and Walt Whitman.

MacDonald's use of fantasy as a literary medium for exploring the human condition greatly influenced a generation of notable authors, including C. S. Lewis, who featured him as a character in his The Great Divorce. In his introduction to his MacDonald anthology, Lewis speaks highly of MacDonald's views:

This collection, as I have said, was designed not to revive MacDonald's literary reputation but to spread his religious teaching. Hence most of my extracts are taken from the three volumes of Unspoken Sermons. My own debt to this book is almost as great as one man can owe to another: and nearly all serious inquirers to whom I have introduced it acknowledge that it has given them great help—sometimes indispensable help toward the very acceptance of the Christian faith. ...

I know hardly any other writer who seems to be closer, or more continually close, to the Spirit of Christ Himself. Hence his Christ-like union of tenderness and severity. Nowhere else outside the New Testament have I found terror and comfort so intertwined. ...

In making this collection I was discharging a debt of justice. I have never concealed the fact that I regarded him as my master; indeed I fancy I have never written a book in which I did not quote from him. But it has not seemed to me that those who have received my books kindly take even now sufficient notice of the affiliation. Honesty drives me to emphasize it.

Others he influenced include J. R. R. Tolkien and Madeleine L'Engle. MacDonald's non-fantasy novels, such as Alec Forbes, had their influence as well; they were among the first realistic Scottish novels, and as such MacDonald has been credited with founding the "kailyard school" of Scottish writing.

Chesterton cited The Princess and the Goblin as a book that had "made a difference to my whole existence", in showing "how near both the best and the worst things are to us from the first... and making all the ordinary staircases and doors and windows into magical things."

Later life

In 1877 he was given a civil list pension. From 1879 he and his family moved to Bordighera, in a place much loved by British expatriates, the Riviera dei Fiori in Liguria, Italy, almost on the French border. In that locality there also was an Anglican church, All Saints, which he attended. Deeply enamoured of the Riviera, he spent 20 years there, writing almost half of his whole literary production, especially the fantasy work. MacDonald founded a literary studio in that Ligurian town, naming it Casa Coraggio (Bravery House). It soon became one of the most renowned cultural centres of that period, well attended by British and Italian travellers, and by locals, with presentations of classic plays and readings of Dante and Shakespeare often being held.

In 1900 he moved into St George's Wood, Haslemere, a house designed for him by his son, Robert, its building overseen by his eldest son, Greville.

George MacDonald died on 18 September 1905 in Ashtead, Surrey, England. He was cremated in Woking, Surrey, England and his ashes were buried in Bordighera, in the English cemetery, along with his wife Louisa and daughters Lilia and Grace.

Personal life

MacDonald married Louisa Powell in Hackney in 1851, with whom he raised a family of eleven children: Lilia Scott (1852), Mary Josephine (1853-1878), Caroline Grace (1854), Greville Matheson (1856-1944), Irene (1857), Winifred Louise (1858), Ronald (1860–1933), Robert Falconer (1862–1913), Maurice (1864), Bernard Powell (1865–1928), and George Mackay (1867–1909?).

His son Greville became a noted medical specialist, a pioneer of the Peasant Arts movement, wrote numerous fairy tales for children, and ensured that new editions of his father's works were published. Another son, Ronald, became a novelist. His daughter Mary was engaged to the artist Edward Robert Hughes until her death in 1878. Ronald's son, Philip MacDonald (George MacDonald's grandson), became a Hollywood screenwriter.

Tuberculosis caused the death of several family members, including Lilia, Mary Josephine, Grace, Maurice as well as one granddaughter and a daughter-in-law. MacDonald was said to have been particularly affected by the death of Lilia, her eldest.

Theology

According to biographer William Raeper, MacDonald's theology "celebrated the rediscovery of God as Father, and sought to encourage an intuitive response to God and Christ through quickening his readers' spirits in their reading of the Bible and their perception of nature."

MacDonald's oft-mentioned universalism is not the idea that everyone will automatically be saved, but is closer to Gregory of Nyssa in the view that all will ultimately repent and be restored to God.

MacDonald appears to have never felt comfortable with some aspects of Calvinist doctrine, feeling that its principles were inherently "unfair"; when the doctrine of predestination was first explained to him, he burst into tears (although assured that he was one of the elect). Later novels, such as Robert Falconer and Lilith, show a distaste for the idea that God's electing love is limited to some and denied to others.

Chesterton noted that only a man who had "escaped" Calvinism could say that God is easy to please and hard to satisfy.

MacDonald rejected the doctrine of penal substitutionary atonement as developed by John Calvin, which argues that Christ has taken the place of sinners and is punished by the wrath of God in their place, believing that in turn it raised serious questions about the character and nature of God. Instead, he taught that Christ had come to save people from their sins, and not from a Divine penalty for their sins: the problem was not the need to appease a wrathful God, but the disease of cosmic evil itself. MacDonald frequently described the atonement in terms similar to the Christus Victor theory. MacDonald posed the rhetorical question, "Did he not foil and slay evil by letting all the waves and billows of its horrid sea break upon him, go over him, and die without rebound—spend their rage, fall defeated, and cease? Verily, he made atonement!"

MacDonald was convinced that God does not punish except to amend, and that the sole end of His greatest anger is the amelioration of the guilty. As the doctor uses fire and steel in certain deep-seated diseases, so God may use hell-fire if necessary to heal the hardened sinner. MacDonald declared, "I believe that no hell will be lacking which would help the just mercy of God to redeem his children." MacDonald posed the rhetorical question, "When we say that God is Love, do we teach men that their fear of Him is groundless?" He replied, "No. As much as they were will come upon them, possibly far more. ... The wrath will consume what they call themselves; so that the selves God made shall appear."

However, true repentance, in the sense of freely chosen moral growth, is essential to this process, and, in MacDonald's optimistic view, inevitable for all beings (see universal reconciliation).

MacDonald states his theological views most distinctly in the sermon "Justice", found in the third volume of Unspoken Sermons. (Source: Wikipedia)